Piece by Piece

Author's note

This story contains topics that might be triggering for some readers like domestic abuse, sexual assault, trauma, etc. For a more detailed list, check the trigger warnings on my website

www.jarahwrites.com

Other books by Jarah Aurel

Sommerstall Academy
Arcane
Serendipity
Untangle Me
Only you
Little Nymph
In Shadows We Rise
Effervescent

Chapter 1

Aliena

My eyes are closed. My hips are swaying. My head is tilted back against the broad chest of the man behind me.

His hands are on my hips, holding me without restricting my movements like he knows I like. I'm dancing, I'm leading, and we're both getting something out of it. Me, the comfort of being held and the validation of his attraction. Him, well, the kind of dancing that could pass as a lap dance from one hell of a woman.

The loud music and pounding beat warm my blood, intoxicating me like no drink or drug ever could. I can feel it in my veins, that familiar hum I crave. This is me. The music, the parties, the hands on me. This is where I'm free.

The fingers splayed on my hips give me a little squeeze and Mattheo's head comes down next to the side of mine. Pushing my messy hair over my shoulder so he can speak into my ear, he says, "I'm sorry, *seduttrice*, I can never keep up with you. What do you say we take a small break?"

I enjoy the way his words brush against my skin, letting the sensation add to the warm bundle of feelings inside me. Then I turn to him with a smile, take his hand, and nod.

He easily pushes past the crowd of dancing people, towering over them all and finding his way to the base of the stairs without a problem. Meanwhile, little old me has to dodge two elbows in the course of the short trip to avoid a bloody nose. Tall men should really have a separate section on the dancefloor to go crazy because they do not have any spatial awareness when it comes to anything below their chin.

The security guy making sure no one gets to the second floor of the apartment without permission barely glances at Mattheo before stepping aside for us. Another perk of keeping company with the host's best friend.

As we climb the stairs, I watch the dancing strangers below through the glass railing, smiling since I know I'll be back among them in no time. It's not often I'm away from the dancing crowd.

Mattheo and I walk into the private room on the second floor, heading for one of the black leather couches assembled in a sort of circle. Our friends and some people I know in passing are already seated there, nursing their drinks and talking in the blue glow of the LEDs above.

When Lilianne sees us, her flushed face lights up. "Aly!" she exclaims, clumsily freeing herself of her boyfriend's hold to greet me with a tight hug. As if we hadn't come here together a few hours ago. "You were gone for so long! I missed you!" she announces, her words drawn out and slurred. Her grubby hands come up to cup my face, as if to hold it in place when it's really her swaying. I bite back a grin as she turns to my friend. "You need to stop stealing my friend!"

Mattheo laughs and gives her a gentle pat on the arm. "Sweetheart, she is the one always keeping me away. The woman never tires of dancing. Keep her, I need a break and a drink." He winks at me and walks over to Andrew. I can still hear him ask his friend, "Did you miss me? How come

Jarah Aurel

Piece by Piece

© 2025 Jarah Aurel
ISBN: 9798312343137

To everyone who's too used to doing things alone...
May you find your Sebastian

I'm never greeted that nicely?" over the music before Lily demands my full attention.

"Come, let's sit down," she proposes and starts pulling me to the couches without waiting for a reply. Chuckling, I follow her lead. When we sit down on the couch next to the one the guys are on and I note Andrew's frown, I elbow Lily gently.

"I think your boyfriend misses you," I tell her.

"I sure do," Andrew pipes up, his dimples showing.

Once again, I can't help but notice how handsome he is. Light brown skin, sharp cheekbones, shorn black hair, and dark, friendly eyes. His grin is ever lasting, and it's a damn good thing too with my best friend being who she is. Not only is she the most gorgeous, flawless woman I know, but she's a walking ray of sunshine. It's good to see her with a man that matches the happy energy she exudes.

Lily throws her arms over me. "You've had me for hours now. Enjoy the break, my bestie needs some love too." Andrew has the grace to chuckle it off, even though I'm sure he doesn't exactly need a break from her. They're joined at the hip most days, a fact both seem to be very happy about.

"And what have I been giving her for the past hours?" Mattheo demands playfully.

"I don't know. Probably tingles and damp underwear," Lily replies before I can fire anything back. My jaw drops and Mattheo's laughter booms.

"Christ, Lil!" I mutter, stifling a laugh of my own. Here she is, my shy, introverted, sweet best friend after a drink or two.

My eyes meet Mattheo's awaiting ones, and I'm tempted to stick out my tongue like a child at his raised brow and knowing smile. Idiot.

A guy from a nearby couch pops our little bubble, screaming over the music to be heard across the room. "Eyo! Mat, A, where's Sebastian? Haven't seen him all night. I wanted to thank him for putting me on the VIP list," he explains loudly, throwing his head back to get his blond hair out of his eyes.

Andrew shrugs dismissively. "He's out tonight."

"Ditching his own party? The lucky lady must be a dream in bed, then," the blond adds, grinning crookedly.

Don't react. Don't react.

Mattheo is still watching me, but I avert my eyes. I have no reason to, there is absolutely no sense in my mood dimming or for the small kernel of guilt or jealousy to appear in my gut. Sebastian is out with a girl as always. I'm enjoying a party as always.

I'm aware of Mattheo's movements as he gets off the couch to head to the bar. On the way, he stops next to me, putting a hand on my shoulder to get me to look at him, and asks, "You want anything? It's important to stay hydrated if we're going back downstairs in a minute."

I smile gratefully. This is why I love this guy; he can read me like a book and is smart in the way he cheers me up. He sees my mood dim and asks me to dance. Problem eviscerated. I'm easy that way.

"I'll take whatever you get," I tell him. Usually, I stay sober at parties, at all other times even more so, but a drink every now and again isn't off-limits in my book.

Mattheo comes back with our drinks, handing me one before reclaiming his seat. Our group picks up where we left off with our banter like we were never interrupted. Then, when my drink is finally empty, I get to my feet and force the Italian to come back downstairs so we can get moving.

We return to our earlier spot amid the crowd downstairs where I'm quick to resume my dancing. I grind against Mattheo, not caring for the heat or the sweat slicking the back of my neck. Then I turn around and throw my arms around his neck, as well as that works with our eight-inch height difference. He holds me close, swaying along to the music with me while shooting me his signature grin.

"You're hot as hell when you look up at me like that, *seduttrice*," he teases.

I smile wider. "Yeah?"

"Oh, yeah. With your face all flushed and lit up like it always does when you dance. Magnificent."

"You're flattering me. You don't look half bad from down here either. If only it weren't for that thing hanging from your nose," I tease him.

He throws his head back and laughs. "There's nothing in my nose."

"How can you be sure? I can see it perfectly from where I stand." I make a show of looking at his perfectly clean nostrils.

"You don't look nearly disgusted enough, that's how I know. No, you're still giving me those eyes. I'm sure you wouldn't if there was something in my nose."

I raise a challenging brow at that. How bold for him to assume anything about me. "How am I looking at you, exactly?" I ask.

His grin widens as if accepting my challenge. He leans down slightly, his lips brushing the shell of my ear once more as he says, "Like you want me to kiss you." We're barely dancing now, and he studies me closely. "Like you want me to be a really good friend tonight and take your mind off things," he adds.

I let my eyes close and imagine it. I'm certainly not opposed. No, I've had one-night stands with much less appealing suspects, and with Mattheo, I don't doubt he could make me feel good tonight and go back to being the friend I flirt with tomorrow. We've been toying the line with our dancing and teasing for months, anyway. The only action I've been getting involves me alone in my room and a hand between my legs whenever unbidden thoughts of a man I shouldn't be picturing resurface and my restraint wavers. Why not indulge tonight? Maybe this is exactly what I need to stop thinking about someone who's never been and never will be mine

Soft lips brush against my cheek, his short stubble awakening goosebumps on my feverish skin. I open my eyes as he pulls back a little, and when our eyes lock, it's clear we've come to the same conclusion. He cups my cheek with one big palm and brings his lips to mine.

There are no fireworks. No world-changing enlightenment as Mattheo kisses me. Still, my body reacts to the physical contact, skin tingling, my lower stomach warming, and at the soft caress of his thumb, my legs become weak.

I've been kissed at parties by many, but so few know how to do it right. They grab my butt and grind against me, anything to take the edge off. They're unaware of how they make me feel like a means to an end rather than a person . It's unsatisfying.

Kissing Mattheo isn't. One of his hands stays on my cheek while his other arm snakes around my back to hold me close. He envelops me, managing to shut out the rest of the party. The rest of the world.

Just with a kiss.

I bring my hands to his hair and angle his face to deepen the moment. I want him closer. Need him to show me more.

Instead, Mattheo pulls away. "*Amo*, either take it slow or let me take you upstairs. People at Hartford University talk, and while I don't particularly mind, I like the idea of being the only one here that knows how your moans sound. And you seem a moment away from doing just that." Oh, that infuriating smile. I should've kissed it off his face sooner.

"So, take me upstairs," I say.

The second floor consists of the VIP lounge, Sebastian's bedroom, and some spare rooms only a selected few are allowed to use or stay in. Those selected few are Andrew, Mattheo, Lilianne, and me, by default.

Mattheo takes my hand and walks ahead until we reach the stairs. There, I take the lead until we are in the room I mostly stay in. The door shuts and locks behind Mattheo, the automatic low lights embedded in the ceiling turning on to cast an intimate glow over us.

The air around us changes, the playfulness morphing into something deeper. Mattheo's no longer grinning. Instead, his eyes are almost feline as he takes measured steps toward me. He cups my face with both hands, enveloping my cheeks entirely. "You are sure about this, *amo*? We are on the same page?"

"A casual, mutually beneficial one-night stand between friends that have chemistry. I don't get this type of stuff mixed up, Mattheo. Do you?" I challenge, bringing my hands to his shoulders and caressing their breadth with my nails.

Now he's grinning again, shaking his head like he can't believe me. "I should have known better than to even ask. I call you *seduttrice* for a reason, after all."

Before he can say more, I stand on the tips of my toes and pull him down so I can kiss him again. My shoes elevate me a few inches, but he still has to lean down to reach my lips. He seems to notice the inconvenience and decides to take matters into his own hands, bringing his hands to the backs of my thighs and picking me up easily. I go along with it and lock my legs around his slender hips.

Thank god for his years of swimming practice. His body feels lethal under my touch. He's solid muscle, but not in a threatening way. Not like a certain man who owns the apartment. No, Mattheo is lean and defined in a delicious way. I've been to enough of his tournaments to know exactly what he looks like. Now it's time to learn how he feels.

I grab the hem of his shirt and pull it over his head. As soon as the fabric's gone, he tries to bring his lips back to mine but I pull away. "Give me a second. I've been dreaming about this," I tease. While dreaming might be an exaggeration, I can't deny I have thought closely about his body when we were dancing, so I will take my time.

I carefully move my fingers from his shoulders to his pecks, feeling every dip and groove under my fingertips. He flexes beneath my touch, and I give him a look. "Really?"

With satisfaction written all over him, he just shrugs. I chuckle and resume my mission to get to know his torso. I feel his ribs, over his shoulders and down his back, along his spine, then back to his flanks. My touch is featherlight, so much so Mattheo shivers when my digits move over the fine trail of hair vanishing into the waistband of his pants.

"You're driving me crazy. Stop touching me like I'm made of porcelain, Aliena. I'm not going to break," he says, his voice low.

I meet his eyes and smile. "I know you won't. Sometimes it's nice to be handled with care though, no?" I ask. Knowing how I usually get used for hookups, I don't want to know how a man like Mattheo is treated. He's one of the most popular, influential students at that preppy university all my friends go to. On top of that, he looks like he does.

He's a trophy.

And I'm not saying he doesn't enjoy how women treat him or that he minds his one-night stands. I just think at times, we don't realize what we crave. If only for a change.

He looks thoughtful as he holds my gaze, but I didn't come here to lecture him or even talk. No, we've been in here for many long minutes and most of our clothes are still on. That's not my style.

One corner of my lips tips up as my hands leave his warm skin. I bring them to the bows holding together the straps of my dress and pull them one by one. The strips of fabric fall, front and back, exposing my chest completely.

My friend's eyes drop, and he swallows.

"Christ, woman, a warning would be nice the next time," he tells me despite the need in his voice. He likes what he sees.

"Maybe it's time we move this to the bed," I suggest.

With a nod, he carries me there and sets me down gently on the soft mattress. Then he takes a step back to admire me as I did him.

"Come here," I instruct, reaching for him. It brings a smile to his lips, and he shrugs his pants off before complying and climbing over me. But not before I got a glimpse at those mouth-watering thighs of his. Maybe I'll get to kneel between them some other time, touch the defined muscles there like I did with his torso.

"You know how to play, *seduttrice*," he admits before pressing a kiss to the side of my jaw.

"Practice makes perfect," I say, arching my back just slightly. He understands my command and moves his lips further down, trailing them along the curve of my neck before kissing his way over my cleavage.

"Don't I know it," he mutters against my skin a second before his lips close over my nipple.

"Take off my dress," my breathy voice orders. That I'm this affected this early by what we're doing is more confirmation that I haven't done this in too long. Again, Mattheo is happy to obey, and with his help, my violet dress is discarded on the bedroom floor in a matter of seconds.

He looks down at me with a grin. "Oh, heck yes. Red still looks good on you," he tells me, tugging at my red lace panties.

I smile at the familiar words from his lips as I pull his head back to me and kiss him while his body melts into mine. I spread my legs so his hips fit between them, and when I feel the warmth of his erection through the fabric of our underwear, the heat in my lower stomach turns to tingles.

He's holding himself up with one arm and has his other hand on my face, kissing me like we have all the time in the world. Meanwhile, I'm getting impatient, no matter how mindful touches are.

I take his hand from my face and move it down to the hem of my underwear, feeling bold when he hums his approval against my lips. I release his hand, and he takes over, stroking my swollen clit over the lace. He continues at an unhurried pace, again and again, until finally, he pushes the fabric covering me to the side. Two fingers find my entrance and circle it without pushing inside. Then he brings his slick fingers back to my clit and starts rubbing it in earnest. I arch my back at the first circle drawn with just the right pressure, and the faintest moan escapes me. Mattheo swallows it whole.

After minutes of his steady, heavenly assault, my skin grows clammy with a sheen of sweat. Then, his fingers move away and find their way back to my entrance just as he breaks the kiss. Our eyes lock as he pushes them inside of me, and I recognize the satisfaction in his eyes when he draws another moan out of me with a well-placed stroke against my G-spot.

I grab his shoulders and pull him down so I can whisper in his ear, not trusting my voice to be louder than that anymore. "I'm ready, Mattheo. You can feel I am. Stop playing and be the good friend you promised me you'd be."

When he pulls away to look at me, his smirk is back in full force. "I thought that's what I've been doing for several minutes now," he says. He enunciates his words with another stroke against my G-spot. And another.

His fingers curl inside me at a steady pace until I can feel my legs grow weak and tingles explode in my womb, reaching the tips of my fingers and toes. I tense underneath him and close my eyes to catch a break from the intense look in his eyes. Then, I come with his name on my lips.

"Am I being a good friend yet?" Mattheo asks, pulling his fingers out of me.

"I don't know. Better keep trying." I'm still catching my breath, so my snappy reply lacks in delivery. My friend has the decency not to call me out on it. Instead, he arches an amused brow.

"I guess I better," he agrees. He makes good on his words, taking off our remaining clothes while I take a condom out of the bedside drawer. The box is still unopened since I barely ever stay the night here and certainly not with someone else. Not until now.

I open the foil and put on the condom for him, his eyes following the movement. When his impressive length is covered, I give it a gentle stroke.

He curses, pulls my hand away, kisses it, then pins it to the mattress above my head. "I'm going to be the best fucking friend you've ever had, *amo*," he promises as he brings his tip to my entrance.

"I don't doubt it," I whisper. Then my eyes flutter shut with his first thrust, my lower half struggling to accept his intrusion. He bottoms out and holds still for a second, breathing deeply while his body thrums with energy.

"Don't hold back, Mattheo. I can take it," I encourage him, desperate for him to move.

His eyes meet mine with a mischievous glint. "Big, big words for such a small thing," he mutters.

Any retort dies on my lips as he starts moving, pulling nearly all the way out before driving back in. One hand stays on my pinned wrist while his other holds my hip in place. I merely lie there and hang on for the ride, happy to let him lead.

But as our breathing grows harsher and soft moans climb from my throat, something interrupts the otherwise silent room.

A knock on my door.

Mattheo's movements falter for a beat and the lustful haze clears from his eyes a little. He looks at me with a questioning gaze.

"Don't you dare stop," I hiss at him, already feeling the tingles that have been building over the past fifteen minutes recede. Whoever's at the door will leave if there's no reply, I'm sure.

Mattheo shoots me a quick smile and then goes back at it, bringing his lips to mine as he fucks me into the mattress. When the person at my door knocks again, we don't react at all. Some small part of my mind is wondering who the hell it could be, though.

"Aliena?"

One word through the wooden door that should hardly meet my ears. And yet, that voice rings through loud and clear. An unexpected rush washes over me, my body wrecked by an answering shiver.

I close my eyes as a vision crosses my mind too fast for me to stop it. A vision of his words brushing against the shell of my ear rather than through the wooden barrier, one of him moving over me, his dark eyes holding mine. A moan tears from my lips before I can swallow it, and I wrench my eyes open to try and escape this unwarranted fantasy of a man I shouldn't like.

Mattheo recognizes the voice of his best friend too, and his eyes open once again, meeting my wide ones even though he doesn't stop moving. There's a challenge in his gaze, something knowing and wicked, perhaps feeling the flood of my arousal at the sound of Sebastian's voice. I should be ashamed, should be embarrassed, he caught me getting turned on by his best friend while he is inside me, but the glint in his eyes tells me he doesn't mind at all. That he isn't surprised or offended. It's wicked and sinful and what draws the first true moan from me.

The knocking lets up for a second only to return twice as harshly. "Aliena? I know you're in there, the door is locked and only you have the key. Open up!" Sebastian demands, irritation clear in his voice.

Mattheo smiles cockily and whispers in my ear. "Yes, Aliena, open the door," he taunts. I clench around him, moaning even louder now as if my body just can't control it.

Sebastian hears it. He bangs more. "Is someone in there with you? I swear to god, Aliena, open the fucking door! This is *my* apartment!" he rages outside. And, god, I'm becoming unhinged, moaning again. Unbidden images of him standing out there with his chest heaving and eyes dark with rage flash through my mind as I flutter around Mattheo. Is that what he would look like fucking me? Would his voice be as rough then?

Oh, god! What is wrong with me? I shouldn't be fantasizing about him. I shouldn't think of him when he's what I came here to forget. I shouldn't care for his voice, and I sure shouldn't be hearing it when he knows I'm in here with someone. We aren't together. Jesus Christ, we don't even get along and never have in all the months I've been forced to get to know him. Not once after our first meeting.

"Aliena!" his voice booms, shaking now. I shouldn't like it. Shouldn't care what he sounds like when he loses control, and yet I can't deny the warm tingles spreading through me. "Open the fucking door! I won't leave until you do!" he announces. I bite my lip to stifle another moan. There's no need for me to urge him on.

Mattheo's finger drags my bottom lip from between my teeth, his intention clear. *Let him hear.* Then, he turns his head to the door and yells, "You better not! Keep shouting, dude. She's loving it!" Then he winks at me.

A shockwave of heat and shame washes over me as my inner walls pulse around Mattheo's cock.

This time, he groans. "That's it, *amo*," he tells me.

"Mattheo?" Sebastian's disbelieving voice comes from outside the room. The banging resumes. "What the fuck! Open the door, you sad excuse of a friend!"

"In a sec. We're getting her there," he shouts back, thrusting deeper and faster now.

Holy shit, I can hear Sebastian curse outside but gradually, his voice begins to fade to background noise as the sensations become too much for my body.

Pleasure washes over me in waves, and I close my eyes, every muscle tensing. Stars dot my vision, and I distantly feel my mouth open. I think my lips move on a cry, but the sound doesn't register to my own ears.

I come back to myself with heaving breaths and numb limbs. Above me, Mattheo is catching his breath as well, so I guess he tipped over the edge with me. He slowly pulls out of me with one last peck and discards the condom. The banging on my door hasn't stopped.

I join Mattheo as he puts on his clothes. "Want me to give you a ride home or are you staying here?" he asks, acting as if his best friend wasn't on the verge of knocking the door down.

I mirror him, ignoring the sound. "I'm not staying here." Then, seeing as we both have our clothes back in place, I step up to the door with a deep breath. It's a shame I have to open it now and face the menace on the other side when the whole point of this was to forget his existence for just one blissful moment.

Although that ship had sailed the second his voice pierced the air of my bedroom, clearly. Mattheo gives me an encouraging nod, and I unlock the door to reveal the owner of the house.

Sebastian William Henderson, son of William Henderson, dean of Hartford University. One of the most influential and richest students among all the other snobs at the university as well as the most popular, thanks to the parties he regularly throws.

In my opinion, he's also the most infuriating, although I do only know a handful of students.

I look at his flushed, angry face and his heaving chest and try to see what the others do. A broad, 6-foot-1 frame of pure muscle, courtesy of the private gym in the apartment where he takes his anger out, dark hair, shorter on the sides and longer on top, and dark, menacing eyes currently burning into me. He looks good, yeah. That was never in question.

16

As was the weird chemistry between us, which he seemed fine with on our first meeting, not so much on any of the others, though.

Chapter 2

Aliena

Last July

"Look who was sent fresh flowers again!" I say enthusiastically as I step into the room of my favorite resident, 85-year-old Rosie Henderson.

The old lady perks up in her chair and beams at me, stretching out her hands for the lovely bouquet I bought. I hand it to her, and she takes a deep whiff and sighs. "My lovely son. You know, he's so busy he can never visit but he never fails to send me these once a month," she tells me like she does every month.

Maybe it's wrong of me to lie to her, but in the five years of working here, I learned to take some liberties when it comes to bringing these lovely seniors some joy. A year after Rosie's arrival, during which I always had to disappoint her whenever she asked if her son called about a visit, I started buying her flowers and told her they were from him. That was six months ago, and her mental presence has been looking up ever since.

"That's very nice of him. They're beautiful," I agree as I move on to tidy her room. It's very spacious, only the best for the residents since the price sure demands as much.

When I was told what the yearly fee for a residency at Bloomfield Living Care costs, I nearly choked on my tongue. Let's just say, sixteen-year-old me had never heard of such expenses.

The room's equipped with a desk usually decorated with my flowers, a comfortable bed with some bedside drawers, a TV, and a closet. Adjoined with the bedroom is a small bathroom.

In my opinion, the best part of this room is the window looking out into the big yard of the nursing home. A few people are out, playing cards or checkers at one of the tables in the shade, enjoying the July weather. I open the window for Rosie.

"Thank you, dear. Oh, while you're back there, could you please hand me the glass of water from my bedside table?" she asks.

I comply in a beat, smiling as I give her the glass only to feel something inside me twist at the sight of the woman's shaky hands. It's nothing new and almost none of the residents here have a steady hand anymore. Still, it's hard not to notice the little things when I know Rosie probably won't make it into the next year. Cancer doesn't spread quickly at that age but it's vicious, nonetheless.

A soft knock on the door interrupts my thoughts. Rosie looks at me expectantly, and I smile at her, trying to hide my confusion and surprise. In all her time here, she's never had a visitor. What if her son suddenly decided to show up? I just hope he won't expose my little flower scam.

I open the door and come face-to-face with a young man that's certainly not Rosie's son. He looks around my age and fits right in with the classy, expensive interior of the nursing home with his white button-down and his clean-shaven face.

Damn, he's handsome. So much so, that for a second, I forget my manners and just stare at those sharp cheekbones and dark eyes. Finally, I shake myself and speak with a burning face. "Hello, sir. How can I help you?" I ask.

"Hi, I'm Sebastian Henderson. I'm here to visit my grandmother," he tells me with a polite smile. I can feel my brows rise but step out of the way, knowing he wouldn't be here unless the receptionist checked his identity.

"Rosie, would you look at that? Your grandson came around for a visit," I tell her, taking the glass of water away again.

The woman beams wider than ever before. "My Sebastian! Oh, today is full of surprises. First, your father sends me flowers, and now this." She gets up from her chair with some struggle and throws her arms around the young man.

He hugs her back, but his eyes lock on mine and he mouths, *"Flowers?"* I just shake my head. Maybe I'll explain it later, maybe he won't care enough to ask in private, but I certainly won't risk Rosie overhearing my confession.

When they end their embrace, Sebastian helps her sit back down on the cushioned chair. "I'm sorry I didn't visit sooner, Grandma. I didn't know you were transferred and couldn't find you," he says, and while I don't understand what he means by that, Rosie just nods and pats his cheek affectionately.

"Don't you worry about it, boy. I am happy you are here now. Besides, Aliena here kept me perfectly good company. Isn't that so, my dear? I even taught her to play Cribbage. Between the two of us, she isn't that great at it yet. No match for you." She tries to whisper the last part, but I am very much able to make the words out.

Her grandson's eyes flick to mine, and he gives me a big smile quite similar to Rosie's. "Give her some time. Chinese poker is no easy feat, and I had years to learn from the master," he tells her. Again, something twists in my stomach at the reminder that she won't have enough time to teach me well at all.

I wonder how much he knows about her condition. If he hasn't seen her in one and a half years, he's way out of the loop. I'll have to pull him to the side and give him all the news before he leaves.

I scan the room one more time before piping up, "Okay, I think my job here is done. I'll give you two some privacy. Mr. Henderson, why don't you ask for me at the reception desk on your way out? Until then, enjoy your visit. I'll see you at dinnertime, Rosie."

I head to the door, but gentle, long fingers wrap around my wrist, and I turn back around. "By all means, I don't want to be the reason you miss your Cribbage lessons. Stay, please. I can watch and maybe throw in a tip or two. Oh, and call me Sebastian," he says.

He looks sincere in his offer and since Rosie is nodding enthusiastically and our time together is my favorite time of the day, I agree.

"Okay, sure. Let's all witness another ice-cold defeat of mine. Your grandma is ruthless," I tell the young man. He tips his head back and laughs, the sound like honey to a sore throat. Meanwhile, Rosie watches us with a new glint in her eyes.

———

"Okay, I think I've lost enough for the day," I announce after five games of Cribbage because, despite Sebastian's occasional tips, I didn't stand a chance against the old lady. I feel like I did even worse today than usual.

In my defense, the low rumble of Sebastian's barely contained laughter did little to help my focus, and whenever he'd lean in to whisper something in my ear, I nearly dropped my cards altogether.

"I can't blame you. You really are having a bad day, sweetheart. Are you feeling all right? Your face is glowing red," Rosie remarks, drawing attention to what I know is nothing more than a silly blush.

Sebastian comes around the table to look at me too, a smile on his lips and satisfaction clear in his eyes. "Yes, Aliena, your face is a little flushed. Do you maybe want to get some fresh air?" he teases, just innocently enough for his grandmother not to notice.

It's then I realize he did this on purpose, all those fleeting brushes of his fingers against my arm and so on. He *was* flirting.

"Oh, I think that's a good idea. Sebastian, accompany her, will you? To make sure she is okay," his grandmother adds. To my dismay, she proceeds to wink at me. My face burns even hotter, and the only reason I don't disagree is I have to talk to the young man in private anyway. And maybe because the idea of being alone with him for a minute or two excites me just slightly.

I don't know what's wrong with me. Here I am, acting like some shy maiden when I am anything but. My habits

22

as a partygoer are proof enough of that. I don't remember there ever being a time when I blushed because of a guy. Maybe the innocence of this whole meeting does it for me. It's something new.

"Lead the way," Sebastian tells me, holding the door open for me. Great, I didn't even realize I zoned out. Here's a cute guy and I suddenly stumble over myself like an idiot.

I take a few short, hurried steps to catch up with him and walk through the door, muttering, "Thanks," under my breath.

I start walking toward the closest exit without looking back to make sure he is behind me, keeping my eyes on the floor as I try to gather my wits. The talk the two of us are about to have is anything but funny or lighthearted, so there is no space for me to be so unprofessional.

I'm looking for the right words to start when his hand is suddenly pressed softly against my lower back. I nearly miss a step with how fast my head whirls in his direction.

He smiles comfortingly. "Sorry, didn't know how else to get you to stop running. Are you okay?" he asks.

"Yes. Sorry, this is the first time Rosie has had a visitor, and I'm not sure where to start catching you up," I tell him and watch as his smile dims ever so slightly. He knows what I'm building up to and he isn't surprised.

"I know. The flowers, by the way, I know for a fact my father didn't send them, so thank you." His eyes are sincere, his tone earnest, and I can almost feel the gratitude coming from him. He must really love his grandmother. It makes me want to tell him even less.

"She was just so sad that her son never came to visit, and I couldn't stand it," I admit, feeling my cheeks heat

23

again. I quickly change the subject. "You said you hadn't known she was transferred? May I ask what you meant by that?"

His expression sours, and his hand leaves my body to rub over his face. "My father thought I wasted my time with all the visits I paid her at her last nursing home, so he moved her and wouldn't tell me where to. I had to scour every nursing home in and near Hartford. I can't believe it took me this long." He blows out a breath. "How's she doing?"

I keep leading him down the corridor until we finally reach the door to the yard. Once we're outside, I slow down and turn to look at him. "She is happy. Mentally, she's doing very well other than some minor short-term memory lapses. She has a few friends here and her spirits are always high." I take a quick break and hesitate.

"And what about her body?" he asks when I take too long to go on.

I shake my head a little. This is the worst part about this job. Sure, some of the time, we have doctors to give the really bad news to loved ones but most of the time, we nurses have to do it. "She's had cancer for many years now. Her body is growing weak, and she doesn't like taking her medicine. We can't force her, and your father hasn't given us any specific orders, so her condition has been worsening." I swallow the lump in my throat and force the last words out. "It's likely she won't make it into the next year."

Five months. I just told him he has no more time than that with his grandmother.

Sebastian runs a hand through his hair and nods to himself, his eyes a little unfocused on the ground. "Okay. Well, thanks for telling me. And for being here for her. I'm glad she wasn't alone." When his gaze meets mine, I can see they've become glossy. He clears his throat. "I'll be right back with you, okay? Would you mind getting back to her?"

I've always been good at taking hints. "Sure, take your time." I give him my best smile and lay my hand on his arm for a second. When he returns the small smile, I force myself to turn on my heels and return to my favorite senior, trying to lift my spirits on the short way.

Chapter 3

Aliena

I no longer recognize the boy I met at the nursing home four months ago. No, the man staring at me now, with his eyes narrowed and a vein in his neck pulsing, looks nothing like Rosie's sweet grandson. He looks through and through like his dipshit father's son.

In this house, at these parties, and with his friends, he always carries himself with an air of superiority. He thrives on the undeserved respect his fellow students give him because that's how their rich parents told them to behave. They kiss his ass and allow him walk all over them. And all for what?

To make a good impression on the dean of the university and heighten their chances of an invitation to the VIP room. If only they knew the dean and his son don't actually talk, least of all about Sebastian's friends. They could all stand up to him and would never have any troubles with the school.

Sure, Sebastian would beat them to a bloody pulp if anyone crossed a line and openly disrespected him, but one day or another, he'll meet a worthy opponent to push back.

I'm eagerly waiting for the day. It would do him some good to be humbled.

He and I are locked in a staring contest, both unwilling to look away. His gaze flicks over my appearance, lingering on my messy hair and my no doubt kiss-swollen lips, all evidence I'm freshly fucked. I can see the fury in his crazed eyes and the slight twitch of his jaw. The unfamiliarity of seeing those dark irises reveal so much is unsettling. Usually, he is collected, always cool. Now he looks a breath away from losing his mind. I don't understand what has gotten into him.

He loses our game as his eyes flick over my head and to his friend behind me. I watch as the wall comes down over his emotions, shutting them away, until he is nothing but a shell quaking with anger.

He shakes his head, the motion nearly unidentifiable, and before I can act, he pushes past me and heads straight for his friend. He grabs the collar of Mattheo's rumpled dress shirt and slams his fist into his cheek before anyone can make so much as a sound. Mattheo doesn't move to defend himself or to get his friend away. He just stands still, his face stoic while I cry out and scramble toward them.

Adrenaline floods my veins, and I almost can't believe what I'm seeing. What has gotten into him? Why the hell is he upset enough to hurt his friend? Just because he had to wait in front of my door for a few minutes instead of getting what he wanted immediately?

A cold shiver rushes down my spine. God, I hate violence.

"Hey! Stop! Sebastian, let go of him!" I yell, pushing him from the side so I can wriggle between the two idiots.

My heart is racing so much my chest hurts. I hold out my arms as one of Sebastian's hands clamps down over my shoulder for stability. He is clearly seeing red and only notices it's me in front of him after a second. His fist is already cocked to land another hit when the recognition sparks in his eyes, and out of muscle memory, my whole body locks up as I flinch.

That has him dropping his hands quickly, and he takes a hasty step back, shaking his head. He huffs. "You thought I'd hit you," he mutters, as if not quite sure of the words. Then his face hardens again. "I can't believe you. I gave you permission to use this room in case it got late and you didn't want to go home alone at night, not to spread your legs for anyone with low enough standards." He gives me a withering look.

"Dude," Mattheo interjects, looking ready to say more in my defense—or maybe his own. I stop him with a subtle shake of my head, and Sebastian, who sees the silent interaction, looks like he's about to burst.

I speak up before he can. "You have zero rights to shame me for this, much less any reason to be angry. You have no claim over me, Sebastian. None at all. Now get out!" I snap. Who does he think he is? It's all the more ironic because he was with a girl tonight. Like he was many nights before since we got to know each other. Occasionally, he picks them up right in front of me.

He has no right to shame me and cause such a scene. It's not like Lily and Andrew don't sleep together in their rooms all the time. Besides, he was the one shutting down whatever weird chemistry we'd had on that first meeting, not the other way around. He can't not want me and not want anyone else to have me either.

28

He glances between his friend and me a few times, his beautiful face twisting into something ugly and bitter. Finally, he gives me a short, disgusted glance and says, "You know, I really didn't peg you for the type. I'm sure Rosie would be so proud if she saw you now," he snarls.

With that, he turns and leaves while I stare after him, surprised by how much his words sting. Most of all, it was just wrong of him to bring up Rosie knowing how much she meant to me. Knowing how much her opinion meant.

In a matter of seconds, I shake myself and remember that he's just a coward who's acted like an ass ever since I first stepped into his house because he didn't like me knowing he was a big softie for his grandmother rather than the spoiled brat he pretends to be at school.

He has no right to be angry. His words mean nothing.

"Are you okay?" Mattheo's low voice is hesitant. With a deep breath, I turn around and give him my best unbothered look.

"I'm fine. He's the one with the problem. How's your cheek? I can't believe he hit you. God, what is wrong with him!" I huff a breath and then take a closer look at my friend's cheek. What an interesting mess I got us in.

"I can," he admits, rubbing the red bruise forming right on the bone. When I reach up to touch it, he brushes me off and shoots me a grin. "Was still worth it. He barely put his weight behind it," he assures me.

"Fool," I mutter playfully. "Anyway, I'll get going now." I step up to him. "Thank you for being such a great friend tonight. You really did make me feel amazing," I say, locking my arms behind his neck. He smiles coyly and I allow myself to kiss those soft lips of his one more time.

29

He muses, "You are flattering me, *amo*. Besides, I think I only deserve half the credit. Especially after you called *his* name when you came the second time," he teases.

My body jolts and I pull back, searching his eyes to see confirmation that he's joking. There's a glint in his eyes, amusement shining through.

No, he's joking.

I roll my eyes and shove him. Of course, that was a joke. Before I can turn to get on my way, his arms are back around me, and I find myself enveloped by his massive body. It takes me a second to realize he's hugging me, and when that registers, I can feel my heart crumble just slightly in my chest.

It's embarrassing how much I crave comfort, and it really is something nothing other than a sincere hug or a sweet caress can provide. I've been scrambling for scraps of this affection for years, giving up my body willingly to anyone with *low enough standards*, to put it in Sebastian's words. It was disappointing when I first realized sex and comfort weren't the same.

I soak up this moment and store it somewhere inside me for as long as I dare. Then I pull away and pat his shoulder. "Goodnight, Mattheo."

"Night, *seduttrice*. Get home safely."

Chapter 4

Aliena

Last July

"Do we have to go out tonight? Work tired me out and I'd be happy to just pass out in my uncomfortable bed," I whine while Lily adds some last-minute touches to her makeup. She throws me an unimpressed look over her shoulder.

"People looking as good as you do right now don't talk like that. Get up, or you'll wrinkle the silk. We're going tonight," my best friend declares, leaving no room for arguments. I groan again and roll onto my back, ignoring her comment about wrinkling the dress she bought me for my birthday last year.

"Since when do *you* drag *me* out to parties? You never want to go out. That bloody Anders is changing you," I pout.

"His name is Andrew. Don't act like you don't know. You've met him. And yes, he's forcing me to come out of my shell like you have been doing for years. Don't act like a baby just because you aren't the only person influencing me anymore." Before I can deny her accusation, she shoots

31

me a look in the mirror telling me to keep my words to myself.

She goes on. "It will be fun, A. The host's parties are legendary at my school, and we're VIPs since he's one of Andrew's best friends. Plus, you'll love the company my boyfriend keeps." That last part is followed by a wink.

I raise a brow. "Oh yeah? Anyone attractive you can brief me about?" I ask.

"More like *everyone* attractive, babe. I'm sure you'll find someone to your liking there."

"But they're all preppies!" I whine again. It's hard having a rich friend at times. While she is out getting to know the future presidents and first ladies, the only company I keep is the next generation of funerals.

"I'm a preppy and you like me just fine," she insists, fluffing her blond hair again before pouting at the mirror.

I must say, I enjoy seeing her this confident. Andrew is good for her. Not that I'd ever tell her that. Or him, Christ, no. He does not need that ego boost.

She finally turns around and eyes my starfish position on her bed. "Aliena, up! Now," she orders. With a laugh, I comply and head to the mirror too. Great, her boyfriend is supposed to pick us up any minute now and I have bedhead. I reach for the hairbrush, but Lily stops me.

"Don't! Leave it like that, you look hot." She appears at my reflection's side and rests her head on my shoulder with a wistful sigh. "God, it's unfair how fantastic you look." She gives me a once-over, keeping her eyes on my exposed cleavage for a long second. She smiles bashfully. "Oh, everyone will be drooling over you there."

I laugh and brush her off though I do give my reflection a lingering look. Red silk is molded to my body like a

32

second skin, the cleavage drops just low enough for it to be safe to dance without a bra on, and the hem reaches just the top of my thighs.

With an outfit like this, I kept my makeup simple. Highlighter, mascara, and red lips. I smile at myself and check my teeth for stains. Lilianne groans behind me.

"I will never get over your fangs. They make me want to ask for a bite and I'm straight." She cups my face and turns it to hers to inspect my mouth more closely. I roll my eyes.

"They're not fangs. Just very pointy canines," I explain for the millionth time.

"Yes, yes. Semantics."

The doorbell interrupts the moment, and my friend releases me. I snap a quick picture of myself in the mirror before trailing after her as she heads toward the door, grabbing my heels on the way.

"He walked up to the door? He couldn't have just given you a call?" I tease, even though I find it very cute.

"He was raised well," she tells me over her shoulder, grinning.

Good for him. My best friend deserves no less than a gentleman. She opens the door, and Andrew is quick to swoop her up in a kiss. I turn away, giving them a moment of privacy as they pull away and banter playfully.

"You look like a dream," Andrew whispers. Then he turns to me. "Hey, Aly. You look very lovely too." He gives me his winning smile, keeping his gaze on my face, and I thank him with a curtsy. I only met him twice before, but he seems like a good guy, so we get along well enough.

"Are you two ready? Mattheo is waiting in the car," he tells us.

Once we've confirmed, we're on our way downstairs. A slight breeze brushes against me as we exit Lilianne's dorm building, and chills prick my skin at the comfortable sensation. The days have been unbearably hot this summer, but now the sun is setting, the temperature is heavenly.

We head straight for a black Mercedes, and I smile at the sight. It's an elegant vehicle, low and broad from the front with sexy-ass lights. As we draw closer and the driver, Mattheo, I suppose, sees us, the motor purrs to life.

I don't have a lot of experience when it comes to getting rides in cars this fancy, and dressed up as I am, I must admit I feel like some supermodel or movie star. Especially when Andrew opens the back door for me after having done the same for Lily in the passenger seat. My will to go out tonight is certainly with me now.

"You know, I really wouldn't have minded sitting in the back with Aly," my friend says from the front, looking back at her boyfriend.

"I know, baby. In case my troll of a friend crashes his car, you have better survival chances in the front though." He winks at her, and so the discussion is closed. I still catch Lily's blushing cheeks and subtle smile before she faces forward.

"I know how to drive!" the man at the wheel suddenly protests. Then, his hazel eyes meet mine in the rearview mirror and he winks. "I'm Mattheo, by the way. And I must say, in all the many times Lily talked about you, she never mentioned how breathtaking you are."

"What a charmer," I joke even as my cheeks heat. I guess Lily wasn't exaggerating when she said I'd be intrigued tonight.

We stop at a red light and Mattheo turns in his seat to give me a slow, casual once-over. "Red looks good on you," he finally concludes, still grinning.

I'm rescued from scrambling for a reply when Andrew pipes up. "It's green, moron. Watch the road. You can flirt with her all night," he tells his friend.

Mattheo turns to the front but not without mumbling, "Oh, I sure plan to."

———

"Jesus Christ, Lil, you didn't warn me the party was at a palace!" I accuse my friend under my breath, looking up at the giant apartment complex. As soon as we drove into the neighborhood, where in between every house another five could fit, I knew we were headed somewhere fancy. I just didn't know how fancy.

"And you let me come with bedhead. If we're about to walk into a damn cocktail party, I'll shave off your eyebrows," I threaten, not entirely joking.

"Relax, A. I would never trick you like that. Trust me, his parties aren't any less wild than those you normally drag me to," she assures me right as Andrew throws an arm over her shoulder.

"If I had to guess, I'd say they're much crazier," he adds. "No one throws parties like Sebastian, the brilliant bastard."

35

I frown at the host's name. It's the first time they've mentioned it, and my mind goes straight to the young man I met at the nursing home two weeks ago. I have to admit, it isn't the first time my mind has strayed to his handsome face since then. Whenever work is slow, I imagine him walking back through the big double doors to visit his grandma. And maybe give me some tips at Cribbage and look at me with that adorable smile of his again. It's not every day you meet a sweet, gentle guy that's simultaneously incredibly good-looking, after all. I think it's fair for a girl to daydream.

"I guess I'll be the judge of that at the end of the night," I say, forcing my mind to stay on topic. Mattheo appears at my side, and we enter the building, only to be greeted by two buff men in suits on either side of the elevator.

Before I can question it, one of them says, "Have a good night, sirs."

The elevator doors open and the other stranger turns to us, his stoic expression giving way to a polite smile. "And you too, ladies." With that, the door closes, and we're heading up.

I watch the glowing numbers grow bigger and bigger until we reach eleven. By then, my mouth is slightly dry, and I feel myself grow a little nervous.

I'm not opposed to new things, but this … well, I have no idea what's waiting for me, and the elevator doors are thick enough to not let any sound seep through. Well, that or the party is incredibly silent.

But then the doors slide open the first inch, and I nearly jump at the blast of music flooding the tiny space. It's surreal and the feeling that this is a dream only intensifies when I look ahead and see the elevator brought us right into the apartment. Andrew and Lily step inside, completely

36

unfazed, and I jolt ahead too when Mattheo's hand finds my shoulder to lead me.

There are dancing bodies everywhere. And I mean dancing, bouncing, and jumping, not the lame swaying that some people consider party appropriate. All along the wall on the right, booze is displayed on a massive, illuminated glass shelf, a long bar parting it from the dance floor. The shelf is equipped with LEDs, each row a different dark color while the rest of the apartment is flickering with neon lights and lasers.

Hell, how can anyone live here? This looks more like a high-end club than a home.

"Not bad, huh?" Mattheo asks me, leaning down so our faces are on the same level. Even in my five-inch heels, I have nothing on his height.

I'm sure I look starstruck, so I don't bother playing it off. Instead, I just shake my head and feel a massive smile take over my face. Thank Lily, that beautiful goddess for dragging me along. This is where I should have always come to party.

Without thinking, I take Mattheo's hand in mine and drag him deeper inside the crowd of strangers, eager to lose my mind in the heat of the moment. If only Mattheo didn't stop me before I could even start, leaning down to tell me something again, "You know, I'd truly love to dance right now, Aliena, but we should say hello to the host first, no?"

I lean back and pout, giving him my best eyes as I look up through my lashes. He just chuckles.

"Damn *seduttrice*, you're good. We'll make a quick appearance, then we'll dance, okay?" he asks.

And just because I am happy as hell to be here and hopeful to secure an invitation to the next party, I smile at the giant and let him lead the way. I guess it's time to meet this mysterious Sebastian that lives in this mansion.

I'm not sure if it's just nerves or hope making my stomach queasy as we walk past the lone bouncer and up the stairs, but I feel my hands growing clammy. Partially because I'm letting a giant stranger lead me away from the party, though I'm not so worried about Mattheo. I'm more scared that I'll make a bad impression on the host.

What if it really is Rosie's grandson? I mean technically, he mentioned Hartford, which is where we are, and if he's the son of the person paying for Rosie's residency, the palace would make sense. Butterflies go off in my stomach as the pieces click into place.

God, I hope I'm right. I think. I mean, it would certainly be fun to meet the sweet young man again and another familiar face at this party wouldn't hurt. I really can't picture Sebastian in his white button-down among these party people though.

My questions go up in smoke as I'm led into a room down the hall on the second floor, and my eyes find those hauntingly beautiful dark ones. It's him. Oh damn, it really is him. My cheeks blush and I smile to myself as he looks at me, recognition clear on his features. It's good to know I made a well enough impression he remembers me after weeks and when I look completely different.

Mattheo lets go of my shoulder and walks toward the couch where Andrew, Sebastian, and Lilianne are already seated. He greets the host, momentarily stealing his attention. In the meantime, I walk over too, feeling uncharacteristically shy.

I force myself to stand straight and smile naturally when I stop in front of the couch, unsure how to proceed. Like, do I shake his hand? It's not like he's getting to his feet to greet me as he did with Mattheo. No, he's just sitting there, giving me an unimpressed look.

The butterflies shrivel. What the hell? Where's that sweet smile of his?

"Hey there, thanks for the invitation. The party looks like so much fun," I greet him, trying not to let his cold stare intimidate me.

He arches a brow. "Yeah sure. And you are?" he retorts, none of the politeness of our first meeting to be found.

"That's Aliena. You know, the best friend I never stop talking about? The one I grew up with?" Lily pipes up and I can hear her irritation. No matter how shy she is, she's never too shy to stand up for me. I shoot her a quick smile, and she responds with a quick nod.

The short moment of triumph is broken by Sebastian's unimpressed voice. "Huh, doesn't ring a bell. Do you go to our school?" he asks lazily, leaning back further into his seat. Really now? He's going to pretend not to know me? I'm sure he remembers how I told him I didn't go to university or college but worked instead. He met me there, after all.

But fine, if he wants to play this game, I can too. This isn't the guy I met at the nursing home anyway. "No," I reply, my voice dry, before taking a seat on the couch next to Lily, who leans closer to whisper something in my ear.

"I'm sorry about him. I don't know what's gotten into him. He's usually not half bad," she says.

I just brush her off. I'm pretty sure I know exactly what's gotten into him. He doesn't like the fact I saw him vulnerable and human when he visited his sick grandma, and now, he's trying to make up for it by being twice the "man". A.k.a., being a jerk.

I really misjudged him.

And as if my mood hadn't soured enough, a beautiful, tall, slim woman appears next to the couch in the next moment and conveniently falls onto the host's lap. She giggles, throws an arm over his shoulder to play with his hair, and whispers something in his ear, all the while shuffling around on his lap.

His icy expression thaws, and he gives her a small smirk, touching her thigh briefly. The similarity of the touch to how he flirted with me those weeks ago only makes me madder, and I can feel my face burn. Great, so this is just a regular thing for him, picking up women wherever he goes. I'm an idiot. I wish I hadn't spent all that time daydreaming about him.

Suddenly, his eyes leave the pretty girl's face and lock straight onto mine. His grin widens. And I've had enough. I get to my feet, smile at Mattheo, and hold out my hand to him, making sure my movements are extra smooth. If there's something I know, it's seducing and appealing to men. Better use that talent now.

My new friend doesn't need more encouragement and gets to his feet, grinning like a Cheshire cat. As we walk away, there's a new swing to my hips.

So what if the guy I had a silly little schoolyard crush on for a few days turns out to be an idiot player? I look great tonight, and the party downstairs is awesome. I'm going to enjoy the hell out of it.

Plus, I know I didn't imagine the host's clenched jaw as I walked off with his friend. What can I say, I couldn't help a small glance back at Lily. Since Sebastian was right next to her, I saw him by default.

I look up at Mattheo as we walk toward the stairs, past all the doors on the left and right. "I hope you're ready to dance, big guy. Try to keep up."

Chapter 5

Aliena

It seems during the time Mattheo and I were in my room, the party ended and most people have left by now. Some are already cleaning up, although I'm sure they aren't the ones that made the mess but hired people instead.

I make my way through the big apartment with my gaze lowered and head straight for the elevator. Maybe I should check if Lily is still here, but she'll probably go home with Andrew anyway, and I really want to get out of here before I run into Sebastian again. No, one argument is enough for tonight.

I throw my black coat over my shoulders, grab my purse, and leave. A shudder wrecks my body as soon as the November chill surrounds me, making me draw the fabric closer around me. Yeah, it's definitely time for a new coat. At the very least it's not raining like it was when we arrived.

I walk for twenty minutes until I see a familiar, tall shadow in the distance that always makes my strides lengthen. Another shiver goes down my spine, this time not from the cold. The old phone booth standing at the corner of this mostly deserted street is way too creepy. It's old and

I doubt it even works anymore. The only reason it still stands is that only three houses are around, and even they look like they are deserted, so it's simply not worth the trouble to tear it down.

I'd like to sign a petition to get it removed. In the dark and with the lack of streetlights, I mistake it for a giant person every time I see it in the corner of my eye. That damn thing.

I quicken my pace and draw my coat around myself more tightly while my eyes flick around my surroundings. My skin crawls with wariness. I should have accepted Mattheo's offer to give me a ride home. At the time, I just wanted to be alone and not mix things up further. I can deal with one-night stands just fine but part of that is being gone before the other person realizes it.

I never spend the night, and I never take people to my place. Anything to avoid rejection and seeing regret on someone's face in the morning. No, I'll pass. No one has to awkwardly tell me to leave. I never stick around that long.

But Mattheo is different anyway. He's my friend and has given me rides home several times. I'm an idiot, and now I have another twenty minutes of freezing my ass off ahead of me.

I turn the corner and finally put some distance between me and the horror cabin when I hear footsteps behind me. I don't pretend not to hear it, not with the fast, urgent pace from the person behind me. Instead, I whirl around and come face-to-face with a hooded figure. A shriek claws its way out of my throat. Where the hell did this person just come from? Whatever they want, it can't be good seeing as they are heading right for me.

43

I don't try to run. Not with my heels on. There would be no use. Instead, I walk backward to keep an eye on the advancing stranger while searching my purse for my pepper spray or my phone. Whatever my fingers might grasp first.

The person starts running, and my stiff fingers are still searching. More panic burrows itself inside my stomach, and I feel sick as I scramble back.

"Stop!" I finally yell in a pathetic attempt to change their mind. They're only mere feet away now. I scream again, this time for help.

Where's my phone? Where's my pepper spray? My numb fingers shake too much to identify the objects in my overstuffed handbag, and I curse myself for not having taken just a clutch with my essentials tonight.

I resort to clutching my bag's handle with both hands and ready myself to swing it at the stranger. My heart is racing painfully in my chest and my hands are clammy around the handle. I've had more than enough violence tonight as it is. Why the hell is this happening now?

The person launches for me, and I yank the purse forward. Before it can make contact with my attacker, they have their hands on the item and pull at it instead. I stumble forward and try to hold my own, but with the strength behind my attacker's yank, I'm guessing it's a man.

A fresh wave of panic fills my veins. *Why a man? Why is it always a man?* Fears of possible outcomes flood my system, turning my shrieking broken. It's all I can do to hold on to my bag, the one thing between me and my attacker, as if that might protect me. As if it could work as a shield.

Something dark flashes in the corner of my eye, but the danger doesn't register until the fist collides with my jaw, snapping my head to the side. The taste of blood invades my mouth as my lip splits, and as I stumble, I fall back. My tailbone hits the pavement with so much force I see stars, and the palms of my hands scrape over the tiny rocks on the ground as I move away from my attacker. *Don't focus on the pain. Get away.*

But it seems like there was no reason for that last attempt, anyway, seeing as my attacker is now running in the opposite direction, my belongings in tow. I watch his shadow disappear into the night, numb for a beat until the first broken sob falls from my split lips.

I didn't feel the sound coming, and I startle myself as it pierces the otherwise silent night. One hand comes up to cover my mouth, to stifle any more cries, but I can't get myself to move otherwise.

The longer I sit there, the more the cold registers again, and I realize I'm shivering. My jaw and the entire side of my face are throbbing numbly. The familiarity of it all is enough to make me cry even harder. I close my eyes, and for a second, I'm not out here at all. Instead, I'm out in the garden with my father on a chilly Christmas Eve many years ago.

My lip was bleeding then, too. Or maybe my eye was. And six-year-old me was crying and shivering just like I am now. But I was not alone then. No, my dad was with me, pacing the small, unkept lawn in an anxious habit. *"You don't understand. Just be quiet, Aliena. Just stop being so needy and asking for things you cannot have! You are agitating your mother!"* he pleaded with me, as desperate as he was angry.

45

I didn't understand back then. Didn't understand how much he had to do to pay our rent and make sure our little family had food on the table. He was grasping at straws, and there was little me asking for more. I don't even remember what it was. Some doll or something that my classmate talked about the week before at school.

I wanted that stupid toy so much that when my parents told me there were no presents, I made a scene. My dad, stressed as he was back then, saw that my mother became upset too and didn't know what else to do but force me outside and punish me with a punch to make me shut up.

In retrospect, I know he didn't mean any harm. He always cared about me. It's just that he cared about Mom too, and nothing good ever followed when she was agitated. She had developed a habit back then, and I was a stupid kid that didn't understand I was only making things worse.

She'd lost her job and started stealing from Dad, who was already struggling to make ends meet as it was. That Christmas, he got an old tree that was supposed to be thrown away at the market for free so we could decorate it like we always had. Of course, I didn't understand how much effort he put into that and demanded more. Always more.

I was a shit kid.

Small stones dig deeper into my palm and the memory fades. For a beat, I hardly understand where I am, and my stomach turns with nausea like it tends to do after flashbacks. I grit my teeth and get to my feet, nearly falling back down as a wave of disorientation hits me. Shit, I'm dizzy.

Not confident in my ability, and sure of my disinterest in walking home the rest of the way, I decide to do the only thing left for me to do and walk toward the nightmarish phone booth. My heart is still racing, and it only worsens when I try to recall the number of any friend of mine. I start crying more.

I always knew Lilianne's number by heart, but she just got a new one and I never bothered to memorize it. I sure as hell don't know any of the others. Except for one, that is. The last person I'd like to call or have with me right now. Not when I'm crying and dizzy and lost.

I finally reach the booth, and a weight drops from my chest when the door opens easily. My confidence I could even get inside was below the ground the closer I got to the old thing. I type in Sebastian's number with shaky hands and dread in my chest. What if he doesn't pick up? Would he bother to pick me up after what happened tonight? Maybe he'd at least tell Lily or Andrew that I could use some help. I don't doubt they'd come in a heartbeat.

The only reason I know his damn number in the first place is that I used to catch glances at it at the nursing home after his first visit and dream about it lighting up on my screen on boring days. That was before I truly met him. And, of course, there was one time I had to dial his number over and over again because, not unlike now, my vision was blurry from too many tears.

I hold the receiver to my ear and listen to it ring, suppressing a sob as the seconds drag on and my hopes shrivel. I count the high-pitched sounds, growing more anxious the higher the number becomes. How long until it disconnects? And what do I do when it does? I really don't want to walk home alone anymore. I'm too shaky. Too dizzy. And my head is throbbing.

Shit, did I hit my head? I thought I only fell on my ass but I'm not sure. My head sure feels as if I hit it. Unless the person who robbed me just put much more force behind the punch than I was used to. My dad probably always went easy on me.

I sob again on the fifth ring, clutching my stomach with my empty hand as more nausea rolls over me. Finally, just when I'm sure I'll have no choice but to walk the rest of the way, the most beautiful sound reaches my ear.

"Sebastian Henderson. Who's this?" he asks when he picks up the call.

Chapter 6

Aliena

Last September

"Sebastian Henderson. Who's this?"

Shit. He picked up. He actually picked up. Fuck, I'm not ready for this. I really, really am not. I don't have the right words. I'm not calm. Shit, I should have let a doctor do this. Or another nurse. Someone who was less personally involved in the situation. Anyone but me. I really shouldn't have called.

But I wanted it to be me. I thought that maybe it would help to get the news from someone he knows, someone who shares some of his pain. Or maybe I did it for my sake. Because I wanted to hear his familiar voice. No matter how rude he is to me at times, he's still my friend. I need that now.

I swallow a sob, biting down on my tongue behind the hand that's clasped over my mouth. I've been crying for an hour already, why can't I stop now? I wanted to stop before making this call, that's why I waited this long in the first place. But I couldn't put it off any longer. It isn't fair to keep this from him for so long. We're to notify the loved ones as soon as possible after the death of a resident. God, I really am messing this up.

If only I hadn't gotten so damn attached to someone I knew was on borrowed time. After nearly six years of working here, I should have known better. If only I hadn't gotten so used to her asking about my day or weekends, her sweet smiles, and those Cribbage lessons. Maybe then it wouldn't feel as if something was stolen from me now. Taken unjustly. Broken right out of my chest.

I hold the phone away from my face and take a shaky breath. "Sebastian, hey. It's Bloomfield Living Care. Um, it's Aliena." I hiccup, remembering the time Rosie introduced me to him. If only I hadn't met him then. Maybe I never would've been able to imagine the sweet man he could be. I never would have met the loving, polite side of him I never got another glimpse of since that first meeting.

I saw on the visitor list he kept coming, but only ever when I wasn't there, and whenever we were forced to hang out together with our friends, he was different.

Relaxed and funny with his friends and Lily. Occasionally he even spared some humor for me. After our rocky start at his party, he never really warmed up to me though, and I never tried to change that. He was laid back and left me alone outside those stolen, rare moments where our chemistry would bubble up unexpectantly.

One time I stumbled on the sidewalk, and he had to steady me by my elbow. I looked up at him, and for a second, something warm flickered to life in those dark eyes. Another time, I spilled some of my drink on him and stupidly tried to clean it. Again, our eyes locked with my hand on his chest, and in that short moment, I almost kissed him. I thought he almost kissed me.

Both of those times and many other similar ones ended with him pushing me away. Every flirty comment he'd sometimes throw at me was followed by even more distance as soon as he realized what we'd done.

He was a player, he was rude, and he was nothing like the young man he pretended to be around his grandma. Or maybe he's pretending around us. Either way, I'm about to deliver bad news, and I've never hated my job more. No matter how expected this was.

"Yes?" the man on the other side prompts, his voice impossibly colder. He knows what's coming. He must.

"I'm calling about Rosie. I'm so sorry to inform you she passed away this afternoon." I can't keep down my sob this time, memories of the alarm going off in the break room for us nurses as her vitals dropped tormenting me. I don't think I'll ever forget how my heart froze over and dropped to my stomach. Or how I started running to her room before anyone else reacted.

I broke down at her bedside and took her hand as if it were my grandmother. Meanwhile, I guess I stole that opportunity from her actual grandson by waiting so long to call him. Maybe he could've seen her one last time. By now, they must have taken her away.

The guilt is making me sick. I force the last words out, not unlike how I had at our briefing when we first met. "She went quietly during her nap. I am really sorry for your loss." Okay, there it was. That's it. I cover my mouth again and try not to sniffle too loudly as I wait for his reply.

It takes him a few seconds but finally, he snaps, "God, get your act together. What is wrong with you? This is your job, stop crying." With that, the line disconnects, and I finally set the phone down, curling in on myself like I've wanted to for the last hour.

I can't even blame him for how he just reacted. I couldn't even tell him about his grandmother's death without falling apart and making it all about me. It's like I'm that needy kid on Christmas all over again.

No, he's hurting too, and if the roles were reversed, I'm sure I would have wished for someone more professional to deliver such news. I'll just take this as a lesson not to ever get this close to a patient again, for one, and to be what the person losing a loved one needs the next time. I need to stop looking for scraps of affection wherever I can. This isn't the place.

Chapter 7

Sebastian

There's no reply from whoever called for long enough to make me contemplate just hanging up. It's way past midnight, after all. Certainly not the time to get a call, which is why I'm curious enough to stay on the line, even though it's a time when most people would be asleep. A time when I sure as hell should be asleep rather than abusing my punching bag to release some of this undying, unjustified anger within me.

All because of a certain honey-eyed, golden-haired girl and her stupid decision to fuck my best friend in my home. Now, her moans are the only thing I can think of whenever I want to walk down the corridor leading to my room.

Yeah, I'm not getting any sleep tonight. I'll just stay in my gym until it's time for my morning run and hope I can finally pass out after that.

At first, I even contemplated calling the girl I was with earlier tonight, but that idea was quickly discarded. I already turned her down once today. Inviting her over just to do it again would make me a jerk. And there's no way I wouldn't turn her down when it's all I've done with any girl for months.

It's the same thing every time. I indulge in flirting and maybe kiss a girl, but in the end, I never feel like taking it further even when there's nothing wrong with her.

Ever since I met that infuriating nurse who turned out to be a lot less sweet than first anticipated. It's funny how I thought I met an angel only for her to turn up at my party looking hot as sin in the same month.

Of course, she and my friends think that I haven't changed my ways since I can't seem to stop picking up girls in front of them. They don't know that I just get a kick out of the jealousy in Aliena's eyes whenever I turn my attention to someone else.

It's only fair I pay her back for how she flirts non-stop with my best friend. Call me stupid but I guess I thought it was just a game we were playing.

As it turns out, we weren't on the same page about the rules. She confirmed that when she fucked Mattheo while I left my date after watching a movie without so much as a kiss.

My agitation grows, and I'm about to either snap at the person over the phone or simply end the call when a soft noise stops me. A sniffle. A sound that's eerily familiar.

"Seb?" a shaky voice asks. Her voice. Just a much softer, flimsier version of it that triggers all the wrong emotions and instincts in me. I stand up straighter, the hair on my arms rising.

"Aliena? Whose phone are you calling me from? What's going on?" I ask, no longer feeling my earlier rage. Just a whole lot of confusion. And maybe a little worry as I squint at the foreign number on my screen.

She sniffles again. "I'm using the telephone booth. Someone stole my phone."

I'm already moving toward the door when I ask, "Stole your phone? Who stole your phone, Aliena? Someone at the party? And what are you doing out at this hour? Didn't Mattheo give you a ride?" Too many questions are buzzing in my head. I don't know what to focus on.

"No. I was walking home when someone attacked me." She hiccups and I can feel my stomach tighten. Someone attacked her. What the fuck? "Seb, I don't feel too good."

Those words have a whole bucket of ice crashing over me, and I stop dead in my tracks, giving her my whole attention.

"Are you hurt, Aliena? Where's the booth, exactly? I'm coming."

"I don't know. Um, he hit me and took my bag. And I fell but... I don't know if I hit my head. I'm just really dizzy. I don't want to walk home anymore," she says, her words breaking off with a choked sob. I press the elevator button repeatedly, my mind racing.

"You don't have to, baby. You don't have to go anywhere. I'm on my way, okay? Just stay on the phone. Is the booth on your way home?" I ask urgently. What is wrong with Mattheo for letting her walk home alone at this hour? First, he fucks her, and then he's too good to make sure she gets home safely. I'll kill him. Right after I find whoever made her sound so fucking scared and shaken and kill him too.

Finally, the elevator opens slowly, and I burst out of it. Everything is moving so damn slowly.

"Mhm," Aliena replies as I get into my car. She sniffles again. "I'm really dizzy, Sebastian. I think I have to sit down and close my eyes for a second," she adds.

I'm already shaking my head. "Don't close your eyes, Aliena. Just keep talking to me until I'm there. Can you tell me more about the person that robbed you?"

"He was hooded. It was too dark to see anything. Um, he has a mean right hook though," she mumbles, and I don't like that wobbly sound at all. It doesn't suit Aliena. She's loud and cheery and obnoxious most of the time, but she's not weak and unsure.

Jesus Christ, and did she say he hit her? My hand tightens around my phone and my blood starts boiling at images of Aliena being jumped on her way home. The thought of her taunting, pretty face with even a single bruise makes me want to snap.

I'm absolutely killing Mattheo for letting her walk home. And I hope she's ready for a lecture about how stupid she was to go out alone and unprotected this late. She lives a twenty-minute drive away. By foot and in those ridiculous heels she insists on wearing everywhere, it would take her forever. What was she thinking?

I can hear her take in a choppy breath and realize I stopped talking. "Where did he touch you? What hurts?" I ask even though I sure as hell don't want to hear the answer to that.

"Just my face. Just one punch. Nothing new. I don't know why I'm feeling so bad."

I'm too busy worrying about how slurred her words are to stumble over the nothing new part. That only registers when I'm in my car, racing down the street way over the speed limit.

I'm sure there are better things to ask about now. Still, it bothers me too much to drop my prompt, "Nothing new?" It takes a second until eventually, I get a reply in the form of a crashing sound and a thud that reminds me way too much of a body hitting the ground. My heart misses a beat. "Aliena? Hey, what happened? Are you okay?"

There's no reply. I accelerate my car further, scanning the sides of the road as best as I can in my search for that stupid booth.

"Aliena? Come on, answer me," I urge her. "I'm almost there. I'll be with you in a second and then we'll get that pretty head of yours checked at the hospital, okay? You're gonna be okay. I'll pick you up in a sec. Can you hear me? Just make a sound so I know you're still there."

It's useless for me to keep talking, and I know it. But the thought of her passed out in a creepy old booth makes me feel sick with worry, and I don't know what else to do. She said she didn't hit her head. She shouldn't have passed out.

Finally, after excruciating minutes, I see the tall frame of the telephone booth, and my car screeches to a halt. I don't bother to turn it off, letting the lights give me a better view as I run for it. When movement to the right catches my eye, I turn and nearly trip over my feet when I recognize what I'm looking at.

"Hey! Get your hands off her!" I yell at the strange lady dragging a limp Aliena away.

At my words, the stranger's head snaps up and she drops Aly, letting her head fall to the ground as she shies away from me, looking terrified. She fiddles with something in the waistband of her pants and finally pulls out a small gun, pointing it at me. I slow down.

57

"Don't come any closer! Get away from us!" the woman yells. It's now I see she must be even younger than me. In her late teens, at most. The weapon is trembling in her hand.

"Listen, that's my friend you're dragging over the ground. I'm asking you again to step away and put the gun down, please. I won't hurt you."

The girl looks unsure but shakes her head, lifting her chin a little. "No, I won't let you take her! Not without proof. I live over there, and I heard her call for help. That's what I'm doing," she tells me. I relax a little further. At least she's no danger to Aliena, and I respect her for coming outside in the dead of night after hearing someone call for help. Alone, at that.

"Okay, I'm glad you wanted to help. I can show you that she called me from the booth just now, okay? I can show you the number," I say, carefully holding my phone out more. It's still in my hand from when I was talking to Aliena.

The girl nods and I carefully walk closer, showing her the strange number at the top of my calls list. With a relieved sigh, her shoulders drop, and she lowers the gun. "Thank god, I had no idea what I was doing. Can you take her to the hospital, please?" she asks, looking even younger now.

"Of course. And thanks for looking out for her." I'm glad she wasn't ready to hand a passed-out woman to just some shirtless man that randomly showed up on this abandoned street. I must look like a maniac. In my hurry to get to Aliena, I completely forgot about getting dressed.

My eyes drop to the girl on the ground and every bit of relief I briefly felt vanishes as I crouch down at her side, cradling her head and thin shoulders. "Aliena, baby? Can you hear me?" I ask quietly, weirdly aware of the stranger observing us from behind me. It's unsettling to have my back turned to an armed person. Not that I think the girl will attack me.

I curse under my breath at the feel of Aly's icy skin. I gather her in my arms and lift her up. Her head rolls against my naked chest, and when I look down, something fierce grabs ahold of me. My stomach is in knots and chills have spread over my skin at the subzero temperature, yet my chest feels warm.

I shove that realization to the side and turn back to my car without wasting any more time. "Have a good night," I tell the girl as I start striding away with long steps. The first thing I do inside the car is turn up the heat. Then I get a good look at her split lip, instantly wishing I hadn't looked at all.

I can't believe she was attacked and injured. I also can't believe she called me, of all people. Especially after how much of a dick I was earlier.

Turning on the engine, I race to the hospital. "I'm so sorry this happened. You're safe now. We're almost at the hospital where they'll take good care of you," I promise her uselessly.

At least I take a bit of comfort in the fact her face looks fine other than the split lip, though I don't like that she passed out in the tight booth and how the girl later let her head drop. Still, my best guess is she passed out from adrenaline or a mixture of different factors. I'm sure she'll be okay.

She'll be fine.

Chapter 8

Sebastian

Last August

"Dude, stop speeding just because you can afford the fine. I don't know about the others, but I'm too pretty to die, and we're not even in a hurry. Slow the fuck down," Mattheo whines from the backseat, earning himself another one of those laughs from Aliena.

My fingers tighten on the steering wheel enough to turn my knuckles white, and without my brain's command, my foot presses down harder on the gas pedal. Mattheo might not be in a hurry, but I need nothing more than to get out of the car and distance myself from the girl laughing in my backseat.

We just picked her up at her place since we're going to a club tonight, and as soon as she got into the car, her addictive scent invaded my nose. It's like she put a spell on me, and now all I can think about is her. The way she looked as she walked to my car in her short black dress. The way the hem of said dress rode up further on the back of her thighs when she hugged Mattheo hello. Or how her bare, slender back flexed when she squeezed him tightly.

My eyes flick back to the rearview mirror and instantly find the golden-haired menace. Of course, her gaze is trained on my friend on her left side. The friend whose hand, I now notice, is placed on her naked thigh as he smiles at her.

I hate their relationship. Two flirts in their natural habitat. It's like they can't help but be obnoxiously teasing whenever they're together. Not even when there are three other people in the car, who absolutely don't want to witness this shit again.

Well, I don't know about Andrew and Lily, but I sure as hell don't want to see it. Of course, the other two are unlikely to even notice what is going on in the car with how lovestruck they are. Even now, my friend is giving his girlfriend moon eyes from where he's sitting in the back. She's no better, always turning around in the passenger seat to meet his eyes.

And then there's me. The driver. The newly appointed fifth wheel. I speed up further, enough to get Mattheo's attention again.

"Dude, I wasn't joking."

"Dude, I don't care," I mock him. And again, my treacherous eyes find Aliena in the backseat. Only this time, she's looking at me too, and our gazes lock. There's a challenge behind those honey eyes, a silent question, and an understanding I absolutely despise.

She smirks and my gaze drops to those full lips. I hate how beautiful she is.

I force myself to look back at the street so I don't crash the car. Whether I like it or not, everyone I consider a friend is in this vehicle, and I don't need that number to go down any further by killing one of them.

Even though at the moment I'm not sure I would mind if it was Mattheo. I mean, I know I would mourn him since we grew up together and all, but right now, I'm just not feeling it.

I take a deep breath and ease the pressure on the accelerator. My friends all visibly relax, though some of the tension my outburst created lingers. That's why I force myself to loosen my fingers around the steering wheel and throw a lazy smile back at Mattheo.

"There you go, princess. Any other demands?" I tease, attempting to sound a lot more at ease than I feel. Meanwhile, Aliena's eyes are burning the side of my face. I don't indulge in meeting her gaze this time. It's not worth the satisfaction she would get out of it. No matter how exceptional the view may be.

When we reach the club, I park my car and finally leave the torturous confines of the vehicle. I walk ahead until we reach the entry, greet the bouncers with a nod, and thank them as they let my friends and me inside. Then I fall back a few steps and let the others go ahead right before we reach the main hall.

As expected, Aliena stops in her tracks at the railing, looking down on the dance floor, her eyes wide and her body eerily still as she marvels at the sight. The others move on toward the VIP section, oblivious, but I linger, watching her watch the people below.

She's so predictable. Every time we take her to a new location I've long since gotten used to, she takes a minute to take it all in. I noticed it when she entered my upstairs lounge at the first party and every time since.

I think it's good for me, the reminder that what I have isn't as natural as it sometimes feels. She makes me look at the beautiful places we go to, really look at them like a newcomer might, and I can't deny the gratitude it elicits inside me for all I have.

After some time, Aliena comes back to herself and notices me standing behind her. She looks at me over her shoulder, then turns fully so her back is at the railing. It's then that I notice how close we are. Close enough for me to see the faint freckles on her face, and the dark specks in those brown eyes that are actually golden when the sun hits them right.

"I don't think I'll ever get used to this," she says, her voice breathless and low as if she was scared to ruin the moment. I feel it too, the fragile spell that ties us together right now and grants us another one of these rare seconds of peace. Moments we might have had more of if only I hadn't met her at the nursing home first. If she hadn't seen a piece of me she shouldn't have, the type of vulnerability no one is supposed to witness.

"Love makes you weak, boy. See how easily I can exploit your love for your mom. You stay in line because you know what the alternative is. You know she can't survive without me, and you would never risk that no matter how much you hate it. As long as you keep your cards wide open, you will always be powerless."

I keep watching her, unsure of what to say. All I know is the spell between us is calling me closer, making me step forward to erase some of the distance between us. So much until she's looking up at me through her lashes, smiling softly. Fuck, she's beautiful. It's moments like this when I really understand why Mattheo calls her seductress. When she looks at me like this, in a moment as such, I'm not sure there's a thing I wouldn't do if she only asked.

"Thank you for bringing me here," she whispers, reaching out to touch my arm gently. My breath hitches at the electric current that comes to live inside me at the skin-to-skin contact. Is this the first time she has touched me? I can't remember, but I know she hasn't done it enough. Why does she, of all people, have to be the one that makes me feel this way?

Her eyes drop to the ink on my right bicep, so close to where her hand is, and she starts tracing my tattoo lightly. I use that momentary lack of her attention to take a deep breath and close my eyes. In a second, we'll join the others, and the spell will be broken. I know that. That's why I'm allowing myself to just soak it up now.

"How many do you have?" she asks. I reopen my eyes to find her still gazing at the sun on my arm, tracing each fine line.

"Eighteen," I reply. Her eyes meet mine and for a second, and I could swear they were asking me to kiss her. Before I can decide if I'm reading her right and if I should just give in and lean down, she looks back at the sun.

"What does this stand for?" she asks.

"Argentina. It's where my mother is from," I tell her, surprised by how easy it is to tell her something private about me.

As if she didn't know enough already.

I shake myself. It's time for me to pull myself together. The moment has lasted long enough. Better to just get back to reality before I lose all my will to ever do so.

I take a step back with a deep breath and feel the regret bloom in my chest. In the end, I can't deny myself the small pleasure of brushing the palm of my hand against her arm to lead her in the direction of our friends, saying, "Come on, it's time we join the others."

———

"You're insatiable. And don't give me those eyes, *seduttrice*. I'll be back on the dance floor with you in a second. I just need a drink and a moment to catch my breath," Mattheo complains, falling back onto the leather couch like a bag of rocks.

I try to look as unfazed as possible as I lazily let my gaze slide over to them, but the sight of her smiling at him as she ruffles his hair makes me feel anything but. I don't even know why. I'm attracted to her, so what? I'm attracted to many people, but I never give a damn about who else they give their attention to.

Aliena must feel me staring because she turns around the next second, giving *me* her attention for a change, rather than my friend. To my great satisfaction, her face sours as her eyes flick to the girl in my lap. She does not have the same control over her features as I do, that's for sure.

The girl in my lap gives my hair a tug, eager to be the center of my attention again, and I play along as if she'd ever been it in the first place. She smiles down at me, pouting just slightly before leaning in to whisper in my ear.

"I'm thirsty," she tells me.

Her innuendo isn't lost on me but since I have no interest in taking her up on *that* offer, I just smile and say, "Get whatever you want. It's on me." She seems happy enough to hear that and gets to her feet, giggling when I give her ass a playful parting slap.

I make sure to look after her for a few seconds before allowing my eyes to wander where they actually want to be. I'm not surprised to see Aliena still watching, and the pleasure it causes me is unheard of. I bring my drink closer to my face and give her a small nod before taking a sip, never breaking eye contact.

That's when an unsettling smile spreads over her face. For a short second, I'm scared she tampered with my drink. Then she throws an arm over Mattheo's shoulder and falls into his lap, looking really pleased with herself. Mattheo doesn't miss a beat and places a hand on her thigh, thereby making me want to put a hand around his throat.

My hand clenches around my glass and I only realize I'm staring a hole into my friend's hand when Aliena laughs softly. Mattheo's whispering something in her ear but her eyes are locked on me. I don't doubt that laugh belonged to me too.

As if that wasn't enough, Aliena takes the game a little further and shimmies back on my friend's lap. His smile turns wicked, his hands find her slim waist, and I watch with simmering fury as he pulls her against him the rest of the way, bringing her back right against his chest and placing her ass perfectly on his groin, no doubt.

I see red, but of course, Aliena isn't done playing now. No, she loves the reaction she's getting from me, I know she does, and yet, I can't bring myself to look away and put an end to this. Maybe I secretly get a kick out of it too. Of knowing that it's me she's doing this for, not Mattheo. That it's me she's focusing on and maybe, just maybe, it's me she wished she was sitting on top of.

I'm crazy to think her eyes become lidded because she follows my stream of thought and is thinking of my touch.

66

That's when I realize Mattheo is peppering her neck with small kisses while she holds my gaze.

My hands ball into fists, but I don't look away. No, I won't do it if she doesn't. I won't extract myself from the moment and let it belong to him when it's still me she's giving that look to. Her hands rise to her neck, and she brushes her hair over her shoulder and tilts her head, giving Mattheo perfect access to deepen the kisses against her skin. Then, her fingers move into his hair and her eyes briefly flutter shut.

When she opens them again, I know it's me she wants. The eyes she's giving me, the way her body is gradually turning more toward me. Seductress is right. I can feel myself getting turned on by the little show she's putting on, but it's enough for me to know I'm not the only one. No, she's getting restless too, I can see it in the way she keeps crossing and uncrossing her ankles, flexing her legs before relaxing them again.

Shit, and now I'm looking at her long, smooth legs.

I'm saved from drooling all over her when my date of the night returns with her drink. She gets my attention by gently squeezing my shoulder, and when I lean back in my seat, spreading my legs just a little wider, she quickly reclaims her place on my lap.

Not unlike how Aliena did it, she moves all the way back on my thighs. For just a second, I let my head lean back on the couch and just feel. Feel and imagine that maybe, it's a woman dressed in black on my lap, rather than the raven-haired one in her silver skirt and halter top.

It's a minor slip-up that lasts a mere beat of the pounding music, but it's enough to make me harder than I've gotten for anyone in a month. I open my eyes, look at

Aliena, and then finally turn away to take another big sip of my drink. That's it, we're done. The spell's broken.

I'm aware of Aliena getting to her feet, of Mattheo doing the same, and of them disappearing into the crowd outside the VIP section. Finally, I relax in my seat, knowing things are back to what they always are now. The two of them are dancing out of sight, and I'm people-watching with a nice girl in my lap, occasionally conversing with Andrew and Lily whenever they aren't busy eating each other's faces.

This is familiar. This is reliable. This is safe

Chapter 9

Aliena

I felt like an idiot when I woke up at the hospital. I felt even more so when the doctor gave me a quick sum-up about how I was brought here because I passed out after I couldn't handle all the adrenaline that flooded my body after the attack. Or something like that.

But what made me feel most like a fool was the disappointment that flooded me when I opened my eyes and was met with the sight of Lily, and when it was her scent that invaded my nostrils as she hugged me tightly, not Sebastian's. More than that, I started feeling guilty as soon as I identified the emotion.

There was my lovely best friend telling me how glad she is that I'm awake and well, and how she can't believe I was attacked, and I was feeling upset that Sebastian didn't stick around rather than be grateful for what I had. It's moments like that when I feel like the selfish little girl I used to be. I hate myself in such moments but maybe there are just traits about me that I cannot lose, no matter how hard I try.

"When Seb called me, I didn't want to believe him. I was asleep when the phone went off and didn't hear a word for the first two minutes he spoke. Then he said you were at the hospital, and I thought he was joking.

"I woke Andrew and forced him to give me a ride. He wanted to stay and wait with me, but I sent him home again. Figured you didn't want a bigger audience, right? I'm sure he won't mind picking us up as soon as you're ready to go, though," she told me, practically rapping the words in a nervous beat.

Then she forced me to tell her what had happened, and why I called Sebastian instead of her. I did my best to catch her up, but my memories were jumbled and my thoughts scattered.

That's when the doctor came in to brief me about my condition and basically told me I was in perfect health other than my split lip. Of course, he gave me the whole lecture about how I should go to the police once I'm out of the hospital and that I should be careful, and something about having gotten lucky.

And lucky is what I felt when I went to the receptionist after being released to ask for the bill only to have her tell me it was already paid for. Since Lily swore it wasn't her, it only leaves one person that could have covered it.

I was tempted to call Sebastian right then to thank him for getting me last night and for paying the bill, but then I remembered we weren't that kind of friends. I'd only called him twice since I met him and those were due to absolute necessity. I decided to just thank him when I saw him next despite not fully being over his outburst earlier last night. Since I'm in no position to refuse his generosity, it's all I can do to offer my gratitude.

I don't feel so lucky now that I've been awaiting my turn at the police station for a damn hour. With nothing to entertain me other than some old gossip magazine I found lying around.

Andrew dropped me off here and then went home with Lily since she wanted to change out of her pajamas. Yeah, she didn't think to do that before she rushed to me in the hospital as if I were dying or something.

I love my best friend.

Either way, they left me here an hour ago. Since I'm still phoneless after last night, I can't even ask her when she'll be back. The silver lining is Lily kept her old, still intact phone when she got her current one, so I don't have to spend all my savings on a replacement. It looks like I'm even getting an upgrade on that front, since my phone was ancient and had a broken screen.

The station door opens, and like I do every time it does, I look up from the magazine and check who it is. This time, I'm relieved to finally see my friend and her boyfriend enter, already looking around the room in search of me. I stand and wave them over, unable to contain my smile when Lily teasingly waves my new phone in front of her as she comes closer.

I hug her as soon as she's within reach. Then I do the same with Andrew, and finally, I hug the shiny phone with its fluffy case to my chest. Yeah, the case will have to go, but I'm still happy to have a phone again, no matter that I don't have any of my stuff on it yet. Just the weight of it in my hand is reassuring. It's scary how lost I felt without one.

"Thanks for coming. I was about to die of boredom. I don't know how people did it back in the day," I say, exaggerating just to see them smile and roll their eyes at my theatrics.

"Have you given your statement?" Lily asks.

"No, they keep telling me to wait," I reply and already, my mood is dimming. I just want to go home, take a shower, and change out of my party clothes. I wish Lily had brought me something to change into. I can tell the people here disregard me more than they usually would because I look the way I do. That is to say, like a hooker who was beaten up.

"What? You've been here for over an hour. Hang on, I'll handle it," Andrew pipes in. Before I can accept or deny the offer, he's striding toward the officer behind his desk, muttering, "Unbelievable." His strides are purposeful in a way I've never seen before, the serious demeanor so at odds with his usual carefree attitude it seems completely unnatural, and yet it's clearly enough to intimidate the officer when Andrew stares him down at his desk.

I'm about to crack a joke about the surreality of this situation, but Lily just looks at me and shrugs. Like it's normal that law enforcers respect Andrew naturally. I frown a little.

Andrew is a man, yes, but he's a man of color. Unless I'm missing something, this interaction seems most uncommon.

I watch the men exchange a few words too low for me to hear and then Andrew is back with the officer at his side in a matter of minutes. I'd be offended by the favoritism if I didn't just want to get this over with.

"Hello again, Miss. I'm ready for your statement now," he tells me, smiling nervously and glancing over my shoulder for a split second, where I'm sure Andrew's standing. What I want to retort is that he would have been ready for me half an hour ago if he had just stopped watching a recorded football game on his laptop with the screen turned away from me in the hopes I wouldn't know.

But seeing as Andrew probably already gave him shit for his lack of professionalism and my inconvenience, I decide to smile back just slightly and say, "That's great." We go to his desk where I have to tell him every little detail from where I was robbed to any characteristics I can list about the person's appearance.

Finally, he nods to my split lip and bruise and asks, "That's from the man that robbed you?" I nod, but to my surprise, the officer, who didn't waste a moment second-guessing any of my replies so far, gives me a skeptical look. Then his eyes flick to Andrew.

I understand what he's building up to and my protectiveness for my friend grabs me by the throat, making my next words come out sharper than they should. "I tried to swing my purse at my attacker. He grabbed the thing and pulled it. When I wouldn't let go, he hit me. That's what happened, as I told you twice now. Are we done, here, officer? I'd like to go home and change, and I believe you have a football game to finish watching."

The man's round face turns purple as he nods his head vigorously. "Yes, of course. Have a nice day." With that, he's off his chair and rushing to the bathroom. Lily and Andrew are with me the next second.

"Ready to go home?" Andrew asks as Lily throws her arm around my waist.

"Oh, yes, please."

———

By the time my birthday rolls around two weeks after my mishap on the way home, I still haven't had the chance to thank Sebastian for coming to my rescue. He hasn't hosted any parties, and we didn't go to any clubs. If it weren't for the fact all my friends have been busier than usual, I would've thought he was avoiding me.

At least there's no way I won't see him tonight at the birthday party Lilianne insisted on throwing me. The party I don't know the location of or dress code for yet. All I know is that Lily's picking me up at three p.m. to do god-knows-what with me. Later, she said, we'll get ready together, so I guess I'll be in good hands.

That leaves me with six hours to spare, which I cannot spend pampering myself since I have been given instructions to be bare-faced and unshowered when my friend arrives. I'm scared to find out what she has planned for me.

For now, I'm working up the courage to step out of my apartment building to get my mail. I eye the short distance to my mailbox through the glass door before looking down at my outfit. Fuzzy socks in my slippers, shorts, and a fuzzy sweatshirt. I'm so cozy but even the sight of the outside makes goosebumps prick my legs.

I take a deep breath and force myself to push through the door, damn near howling when the icy December cold envelops my body. I make my way to my mailbox in jumpy steps, fumble to get the key inside to open it, then make a clumsy sprint back inside the building with my letters in hand.

As soon as I'm back in my tiny, warm apartment, I grab a fluffy blanket and wrap it around myself to chase away the lingering chill. Then I sit at the table I threw my mail on and start opening the letters.

Happy birthday to me is all I can say to the stack of bills. And then there's the envelope with the neatly written address on the front. I recognize my mother's handwriting and quickly decide I'm not in the mood to open that just yet. Besides, I'm fairly certain I know what it's about.

My parents have been begging me to come over some time to catch up, which I have. A few times... in the three years since I moved out.

It's not necessarily that I don't want to see them. It's just that I'm busy with work most of the time, and whenever I'm not, I'm out with my friends or in need of some me-time.

There's nothing better than a hot bath with some cheap scented oils and a few candles to make me feel like the royalty I'm sure I was in another life. I kept the attitude from back then, for sure. The wealth? Not so much.

Anyway, it also doesn't help that every meeting with my parents is so damn strained. Ever since my mom got clean and it dawned on her what went down at home while she was busy spending money we didn't have on drugs, she became horribly nice. In a very forced way.

We don't talk about my childhood. Neither my dad nor my mom ever tried to pick up the topic, and while I'm fine with that and don't hold a grudge for whatever flaws they might've had, the awkwardness between us makes it hard to be with them.

I know my mom feels guilty for not having been around. In the sense of not having helped financially, not having been there to make my meals or help me with school, and not having been mentally present enough to share any of my firsts. Again, I don't blame her, but I also don't feel the need to make up for lost time.

It's hard to see your parents as such after you take up the role as their caretaker. I've gotten too accustomed to dealing with everything by myself to try and form a parent-child relationship now. I don't need that sort of connection. Not anymore.

My dad's a little more complicated. It's not that I'm scared of him. I love my father very much and am eternally grateful for how he managed to step up and provide me with a stable enough home. There is no reason for him to hurt me anymore and I know he wouldn't. Sometimes, when we're left alone though, I'm just not that comfortable, but that's my issue.

Yeah, I'll deal with that letter some other time.

That leaves me with one more envelope, a cream-colored, expensive-looking, narrow thing. I eye it suspiciously, then open it. The letter inside has been folded twice so the paper's parted in perfect thirds once I open it. That's my first indication that this letter is too fancy to fit the others.

The extravagant font is the second giveaway.

I scan the words quickly, my heart racing a little more the further along I get. When I'm done, I reread it two times, wondering if this is to be trusted. After the fourth read, I decide it is and jump to my feet, squealing like an idiot.

Oh my god, I'm going to kiss him. His signature isn't anywhere on here, but I know it's him. The name of the gallery I just got an invitation to is proof enough. Rose

Gallery is the biggest art exhibition within a hundred miles, the one Sebastian's grandfather sponsored at one point in the last century. The first owner gave him the right to name it, so old Henderson named it in his wife Rosie's honor.

I can't believe I get to go! There's usually an outrageous entrance fee but not with this. Not with an invitation.

I'm going to fucking kiss Sebastian's stupid, privileged face until he regrets ever having given me a present like this. I had no idea he even knew of my love for art. It's not like I always talk about it when I'm out dancing, though maybe I mentioned it at a dinner once.

Which solidifies my point, I can't believe he knew to get me this. Stupid, brilliant, attentive idiot. He's so going to regret having done this. It's the second time he's been nice to me in the span of a month. Maybe this is him calling a truce.

I can go to the Rose Gallery!

I have to get ready! If I take a cab, I can be at the gallery in fifteen minutes, but I certainly can't go looking like I am now. Luckily, my hair still looks good enough I don't have to wash it, but I have to change and put on some makeup.

I'll take it off for Lily later, but there's no way I'm going to a gallery looking like a zombie. No, it's all about the aesthetic.

Twenty minutes later, I'm sitting in a cab, wearing my most beloved, classiest simple silk dress I thrifted recently, paired with some knee-high boots and a thick coat, clutching the beautiful invitation tightly. As I dreamily look at the beautiful font, I can't help but think this is already the best birthday of my life.

77

There's no way I'll ever be able to repay Sebastian for this.

Chapter 10

Aliena

15 years ago

Daddy's angry. He's walking back and forth in the small kitchen, muttering to himself like he sometimes does. I can't hear what he's saying and that's okay. The words aren't for me. They are because of me. Because I made a mistake. But they aren't for me to hear.

One day when he was talking to himself, I waited until he calmed down and asked him if he was praying. We aren't the type of family that prays before dinner, and we never go to church, but whenever Daddy is very restless, he talks under his breath and keeps looking up or closing his eyes. It looks like he's praying.

That day, he smiled at me and ruffled my hair like he knows I hate. He makes some strands stand out in all the wrong ways. Then he told me, "Something like that, princess."

I wasn't happy with that reply because I didn't know what it meant, but I didn't keep asking. He had just called me princess, a nickname he used to give me a lot more when I was younger and Mommy was still feeling better. I didn't want to make him take it back when he got mad at my questions.

Sometimes when I ask too many questions—like why Mommy is sick and always sleeping—he gets angry and tells me to shut up. I don't like making him angry, but I never understand what exactly makes it happen. I think it's worse when Mommy is around, though. At those times, it's best for me to just stay quiet.

Today, I didn't say anything to make him angry. I did something.

I was home alone with Mommy, like I always am when Daddy's working, but she was asleep, and I got bored. I took her phone and started playing with it. Then I asked YouTube what I should do on my seventh birthday, and it showed me how to make an easy cake.

It only took a few ingredients, and I found most of them at home, so I tried it. I preheated the oven and mixed everything the way I was told. When I finally put the pan into the oven, I knew it was almost time for Daddy to come home.

I was so excited to show him what I made.

While the small cake was baking, I did the dishes to make sure everything was clean before he saw. Right when I was done and about to check if my cake was done, my mother called out to me from the couch.

Her voice was croaky, like that of a frog queen, and I quickly went to her. "I need water," she told me without focusing on my eyes. I turned around without replying, running to get her what she needed. Daddy had told me I always have to help Mommy as quickly as I can. He said it was very important.

"Here you go," I told her, leading the full glass to her lips. She tried to swallow it where she was lying, keeping her eyes closed, and when the liquid went down the wrong pipe, she coughed it back up and it splashed right in my face.

My body flinched away, and I accidentally let go of the glass, making it fall to the floor and shatter into many pieces. For a second, all I could do was look at the mess I'd made, and my heart started beating painfully in my chest. It always does when I make a mistake. It feels like someone is stacking weights on top of it and it becomes hard to breathe.

I wiped the spit away from my face with the sleeve of my favorite sweatshirt. Then I looked at the clock hanging on the wall and even more weights fell onto my heart. Daddy was about to come home any minute.

I quickly scrambled forward and gathered as many broken pieces in my hands as possible. I threw them into the nearest trash can and went back to the couch until I saw no more glass on the floor. Then I grabbed a rag and started wiping the floor until it was dry so Daddy didn't have to see I made a mess in the first place.

I'd just thrown the rag away when Daddy came home. I ran toward him, happy to finally have someone to celebrate with, but he already looked weird when I reached him. His head was turned up and he was sniffing the air. His eyebrows turned down in the middle and then, he finally looked at me.

"What's that smell, Aliena? What did you do?" he asked.

I didn't immediately understand but then I noticed the burned smell in the air. I'm not sure if my heart kept beating at all, and my head grew light and dizzy as I ran into the kitchen. I opened the oven, and a cloud of black smoke blew in my face. Daddy was right behind me and coughed.

I reached inside the oven blindly because I wanted to take a look at my cake, but I forgot that the oven was still hot. My hands clasped around the small dish, and I instantly cried out and pulled them out again, clutching them to my chest.

Daddy said a bad word, and I heard him turn on the faucet. Then he picked me up, placed me on top of the kitchen counter and pulled both of my hands under the cold water. That made my burns hurt even more, but when I tried to pull them away, Daddy held them in place.

"Keep them there," he ordered. He grabbed a towel and took the burned cake out of the oven. He gave it a long look, then shook his head as if he was disappointed in it and threw it into the trash. Along with the dish.

I was glad I was already crying because I would've started then if I hadn't already.

Then Daddy started pacing. He hasn't stopped. I'm still sitting on the counter, keeping my hands under the cool water as I watch him walk back and forth. I'm still crying, scared of what he might say. I don't want him to yell at me. I really didn't mean to make a mess. I just wanted a birthday cake.

When Daddy finally walks over to where I'm sitting and reaches out, he does so to cradle my face gently. Not to punish me. I hold very still as he looks at me and try to stop crying.

In the end, he sighs and leans down to give my forehead a long kiss. "Happy birthday, princess," he whispers. I cry a little more when he pulls away and I see he has tears in his eyes too. If there's one thing worse than making Daddy angry, it's making Daddy sad.

I want to apologize but I can't speak. My throat is hurting and closed off completely. I can't say a word.

Chapter 11

Aliena

"Don't say a word. I can tell you want to ask again but the answer stays the same, I won't tell you where we're going," Lily cuts me off before I can even formulate the question for the fifth time. We've been in the car for forty minutes and I don't recognize our surroundings anymore.

I hate surprises. I trust Lily though, so I guess I'll do as I'm told.

"Now, tell me about your day. All we've talked about so far is what will happen later," she adds.

I just shrug. "Didn't really do anything so far," I lie before my brain registers the deception. I'm not sure why I'm keeping my visit to the gallery a secret from her. It was fantastic and I should be bursting at the seams with the need to talk all about it.

But she'd ask me how I managed to go, and I'd have to tell her that Sebastian got me an invitation. Then I'd have to tell her why he'd do such a thing, and I have absolutely no idea what to say to that since it's a widely known fact he and I cannot stand each other. Not really.

"You're a bore. What would you only do without me?" She sighs dramatically, and I shove her shoulder. "Careful, I'm driving!" she exclaims. I ignore her.

"Without you, I'd still go to parties but with cheap beer and crackling stereos. So, thanks for getting a very awesome, very preppy boyfriend with very useful ties," I tell her.

"You forgot to mention you'd be absolutely devastated. Don't forget about that part," she adds. I roll my eyes.

"Yes, yes, I would be in pieces."

"I know. Now, we're here, look!" she says, motioning to the spa right in front of our parking space. Not the hole in the wall kind, either, but one with big glass doors and clean walls. I look over at her, feeling a little guilty.

"Lily—" I start but she cuts me off.

"Don't even, Aliena. I know what you're going to say. That I didn't have to do this and you'd be more than happy to just drink cheap wine with me on my couch and blah, blah. Just accept I'm conveniently using your birthday as an excuse to go to the spa, okay?"

"I can never pay you back," I tell her, hating how pitiful I sound.

My friend places a gentle hand over mine. "I don't care about that, A. You know that. Now, can we please go inside? I booked a couple's massage. I hope it's okay that I asked for a male masseur for you." With a wink, she leaves the car while I scramble after her, laughing to myself.

This woman.

And so we get a couple's massage. And no, I don't mind having a male masseur but not for some questionable reasons. I just like the feeling of big hands on me, and I prefer a lot of pressure. It gets awkward asking a tiny woman to knead me more thoroughly again and again until I eventually have to accept she simply doesn't have the right leverage and strength for that. The guy working on my muscles today does wonders to relax me.

"All right, what's next on your plan?" I ask, my words almost slurred with how blissed out I feel.

My friend smiles at me and pulls me deeper into the building. "We get our nails done. I don't remember the last time you painted yours. Meanwhile, you have such fantastic, natural long nails. They're wasted on you," she complains.

"I just have other priorities. And yes, please take them. They grow too fast, and it's always such a waste of time to shorten them." If I got a dollar for every time someone commented on how jealous they were of how I could grow out my nails, I'd live in a much better apartment.

"I don't know how I put up with you," she huffs, even as she throws an arm over my shoulder.

"You love me. Now, be nice. It's my birthday."

———

Three hours later, we're at Lily's with painted nails, hands and feet, and a clean face from another treatment she decided to spontaneously book when she saw the flier. I don't think anyone has ever wasted so much money on me in the span of a few hours, and while I appreciate every part of her surprise, it's also making me feel like shit.

The gallery plus this plus wherever we're going tonight is just too damn much. I didn't do anything to deserve all this.

On Lilianne's birthdays, the best I can manage is a nice picnic with some of the wine she prefers or a trip somewhere all right for dinner. And I save up for months to manage that no matter what a downgrade it turns out to be from Lily's day-to-day life. It makes it even harder for me to accept her presents.

"Okay, you shower first while I set out a bunch of clothes you have to choose from for tonight. Then we do our makeup. The guys are picking us up in two hours," she tells me.

I nod without further protest, keeping my inner war to myself. Now's not the time to voice them. Today's not the day.

——

The first thing I notice when we go outside to meet the guys is it's not Sebastian's McLaren waiting for us, so I already know he won't be in the car. When he's with us, he drives. I don't think I've ever seen him in the passenger seat.

As I get in the backseat, I realize that Mattheo isn't here either. It's just Andrew behind the wheel, turning around to beam at me.

"Hello, birthday girl. Sorry for the piss-poor greeting. I'll make up for it once we reach our destination," he promises. Then he leans over to give his girlfriend a kiss. "Hello, gorgeous."

87

She pulls away first. "Shut up and drive," she teases with feigned huffiness, then softens the blow with a kiss on the cheek.

"Bossy," he mutters even as he starts driving. "So, did you two have a good day?"

"Definitely. Your girlfriend spoiled me rotten. I'm already scheming for her birthday in three months," I respond, acting like I'm under a lot less pressure than I actually am. Internally, I'm freaking out.

"Oh, we'll have to put our minds together for that. I have an idea or two as well," Andrew interjects, surprising me when it shouldn't. My first instinct is to turn him down since it's Lily's and my tradition to organize something for the other's birthday, but I keep quiet. Andrew's her boyfriend, so it makes sense he wants to plan something for her.

It's nice, I guess, and it would certainly allow us to go a little more overboard since he has access to more resources than me. If only I were a little better at handling change.

"Hey! There she is!" Mattheo cheers as soon as I step onto the VIP platform of yet another club I've never been to. It's beautiful; classy and spacious with a raging dance floor. A crazy light show's going on with colorful beams of light jumping over the room.

There are more lights, steady ones, casting the room in a blue hue whenever they don't shut off to leave only the tiny lasers and spotlights to provide light. I don't want to know what all happens on the dance floor in the safety of the darkness.

And then there are the flashing lights occasionally disrupting the steady sounds of the club as the crowd erupts in cheers. To say the party's already in full swing would be an understatement, and I'm convinced it'll only get better.

The VIP part is slightly elevated so we can see over the dancing crowd. It's equipped with three black satin couches, which look surprisingly clean, and some space for dancing if anyone wants to put on a private show, I guess. Oh, and there's a small box that looks like a minibar and a button on top that says "service".

Fancy. This seems like my kind of place.

Mattheo is sitting on the couch, and I make my way over to him before he can bother to stand up, throwing myself into his welcoming arms. I haven't seen him since the night I was attacked, and I missed the idiot. I clumsily settle on his lap, hug his narrow middle and bury my face in his neck, sighing contently. Oh, how I adore tight hugs. Especially the ones coming from giants like Mattheo that can envelop me entirely.

It's been too freaking long since I got a hug. One from a guy, at least. A guy that isn't my best friend's boyfriend, since Andrew hugged me once we got out of the car in front of the club. Embraces like that are obviously appreciated too but it's not the same. I don't know.

"Someone's happy to see me. How are you?" he asks, letting me pull away slightly to look at his handsome face.

"I'm great, thanks. This place looks awesome!"

"Did you expect anything else? You know your best friend has taste," Lily pipes in from another couch. I smile at her over my shoulder.

"She does. She also spends way too much money on me though!" I insist again.

89

"We split the price, sweetie. Don't worry about it," she brushes me off, like that would make me feel any better.

"You all paid for this?" I ask, looking at all of them. They nod.

"Seb too," adds Andrew.

That reminds me. "Where is he, by the way?" I ask, looking around the empty space apart from the four of us again.

"In the bathroom, I guess. I'm sure he'll be back in a second," Mattheo replies, caressing my arm sweetly. I nod at him and smile.

"Well, I'm not waiting for him. Come dance with me," I say, getting off his lap in the hopes he'll follow. Only he doesn't. Instead, his face turns apologetic, something I don't like at all.

"As much as I'd love to, and you know how much I would, I'm afraid there won't be any dancing for me tonight," he tells me.

"What? But it's my birthday," I protest, trying not to sound too pouty or upset. No dancing? What is he talking about?

He reaches out and gives my hand a squeeze. "I know, *amo*, I'm sorry but one must follow the doctor's orders," he teases, nodding to his right leg. That puzzles me enough to forget being upset.

Instead, I ask, "What? What's wrong with your leg?"

"Dislocated my knee two weeks ago. It's still healing. I actually went back to the doctor today for a check-up, but I'm afraid I'm blocked for the night. That's why I met you guys here. Sorry, I really tried," he explains, but I'm already shaking my head.

"But how did that happen? Did you do something wrong at practice?" I prod.

"Not exactly," he replies wryly. Before I can push him for answers, Sebastian joins us on the platform and redirects my focus.

"Look who decided to make an appearance. How lovely," I tease. He just rolls his eyes at me and falls back on the unoccupied couch.

"What are we talking about?" he asks, looking between Mattheo and me.

"Nothing," my friend replies at the same time as I say, "He won't tell me how he hurt his knee." My eyes briefly snap to Mattheo's in question at his dismissal, but he keeps looking at his friend across the platform. I follow his gaze. The men share a look I don't understand until finally, Mattheo looks away glumly while Sebastian turns his eyes to me, arching an amused brow.

"Well, Aliena, sometimes people just don't want you knowing all their business," he provides unhelpfully. The innuendo about how we first met and how he still holds a grudge because of that isn't lost on me, but there is a part of me that is surprised. Maybe it was naive of me, but I was thinking his nice gestures of the past few weeks were meant as an olive branch. I mean, why would he get someone he couldn't stand a birthday present. And such a customized one at that.

Clearly, I was mistaken to believe that anything had changed. His cold tone is enough of an indicator of that. Sometimes, I really don't know what goes on in his head. I think we could've gotten along great if only he hadn't been a dick to me the second I stepped into his house.

As if I wouldn't have stayed quiet about our first meeting if only he'd asked me to. It could have been our little secret. Instead, he made it the reason we can't be friends. Idiot.

"It's her birthday, dipshit. Be nice," Andrew pipes up. Sebastian just raises his hands in surrender and melts into the couch cushion. For a second, I'm just standing amid them, unsure of what to do. Then I decide this isn't how I want to spend my birthday, and I let go of Mattheo's hand.

"Well, it's a real shame you can't keep me company, but I'm sure I'll find someone else to dance with. Y'all have fun sitting here, losers."

Chapter 12

Sebastian

I watch her in the crowd as my friends talk around me, unable to look away. It's like she hypnotized me, that silhouette dressed in green silk. It should have been impossible for me to find her once I lost sight of her on her way to the middle of the dance floor. Yet, there she is, just another dancing body. One that's infinitely more interesting to watch.

This isn't the first time I've seen her dance, but even after months of getting used to it, I don't think I'll ever tire of it. The way her eyes stay closed, and she moves with the music as if it possesses her, surrounds her, and uses her as a marionette to express the meaning of its beat.

The downside is I'm not the only one that sees. The other people are just as drawn to the dancer amid them, and I have a perfect view of all the guys looking at her longingly. And the ones who try to do more than look.

She entertains a few, innocently dancing with them for a few minutes, before leaving them and moving a few feet away. I enjoy seeing those slugs' greedy hands on her about as much as I'd enjoy being shot.

93

I roll my eyes at the next dude that clumsily dances up to her and take a sip of my drink. And then another when I see him standing right behind her, whispering something in her ear. When his hands find her waist and they start dancing, his eyes closing in pleasure, I down the rest of my drink.

Then I get to my feet and excuse myself from my friends with a quick, "I'm getting another drink." I walk into the crowd, heading toward the bar rather than straight for Aliena in case my friends are watching. Of course, they're too invested in whatever they're talking about to care, but I like to take precautions.

I finally turn halfway to the bar and find the girl in her green dress in a matter of minutes. The closer I get to her, the more urgent my steps become.

"Really, I should get back to my friends." I faintly make out her protests as she tries to extract herself from the guy behind her. He just shakes his head and tightens his hold on her. I see her wince, and my hand shoots out to grab the guy's hand the next moment, twisting one of his sweaty fingers. He cries out and takes a step away from me and thereby also from Aliena. That's good enough for me.

I let go of his hand and level him with my most withering glare. "She told you to piss off. Try to take the hint next time. When you have to beg someone to keep dancing, you're just proving you're better left untouched," I yell over the music.

He just averts his eyes and flees into the crowd. I turn to Aliena. "You okay?" I ask.

She grins softly and nods. "Thanks. Oh, that reminds me, I have more to thank you for. I'm very grateful you came so quickly that night, first and foremost, and I can never repay you for the invitation to the gallery and the hospital bill. So, thank you for all of that."

Her words combined with the sincere look on her face have something warm taking over my chest. I take close care not to let my face give away too much of what I'm feeling.

"It was no big deal. I'm glad you liked it," I brush her off, uncomfortable with the intimacy. It's not entirely true since I had to ask my father for the invitation, and everything including him is no easy feat—most of all asking for his help—but I survived. Besides, Mom was happy to see me swing by no matter how short the visit was. That made it a little more worth it.

"I loved it. It was unbelievable. Just the building is art itself. I'm pretty sure I walked in with my jaw on the floor. And then there were all the paintings! I've never seen anything like it. I felt like I was a royal back in the day or something. I don't think I've ever been to a place that hurt so much to leave," she rants, her eyes lighting up.

The unbidden thought that she's absolutely enthralling takes firm hold in my mind again.

"I can take you there again sometime. You don't need an invitation when you're with me."

At that, she perks up further. "Really? You'd go with me?" She breaks out in the biggest grin. "I mean, yeah, sure. I'd definitely be down for that. I'd let an ogre take me if that was what it took."

For the first time today, I laugh. "You just compared me to an ogre?" I ask, a little flabbergasted. This woman.

"Well, occasionally you do share some similarities. When you dance, for example, you certainly look like some creature of the mountains. Just one undercover in a very beautiful shell," she jokes. Immediately, her face turns darker under the blue lights, and I know she's blushing.

"Careful, that almost sounded like a compliment," I warn her teasingly.

She shoves me. "Was it enough to charm you into dancing with me? I mean, that way we can minimize the chances of you having to come to my rescue when someone gets too handsy again. Besides, Mattheo is not an option tonight so you're the next best thing." She's teasing. I can tell by the look on her face.

And yet, the happy little balloon in my chest deflates a little. My best friend is a no-show and I'm the next best thing. That feels good to hear. I'm ready to say as much or turn her down but her hopeful, expectant expression stops me.

Fine, this time, I cave. "Hardly, but I'm feeling generous since it is your birthday," I tell her and let her take my hand, acting as if she was about to lead me to the gallows despite the secret spark in my chest at the prospect of it being *me*. Of being the lucky bastard who not only gets to watch her up close but also feel her this once.

My whole body ignites at the single, innocent contact with her. Not for the first time, I ask myself why. Why does she have to make me feel this way? Why is she the only person that can excite me anymore and bring my every last cell to life?

Her face lights up as if she feels the same as I do, then she twirls, letting her hair fly in a wide arc and then flop over her shoulder as she stops with her back to me. For a few beats, there's a distance between our bodies. Then she looks back at me with a challenge in her eyes, and I take a step forward, letting the hand that isn't holding hers find her waist like I've watched Mattheo do way too many times before.

Her body molds to mine, and it makes my next breath stall in my lungs. If this isn't what heaven feels like, I don't want it. She feels perfect against me, eerily *right* in my arms.

As if agreeing, she moves backward until our bodies are pressed up against each other tightly and we're swaying to the beat together. Her movements are big and decisive, an infuriatingly deadly combination when they make her ass move over my crotch repeatedly, her hips moving in a wide loop again and again while her arms move in all directions.

I'd say I'm doing a good job at keeping up with her for an ogre, despite the distraction my hardening dick is providing. My body feels tingly and warm like it never has. Maybe it's because of how long it's been since I had sex and a proper release. Maybe it's just that it's *Aliena* I'm this close to.

Either way, I despise that she has this sort of power over me. And I despise it even more that I can never act on these feelings and find out what it would be like to take this further. To touch her without the barrier of her silk dress between our skin. To fuck her and be the reason a room is flooded with the sweet symphony of her moans—moans I know the sound of since they've been engraved in my mind ever since I interrupted her and *Mattheo*. I must be losing my mind because even though it was my best friend in that room with her, I thought I heard her call out *my* name before they went silent. It's been keeping me up at night.

One of her hands finds mine on her hips, and she clasps down over it, making me hold her tighter as she rests her head against my chest, her moves never faltering. Then she moves my hand further down, over her hips and, to my great dismay, to her bare thigh.

Her skin is smooth and soft and incredibly warm. My fingers dig into the taut flesh, images of those thighs spread for me momentarily occupying my mind. Then I catch myself and bring my hand back to her hips, holding her just enough to not restrict her movements. I wouldn't dream of limiting her.

We keep dancing and I lose track of time. Sweat lines my hairline, neck, and even my back. I can feel it and yet, I'm surprisingly unbothered by it. Me, someone who's not a fan of dancing, losing myself to it so thoroughly I don't mind my shirt sticking to me. Aliena is a witch.

She eventually turns around, her face bright, and throws her arms around my neck. Then she keeps dancing, making my whole situation so much worse with how she looks up at me as her lower stomach rubs against my erection.

She knows exactly what she's doing, what she's making me feel, and she's loving every second of it, the wicked woman. There's no way she's unaware of my reaction with the way we're dancing, but I'm not the only one who's getting turned on by this. No, her body's like putty in my hands, and even her fingers move at a sultry pace in my hair. Most importantly, her lidded eyes are telling me exactly what she's thinking about as they drop to my lips.

She comes impossibly closer, her arms tightening around my neck. Then she looks at me expectantly, almost hopefully, and I nearly cave right there. Nearly lower my head a few inches to bring my lips to hers and devour her like I've been thinking about ever since I first met her.

But I can't. I can never take it as far as I want with her. Whether I like it or not, she's a lasting person in my life and it would be impossible to stop seeing her after we took things where my mind is currently going. And since I could never be in a relationship with her, all crossing that line would do is complicate things.

Mattheo might be okay with sleeping with her and then seeing her with others, but I could never. Once I had her, she'd feel too much like mine, and the possessiveness and jealousy I already feel when it comes to her would be too much to take.

No, there's no way I'll go there.

I pull away, take my hands from her hips and take one of hers again, trying not to make things too awkward with a harsh rejection. "Let's rejoin the others. I'm sure they're missing the birthday girl by now," I say and start leading her away before I can take a too-close look at her faltering expression.

The closer we get to the VIP platform, the more her hand in mine starts to feel wrong, and I become unsure of what to do. Our friends aren't aware of our occasional *moments* and since changing that would only bring up unwanted questions, I refuse to do it.

I release her hand and meet her eyes over my shoulder, my face impassive even though I hate the way it makes her frown. "I don't dance," I remind her, knowing she'll take the hint. Her face loses the last of its glow as she huffs.

We get onto the platform together, but while I return to the empty couch, Aliena plops down next to Mattheo. That's another reason why I wouldn't fuck her. It's clear I'm her second choice, and I don't do second place.

And so, the night resumes with the girl I just danced with and my best friend flirting loudly while the couple on the other couch is making out or talking intimately. Then there's me, pretending to watch the crowd as I down drink after drink, trying to tune out the idiots on my left.

Yeah, I love fifth wheeling.

Every now and again, someone throws a question around and a group discussion breaks out. That's when I'm forced to look at Aliena when she speaks, instantly wishing I hadn't when I note her legs thrown over Mattheo's while he gently caresses her skin.

That's about enough for me.

My eyes flick back to a girl in the crowd I've been watching for a few minutes now. She has shoulder-length brown hair, a heart-shaped face, and nice, full lips. She looks good and since she's dancing right in front of the platform, I noticed her. She noticed me too and has been throwing me glances every now and again as she swayed her hips to the beat.

I get up from my seat and walk toward the end of the platform. "I'll see you later," is all I say to my friends, and I don't miss the way Aliena's eyes narrow on me, then jump to the girl. I guess she has been paying enough attention to see our silent interactions before. My intoxicated mind finds that very interesting, and I'd be lying if I said I didn't get a small kick out of getting a reaction.

I meet the girl on the dance floor and shoot her a lazy grin when she smiles demurely and says, "Hey."

"Hey, gorgeous. What do you say we go somewhere a bit more private? My friends are too curious, and they already noticed me watching you. I don't need to give them any more reason to talk," I tell her, laughing softly. She joins in and coincidentally touches my shoulder.

"Sure, I'd like that," she agrees. I take her hand and start leading her away with one last fleeting look at my friends, who are already watching me as expected. Oh well, let them watch if they get off on it, I guess.

I take the girl back to the corridor lined with bathrooms, doing my best to walk straight so as not to seem too drunk. I might've had one drink too many, considering I don't like to lose control of myself, but I'll be damned before I let someone notice it.

Once we're alone, the girl doesn't waste any time grabbing my face and kissing me. She's tall, enough so I don't have to lean down. That's a blessing since any acrobatics I'd have to attempt right now would surely end with me sprawled on the floor.

She kisses well, gentle enough for the beginning, though there is something demanding in her touch I don't mind at all. My hands find her waist, and I pull her a little closer, enjoying the fact there are no overwhelming fireworks as I touch her. This is simple. Forgettable.

A throat clears obnoxiously somewhere nearby, and the girl in my arms pulls away to find the source of it. I know who it is before I see the cross-armed birthday girl a few feet away. I give my hookup who still hasn't introduced herself a pat on the arm and nod toward the nearest door to one of the private bathrooms.

"Why don't you wait for me in there while I deal with my friend? I'll make it quick," I tell her, lowering my voice.

She nods and leaves, but not before saying, "Just for the record, I only believe that isn't an angry girlfriend because I saw her on your friend's lap before. I'm no homewrecker." I smile and nod solemnly. That's something to respect her for.

I'm still smiling when I stroll toward Aliena. The closer I get, the more amusement fills me. God, her face is red. She's *mad*.

Before I get the chance to speak, she snaps at me, "Is it that hard for you to keep it in your pants for one night?"

Mh. It's clear to say the unjustified accusation wipes the smile right off my face. Indignation fills me, so hard and fast that I almost get whiplash. Maybe the alcohol is making me sensitive or maybe I've been holding on to this since she pulled that move with Mattheo, but I feel almost unhinged when I retort. "Look who's talking!"

She huffs at me. "One person. One time since I've known you, Sebastian! What did you expect me to do, live a celibate life because you don't want me, but you also don't want anyone else to have me? Meanwhile, I get to watch you have a different girl every night?" Her voice is shaky and breaks at the end of her sentence, but I don't let it get to me. No. No matter what reasons she might think she has to be upset, she's fucking wrong.

I decide to finally tell her that. "There are no girls! There haven't been any since I met you, Aliena, so to answer your question, no, it isn't hard to keep it in my pants for one night. It just doesn't appeal to me this particular one. Now crawl back to Mattheo, will you, because you're right, I don't want you." I practically spit the words, and I can see them hit the bullseye when she clamps her mouth shut. A part of me rebels against leaving her like this with her stupid hurt expression and those damned tears shining in her eyes. The sight doesn't make me feel nearly as triumphant as I thought it might.

And now we're here, both our chests heaving with deep breaths as we stare at each other in shocked silence. Before I can cave and even think about apologizing, I turn and join my hookup in the secluded room. Just like that.

I lock the door behind me and slam my lips to hers, hoping to drown out the war raging in my head. This serves her right. After what she pulled with Mattheo in *my* house, she deserves to think I can enjoy someone else just as much as she clearly can.

Even though I know I can't, and I know I won't. Tonight, despite the alcohol and my anger, won't be any different from all the others. I'll entertain this nice woman, make out with her for long enough to let Aliena's mind run all sorts of scenarios about what I'm doing to her, and then go back out as if nothing happened.

That time turns out to be around forty minutes. Forty minutes that felt like a lot longer. Luckily, my company was nice enough and she seemed to enjoy my approach of not taking any clothes off either one of us. After telling her some excuse and it was nice to meet her, I leave the bathroom and return to the VIP section of the club.

The party's still going strong but somehow, the colors seem a little duller as I make my way to my friends. If only my conscience would stop bothering me with the image of Aliena's silly hurt expression. So what if I offended her a little? She didn't care about my feelings two weeks ago.

The thing I immediately notice is only three people are on the couches of our VIP lounge. The birthday girl is missing, and it doesn't sit quite right with me. Overall, I'd describe the mood up here to be somber as hell considering where we are. Even the lovebirds don't have their heart eyes on.

103

I force my lazy smile to remain as I casually ask, "Where's the guest of honor?"

"Home. She just texted," Lily replies. That has me halting in my tracks, and I can feel a brow rise on my forehead as I turn to Mattheo.

"And how exactly did she get there?" I ask him, my harsh tone betraying my cool façade.

"I don't know since she left without notice after following *you*," he says through gritted teeth. And here I thought messing up his knee would teach him a lesson about making sure our friend got home safely. If I didn't already know she made it home tonight, I'd have to give him another friendly reminder.

"You wouldn't know anything about that, would you?" he adds, clearly blaming me for her departure.

"What's that supposed to mean?" I demand.

"It means that she was fine before you started eye-fucking that girl and left with her," he retorts without missing a beat, being more direct than he's ever been about my situation with Aliena. I just shrug, unwilling to agree that he has a point.

"Why would you connect those two occurrences? What I do and with whom is none of your business, and it certainly doesn't concern Aliena."

"Oh, please, we all know that's bullshit. I don't understand what the hell is up with you two, but it's clear something *is* up!" he has the nerve to exclaim. That does it for me and I snap.

"Oh, so there is something between us, huh? You didn't seem to think that when you *fucked* her in *my* house. No, of course, I'm the bad guy as soon I do the same. Fuck you!"

"Whoa, what? You slept with Aly?" Lily interjects.

"Yeah, she didn't tell you? Funny considering you saw her hours later. You know, at the hospital after she was attacked on her way home since Mattheo didn't think to give her a ride home after he was done with her."

Lily mutters something more, but it's Mattheo's loud voice that demands my attention. "*What*? What do you mean she was attacked?" he demands.

I shrug. "It seems I was the only one here with all the information. Ups." I give Mattheo a look. "What did you think I banged your knee up for?" Not that I feel particularly sorry about it. I'm just curious what explanation he came up with for our altercation.

"I thought you did it because you are a psycho!" he's quick to reply.

Of course, he's not fully wrong. After the way he taunted me through that locked door, I really didn't need much more motivation to take some of tumultuous emotions out on him.

Andrew sputters from where he's sitting, entering the conversation for the first time. "Whoa, hang on. *You* dislocated his knee?" he demands. *Ups*, I guess I forgot how twisted the whole story was and how little Andrew knew of it all. It looks like I'm going to be here for a while.

Cheers to that.

105

Chapter 13

Aliena

I'm still crying. I haven't stopped crying since Sebastian locked himself in the bathroom with that girl and left me standing in the hallway like nothing more significant than a stray dog.

At first, I contemplated knocking on the door and demanding he got the fuck back out here so we could … I don't know, talk this out? To do anything other than have him sleep with that woman. Especially after he dropped that little bomb about not having been with anyone since he met me.

That has to be a lie though, right? He's picked up girls every other night and eventually disappeared with them. There's no way he didn't sleep with any of them.

In the end, I realized banging on the door would leave me in the exact same position he was in two weeks ago and thereby put me exactly where he wanted me. I didn't want to give him the satisfaction. I also didn't want to humiliate myself even further. All I really wanted to do at that point was go home and curl up in a ball in my comfortable bed, wearing some fluffy pj's.

So, I snuck out of the club and walked home to do exactly that. I learned my lesson from the last time, though, so I only walked along the main roads and clutched my pepper spray tightly in my hand. It was still early enough for a Saturday night, after all, so there were other people out and about.

Other than getting catcalled by a group of drunk men outside a bar in the less extravagant part of the city, I got home safely and untouched. I made quick work of taking off my makeup and changing.

Now I'm here, crying into my fucking pillow as I hold it tightly against my chest. On my birthday. Like a fucking idiot.

It's a shame. No matter how hard Lily, or the rest of my friends try, my birthday curse just seems to stick with me. Something always goes wrong, and I'm particularly sensitive because I already got my hopes up that one year it would be different.

I'm a moron and I feel like a bitch for ditching my friends without having said goodbye. I just didn't want to face them in the condition I was in. They would have asked too many questions, and I didn't feel like talking.

So, I texted Lily I was home and apologized about how I left. I also thanked her another million times and insisted on what a great friend was. Because she really is.

Knowing she'd want a better explanation for my sudden departure than that, I turned off my phone before she could reply. It's better this way. I'm done with the day.

I wake with a headache and swollen eyes not long after noon. I hate sleeping in, but despite that, all I want to do as soon as I open my eyes is close them again. Instead, I force myself to turn on my phone and face a million texts my friend sent me, scared that she might come over and bang down my door if I didn't reply soon.

The last thing I want is company. I've always been this way when I'm upset, and luckily, I know Lily will respect that. To a certain point. She won't accept being ghosted, though.

I start scrolling through the messages on my way to the kitchen to get some juice, surprised I have a few from Mattheo and even some from Andrew. My heart feels a little lighter at their concern, but at the same time, it has pressure building inside me. Now I have more people to reply to and appease.

I look up from my screen to search my fridge for the juice I was so sure I bought recently. To my dismay, it's nowhere to be found. For God's sake, another let down isn't what I need now.

With a sigh, I turn to my coffee machine instead. Caffeine it is, then. As that's getting done, I lean against my counter and breathe heavily. I feel like shit, and it doesn't get much better when my eyes fall on the letter my parents sent me. Without thinking much about it, I push myself away from the kitchen and pick up the letter. I already feel bad, how much worse can it get, right?

When I open the folded paper, I'm glad to see that the message isn't too long.

Dear Aly

First things first, happy birthday, dear. I hope I did everything correctly and this letter reached you on the right day. If not, let's just pretend it did ;) I hope you have a great day! Maybe you can tell us all about what Lily planned for you this year when you come to visit us soon? Your father and I miss you greatly.

I'm afraid I don't have much good news for you, my dear, and I hate to tell you this on your birthday, but you have the right to know. Your father had a heart attack and had to take leave from work. He is recovering, don't worry, but I'm sure he'd be very happy to see you. Feel free to swing by whenever you're free, dear, we know you're busy.

Love, Mom

By the time I finish reading, my heart is a cold rock in my chest, and the tears I managed to hold back so bravely when I realized I didn't have any juice are now an unstoppable force behind my eyes. I sigh, my body deflating before I drop my head in my hands and just start sobbing.

My dad's sick and had to take leave from work. Shit, they can't afford that. I already know what that means, why my mother wrote to me now. She came to the same conclusion and wants my help.

Panic seizes my chest, and I take a choppy breath. I can't believe this is happening again. I don't want to do this. I can't take care of them again when I'm barely staying afloat myself. I don't have the resources or the emotional capacity for it.

I rub my knuckles over my chest, feeling the space inside it tightening and tightening until my lungs barely feel able to expand enough for my next breath. I cry harder

109

despite my best efforts to pull myself together. It seems I'm too tired to get myself back on track right now.

I wish Lily was here. She always knows what to do and she's the only one that can understand what I'm feeling right now. She knows about my past, almost every feeling and situation little me had to go through.

But if I told her about this, I know what she'd say. She'd say I needn't worry about it because she can support me and my family until they get back on track. She'd do whatever it took without hesitation because that's the kind of person she is.

But I can't let her do that. No way. Least of all before I have a talk with my parents and get a better idea of the situation they're in. I don't think I could ever look Lily in the eyes again if I let her do this for me, on top of everything she's already done.

I force a painful breath into my tight lungs. No, I got it. Of course, I do. I just need to survive this moment, take deep breaths, then figure out a game plan. I have things under control. It'll be okay. I'll be okay.

But first, it seems I have to pay my parents a visit.

———

"Oh, hey, dear. What a lovely surprise! Does this mean you got our letter? Come in, come in," my mother gushes when she opens the door for me, her smile too wide for the circumstances. She steps aside, yelling, "Albert, it's Aly!" Then she pulls me in a tight hug.

I pat her back awkwardly, really just wanting to see my dad. When she finally lets go, I shoot her a forced smile and ask, "Where's dad?"

"On the couch, come on," she replies, already leading me there as if I didn't know the way. She seems awfully fidgety.

When I see my dad lying on the couch, his face pale despite the small smile playing on it, my steps falter. Fuck, I didn't think it would be this hard seeing another parent look so weak in the same spot my mother always used to suffer her crashes on. But now I'm here, struggling to keep any flashbacks at bay and my voice even as I greet him.

I can't stand this house.

"Hey, Dad," I say, crouching next to the couch to be at eye level with him.

"Hey, honey," he replies, gently placing his hand on mine, a gesture oddly affectionate for him. He's normally not very touchy, and I try not to react to the discomfort it invokes. He looks past me to my mother, shooting her an apologetic smile that seems to hurt. "Linda, I think I left my phone upstairs, if you could be a dear and get that for me?"

If she notices anything off about his expression, she doesn't show it. "Of course," she agrees, already turning on her heels. He gives me his attention again as soon as her steps disappear. "How have you been, Aly?"

I give him a look. "I've been good, Dad. I'm not the one who had a heart attack."

He keeps smiling, undeterred by my flat voice. "That's good to hear."

I can't believe him. "Dad, what happened?" I ask. I mean, a heart attack. Really? I know he hasn't had the least stressful life but he's not that old yet. Definitely not the age

111

where I should have to worry about him *dying* of natural causes.

"The doctor said it was just due to stress. I'll just have to eat a little healthier, exercise a bit, and take my medicine, and I'll be just fine. It looks like I won't even need surgery."

Thank god for that. There's no way my parents could afford heart surgery. He squeezes my hand before his face turns somber. "I'm afraid it's not me we have to worry about," he adds, his voice taking on a hush.

I'm sure my confusion is clear in my features even when he gives a meaningful look in the direction of where my mother disappeared.

My dad lowers his voice impossibly further. "Honey, I think your mother relapsed. It was a great shock for her when she found me out cold on the floor and had to call 911. She was upstairs when it happened, you know, and heard me fall."

Relapsed? The word hits me like a lance to the chest, nearly knocking the breath right out of me.

"What? No. What makes you think she relapsed? She's been clean for years," I protest, aware of the panic I'm unable to mask rising with every word.

"They gave me pills after I was released from the hospital. Morphine, among others. A week ago, I was unable to find the nearly full bottle of them, and when I asked Linda about it, she said I probably just misplaced it when I know I didn't."

His last words barely reach me through the fog clouding my mind. My mother stole my dad's morphine? That's not possible. She wouldn't relapse after so many years of being sober. Especially not at a time like this when my dad needs her. She's the only one able to work at the moment and she knows it. If she loses her job, they're screwed. She wouldn't take that risk. Not because of a little stress.

She can't be that selfish. I don't want to believe that. Plus, she doesn't seem high right now. I'm sure I'd recognize that.

My dad keeps talking while my mind is reeling. "I know how hard this must be for you to hear, and I hate to burden you with this. I just think it might help if you came over for visits a little more. Only if you can squeeze it into your tight schedule somehow, of course. But maybe that could give your mother something to look forward to and distract her. She always talks about how much she misses you." He gives me a pained smile as if he knew exactly what he was doing to me with those words.

Every one of them hits me right in the chest and fills my stomach with more and more guilt. I can't believe we're having this talk. My father had a heart attack for god's sake, and I only learn about it two weeks later. What kind of child does that make me?

And now my dad tells me my mother's addiction might become a problem again because I couldn't be bothered to visit them some more. After everything they did for me growing up.

They need me and, my head still manages to make this about me as the panic within me rises. I don't want to do this again. Hell, I can't do this. Not when I'm already struggling to keep my own head above water with the low salary I get. How am I supposed to take care of an addict for a mother and a sick father while working every shift they let me?

113

"How long is your leave of absence? Is it paid?" I ask, hating how selfish the motives for this question are.

But my dad just shakes his head. "I didn't take leave from work, honey. That's what I told your mother so she wouldn't panic."

"What do you mean?" Damn, I almost sound like a kid to my own ears. A hopeful kid that knows, deep down, it's about to get some terrible news.

"I was laid off, honey. I'm already looking for a new job but it's hard with the condition I'm in." Just like that, the world starts spinning.

"They fired you? How? Is that even allowed?" I demand shakily.

He ignores me and squeezes my hand again. "I am really sorry, Aly. Please, don't worry about it too much just yet, okay? I'm sure everything will be just fine. Maybe I'm wrong and your mother just slipped. It doesn't mean she'll go back to the way she was. And I'm looking for a job all day, every day now that I have the time. Until I get one, we have a few savings we can survive off, and if need be, we can always sell the house and move into a smaller apartment," he tries to assure me.

It only makes me feel worse. If he's already thinking about such matters, things can't be as good as he wants to pretend. Besides, he should be *recovering*, reducing the stress in his life so he can get healthy again. Instead, he's busy job hunting.

"I want to help. Tell me what I can do," I insist. He could *die* if I don't help him.

"For now, I have things under control. Just promise you will visit a little more, please."

114

"Yes, of course. I'm sorry I didn't come sooner, Dad. You need to keep me posted from now on. On your health and Mom. Give me your phone, I'll put in my new number," I say.

I never bothered to give my parents my number, most of all because I didn't want them to be able to reach me so easily. I wanted an excuse to only reply to their messages after some time, but things have changed now. I need my dad to be able to reach me if he needs to. I'm the only one he can count on.

Chapter 14

Aliena

11 years ago

"Aliena, honey, is the food almost done?" my father asks as soon as he returns from work. My heart rate picks up at the sound of his voice and nearing footsteps, but I'm not scared, just nervous I did something wrong.

Daddy works hard all day so we can keep living at home, finance Mommy's medicine and have food in the fridge for me to prepare, so the least I can do is do my chores right. I want to do them right and make Dad happy. He deserves as much. I know he is stressed because Mom is still not feeling better after so many years of being sick, and I'm happy to ease his stress.

"I'm plating it right now," I shout back, hurrying up just enough not to mess up. When I am done with the plates, I carry two to the table and sit down opposite Dad, eager to see his reaction. I think I've gotten pretty good in the kitchen, or at least better than all my friends. None of them know how to cook anything. I had to learn my way around over the years and try to get better by watching cooking videos whenever I have the time. Still, there are always butterflies in my stomach while I wait for Dad to take his first bite.

Before he picks up the fork, he says, "Thanks, honey. Did you make enough for Mommy?"

"Yes, her plate is in the kitchen," I tell him. I'll have to beg her to eat some of it later. She rarely has an appetite because she occasionally sneaks into the kitchen during the day to snack. It comes and goes in waves. She never eats with us.

"Has she eaten anything so far?" he asks, his voice weary.

"No," I say, hating that that is the answer. I know Daddy doesn't want to hear that.

He sighs and nods to himself, pushing his chair away from the table again. "I'll check in with her and bring her the food. You should eat while it's hot," he tells me, forcing a tired smile, but I'm already getting to my feet anyway.

"Let me do it. You only just got home, Dad. Eat, please. I'll take care of Mommy," I argue.

If anything, my words seem to make him even sadder, and my heart grows cold. I hate how tired he looks. There are days when he looks almost as sick as Mommy, and it scares me.

"Okay. Thank you, Princess. You're a blessing," he says, sitting back down, and the pressure in my chest eases again. Daddy starts eating, and I go back into the kitchen.

Upstairs, I enter my mom's dark room and turn on the bedside lamp before sitting down on the chair next to her bed.

"Mom, it's time for dinner," I tell her softly. She's sleeping and doesn't react. I lean over to shake her bony arm. "Mommy, you haven't eaten all day. Come on." She still doesn't stir and my shoulders slump slightly in resignation. Yeah, I'll be here for a while. Maybe I'll get to eat dinner with Daddy tomorrow.

——

By the time I go back downstairs, Daddy is asleep on the couch. The tightness in my chest has returned and is only getting worse. Daddy often tries to stay awake in the evening to spend some time with me, so he stays downstairs instead of going to bed. In the end, he can't help but fall asleep, then he wakes up with bad muscle aches.

I never know what to do. I don't want to wake him, but I also hate he's in pain because of me. I've told him before he should just go to sleep in his bed if he's tired, but he said he looks forward to seeing his little girl all day and doesn't want to miss it for another twenty-four hours.

He never learns.

I do the dishes as quietly as possible and clean the kitchen with the same care. Then, I eat a few bites of my cold food before packing up the rest for Dad to take to work the next day. I didn't get the ratio quite right today because Mom had unpredictably much appetite. It's okay though, I'm not hungry and Dad needs the food more than I do.

If I eat really slowly and drink a glass of water beforehand, anything can make me feel stuffed, no matter how small the amount.

After cleaning and drying my plate, I cover Dad with a blanket before heading into my room where I finish folding all the laundry I haven't done yet. Earlier, I washed all the bed sheets and towels that have been used in the house.

Then I did all our dirty clothes, which took so many turns it took all day.

By the time I'm all done, my eyelids are nearly too heavy to keep open. I fall back onto my bed like a sack of potatoes and curl up in a ball, mentally going through the list of things I had to do today and checking them off. Between attending a few lessons at school, finishing my homework, taking care of Mommy, doing laundry, and preparing dinner, it was a busy day. I'm just glad I didn't stupidly forget something.

I grab a crumpled edge of my blanket and pull it over me, huffing in annoyance when I realize I'm lying on a part of it which means I have to move. I do so, then cover myself up to my nose and let my eyes glide over my messy room. It's funny how I make sure the whole house is neat and clean yet cannot seem to do the same with my room. The space is smaller, so it should be easy. But the mess keeps reappearing, and sometimes, I just can't be bothered to make it disappear. I'm the only one that's ever in here, after all, so it really doesn't matter.

Everything that only concerns me isn't important. Not with all the urgent things going on in this house.

Chapter 15

Aliena

I manage to avoid a confrontation with my best friend until eight p.m. when I finally leave my parents' house. On my way home, I decide to pick up the phone when she calls again.

"Oh, so she is alive! How good to know! What the hell have you been up to, A? I've been trying to reach you all day. I even went to your apartment only to find it empty! I thought you'd been kidnapped!" she immediately chastises.

"I'm sorry, Lily, I was busy. But I told you last night I made it home safely, and I texted you this morning."

"Yes, but I still haven't gotten an explanation as to why you snuck off last night. I think I deserve as much, don't you? You didn't even say goodnight."

If I weren't so tired, hearing my friend's sad, disappointed voice would certainly make my chest ache with guilt. As it is, I think I've felt too many emotions for today already. I'm empty.

"I visited my parents today," I decide to tell her. There's a pause where both of us are silent. Then, I go on, "I didn't feel like talking about it on my birthday, you know how it is, but I figured I shouldn't stay out all night before meeting them. I panicked and just left. I'm so sorry." It's not the truth. Not really.

When I left last night, it had everything to do with Sebastian. I didn't even know I'd have to visit my parents so soon. But if there's one thing I want to talk about less than my parents, it's Sebastian.

"Do you want to talk about it now? I could come over and bring some snacks," she offers. Bless her soul.

"I really appreciate it, but I don't think I'm up for it today. I wouldn't mind a distraction though," I say, knowing she'll accept that as an answer for now. No matter how curious she is, she's never pushed me when it comes to my parents. She knows I need my space.

"That can be arranged. Have you had dinner? We could go to a restaurant with the guys."

Somehow, my stomach knots further at the thought of seeing Sebastian. Despite that, I recognize the anticipation too. Maybe I'm a glutton for pain hoping for a rare good moment with Sebastian when I'm much more likely to get hurt.

"I haven't. That sounds great." I cooked for my parents before I left but couldn't bring myself to swallow a bite myself. It felt too much like old times and all I wanted to do was get the hell out of that house.

"All right, we'll pick you up in a minute. Be ready."

"Aye, aye."

———

121

"There's our little fugitive. How's it going? Do you feel different now you're twenty-two? Other than the urge to retire a lot earlier on a Saturday night?" Andrew teases me when his girlfriend and I sit down at the guys' table.

Today was one of the rare times Lily used her driver's license and car to pick me up instead of asking Andrew to be her driver. I guess she wanted to make sure I was okay before we met our friends.

I just brush off Andrew's comment with a laugh and hug the man. I really don't have an answer for him. Do I feel different now I'm twenty-two? The obvious answer would be no, but I can't deny I feel a hell of a lot more tired than I remember having felt in years.

Still, just seeing my friends helps a little. Even Sebastian, who hasn't looked at me yet.

Mattheo gets to his feet, and I notice how he puts most of his weight on his uninjured leg. That reminds me that he still hasn't told me how he injured himself.

"Hey, Quasimodo. Do you still refuse to tell me how you injured yourself?" I tease him as he pulls me into a tight hug. He holds me for longer than would be appropriate, and I have zero inhibitions to make myself melt into the embrace. It still bothers me I don't get a reply.

"How are you?" Mattheo whispers in my ear instead.

"Better now," I tell him truthfully. He doesn't ask what that means. Just holds me for a little longer before he pulls away and gives me a nod. I don't miss the way Lily is studying us curiously. Weird.

That makes Sebastian the only person I haven't greeted, and the moment gets really awkward really quickly. For me, at least. He just keeps scrolling on his phone, still refusing to look at me while I stand between his and Mattheo's chairs.

It's awkward because I don't know how to say hello. We've never hugged, but it's always been easy since normally we meet at his car. He simply never gets out of the driver's seat to hug Lily and me as the other men do.

But now I hugged the other two right in front of him, I wonder if I should just do the same with him to complete the circle.

Before I can come to a conclusion, his eyes lazily meet mine, and he arches an arrogant brow. "Did you need anything?" he demands.

Wow, I almost forgot what a jerk he was. Despite the uncomfortable feeling of rejection, I force myself to smile sarcastically. "Oh, so he did notice our arrival. And here I thought rich parents taught their children manners. Or had someone else do it, at least. No worries, I'll give you a crash course. When a friend arrives, you put your phone away and say hello," I explain very slowly so the peabrain may understand.

He gives me a flat look, then turns to Lily. "Sorry for my lack of manners, Lil. I was trying to finish an important email, but I should have said hello first." Then he turns back to me. "Happy now? I said hello to my friend."

I huff and take my seat between Lily and Mattheo without another word to him. Partially because I'm scared my voice might break if I tried to speak. I'm tired and too vulnerable to keep up with his open hostility. It's okay, though, all I need is a sip of water to make the lump in my throat disappear. Then, I'll be fine again.

Mattheo must have a hunch I'm not as unbothered by Sebastian's rejection as my expression suggests because he places a gentle hand on my thigh beneath the table and gives it an encouraging squeeze.

I smile at him. After a second, my eyes flick to Sebastian, who is eyeing the spot where Mattheo's arm vanishes under the table with an odd intensity. God, what is wrong with him? Why does he have to be so fucking confusing?

I try not to focus on him as the rest of my friends try to lighten the mood and fill the air with all sorts of nonsense topics. It quickly becomes clear that despite not knowing what's going on with my parents, my friends somehow all know I need a distraction and some cheering up. It makes me wonder what happened last night after I left.

It hasn't even crossed my mind, but now I can't help but think I missed something. There are looks exchanged between them I don't understand, and I hate it. Despite being the only one not going to their preppy school and our vastly different financial states, they've never made me feel like an outsider. Never until now.

I don't have an opportunity to subtly ask about it since they all steer clear from the topic of my birthday. That is until Sebastian breaks that rule.

"So, Aliena, will you tell us what happened last night to make you leave without saying goodbye?" The three others at the table immediately shoot him glares, so he raises his hands in surrender. "Hey, I'm just asking. I feel like after we spent all that money on the location, a short explanation is the least we deserve. She's the one that talked about manners. Or lack thereof."

Before any of the others can reply to him, I beat them to it. "Guys, he's right. It was rude of me to leave so suddenly and without notice and I'm really, really sorry. Something personal came up and I didn't want to explain or talk about it. It was selfish and I owe you an apology. I'm sorry if I ruined the rest of your night."

Now it's Lily that reaches out to touch my arm tenderly. "Don't worry about it, babe. We understand." She gives Sebastian a hard stare. When I follow her gaze, I find him studying me curiously. Like maybe, despite knowing the true reason for my departure, he believes there's some truth in what I just said.

"Lily's right. There's always another night out to make up for it and prove you aren't retiring from being the life of the party just yet," Mattheo adds with a wink.

"And that is next Friday's party, I believe. Seb hasn't hosted anything in too long."

"Yeah, sure, you decide when I open my house to hundreds of people. And why Friday, my parties are always on Saturdays," Sebastian wonders, though his voice lacks any kind of bite. It shouldn't make me jealous. I'm glad he's treating Lily with an appropriate amount of respect.

But a part of me also burns at the clear contrast between how easily he can be polite when he's always so rude to me.

"Aly works on Sunday," Lily provides. My angel.

Sebastian shrugs like he couldn't care less and doesn't understand what it has to do with him, but he doesn't protest, much to my surprise.

"All right, Friday it is, I guess. You're right, I have to host again before the students of Hartford U think I've lost my touch."

———

"Tell me, big guy, are you allowed to dance already?" I ask Mattheo when I join my friends in the private lounge upstairs. I was at my parents' before to check in on my dad and get an update. Then I cooked for him and Mom, who came home from work suspiciously late, which Dad tells me she's been doing for a few days.

He suspects she's meeting with an old dealer instead, and when I saw her come home that night, her pupils dilated and her voice chirpy, I couldn't deny his suspicion seems likely to be true.

I was almost scared to leave the house again, no matter how badly I wanted to get out. I guess a part of me thinks if I just stay on top of things, nothing else can go off the rails. Maybe if I keep a constant eye on my mom, she'll stop messing up and pull herself together before it's too late and she starts withering away like she used to.

But if she already reconnected with her old dealer, I'm not sure things haven't already gone too far for her to bounce back unharmed. God, it's such a mess. How could she do this? After so many years of Dad taking care of her, she can't support him for a few weeks until he's healthy when he's in need? No, she has to ruin everything and make shit about herself.

I guess I know where I have the selfish gene from.

It feels like the first time Mom developed a habit. Of course, I was way too young to understand back then, but even so, it felt like she got sick from one day to the other. Too fast for anyone to stop it.

Now I'm scared to confront her about it. If we're right, she's in a very fragile place right now, and I'm scared an argument might only make things worse. She's never been able to handle stress well. And if we're wrong, she'd take great offense and be upset for sure.

So instead of talking to her, I stayed as long as I could emotionally handle, which made me late for my friend's party.

It's okay, though. It doesn't seem like I disrupted some natural order or anything. My friends seem to do just as fine without me.

"Two more weeks to wait, *amo*."

"Two more?" I exclaim. That's just cruel. All I need right now is to get on the dance floor and forget the rest of the world. Who better to do that with than my charming dance partner?

Well, there is one other person who managed to make me lose my head and my touch with reality just fine, a voice in the back of my mind reminds me. Maybe even more so than Mattheo ever has. Only that person is currently flirting with a short blonde on the other side of the room, probably unaware I'm even inside his house.

"I'm afraid so."

I pout. "At least tell me how it happened, Mattheo," I push. It's ridiculous I still don't know the source of my misery. And no, I'm not being dramatic.

"Aliena." He sighs and brushes a stray strand of hair behind my ear. "It doesn't matter, okay? I just got into an argument with someone who knew just where to kick a knee to dislocate it."

I sit up straighter at that, reeling with surprise. "You got into a fight? Why?" I demand. Mattheo is usually so peaceful. It's hard to imagine him fighting someone, despite his towering height.

The question is well meant, coming from a place of confusion and concern, but I can tell Mattheo is growing agitated from my constant nagging.

His next words are more strained and lack his usual ease. "I said it doesn't matter."

"It matters to me. Since when are we keeping things from each other?" I demand. Mattheo and I aren't the type of friends that share every detail of our lives with each other, but I never felt the need to actively hide something when he asked. I just assumed he felt the same way.

"That's a rich question coming from you," he huffs.

I pull away from him a little more, unused to the gruffness in his voice. Shit, I think we're having our first fight. In all the months I've known him, we never so much as innocently disagreed on something. Why is everything in my life simultaneously going to hell now?

"What's that supposed to mean?" I ask.

"Really, you're playing dumb now?"

I'm not. I really don't know what he's referring to. It couldn't be my parents. There's just no way.

Mattheo huffs at my lack of a reply. "Why didn't you tell me you were attacked on your way home after you declined my ride?"

Oh, that's what he's talking about. I'm so relieved I could laugh. At least to that question, I have an honest reply. "Believe me when I tell you it totally slipped my mind. I mean it. Sure, it was scary when it happened but it's not like I was really injured or anything.

"Besides, we didn't see each other again for weeks after that, and I didn't think to bring it up on my birthday. It would have been so random. I didn't mean to keep that from you, Mattheo," I explain.

His frown doesn't soften. "You could have called me when it happened instead of Seb. You must know I would have come to help in a heartbeat. It was my fault you were out so late after all." I frown at the way he practically spits his friend's name. Something happened between them.

Actually, I know exactly what happened. Me. I came between two best friends, great. Now they treat each other like they can't stand breathing the same air.

"You offered to give me a ride. I declined. What happened wasn't your fault. And I called him because my phone was stolen, and his number was the only one I could remember." Mattheo doesn't look convinced, so I try to change the topic before the mood in the room worsens further. Of course, Lily and Andrew are dancing downstairs. For once. I could use some backup now.

"So, are we done fighting now? I'm sorry I pushed you about your knee and for forgetting to tell you about that night. Now, let's be friends again," I beg him jokingly, giving him my most exaggerated puppy-dog eyes.

He nods, though he doesn't share a smile with me. "Yeah, of course."

"We're good?" I repeat because he doesn't sound like we are. It makes me uncharacteristically nervous, the thought of him disliking me.

"Yeah, Aly, we're good." He pats my arm softly. Then a red-haired woman strides over with two drinks and a big smile and sits down on the other side of Mattheo. Really close to Mattheo. She hands him a drink, and he accepts it with a grin.

"Right. Aly, this is Miriam. Miriam, this is my friend Aly," he introduces us and no matter how sweetly she smiles at me, I realize I'm interrupting something. Being the good friend I am, I smile back at her before excusing myself.

I get off the couch, intending to go dancing right away, but I linger for a second, glancing at the bar. I'm not usually one for drinking but while drugs are an absolute hard no, I'm more lenient when it comes to an occasional drink. And right now, I feel like I could use one to loosen me up a bit.

I go over to the small bar the private lounge is equipped with and tell the bartender my order. Before I get my drink, I become aware of a presence to my right.

"Looks like your boytoy found a new toy. Poor seductress. That must *really* sting if you end up at the bar," Sebastian mocks me.

I give him a bored look. Maybe if I had any more energy, I'd put up with his teasing. As it is, I opt for honesty. "You know, you're really not that attractive when you try to bully me. I had a shitty day as part of a shitty week, so if you could just leave me alone, that would be great. And for the record, I don't mind Mattheo talking to that nice woman. I'm happy for my friend."

Even though I mean those words with all I've got, especially the part about Mattheo, I feel tears prick my eyes. God, this week was awful. I tried to handle work and visit my parents often, but something else had to suffer under the change. Which, in my case, was my sleep schedule.

I was too busy worrying about so many different things it was impossible for me to get any sleep at night no matter how physically and mentally drained I was.

I let my head drop onto my crossed arms on the counter and try to pull myself together. I faintly hear the bartender greet Sebastian as he places my drink next to my arm, and Sebastian tells him the drink is on the house.

Great, I'm pathetic enough for Sebastian to spare me some decency. I lift my head again and can only hope my unshed tears aren't invisible in the dim light when I say with my best neutral expression, "So, what was wrong with the blonde?"

"Nothing. She just wasn't able to truly capture my attention and keep it. No one can." He shrugs.

"Harsh," I say.

"And sadly true. Believe me, I'm not any happier about it than they are."

I take a long sip of my drink, and no matter how sure I am I shouldn't ask it, my next words force their way past my lips. "What about the brunette a week ago?" Do I sound pathetic? Yes, I do. Do I care? Yes, I do. But Sebastian just seems to have a thing for being around when I'm at my worst so here we are.

"She was a good kisser. That's all I can judge," he says, studying me closely, and even though I have no reason to take his word for it, I can feel a weight lift from my shoulders. I don't know why I care. I know I shouldn't.

Truth is, I do nonetheless.

My face must be showing my satisfaction because Sebastian rolls his eyes. "Try to look a little less happy about my dry streak will you."

I just shake my head, biting back a smile. What a surprise. This interaction took a whole one-eighty. It actually managed to make me feel better.

Chapter 16

Sebastian

She is smiling again. Thank god. For a second, it looked like she was about to cry, and I certainly wouldn't have known how to act then. I've never seen Aliena sad before. Sure, I've been faced with her anger—a lot of that—fear recently, and most of all joy. Not sadness.

And yet there she was for a second; a tired, defeated Aliena who didn't have her walls up. Meanwhile, I hadn't been aware those walls existed in the first place. Now I'm questioning how this girl I have a weird infatuation with is really doing, and my battered conscience is rearing its head.

What if I'm the reason behind her sadness? I was cruel on her birthday, and I was cruel the day after trying to stick to the status quo. That's safe. That's familiar. And I never thought my harsh comments actually got through to her much less enough to hurt her. The thought leaves me feeling uncomfortable.

But when Allie cracks an innocent smile, the tension leaves my chest. Maybe I imagined the flicker of emotion in her eyes. She seems good now.

"I don't know what you're talking about. Your dry streak doesn't concern me in the least. You must be imagining whatever happiness you're seeing on my face," she teases, looking smug as hell.

I'd like to tell her she has everything to do with my dry streak, that she is the very source of it. Instead, I say, "Yeah, sure I am."

She downs the rest of her drink and jumps off her bar stool, standing almost up against me. So much so she has to crane her neck to look at me with that big smile. "If you're not busy losing interest in a nice girl right now, how about you come dance with your friend? You did well enough the last time, I'd say."

What a fucking flirt. Here she is, the little troublemaker, blinking up at me through her lashes, her breasts faintly brushing against my chest with every soft breath she takes. My inner eagerness to tell her yes, that I'd be more than happy to dance with her, is just more proof that she has me wrapped around her finger.

I hold out my arm for her to take, mumbling, "If you insist."

She takes it and leads me toward the door. As we walk past the couches, I can't help a glance in Mattheo's direction. As expected, his attentive eyes follow his friend and me suspiciously. I try to hide the satisfaction I get from it.

"Stop acting like I'm leading you to the gallows. If you don't feel like dancing, I'll go look for another partner," she finally says as we reach the stairs, and I realize I must've tried hiding my satisfaction a little too hard.

Great, and now the image of her dancing with another man is stuck in my mind. Maybe that's why my voice is so urgent when I protest. "No."

She chuckles and keeps pulling me down the stairs. At the bottom, she leans in to speak into my ear since the music is too loud to understand otherwise. Her gentle touch on my shoulder spreads awareness through my whole body.

"But if you're going to be rude about it again once we're done, you better think again," she says, then pulls away enough to level me with a hard stare.

So. Fucking. Beautiful.

I nod, then lean down to talk into her ear. My heart races at the close-up of the elegant swing of her neck and the scent of her sweet perfume. "That's fair. I'm sorry for last week. All of it, other than the dancing. What I did with that woman was petty and I'm sorry for what I said. Especially on your birthday.

"Just know you drove me absolutely crazy with what you did with Mattheo, and I still don't think I'm over it. Nonetheless, I was a jerk last week," I say, struggling to find the right words to apologize. I was never good at it. Never had much practice either. I get that from my father.

She pulls away enough to look at me when she asks, "Why? Why did it drive you so crazy, Seb?"

"Why did I make you cry when I followed her into the bathroom?" I shoot back.

After a thoughtful second, Aliena nods to herself. "I don't understand what we are," she remarks bluntly.

At that, I chuckle. Look at us agreeing on something. "Neither do I."

She nods again, then smiles. Without another word, she pulls me into the middle of the crowd and starts dancing again, with her front against mine and her face near the crook of my neck.

"Let's recap," she starts, dancing as if it's all she's ever known. I can't see her face now and it makes it easier to talk. She's so pretty it's distracting. "It drives you crazy to see me with someone else."

I lean down to talk back, grinning against her skin. "And you hate it when I pick up girls."

She tightens her hold on my neck and keeps dancing. Then she pulls away, twirls once, and returns to our previous position.

"But you told me you didn't want me," she provides. "And you act like you can't stand me most of the time."

"Because you're infuriating," I tell her. She shakes her head.

"Because we met at the nursing home and you don't like that I got an insight into your personal life. Because you feel the same attraction I do but are too scared to act on it," she counters.

"I am not scared," I insist.

"Then why would you not kiss me? I know you wanted to the last time we danced. And a few times before that. Yet, you never go through with it."

"I can't go through with it. We can't."

"Why?"

"Because one kiss wouldn't be enough. Nor would two, or ten, or fifty. Once I felt your kiss, I'd want to feel it all, Aliena. And we can never go there."

She pulls away and her eyes meet mine. Once again, her desire is apparent and it's gnawing at my restraint. "Why's that?"

I sigh, bringing one hand up to cup her cheek. God, just once. I'd love to touch those lips just once. It seems impossible that I plan not to. Ever.

"For better or worse, we're forced to spend time with each other since we have mutual friends. We can't change that. If I kiss you, if I take you upstairs, it's a one-time thing. I'm not made for anything serious. Still, we'd be forced to see each other again. It's too complicated," I explain.

I can tell she doesn't agree with me even before she opens her mouth. "Then why not indulge one time at least?" she challenges.

I huff. "I'm not Mattheo, Aly. I can't be chill about watching you go off with another guy. It would be a bad idea." She must see that. What I'm saying is logical.

But of course, she doesn't. "You're already anything but chill about me being with others," she argues. "It really can't be worse than it is already."

Oh, but it could. What if sleeping with her would feel like touching her does? Just so much stronger. I wouldn't be able to handle it. I'm afraid I'm already addicted to these brief sparks of electricity. If I slept with her, I'm not sure I could stay true to my words and not try to have her again and again.

And that sort of deal is absolutely too messy to risk with someone you share your best friends with.

"I'm not trying to convince you, sorry. I just think we can't go on like this. Either we get over this weird stage of attraction and jealousy or we do something about it," she says.

"The first option is not possible. I don't see myself ever being happy for you if you found someone else like you are for Mattheo." That, at least, I'm sure of.

"Me neither," she agrees. Then the beat drops and flashing lights blind the room, disorienting me. I only see enough to know Aliena is smiling and jumping up and down with the rest of the crowd. Wearing heels and all.

I watch her, allowing myself a moment to do nothing other than look at the way she comes to life with the music.

When the song changes and the hurried beat is replaced by a slower rhythm, Aliena finds her way back to me without a problem. Her back fits perfectly against my front and this time when we dance, she doesn't look at me. As if, maybe, she's trying to ignore the question lingering in between us like I am.

Or maybe because she's waiting for me to make a decision since the ball seems to be in my corner. She told me she'd be ready to indulge. I'm the one that said we shouldn't.

I am seriously questioning my sanity as she keeps rubbing her perfect, lethal body against me. Yeah, no red-blooded straight man would hesitate in my place.

The next time she throws her hands in the air, I take one of them and twirl her so we're face to face. She laughs, adding an extra turn before she meets me in the middle. I cup her face, and her laughter dies instantly.

"Just one kiss. Tell me you are with me. Nothing more. Don't let me take you upstairs," I tell her, practically begging her to keep a clear mind since she stole my ability to do so. Without hesitation, she nods, stepping impossibly closer.

137

There's a small, infuriating smile on her lips as her arms lock behind my head. "You better make it count then," she whispers.

So.

Fucking.

Infuriating.

I crash my lips to hers, nearly toppling us both with the force. Luckily, she manages to hold her own against me and pushes back, tugging at my hair in warning. All it makes me want to do is hold her impossibly tighter.

I was right, kissing her is unlike anything I've ever experienced. Her scent, her warm skin, those soft lips, they all have my body burning up. I adjust our position, keeping one hand on her face while my other arm snakes around her waist to pull her close. We're not dancing anymore. We're barely moving at all. Still, our chests are both heaving. So much so I can feel her heart pounding against my pecs.

"Shit, what did I promise you again?" she breathes out against my lips when I let her pull away a little.

I just shake my head. "Don't pull away. I'm not ready for this to end. We said one kiss," I mutter, keeping my eyes closed. People are still dancing around us, and the music is still blaring. Both of those things disappeared when I had Aliena's lips on mine and both are slowly registering again. I don't want them to register. I want to stay in this bubble with Aliena for a little longer where only we and our chemistry exist.

She gives my lips the softest of pecks. "Always," she whispers as she pulls back. Then she gives me another one. "So"—another kiss—"fucking"—one more—"bossy," she finishes with one last kiss.

I don't let her pull away again, deepening the kiss instead by softly scraping my teeth against her lips. Her reaction is a soft moan, one so similar to those haunting me in my dreams I'm about ready to snap.

"Make that sound again and I'll fuck you up against the closest wall. Don't test me," I warn her.

"Don't tempt me," she retorts, bringing her lips back to mine with a soft sigh. That reaction is almost as bad as if she moaned my name. Fuck, I'm way too attuned to her.

"That's even worse," I groan.

"Mhm, am I making you ache?" she teases while I know she feels how hard I am for her.

"You fucking know you are," I bite back. Just because she's the vixen she is, she rubs her tummy against me once more.

My eyes close more firmly.

"Poor baby. Such a shame you made me promise I won't take care of you upstairs," she goes on, still moving.

"You are a demon," I mutter. "A goddamned succubus."

When she speaks again, her lips are brushing against mine. "You love it."

Then she kisses me again, though she never stops moving against me and my aching erection. She doesn't stop when I tighten my hold on her hips because I can't decide if the pleasure is torture or heaven. She also doesn't stop when I pull away, breathing heavily, and whisper, "What are you doing to me?"

"Trying to make you come, currently," she replies without missing a beat. I'd laugh if only I wasn't afraid that was exactly what this was leading to.

"You can't," I tell her, sounding pained to my own ears.

"Try me," she retorts, but I shake my head.

"I don't doubt your abilities, Aliena. Everything but that. But you can't. There are people around," I try to reason.

"And all they see is just another horny couple that can't keep their hands to themselves. We're just kissing, after all," she says, her movement undeterred. And that's when the familiar tingle at the base of my spine starts to register, and I start to worry I truly am about to come from just making out. Like a teen. God.

"You're horrible," I tell her, then feel her smile against my lips.

"Tell me to stop," she challenges.

"Please, don't," I say instead, my breathing growing harsher by the second.

She hums gently. I can feel the sound reverberate from her chest. "Are you close, Sebastian?" she asks.

"Too fucking close considering you're not even touching me," I grit out. Only she could do this.

She laughs again, and the sound almost feels too precious to be part of this moment. It's enough to make me momentarily question what I'm doing right now.

When my hand tightens on Aliena's waist this time, it's enough to stop her movements. I pull away to look into her eyes.

"What's wrong?" she asks when I don't say anything for a few seconds.

"That's what I'm trying to figure out," I reply, confused by the lack of light in those beautiful honey-

140

colored eyes. She looks happy enough, but something just isn't right about her eyes.

"What?"

"How are you?" I ask instead of reacting to her question.

Her eyebrows move up on her forehead and she swallows loudly. "What are you talking about? I'm good," she insists. "I thought both of us were more than good a second ago, but I clearly did something wrong if you're changing the topic this way."

"You did nothing wrong, Aliena. Other than maybe embarrassing me slightly by nearly making me come in my pants. No, I just came to my senses and realized I promised you a kiss, not to rub myself against you until I came." God, that even sounds disgusting.

Aliena smiles. "That's not what you did. Actually, I rubbed myself against you to make you come."

"You know you don't have to do that, though. Right?" I ask.

"Yes, of course," she tells me, blinking two times too many as she does.

No, I feel like something's still wrong. I lean in to gently kiss her, then caress her cheek with my thumb. That does the trick, and she melts against me like butter.

I rest my forehead against hers, keeping my eyes closed. "You know what else I find infuriating about you?"

That has a surprised laugh bubbling out of her. "No, tell me."

"You are so beautiful it's hard to believe you're real at times."

She pulls back, looking at me with furrowed brows. "What are you doing?" she asks.

"Talking to you," I simply say.

"Why?" She seems so genuinely confused, and it sits very wrong with me. My reply was simple enough. How can it be so hard for her to believe that, yes, I'd choose to talk to her over a quick orgasm? It makes me all the gladder I didn't let it come to that.

"Because you're my friend," I tell her due to a lack of a better description.

"Am I?" she challenges me.

"A friend I am dangerously attracted to and have been treating unfairly. What do you say we try to start over," I propose, feeling uncharacteristically nervous about her reply.

To my surprise, she doesn't hesitate to shoot me down, "No."

"No?" I repeat like an imbecile. Not to sound too full of myself but that was not the reaction I was expecting.

"I don't want to start over and erase our history. I like the way we met, and I like knowing Rosie was very important to you like she was to me. You're my only tie to her. It's more than that, though. I don't hold a grudge for how you've been treating me. We've both made mistakes, all I need to know is if you can treat me differently from now on."

This is the first time she's ever brought Rosie up to me, and it's enough to stun me for a second. Thinking about my angel of a grandmother still hurts. Sure, she might not have been the best mother to my father, but she was always great to me. We were close. It's been a few months since she

142

passed, and this is the first time I've heard her name since the funeral.

It's not hard to believe that Aliena cared about her as well. She looked after her nearly every day for over a year, after all. It has just never occurred to me she made such a strong link between her and me.

"Yes, I can do better," I finally confirm. A nagging voice reminds me why I acted like a jerk in the first place; the old mantra my dad pounded into me from a young age coming to the forefront of my mind. *Love is a weakness, it's exploitable. It makes you a powerless fool, easy to manipulate.* I wish his words didn't still have any control over me, but they clearly do. I didn't like someone with the knowledge of how soft I am for the people I love suddenly at the parties I throw for my peers. Worse someone who knew all about my strained relationship with my father, the headmaster of those who all know me so differently. People who *need* to see me differently because it keeps me protected and well-respected.

To have them doubt my credibility, worse, my relationship with my father would be to give up the illusion of power I now have at the university.

I was an idiot, and I panicked, falling into an old pattern because it was easy and felt safe, and she paid the price for it in the months to follow.

"Good, then we're friends," she confirms. I might not understand why she's so quick to forgive me, but I'm greedy enough to shake her hand on it.

Friends... I guess we're both ignoring that it's no solution for the jealousy issues we both have.

Chapter 17

Sebastian

Last July

I spent three hours with my grandma and Aliena at the nursing home. It's funny how quickly the time passed. We were playing Cribbage and messing around and suddenly, it was time for dinner. When Grandma asked me to stay, looking as hopeful as a puppy, I couldn't possibly deny her.

It also didn't hurt that Aliena accompanied us. She seems like a pretty awesome girl, and Rosie was acting like a matchmaker pro. The innocence of the time we spent together allowed me a short reprieve from reality, allowed me to entertain the idea I could be this guy basking in the attention of a sweet woman with the prospect of actually keeping her.

Sadly, staying that long also meant there was no way my father wasn't going to question my whereabouts. He knows I didn't have practice today since he developed my exercise plan himself, the controlling bastard, and my mother asked me to come home right after school.

I wish I could just go to my place but it's the old man's birthday tomorrow, and I promised my mother I'd stay the night at their place so I could help her prepare a few things for him tomorrow morning in secret. He doesn't deserve it, of course, but my mother insists on constantly doing too much for him. The least I can do is make sure she doesn't overwork herself.

The reason we have to prepare everything so early is that she works in the afternoon, and she wants things to be "perfect". I hate to see how desperately she tries to make sure their marriage is successful and my father has everything he could possibly need with her as a wife. Deep down, I know she's just scared he'll leave her as he did with his last wife.

That's why she never quit her job as a housekeeper. As insurance. That's also why she won't let him hire a housekeeper for their place, afraid the story will repeat itself. Of course, my father has tried telling her she doesn't need a job now she's married to him, but his insistence stems from his embarrassment of having a wife coming from a lower social standing. So low she "doesn't even have a respectable job". Whatever the hell that's supposed to mean.

Never mind that he knew what her job was before they were ever together since that's how they met. Yeah, Daddy fell in love with the housekeeper his ex-wife hired. My mother, bless her heart, was too naïve to recognize him as the pig he was, and when he told her he was divorcing poor Diana to be with her, she was over the moon.

He proposed soon after and my mom saw no red flag concerning the fact he cheated on his ex-wife with her.

Don't get me wrong, I love my mom. All I'm saying is she shouldn't have been surprised when he occasionally worked long shifts... It's exactly as they say, once a cheater, always a cheater. And I'm the one left to pick up the pieces when Mom is crying over my bastard sperm donor.

Speak of the devil. Despite my best efforts to sneak into the house with my key from when I used to live here, my father is expecting me in the living room which I sadly have to pass to get to my old bedroom.

"Where have you been?" he asks, his voice even and stern. I fight the urge to roll my eyes only because my mother enters the room at the same moment, coming toward me with a big smile on her face.

"My boy, hello. How are you?" she chirps, pulling me into a hug.

I hug her back, stocking up on the comfort she provides before my inevitable interaction with my shithead of a father. "I'm good, Mom. How are you?"

"I'm fantastic now you are here. I'm always happy when you visit us," she gushes.

"Which isn't often," my father adds helpfully. Jerk. "You should have been here hours ago, Sebastian. Where were you so late?"

"Oh, William, don't interrogate him. He's young," my mother tries to reason. My dad ignores her.

I take a deep breath and swallow the remark that it's not even ten p.m. Then I reply as calmly as possible. "I was with Grandma."

Now, that has a thick silence swallowing up the room in an instant. Yeah, my father probably didn't expect me to look for his mother after he transferred her without telling me, and this is the only matter even my mother stayed out of. I don't hold it against her though, she's just trying not to disturb the fragile peace that exists in her marriage.

"What was that?" my father asks, his voice dangerously low.

"I said, I was visiting your mother," I repeat provocatively slowly.

"You don't know where she is. I took care of that to ensure you focused on your studies rather than that withering woman."

I clench my jaw as heat licks at my veins. The temper I inherited from him quickly rises. How can he speak of his own mother that way? Did they have differences? Yes. But my relationship with her has nothing to do with him, and still, he insists on disrespecting her in my presence, knowing how much it pisses me off.

The pressure in my body tightens and for a moment, I'm tempted to smash my fist into his perfectly kempt face. Oh, how satisfying it would be to feel his bones break under my clenched knuckles. Just once in my life.

The reminder that my mom is right there, watching the scene unfold anxiously is what makes me relax my fingers and take a deep breath. We all know I love her too much to act on my violent impulses. My father's been taunting me with it for years, yet he never stops trying to push me past the limit of my restraint.

That's my father. Always working hard to keep me on my toes and make my life a little harder. He calls it disciplining me. I call it being a jerk that gets off on powerplays.

"Well, you didn't try hard enough. I found her," I grit out.

Then there's that triumphant smile I hate so much. He melts further into his chair, which he still hasn't bothered to get up from since I arrived.

"I'll just move her again. Far enough that you can't visit her. I'm sure there's a good nursing home on a Caribbean Island. Mother would surely enjoy that."

She wouldn't. She hates the heat. And the beach. He knows that.

"Don't bother. It seems her condition has been rapidly worsening, and she's unlikely to make it into the next year. At least allow me the decency of seeing her a few times in those last few months," I argue, hating how my voice softens without my command, turning into a plea I know he'll take advantage of.

My mother must hear the vulnerability because she swoops in. "Of course, he will." Then she hugs me again and whispers, "I'm so sorry, my boy." I can hear the truth in her words.

My father concedes with a huff. "You were always too sentimental. If you knew her as I did, you wouldn't have put in the effort to find her."

You're too sentimental.

Look at you, boy, so bendable because you wear your heart on your sleeve for anyone to see and use. You're weak.

Stop crying in public. It was just a fucking cat. Leave her, wipe that blood off your hands, and pull yourself together. It's time you start acting like my *son.*

All the times he used his words against me like a sharpened blade rush over me. His comments used to cut back when I was still young and looked up to him. They cut so deeply I still wear the scars in the depths of my

148

psyche. The same psyche that snaps now with the painful reminder.

I can't hold my tongue despite my better judgment. "You know, maybe the reason she was different with me is that you just didn't fucking deserve her benevolence," I snap.

My old man stills, his voice deathly calm when he replies, "What was that?" He sizes me up with an arched brow and sits up straighter in his chair as if he was ready to finally get to his feet. Maybe this is when he finally attacks me and gives me an excuse to hurt him. It would put those boxing skills he's been drilling into me to good use. My nerves are humming at the prospect.

"I said, maybe the reason she treated you badly was that you deserved it. Rosie was never anything less than loving with me. Maybe you just weren't worth the effort!" I seethe, taking a step forward. My mother tries to hold me back in vain.

"Sebastian, please," she pleads silently. For once, her voice isn't enough to make me return to my senses.

William watches our encounter, and when I don't settle down and backpaddle like I usually would, he gets to his feet, bringing us eye to eye. There's a glint in his eyes I don't understand. Like he's happy about my reaction. Like I'm right where he wants me. It unsettles me more than anything else ever could.

"What about your mother? Did she deserve to be called a dirty immigrant? And being told to go back to Argentina?" he challenges, his expression unwavering as he watches me. Waiting for me to crack under the force of his prompt.

He almost sounds as if he cared about my mom and what people call her when really all he gives a fuck about is his own reputation. Whatever he's referring to must've hurt his pride more it than triggered any protectiveness.

But this is the first time I've heard him mention something like this in connection to my grandmother, so I hesitate. She wouldn't really have said something like that, right? I'm aware of the differences the women had because Rosie didn't approve of my dad's divorce and didn't like him remarrying.

What if those problems had a different source than I thought, though? It would certainly hurt my image of my grandmother if she turned out to be a racist.

My mom speaks before either one of us can. "William, that is enough. She's his grandmother," she insists. It's hardly the denial I was hoping for.

"He's wasting his time on her. Time he could be using to get his average grades to be more than that. Or to perfect his skills in the gym," the old man practically spits. "Now stay out of this and keep your mouth shut."

Yeah, that does it for me. I take another step forward, done with him disrespecting women that mean something to me. "You know what, how about I show you just how much I've perfected those skills?" I dare him, squaring my shoulders.

He bristles. "Watch your tone with me, young man. Don't forget your place."

"Don't forget yours. That's your wife you're talking to," I retort, thrusting my arm out to gesture to my mom but never taking my eyes off him. We're nearly standing chest to chest now while my mother tries to force us apart.

"Stop, please. Come on, men. Let's all calm down," she begs. Her voice is horribly shaky and it's enough to make me pause. Knowing she grew up in a household where violence was an everyday occurrence, I'd hate to think we're triggering her.

It takes all my self-restraint, but I finally let her push me back a step. As soon as my old man is out of my personal space, I'm able to breathe again. When I see my dad reclaim his seat like a lazy king and my mother turns to me with tears in her eyes, I feel like shit.

He doesn't care what I do, but she does.

"Alight, I'm going to my room," I excuse myself.

My mom wipes at her face. "Yes, yes. I'm coming with you," she tells me. I don't argue, just step aside to let her lead the way.

"Don't listen to what your father said about Rosie. We had a rough start, but it was a long time ago," she says once we're in my old bedroom, sitting on the edge of my bed. I sit down next to her and hide my face in my hands, sighing.

"She really said those things?" I ask even though I don't want to know the answer. Even though I already do know it.

"She did. At first. I think she was just sad about how William ended things with Diana and how quickly I replaced her as his wife. You know how she was after your grandpa's death. She never even looked at another man. She didn't understand how your father could end his marriage willingly. Don't hold it against her now."

Even though I can feel my chest and head protest at the prospect that my sweet grandma isn't so sweet after all, I nod. People are layered, and just because Rosie was always sweet with me doesn't mean she's entirely good. My mother goes on, "How was your visit today?"

A flash of honey-colored eyes and flushed cheeks comes to my mind, taking it off the unwelcome revelation. At least at that, I perk up a little.

"It was good. She made friends with a nurse there and we all played some Cribbage together." I pay attention to speak nonchalantly, but something must be showing on my face because my mother smiles.

Looking like a dog with a bone she asks, "That's great to hear, although I'm surprised the nurse knows the game. How old is she?"

I grin tugs at my lips. My mom sure quickly got to the point. "She's my age," I confirm. Then, just because I suddenly get the urge to move on, I add, "Her name is Aliena and she's been looking after Grandma for one and a half years. They seem kind of close. It was nice to know Grandma wasn't alone all this time, you know. Aliena even buys her flowers in my father's name every now and again."

I look up from my hands and pause seeing my mother is positively beaming. *Shit.* "She sounds very lovely. Will you see her again?" she asks.

I shrug airily even though I already planned my next visit. I asked about Aliena's schedule at the desk before I left, and I have every intention of using the knowledge to accidentally bump into her again. "If she's working the next time I go, I'm sure I'll say hello."

"Oh, tell her hi from me too," my mom gushes, but I laugh and shake my head.

"I definitely can't do that."

"Why not?"

"Because, Mom, I'd be telling her I told you about her. I'd come across like a sociopath," I explain.

The woman brushes me off. "Please, women like that. She'd surely feel flattered knowing you talked about her."

"Oh yeah, I'm sure she would. I'll still refrain from making any moves that strong for now. Who knows, maybe you'll accompany me on one of my visits and you may meet her yourself. All in due time, though."

"I'd love to meet her." She winks at me and pats my arm. "I'll go check in on your father now. You're okay?" she asks, getting to her feet.

"I'm good. Sorry for how things escalated. He's just so infuriating."

"I know. You two just have a way of working each other up. Sleep now, my boy, we have to be up early tomorrow."

I get up and hug her. "Goodnight, Mom."

Chapter 18

Aliena

I struggle to get the door open with the bags hanging from my arms. I try to push down the handle with my elbow and nearly cry out in relief when I find it unlocked. Thank god. I'm sure I would have dropped all the groceries I bought if I had to get out the key I was given the last time I visited my dad.

"Linda? Is that you?" my dad calls from upstairs, presumably his room. It's where he's been spending most his time, too weak to do anything else.

He hasn't gotten much better in the last two weeks since he told me about what happened and I'm sure our suspicion that my mother relapsed is true. I didn't find any drugs when I looked through her things, but I see the signs. Dad sees them too.

It's been a stressful time and it's only getting worse with Christmas right around the corner. I never liked Christmas, even as a child, but since I spent the last few years with Lily and her family, I learned it could be fun. Sadly, I don't think I'll get to spend the holidays with my friend this year. My parents need me.

I finally set my full bags down in the kitchen and then yell back, "Just me, Dad." I'm embarrassingly out of breath, and it's an unwelcome reminder that I really need to do some cardio.

I can hear my dad make his way downstairs much more slowly than he usually would. I don't know what's wrong with him. He should have gotten better by now. Maybe it's because he hasn't been able to reduce the stress he's confronted with considering his unsuccessful job hunt and the whole situation with my mom. Sure, I've been trying to help but there's only so much I can do.

Between taking care of my parents and working at the nursing home, I haven't even had time to see my friends. I miss them and to say I need a break from looking after others would be an understatement. I can't even remember the last time I took a bath and had some good old me-time.

"Hello, Aly. It's good to see you," my dad greets me with an awkward hand on my back as I start putting all the groceries away. I turn, trying hard to hide my discomfort at the sight of his pale face. God, he looks like shit. I hate seeing him like this, it makes him appear so old.

"Hey, dad. Where's Mom?" I ask. She should have come home from work about two hours ago. For heaven's sake, we're only a week from Christmas now, and it's cold outside. I hate to think she's out somewhere, doing who-knows-what to her body.

"I don't know, honey. I'm sure she'll be home soon," he tries to reassure me.

It doesn't work. I remember the old times when Mom would vanish for days, and we didn't know where she was. Even the thought of those times has a part of me shriveling up inside. I never thought we'd have to go through all that again.

155

One of my biggest worries is that Mom lost her job. She barely made minimum wage as it was, but now that Dad no longer has an income, it's vital to get whatever we can. I'm already covering their expenses for food, but I'm not sure how much more of my own money I can spare. If all their bills come on top of mine, we'll all be in debt. If things keep getting worse, I'm afraid I'll have to stop renting my apartment and move back in with them, but I'll do anything possible to prevent that. I can't live here again. There are too many memories, and this will never feel like home, I know it.

Things are a mess.

"All right. Well, I'll start working on dinner now, okay? You should rest some more."

"I'm fine, honey," my dad insists even though his shoulders are hunched. It's as if the effort to just keep standing is exhausting him.

"Dad, you don't look fine. Have you been taking your pills?" I ask.

He shakes his head and tries to smile softly. "I must've misplaced them," he tries to lie. What he really means is my mother stole the rest of them.

My stomach is in knots, but I try to sound as unaffected as possible as I say, "Dad, I'm no longer a child. Please, stop trying to lie to me. We have to talk about it and find a solution. We can't let her go on like this."

He sighs and just like that, he looks ten years older. "I don't know what to tell you, honey. I feel like I failed you. Again. I don't know how things escalated so quickly with your mother. She was sober for years. I didn't know having the pills around would trigger her. This is my fault," he says.

156

A lump forms in my throat. "Please, don't blame yourself." Not when I should have been around more. It's not his fault Mom relapsed. "Maybe it would help if we talked about it with her?" I propose.

"I don't think that's a great idea. The first time, whenever I tried talking to her about her problem, she just got defensive and left for days. I'm afraid to risk it. It's so cold out now, she could die out there. Especially with all that venom in her veins," he explains.

I nod slowly, turning toward the stove so my dad can't see my expression anymore. I'm so tired, I don't think I could mask my despair at the whole situation.

"What about professional help?" I ask, even though I know we could never afford it. If that is what it takes, I'll just have to find a way.

"I think that might be even worse than if we tried talking to her. The last time, she decided things had to change on her own. Maybe she'll do it again."

She did that after *years*. Hell, how did we get here? I don't understand how my mother could do it. How could she throw everything she worked so hard for away? If there was anything worse than her always being high, it was her withdrawal. There were times when she would scream and cry in pain all night, and she got sick so often, she could barely keep down any meals.

It was hard to witness, to say the least. I was already working at the nursing home by then, so I must've been around sixteen.

I wish I knew what made her change back then but it's not like I can ask. Maybe my dad's right and all I can do is try to get through this and hope my mom will pull herself

157

together soon. Maybe it's not too late for her to go back to how things were again.

I start preparing the healthy meal I went shopping for, letting my tears stream down my face now that my dad is in the living room. If he asks about it, it was the onions' fault. He doesn't need to worry about me on top of everything else.

I'm just about to plate the food for my dad and me when the front door opens and my mom staggers inside, beaming in a dazed way. My stomach drops further at the sight of her, my chest growing cold. I meet her in the corridor before she can reach the living room where my dad is dozing.

Her clothes are disheveled, and the fly of her pants are open. God, what is she doing to get her next fix? I want to scream.

"Hang on, Mom. Let me just fix your clothes," I tell her, speaking in the same voice I use on my confused patients without even noticing. Only I am whispering now so I don't wake my dad.

"Oh, you're sweet. I'm so happy you're always here now," my mom tells me, her eyes wide and pupils constricted. My hands start shaking as I close the buttons on her blouse. This is all wrong. The last time I saw her, her pupils were dilated. Now they're constricted. It's not just one drug she's taking. She doesn't even care what it is.

I have to painfully swallow the lump in my throat before I can reply. "I made dinner. Just sit down at the table, okay?"

"I don't think I'm hungry," she protests weakly, but I just shoo her toward the table. I can't argue about her not eating anymore. I just can't.

On my way back to the kitchen, I gently wake Dad. "Hey, wake up. Dinner's ready," I tell him. He opens his eyes and sits up, smiling weakly. "Oh, and Mom's back," I add, trying to sound as cheery as I possibly can.

He lights up at that. "That's a relief."

I wonder if he would say that if he saw her before I fixed her clothes. Does he know what she's doing? Has she come home similarly in the past? When I wasn't there to shield my dad from it? My stomach twists at the thought.

I go to the kitchen and start plating, though my hands are still shaking, and there are tears in my eyes trying to make my job a little harder. When my mind wanders for a second and I'm too distracted to focus, I blindly reach for another plate behind the pan I just took out of the oven. The underside of my arm presses against the hot steel, and I quickly pull it away, biting my tongue to keep from crying out as I clutch the burned limb to my chest. More tears rush to my eyes, and this time, I'm unable to hold them back. It's too much. It's all just so much, too much.

I drop to the floor, crying as silently as possible as I try to take even breaths. The walls feel like they're closing in on me and an iron fist is squeezing my lungs. I cover my mouth with a tight hand to muffle the sound of my sobs. There's no need for my parents to see me like this. I doubt my mother would care much right now, but my dad would worry about me. I can't make this all about me.

It takes me several long minutes to calm down and breathe somewhat evenly again. Minutes that made it feel like I was dying, but this is nothing new. I've had small attacks like this since I was a kid. It's nothing. I brush it off with one last staggering breath and get to my feet.

When I finally emerge from the kitchen with the loaded plates, my burn hidden underneath my sleeve, my parents are conversing casually. I'm glad they didn't notice how long I took to bring them their food.

"There you go," I say as I return a second time carrying my own plate. My dad smiles at me and immediately digs in, humming as he swallows the first bite.

"That's delicious, honey. Thank you so much," he says.

"Your father is right. It's *so* good to have you back," my mom adds, and I struggle to keep my small smile in place.

Maybe we wouldn't be here if I had only visited more often. Maybe my dad would've never had a heart attack and my mom wouldn't have felt the need to relapse.

Throughout dinner, I barely say I word. It's all I can do to keep forcing myself to eat. Luckily, my mother is in a talkative mood, so she and my dad don't pay me much attention. Still, I see the way she rubs the inside of her elbow through her blouse and picks at her skin. It makes me sick to my stomach.

As soon as everyone has swallowed their last bite, I get up from the table and hastily carry all the dirty dishes into the kitchen. I clean up quickly and transfer the leftovers into appropriate containers. Then I meet my parents in the living room again, eager to get out of here and pass out in my bed.

"So, you guys, the fridge is filled to the brim, and you have leftovers to get you at least through tomorrow. I'll try to come over again soon. Call me if you need anything, okay?" I offer, already inching toward the exit.

"Of course, have a good night, honey," my dad tells me.

When I smile at him, my mother gets to her feet and throws her arms around me. I nearly pull a face at how she smells. A mix of smoke and dirt.

"Thank you for dinner, my dear. I'll see you soon, yes?" she asks, keeping me at arm's length.

I nod, smiling forcibly. "Sure, Mom. Goodnight," I tell her, pulling away. Then I go to the door and put on my shoes, so happy to finally get out of here I can barely tie the laces.

Before I can leave, the lights all turn off at the same time, leaving the entire house in darkness. For a second, we're elevated in a state of silent confusion, and I freeze where I am. Then, my mother starts screaming out of nowhere, and I rush back into the living room, wearing one shoe.

I hurriedly turn on my phone's flashlight to see my mom sitting on the floor with her back to the wall and her hands around her ears. Her eyes are flicking around the darkness almost frantically and she keeps screaming.

Shit, I forgot how paranoid she could get. I head toward her to calm her, but my father's hand on my shoulder stops me. I look at him and he shakes his head. "You've done enough for today, honey. I got this," he tells me.

But he looks so tired that leaving now is not an option. "What happened with the lights?" I ask.

"Your mother usually takes care of the bills. I didn't even think she might forget to pay. They shut off the electricity," he replies.

With his every word, the pressure in my chest builds.

"They can't do that. You can't be here without electricity. Shit, and I just stocked up the fridge. The food will go bad. Give me the company's number, I'll call them," I insist, trying to keep my panic in check.

My father doesn't fight me on it and gives me their number. I disappear into another room to get away from my mother's yelling and call them. Luckily, they pick up. I tell them my name and explain the electricity here just went out. Then I ask if we can get the power back now if I'll pay straight away.

"I'm sorry, miss. We can only grant you the services after we received the payment," they tell me. Tears of frustration clog my throat.

"No, you don't understand. I have food in the fridge that will go bad. Please, I have a lot going on right now and I must have missed the bills you sent me. I just spent the majority of my money on this food, I can't let it go to waste.

"You will receive my payment by tomorrow morning. Just put the power back on until tomorrow. If you don't have my money until then, you can shut it off again. Please." I beg them, not giving a single damn how pathetic I sound.

The person on the other side sighs. "Okay, miss, I'll see what I can do but if the payment is still open tomorrow, there's nothing I can do to help you," she tells me. I thank her too many times until she finally ends the call.

I fall to the floor, sobbing openly in the privacy of this dark room. It's only when the lights turn on again and my mother's screams cut off that I can breathe easily again. Good, all I need to do now is get home and wait for the company to mail me the bill. And somehow manage to pay it on top of my own bills that will come in next week.

Then, I'll sleep. I really, really hope I can sleep tonight.

———

I survived Christmas at my parent's place. I somehow managed to pay all the bills for the month. The only thing I completely forgot about was my best friend's birthday.

Apart from exchanging a few messages with Andrew, I didn't contribute anything to the party being thrown for her tonight. Not a single thing. The two of us won't be spending all day together, and I didn't even get her a present.

Christ, I'm the worst friend on this planet. First, I don't see her for three weeks, then, I ditch her on Christmas, and now I show up at her party empty handed.

It doesn't even end there. Now, with three hours left until I have to be in a room full of strangers and my few friends, I'm crying about the fact that I have to go at all. I made the mistake of looking in the mirror twenty minutes ago, and at the sight of the dark circles under my eyes and the horror that is my unwashed hair, I just broke down. I don't even recognize myself anymore.

I have no energy to socialize, and I'm scared I'll ruin Lily's party. I'm a mess.

After another ten minutes of wallowing in self-pity, I force myself to take a shower as I listen to my usual party preparation music. It doesn't do the trick. I feel just as discouraged when I step out of the shower.

163

Still, I force myself to get ready. It takes a while but, in the end, I look presentable, at least. Almost like I usually would. At least my dark circles are covered so no one will ask me about them. I'm a sensitive mess at the moment, and I'm scared any reference reminding me of my current situation will make me break down.

I just hope tonight will serve as a distraction.

When my doorbell rings and I come face to face with a radiant Lily, I feel like a fraud. Still, I pull her into a tight hug and wish her a happy birthday.

"I'm sorry I didn't organize more or get you a present. I'm begging for a delay," I try to joke, even though I don't find my failure funny in the least. Of course, my best friend isn't aware of what's going on with my parents. It's the one courtesy I offered her since the mess exploded in my face, but she doesn't know that.

"Oh, don't worry about it. You'll never guess what Andrew got me!" she exclaims, thrusting forward her arm to present me with a beautiful bracelet.

"Jesus Christ, tell me those aren't diamonds," I say, forgetting myself momentarily and sounding almost disgusted. I catch myself quickly and force my most convincing smile back into place. "He's spoiling you!" I add.

Lily is undeterred. "I know. He's horrible," she jokes. Meanwhile, I'm still staring at the bracelet as bitterness poisons my veins. What a waste of money. It must be nice to have such a fortune to spare on a trinket.

Hating where my thoughts are headed, I force myself to set my mind straight and remember this is my best friend. I should be happy she has a boyfriend that does so much for her. Sure, materialistic things might not carry much value to me, but one of Lily's love languages is exchanging gifts. It makes my lack thereof so much worse.

"Okay, let's go. The boys are waiting," she says and starts pulling me away. I barely manage to lock my door before she's rushing toward the elevator with me in tow.

"Where are we going, by the way?" I ask her on our way down.

She frowns at that. "You don't know? Andrew told me you helped organize it all," she says. *Shit.*

"I did, but more when it comes to the details," I try to cover up quickly. It's not really untrue since I did give Andrew some tips about decoration and cake and such, all the things a lifelong best friend knows better than a partner ever could.

"Okay, then. Well, he actually rented a clubhouse near campus. I think half the school will be there," she tells me excitedly.

"Oh, and they're all coming just for you," I tease. She laughs and shoves me.

"Sure they are." Then we're jogging toward the car. Apparently, she really can't wait to get going.

I recognize Sebastian's car and for the first time in weeks, my heart starts racing in anticipation rather than panic. Mattheo and Andrew wait for us outside and both greet me with a quick hug. When I round the car to get in the back behind the driver's seat, I'm surprised to find the owner of the car there rather than sitting inside.

Sebastian is leaning against his door, arms and ankles crossed lazily as he faces me. His handsome features are resting in an unfamiliar, easy smile as he takes me in from head to toe.

My heart trips over itself, and I nearly miss a step, my skin heating under his scrutiny. When he's done taking me in, he steps closer and says, "Hey, *friend*."

He pulls me into a hug, and I lose my ability to reply. *What is happening?* This is the first time Sebastian has hugged me hello, and it's enough to make me question whether I've lost my mind. Am I dreaming this up?

His familiar scent invades my nostrils, wrapping around my frayed nerves like a smooth bandage. I just stand there, hugging him back weakly as I soak up the bliss of the innocent contact. Whoever said magic didn't exist has never received a good hug.

Someone slapping the car's hull loudly interrupts the moment, and Sebastian pulls away.

"Come on, let's get going!" Andrew urges. I blink for a second before my brain jump starts and heat rushes to my cheeks.

"Touch my car again and I'll break your hand," Sebastian retorts over his shoulder as he opens the door to the backseat. By the time his knowing gaze swings back to me, my eyes are trained on my legs. He chuckles knowingly and closes my door before getting behind the wheel. I steal a glance at his satisfied smirk through the rearview mirror as he pulls out of the parking lot and try to ignore the wild beating behind my rib cage. *Friend,* he called me. Then why the hell is my reaction to him so not friendly? I'd brush it off and put it down to my exhaustion if it were a new occurrence.

"So, Aliena, what have you been up to? I feel like I haven't seen you in forever!" Mattheo pouts, tearing me from my fantasies about his best friend. I smile at him, glad when that motion doesn't hurt, at least.

166

"I've been swamped with work, sorry. I wouldn't dare miss my girl's birthday though. Twenty-three, you old cow. I remember when you got your first training bra," I tease her.

She glares playfully. "Shush now, we didn't all start growing boobs at twelve!" She laughs and conspiratorially adds, "And stop at fourteen."

"Ey! Below the belt!" I warn her, just joking.

"Wait, what?" Mattheo interjects.

Lily is happy to elaborate. "Our darling Aliena might've thought she was growing boobs early, but she didn't think they'd stop doing so soon though. She had to take the pill to get those tatas we all see and adore now."

I groan as the guys all burst out laughing. "Some friend I have," I mumble though I feel lighter than I have in weeks. I'm glad I came tonight, if only so this short moment could serve as a reminder that not everything in my life is bad. I have friends I can always count on to cheer me up even if they don't know I need it.

I lose myself to the banter as we drive, listening to the familiar teasing while I lean back and enjoy not being needed. When we finally arrive at our destination, there's already music playing inside, the party in full swing. I look around and marvel at what Andrew pulled off. Between the flashing lights and the music blaring through the high-quality speakers, this is almost as good as Sebastian's parties.

The place looks amazing. Extravagant and elegant in an effortless way. It's so Lily. So much more than I could ever have achieved. It feels like a slap in the face, and my earlier disappointment and shame return in full swing, halting me in my tracks.

167

Oblivious to my inner turmoil, my friends head deeper into the party. *Come on, Aly, pull yourself together. This is a party. You love parties. You love celebrating your friend even more.* The pep talk does little to ease the dread in my chest, but it's enough to make me follow them and try not to look like a beaten dog as I do.

Mattheo is off almost immediately, being swept up by the people on the swim team. Lily and Andrew make their rounds saying hi to everyone. I gladly take the out and try to disappear on one of the couches in a dark corner, feeling more like a jerk the more I feel bad for myself.

I don't know what's happening to me. Others are dancing but I can't seem to bring myself to join them. I don't feel like being here at all anymore. I'm tired and the short interactions I had in the car with my friends, as good as they felt, drained me completely.

I hate what's happening to me, but I can't seem to stop it.

I'm torn from my thoughts when someone joins me on the couch, the cushion dipping at my side. I look to my right to see Sebastian getting comfortable. When he's happy with his position, he turns to me.

"No dancing tonight?" he asks throwing his arm over the back of the couch so it's close to my face. Before I can question it, he starts playing with the ends of my ponytail.

I try to muster a weak smile. "I don't know. I'm still waiting for the music to call to me, I guess," I reply lightly.

He frowns a little, studying me more closely. There's an intensity in his gaze that is entirely unnerving, making me fear he can see right through me. "Rough week?" he finally asks. I just nod, which he seems rather unhappy with.

168

Before he can keep questioning me and eager to divert his attention, I speak up, "How come you're not saying hi to all your classmates? Don't you have friends?" I ask as teasingly as possible. It's excruciatingly hard to keep up the façade under his scrutiny, but for now, he doesn't comment on it.

"You know my friends, and I already said hello to all of them," he replies flatly.

I smile at that. Truly. "I am so not surprised. If you don't like any of these people, why do you host so many parties?"

"Because I can. I have the best location for it, and it gets me a good reputation. It's not like I have to clean up the mess afterward, and I get to hang out with my friends in the private room," he explains. I huff softly at that explanation.

He arches a brow. "Is there a problem? The last time I checked, you enjoyed my parties greatly."

"Yeah, they're all right." I play it down.

"All right, huh?" he retorts with a grin, tugging at a strand of my hair.

I swat his hand away. "Hey, that took me twenty minutes to get right. Don't mess with it," I protest, and he raises his hands in mock surrender.

"Aye, aye, ma'am. No touching the ponytail. Message received."

"God, you're an idiot," I scoff, even as my lips tip up without command.

"As long as I'm the idiot that manages to make you smile, I'm fine with that title." He leans back against the couch, his arms on his lap, and I curse myself for making

169

him take his hands away from me. As ill-advised as it is, I like it when he touches me. It makes those little sparks go off wherever we're connected, and they do wonders to take my mind off things. Just like his confession just now does.

My heart does something funny in my chest seeing how casually charming he's being. It's as if our truce really means something to him. As if I mean something.

It feels like talking to Rosie's grandson again at the nursing home. I wish things were that simple.

Shit, there goes my mind again. I promised myself I would stop thinking about the what ifs weeks after Sebastian kept being rude to me in the beginning. But now with him being nice, the old mantra doesn't work, and I'm reminded painfully of just how attracted I really was to him during that first meeting. He keeps watching me closely as my mind wanders, scanning me from head to toe, it seems.

"Will you tell me what's up, Aliena?"

And there goes my fragile good mood.

I swallow thickly and try to keep my smile in place, all thoughts of how earth-shattering it felt when he finally kissed me vanish from my mind. "What makes you think something is up?" I ask.

"You're not dancing, you aren't socializing, and you were uncharacteristically quiet in the car. Plus, there's something off about your eyes."

The last part startles a laugh out of me. It's the second time he's mentioned my eyes. I focus on that oddity rather than the fact he was picking out my flaws while I was mentally drooling over him. I repeat, "My eyes? What's wrong with them?"

"I don't know. There's just something missing. Some spark, or something, if you want me to be cheesy about it.

They just look sad," he observes slowly, every word stacking on top of my heart until my forced lightheartedness slips through my finger like dry sand. Great, not only am I losing myself but it's clear to everyone around. I can't even act happy right.

I just shrug and avert my eyes, which apparently reveal way too much, while a heavy lump clogs my throat. I wish I had something to drink to banish the uncomfortable feeling. *I will not cry.*

Instead of another tug on my hair, two fingers encircle my chin and tilt me toward his handsome face. Even now with that preoccupied line between his furrowed brows, he's beautiful.

"Hey, no, come on. Talk to me. What the hell just put that look on your face?" he demands softly.

I shrug again, feeling those damned tears coming. *I will not cry at my best friend's party*, I repeat to myself. *I will not make a scene.*

I swallow thickly and do my best to reply. "Just tired," I croak, but to my horror, my voice breaks. Just like that, the dam is broken, and my tears start falling. I'm mortified and shove his hand from my face to turn away from him. He shouldn't see me fall apart. I can't believe this is happening here.

"Aliena," he says softly, speaking to my back. My body melts further into the very corner of the couch, anything to disappear.

I ignore him, trying to stifle my sniffles and barely trusting myself to breathe without sobbing. I dig my nails into the palms of my hands, trying to center myself. Sebastian curses, and I feel the couch dip as he gets up from

171

it. Before I can even think that he's leaving, he's standing in front of me, hugging me as well as possible.

I stiffen momentarily, unsure of what to do. I don't remember the last time I cried in front of another person, not to mention when I was comforted by someone. It feels strange and only makes me want to cry more. It hurts. Breathing hurts, crying hurts, and this hug somehow hurts too.

After a few minutes of him holding me while my arms stayed limp at my side, he crouches down so his face is right in front of me and cups my cheeks. "Let's go outside for a second, yeah? We can talk in my car," he proposes but I'm already shaking my head, wiping at my face.

"No. No, this is Lily's party. God, what is wrong with me? I'm fine, really." It's always the same with me. Why do I insist on making everything about myself? I'm such a nasty attention seeker, crying in the middle of someone else's party.

"Aliena, you are not fine. Whatever is going on is taking its toll on you and it shows." He sighs, looking unsure. "Sweetheart, I didn't want to say anything but is it possible you lost weight? Like, a lot in the short time we haven't seen each other? Is that what's going on?"

The more he speaks, the more embarrassed I become. Have I lost weight? I haven't noticed but it's not unlikely with how little I've been eating. What can I say, lunch is expensive, and I have to save money where I can.

Before I can start crying more, I grit my teeth and force my voice to be pure steel as I snap at him, using my defensiveness as a shield. "Of course not! I don't have an eating disorder, Sebastian, I've just been busy. Some of us have to work, you know. Now, I'd be very happy if you could just keep your observations about my eyes and my body to yourself. I said I'm fine. Whether you believe me or not is up to you, but at least take the hint and stop pushing. We're friends but that doesn't mean I owe you an explanation."

At first, he looks taken aback by my outburst, and I think he'll keep pushing. I think maybe my harsh tone just messed up our truce and he'll go back to being mean. I don't think I could handle that, not right now, not from him. I don't even mean to be such a bitch but it's easier than being vulnerable, and I just need him to stop talking before I do something I'll hate myself for forever. Like making an even bigger scene at my best friend's birthday party.

But Sebastian doesn't snap at me. He nods. "Okay, I'll let it go for now. But if you go MIA again or if I feel like you're getting worse, don't think I won't try to talk to you again. I'm worried about you," he insists, and my heart breaks and melts at the same time. Who would have thought Sebastian could be so compassionate?

"Noted and appreciated. I think it's time I get a drink now. Wanna help me look for the birthday girl?" I ask him, relieved we can move past this hiccup. Surprisingly enough, I'm feeling a little better now I'm done with that little meltdown.

Chapter 19

Sebastian

Our first stop is at the makeshift bar where I insist on paying for Aliena's drink. I was raised a gentleman, after all. Technically. She barely puts up a fight and thanks me for it with another one of those fake smiles. I don't comment on it, but I wasn't lying when I said I was worried about her.

Once her drink is empty, the glass discarded on the bar counter, we look for Lily and Andrew, which is no easy feat since there are a *lot* of people here. After searching the whole premises, we move on to the small corridor in the back that leads to all the bathrooms. Surprisingly enough, that's where Lily's voice finally meets my ears.

She's laughing loudly about something, trying to speak as she does, and Aliena and I exchange a puzzled look. Then she shrugs and heads straight for the door her friend is behind, entering without knocking. I have a bad feeling about the whole thing but follow her, nonetheless.

The bathroom is spacious with rosy floor tiles and harmonically matching walls. The lights above illuminate the room much more than the lights in the corridor did, so much so I have to squeeze my eyes shut for a second as they adjust painfully.

"Aly! Seb!" I hear Lily squeal and force my eyes open. She's already holding her friend's hands, swinging them happily as she nearly jumps where she stands. Her face is bright as she smiles but when I look at Aliena, I find the exact opposite. She looks positively horrified.

"Lil? What are you doing here?" she asks slowly, sanding completely still. I don't understand why she's acting like she just walked in on her friend murdering someone. Lily seems fine. A little energetic but fine, nonetheless.

"Having fun!" Lily exclaims, then twirls around. She knocks on the door of one of the stalls and says, "Tip, come out. I want you to meet my friends."

Aliena shakes her head. "Lily, where's Andrew?" she asks, trepidation thick in her voice. I take a step closer to her, worried she might faint any second now. She has turned horribly pale.

"Oh, talking to some friends. I just wanted to come to the bathroom when I met Tip." The stall door opens and a woman with short, spiky hair steps out, smiling charmingly. "That's her. This is Tip, everyone," Lily announces happily.

While I look at the stranger, Aliena gasps. Only she isn't looking at the woman we were just introduced to. No, she's looking past her and into the stall, which I now see has small parcels of cocaine lying around.

I look between the drugs and Aliena, who is now slowly backing away, shaking her head and murmuring, "No." over and over again.

"Aliena?" I prompt softly, reaching out to her. She dodges my hand.

175

"What are you doing? Lily, what the hell are you doing?" She clamps her mouth shut and covers it with a hand, looking sick. Meanwhile, equal parts confusion and worry are raging a war inside me. I'm confused as to why Aliena is reacting so strongly to the whole scene. Sure, cocaine is no joke, but Lily is old enough to decide what she wants to try out herself.

On the other hand, Aliena looks like she's on the verge of death as she studies her friend with a pained expression. Before anyone can say anything more, she turns on her heels and storms away.

"Oh, right. I didn't mean for her to see that. Oh, that wasn't good at all," Lily mutters, but I don't pay her much mind. Instead, I run after Aly. She's already at the end of the corridor when I exit the bathroom, and by the time, I'm at the edge of the dance floor, I've lost sight of her completely.

I start pushing past the dancing people, heading for the exit since that seems like the most plausible place she would flee to. Before I can reach the door, I bump into Andrew.

"Hey, dude, I feel like I haven't seen you all night. What have you been up to?" he asks me happily. He, at least, doesn't have dilated pupils. It makes me remember what Lily said about having wanted to just go to the bathroom.

"Dude, go get Lily from the bathroom," is all I tell him. Then I push past him to get outside.

As soon as I push the door open, I'm engulfed by an icy chill. Shit, the weather is brutal. I really hope Aly didn't go too far. She seemed really upset but we're too far away from her home for her to walk, and I'm guessing she didn't get her jacket when she stormed away. My previous worry

176

spikes imagining her cold and shivering with so much devastation in those beautiful eyes. She seemed at a loss in that bathroom. Completely disoriented.

"Aliena!" I shout, glad no one's out here other than me to possibly obscure my view from her. There's no reply so I start scouting the perimeter with hurried steps, jogging around the house, shouting her name repeatedly.

By the time I hear a nearby bush rustle, my hands have gone numb from the cold. I turn to find the source of the sound, illuminating the ground with my flashlight, and finally, I recognize the purple silk of Aliena's dress.

I run to her, my heart pounding faster the closer I get and the clearer the scene becomes. What the hell? She's cowering inside one of the dead bushes, curled up in a ball as she shakes and sobs, rocking back and forth.

"Aliena? Hey, what are you doing? Come on, we have to get you back inside. You'll get sick," I tell her, reaching out to touch her arm again.

She doesn't flinch away, but she also doesn't react. It's like she can't hear me at all as she shakes her head and mutters. "No. I can't. I can't do this." Over and over she repeats herself.

My stomach drops. I think she's having a panic attack. I cup her face, desperately trying to get her attention. "Aliena! Come on, listen to me. You have to breathe, sweetheart. Come on, just breathe," I tell her.

She's only taking in short rasps, but her eyes finally find mine. She looks crazed, absolutely lost, and it tears at my insides. What the hell is doing this to her?

She keeps shaking her head. "I can't. Please, I can't do this," she cries, and her breathing grows harsher.

177

I do my best to keep my voice calm when I talk to her. I have a feeling my own panic would only add to hers. "It's okay. You're going to be okay. You hear me? I got you. Just breathe with me, come on. Just focus on me," I urge her, injecting my voice with steel. With her eyes still on me, I make a show of breathing slow and deep. It takes her a few tries but finally, she seems to understand my instructions and starts attempting to match her breaths to mine.

All the while, I hold her face tightly in my hands, caressing her cold, pale skin with my thumbs to try and breathe some life into them. There's a small, bleeding scrape on her right cheek and it's driving me crazy. I can't believe she chose to have a panic attack in a dead bush, of all places. She must have hurt herself as she moved deeper into it.

"That's it. I got you," I repeat when she's finally breathing evenly. It's only then I release the sigh that was stuck in my throat. Good, all I need to do now is get her somewhere warm.

"Sweetheart, do you want to go back inside? You're going to get sick out here." She simply shakes her head. "Yeah, no more party. I think that's reasonable. Do you want me to take you home?" I ask next, confused by the fresh tears filling her eyes. She shakes her head again.

"Okay, do you want me to take you to my place?" I ask. That's really the last option I can think of right now. If she says no again, I'll have to kidnap her. I don't want to leave her in the cold for a second longer.

Aliena nods and I don't question her further. I just help her to her feet, wincing at the sound of her hair ripping as strands get stuck in the twigs. She doesn't react to it, which does little to ease my worry.

178

In my car, I instantly turn on the heat, getting a major déjà vu from the time she called me from that creepy booth. Instead of trying to make her to talk here where I can't look at her or provide any comfort, I just reach over to envelop her cold hand in mine, hoping the gesture is enough to bridge her over.

Then I drive home.

———

Once we reach my penthouse, Aliena instantly heads for the big couch in the living room. There, she wordlessly grabs one of my blankets and curls up in a ball beneath it. It does something funny to my chest, seeing her make herself at home at my place.

But the foreign warmth snuffs out as quickly as it took hold of me. Aly looks so small on my couch, so fragile as she quakes. This isn't some cute moment after a night out. Something is wrong with Aliena. Something bad enough that she just had a panic attack, for Christ's sake.

Instead of sitting down next to her, I take a seat on my carpet so we're face to face where she lies. Allowing the silence to linger, I take hold of her hand again. She grasps my fingers tightly and shuts her eyes, squeezing two tears from the corner of her eyes.

"Can we please talk about it?" I ask slowly. For a long second, she doesn't reply.

Finally, she sighs deeply and nods, keeping her eyes closed. "Lily did cocaine," she says, choking on the words. Then she shakes her head. "Why? Why would she do that?

She knows what drugs do. She knows…" Her voice trails off.

"Maybe it just happened in the heat of the moment. A one-time thing. It doesn't have to mean she'll do it again, Aliena," I try to console her.

She finally opens her eyes and moves into a sitting position. "No. It never stays a one-time thing. Never. She of all people should know what stuff like that can do to a person." She tilts her head back as she speaks, trying to keep more tears at bay and it's killing me slowly.

"Why?" I ask. "Why does she know that of all people?" I feel like I'm missing vital pieces of the puzzle here. Aly is a party girl after all, so I would think she should be more accustomed to cocaine, but she just shakes her head.

"I can't tell you. But she knows. She knows I can't do this. Not with her too."

With her too? I have no idea what we're talking about. "Is this related to what's been troubling you recently?" I ask slowly.

A pained sound escapes her. She pulls her knees to her chest but doesn't reply other than that. I try to silently fit the pieces of what she's told me together, but I'm still missing something.

I sigh. "I'll be right back. I'll get you a glass of water, okay?" I ask, slowly rising to my feet. She nods.

When I return with it, she quickly takes a few sips and then sighs, opening her eyes. "Thanks. My throat hurt so badly," she tells me.

"I figured." I put the glass down on the small table behind me and sit on the couch next to her, taking her hand and caressing the back of it with my thumb.

She understands what I'm asking for without needing to hear the words again. "My mother was an addict," she finally shares, startling me. Of all the things I was expecting, I never would have guessed *that*. Aliena quickly goes on. "She's not dead but she got sober," she explains, her voice thicker again.

I return her glass to her, and she takes another sip before cradling it in her lap. "She was sober. For years. But she relapsed recently. That's what's been going on." She takes her hand from mine and buries her face in it, using it to hold her head up like the weight of it is suddenly too much to carry otherwise.

"And my dad lost his job because he had a heart attack, and I'm pretty sure my mom has lost hers now too, and I've been trying to help, but I can't do enough. I don't know how to help my mom and simply being there isn't working. I've been visiting them almost every evening to cook and clean, but she stopped paying their bills, and my dad can't find a new job, and I'm trying. I'm trying so hard to make it work, but I can't do it. It feels like I can't breathe." She shakes her head, dropping it further forward into her hand.

"I take on as many shifts at the nursing home as they'll allow but it's not working. It doesn't pay enough. God, and you're right, I lost weight because I can't afford to eat anymore. I have to buy so many groceries for them I can't stock up on my own." *Dear god.*

"I don't know how much longer I can do it. If things don't change, I'll have to stop renting my apartment and move back in with them." She hiccups and bites the back of her hand. "I don't ever want to live there again." A tremor takes hold of her, and I sense its phantom washing over me.

I fist my hands to stop their shaking at the utter helplessness I feel. Fucking hell, she's falling apart, and I have no idea what to do to help. All I know is I can't stand the sight of her shaking shoulders anymore, so I lean forward and awkwardly pull her into a hug. She returns it this time, moving to climb on my lap and wrapping her arms around my waist as her face presses against my chest.

"I'm sorry," she mutters when I don't speak for too long. She tries to pull away, but I tighten my arms around her like a steel band.

"Don't apologize. You did nothing wrong," I assure her, stroking the back of her head. When I brush against her unraveling ponytail, I start working on getting the tie out.

"I'm such a mess," she adds in despair.

I shake my head against her. "No, sweetheart. You're just overwhelmed and that's completely understandable. It's too much, Aliena. Everything you've been doing is way too much for one person alone to handle. I'm so sorry I didn't know about this sooner."

"I did it before. When I was a child. If only there weren't so many bills," she cries softly. I feel my brows draw closer at that but don't push it now. I can dwell on every word she said later. Dissect them in a silent moment. For now, I need to stay focused.

"I can help you. You should have come to me sooner," I tell her.

"I won't accept your money," she protests instantly.

Stubborn thing. She'd rather work herself into an early grave than accept my help. Good thing money isn't the only thing I have to offer.

"We can talk about that later," I tell her but she's insistent.

"We don't have to. My reply will stay the same. It's why I haven't told Lily." She pulls away a few inches to look at me, a small spark in her eyes as she repeats more forcefully, "I won't accept your money."

The sight of that little spark is enough for me to suck in a shaky breath. She's still in there. "Okay. Move in with me then," I tell her. She recoils almost comically.

"What? You're crazy," she exclaims. But at least there's a hint of life in her voice, her outrage palpable, and it makes me want to smile.

"I'm not crazy. I have the space, do I not? Plus, you already have a room here. It wouldn't be a big deal, and you could save some money without the additional rent and groceries." I can tell she wants to keep arguing but I stop her by holding up a hand. "We can talk about all of that tomorrow. For now, just tell me what I can do to make you feel better."

"You already did too much. God, I can't believe I cried all over you. If you tell anyone about any of this, I'll have to cut out your tongue and throw it off the rooftop," she threatens me.

I make a show out of sealing my lips. "Deal. Now, do you want to eat something? A midnight snack?" I ask.

She considers it for a second before shaking her head. "That's okay, thank you. But...uhm, could I maybe take a bath? I haven't had time for one in forever, and I can't shake this weird chill."

I take her hands and ease her off my lap as we both get up. "Yes, of course. Come, I'll show you everything."

Chapter 20

Aliena

Sebastian surprises me by taking me straight to the last room on the second floor. His room. He does the whole thing so nonchalantly it hardly seems like a big deal, but I know no one is allowed in here. Ever.

Still, he opens the door for me and tells me to go in. Sadly, I don't get much of a look at the whole interior since the lights are off and he's leading me into the adjoint bathroom with a hand on my lower back the next second.

He turns on the lights, and I get a good look at the massive room he brought me to. It's elegant, dark gray, with LED strips embedded along the edge of the ceiling. A big walk-in shower takes up an entire corner of the room, but what takes the cake is the giant bathtub.

Gray steps matching the floor lead up to it, and there won't be any awkward climb out since another small step aligns with the wall on the inside of the tub. It's magnificent. Not so big it would feel like a pool but big enough to comfortably fit two people.

I shoot him a knowing look over my shoulder. "Interesting," I muse.

He laughs and shakes his head. "Incredible where your head is headed again, but I'll have to disappoint you. Believe it or not, I've never had anyone in here," he tells me, which satisfies me on a new level.

"Thank you. Really. Any of your guest bathrooms would have done, though, just so you know."

"Leading you elsewhere would have been a shame. I'm a shower person anyway, so I barely use the tub. You're free to use it whenever you want." The way he speaks, as if I've agreed to his crazy offer to move in. As if it's decided and set in stone.

I cock an eyebrow, feeling my lips twitch. "You're giving me unlimited access?"

"Oh yeah. Make sure to take me up on that offer especially when I'm taking a shower. I'm always happy to put on a show," he teases. Then he starts rummaging through his cabinets while I look at the glass door of the spacious shower. Speaking of temptation.

"A-ha! Here we go. I hope you like lavender," he says, handing me a small glass bottle filled with a dark blue liquid. "Use as much as you want, I have more of them. My mom gives me one for every birthday, but I don't have the heart to tell her I don't actually use it."

I take the bottle and thank him. "That's really sweet of her. When's your birthday?" I ask. That's the only way I can ration the remaining bottles so there are enough until his next birthday.

"January 19th," he tells me.

"Oh, that's soon," I remark as I walk over to the tub. There, I hesitate. "Uhm, what am I looking at?" I ask, studying the different buttons and levers. He steps up to me from behind, placing one hand on my back to stabilize himself as he leans over the tub to explain all the different functions.

By the time he's done, I remember only about half of it. Mostly because I was more aware of his hand on my back and the resulting tingles than the words he said. I just repeat the most important things to make sure I got that right.

"Yeah, that's it. You'll be fine, right?" he asks, smiling softly.

I nod. "Yes, thanks." Before he turns and leaves, his eyes focus on something slightly over the top of my head, and he reaches out, pulling a twig from my strands. I laugh softly. "And thanks for that," I add.

"No biggie. Why don't you turn around so I can get the rest of them? That way I won't have a whole forest in my tub tomorrow morning," he proposes. Instead of resisting, I silently turn around. It's not like I mind his hands on me. Not at all.

For the next few minutes, Sebastian works on freeing the small twigs from my wild strands with utmost care. Then, there's a hairbrush in his hand and he starts brushing out the tangles from the lower half of my hair, slowly working his way up. I relax, surprised by how pleasant this is.

No one has ever brushed my hair, not to mention taken such care of me. It does something weird and fuzzy to my chest.

"You're really good at this," I hum, keeping my eyes closed. It's all I can do not to start purring or moaning where I stand like a weirdo. Sebastian laughs softly.

186

"My mother taught me. She said it was important for a man to know how to properly treat a woman. I'm pretty sure she just used that as an excuse to get me to do her hair."

"Smart woman," I remark, leaning back against him slightly. I could fall asleep right here.

Maybe Sebastian can read my mind because one of his arms comes around my waist to hold me up while his other gently caresses the side of my face. I'm practically fully leaning against him now, but he doesn't make a sound of protest.

"Maybe the bath should wait until tomorrow morning? We wouldn't want you falling asleep and drowning in there," he says.

I softly shake my head against his chest but don't move otherwise. "It has to be tonight. I have work tomorrow, and I'll have to swing by my apartment to change first." God even the thought of that exhausts me.

Sebastian's hold on me tightens. "But tomorrow is Saturday." He sounds confused.

I chuckle. "Well, we can't very well tell the seniors they're on their own on the weekends. I'm lucky though. I have a day off on Sunday." Only I don't, do I? I'll have to visit my parents then. "Well, I don't have to go to the nursing home. I guess I'll still be taking care of people."

I don't know if he understands that I mean my parents or not, but the next thing I know, he's pressing a soft kiss to the side of my head. My mind shutters, all thoughts and worries evading me in a rush. The only thing I can feel are lips on me until he removes them and reality comes crashing back

187

"You're tired, baby. Let's get you to bed. The bath isn't going anywhere." He tries to pull me back toward the door, but I try to resist. No matter that the use of that nickname is nearly enough to make me want to follow him anywhere blindly.

"I can't sleep anyway," I protest and will the butterflies away. My mind is being pulled in too many directions at once, and his distracting touch isn't helping. *Stay on track, Aly. Don't let him lure you into a false sense of security.* "I never can. There's too much to think about and tonight will only be worse. With what happened with Lily, I don't think I'll be able to get any rest."

That gives him pause and he changes tactics, stepping in front of me. "You want to spend the night with me? I can talk you to sleep to keep your mind off things. Or I'll come with you to your room and leave after you're asleep. Whatever you prefer."

Aw, shit. The butterflies come soaring back as an avenging swarm of bees, making me buzz until every last nerve stands on edge. His effect on me is so much stronger now that I'm looking into his eyes.

I try to play it off even as I feel my walls crumbling around me, leaving cracks for him to slip through. "Well, if you put it that way. I'm sure your bed feels like heaven."

He smiles and nods. "Yeah, it does."

There's just one more suspicion to clear up. "How many women have you taken in there?" I ponder.

He rolls his eyes. "None." My heart does a flip.

"You're sure you don't mind?" I ask even though he's already steering me into the adjacent room.

"I wouldn't have offered if I did. Come on, I can give you something to wear if you want. And I have spare

188

toothbrushes. Then it's time to sleep for you." With that, he walks back into his bedroom to get me his clothes to sleep in.

Despite everything, I think I'm blushing.

After changing into Sebastian's clothes—a shirt and some boxershorts—I step out of his bathroom, trying not to appear nervous and make things weird.

Honestly, this is new terrain for me. I've never spent the night with a guy, certainly not one I didn't even do anything sexual with. It's nerve-wracking.

Seb is already lounging on his bed, scrolling through his phone only to look up when he hears me step closer. He's smiling softly, scanning me in a subtle way. If I'm reading him right, he likes what he sees and that has me beaming a little.

I sit down on the edge of the bed, unsure of how to proceed. He laughs at me, the idiot.

"You can lie down, Aliena. I promise I won't bite," he assures me even though his wicked smile tells me a different story. I nearly make a comment, but decide against it. I'm about to spend the night in his bed and shouldn't blur any lines by flirting now. We settled on being *friends* after all...

I just roll my eyes and get beneath the blanket, staying on the far side of the bed so I don't invade his personal space. I'm afraid the reason he never brings girls in here is he doesn't like being close to someone all night, which I really understand. I'm similar, after all. I like my space when I sleep.

"As comfortable as you hoped for?" he asks, lying on his side and leaning up on one elbow to look at me. His biceps bulge where he props his head up, and my fingers twitch with the urge to reach out and brush over his smooth skin.

I close my eyes and let my hand move over the smooth sheets instead. "Close enough," I tease, not bothering to even open my eyes. It feels too nice. The whole moment is surreal, and I'm scared to shatter the spell.

I know this is just a momentary escape from my shitshow life. Tomorrow, I have to work again, and eventually, I'll have to return to my apartment. No matter how tempting Sebastian's offer to move in is, I'm too tired to contemplate such a bizarre change right now.

Some cons invade my mind in an instant of quiet, nonetheless. First off, Lily and our friends would ask questions I don't want to answer truthfully. It still feels unbelievable I told Sebastian practically my whole life story in a matter of minutes. I can't and don't want to do the same with my other friends.

I'm sure to regret it in the morning but for now, I'm enjoying my vacation.

Before my mind can spiral any further, Sebastian's deep, soothing voice catches my attention. "What do you want me to talk about? Give me something to work with," he suggests.

I open my eyes to find him still studying me. My eyes flick to his bookshelf. "How about you read something? I think that would be more pleasant than hearing anything about real life. Only if you feel like it, though. If you've changed your mind and would rather I spent the night in my guest room, that's totally okay," I assure him, scared of being a burden.

"Reading something sounds great. Do you want me to start something from the top or is it okay if I recite from the book I'm currently reading?"

"Of course, it is. I don't care what it is you say as long as you keep talking," I tell him, revealing too much. It's just now that I realize now how very beautiful his voice truly is, deep and velvety in this dimly lit room. Maybe it will be enough to keep my mind from tormenting me all night.

Sebastian reaches over to his nightstand and picks up a thick book, then he starts reading without another look in my direction, presenting me with a very appealing view. He's focused, and I can see it in his sharp features.

The pages pass in a blur, and Sebastian's voice grows distant as he loses himself in the story. Meanwhile, I'm too busy hanging on his every word to worry about anything else. Every now and again, his eyes flick over to me, and he grants me a smile that does funny things to my heart. When his words slowly become more and more slurred, I feel my own eyelids grow heavy. I hug the blanket closer to my chest, curling up further.

Finally, blissfully, I doze off and sink into a deep, uninterrupted slumber for the first time in weeks.

———

When I wake, the first thing I notice is the sweat slicking the hair at the back of my neck to my skin. Yeah, it's definitely uncomfortably warm. I guess that's what happens when two people share a room without a window cracked open.

191

I try to throw the blanket off me only to find my arms pinned. A shockwave of fear bolts through me, and my eyes fly open, but instead of finding some intruder in front of me, I come face to face with a broad chest. A naked, chiseled chest.

I blink at the smooth skin, trying to find a memory of Sebastian taking his clothes off but he must have done it after I'd fallen asleep. I'm sure I'd remember otherwise.

I can't get a good look since he's inches in front of me, my arms trapped in between our bodies while his are wrapped around my back as if trying to shield me from the rest of the world.

It's stifling. I don't know how I slept in this position.

And yet, despite the sticky heat clinging to me, I find myself hesitant to pull away. I've never woken up in someone's arms before and it's kind of nice, I guess. I'm tempted to just close my eyes again and snuggle a little closer.

Before I can do that, I remember my responsibilities for the day and the memories from last night come flying back. Me, breaking down at the party. Like an idiot. And as if that wasn't embarrassing enough, I fell apart completely after finding Lily in that bathroom.

Of course, Sebastian, of all people, had to witness that whole circus.

Suddenly, I don't find our proximity so comforting anymore. Instead, it feels invasive and generally too much. I push myself away from him with a not-so-gentle shove.

He startles awake right as I'm getting to my feet. "Oh, good morning," he mumbles with a yawn. I look at him over my shoulder and make a move to leave his room.

"Morning," I reply. His brows are drawing together, no doubt at my hurried exit, but before he can question me, I say, "Thanks again for letting me stay here, really. I have to get to work now." I'm not actually sure whether that's true since I don't know what time it is.

Sebastian gives the clock on my nightstand a pointed look before bringing his disbelieving eyes back to me. "It's five a.m., Aliena. You slept for barely three hours. Come back to bed."

Oh. My shift doesn't start until eleven. My steps slow but I don't halt. I might as well go home already and do some chores. It's not like I will be able to fall back to sleep anyway.

While I contemplate my next move, Sebastian climbs out of bed and walks toward me, his face neutral. I watch him come closer, trying not to ogle his bare torso too obviously when really it is a sight to see.

I knew he worked out, and seeing his corded arms often when he wore short sleeves, I had proof it showed. Still, knowing and seeing are two different things, and seeing him in his bedroom only makes the sight feel more forbidden. More sensual.

Or maybe it's the lack of sleep making me unreasonably horny.

"What are you doing?" I finally wonder aloud when he stops right in front of me. His smooth chuckle washes over me like a shot of tequila, making heat bloom in my stomach.

"I told you to come back to bed," he offers.

"Well, I told you I had to get to work," I retort. He doesn't buy it. I can see it in his eyes.

193

"What time does your shift start?" he prompts.

Busted. "Eleven," I mumble, looking away.

He tsks. Then, with a smile of angelic innocence, he ducks so his head is near my waist and throws his arms around my middle. I squeal and try to step away, but before I can escape, my feet are off the ground and I'm horizontally in the air.

"Sebastian! What are you doing?" I exclaim, clutching his back. His muscles flex beneath my touch, and I hold on a little tighter. Coincidentally.

"Taking you back to bed," he replies as he starts walking to the four-poster. His steps are even and unhurried as if I wasn't slung over his shoulder like a heavy bag of potatoes.

"I told you I had to go, you caveman!" I protest, slapping his back softly. The next thing I know, I'm flying through the air and bouncing off the fluffy mattress. Once I still, I wipe the hair from my face and glare up at the man, who's now triumphantly smiling down at me.

Then he drops onto the bed next to me, saying, "Much better." He pats the space right next to him and opens his arms invitingly. Like he wants me to cuddle up to him again. "Come back, now, will you?"

I stare at him. "Just go back to sleep, Seb. I should start my day," I tell him seriously even though I'm tempted to ignore all that for a few more hours in his arms.

His smile fades and he shakes his head. "When's the last time you got a full eight hours of sleep?" he asks.

"No one needs that many hours," I protest instead of replying. Truth is, I have no idea when that could have been.

He gives me a look. "What about six hours?" I just roll my eyes. "Aliena, when's the last time you slept?" he repeats.

"Just now," I huff. "It's about quality, not quantity and those three hours just now were great. Really relaxing."

"Good, let's repeat it now," he argues, patting the mattress again.

My restraint is slipping through my fingers, my arguments dying on my lips. Still, I hesitate because I already granted myself such a long break from reality and I'm scared to drag it out. I don't even remember the last time I checked my phone. It must've been at the party at some point. I'm sure Lily texted me by now, and my heart beats a little heavier at the thought. I'm afraid to have received a message from my best friend. I just really, really don't know what to say to her.

Sure, Sebastian was right last night when he said that it's her choice what she does to her body and it might only have been a one-time thing. I just can't help being disappointed in her. And scared for her.

More scared than I've ever been in my life because watching my mother waste away is one thing, but the idea of it happening to Lily is another entirely. She's my family when my own parents feel like strangers, she always has been. I *can't* lose her.

Shit, that's exactly why I should check my phone. I already drove one person back to drug abuse with my apathy and the distance I created. I can't let the same happen with Lily.

When a gentle hand brushes against my arm, I refocus on Sebastian, who's studying me closely. "What's on your mind?" he asks.

What isn't?

But I don't say that. He's too attentive and too interested in understanding or helping me or whatever else his motives are. I shouldn't keep oversharing my thoughts, but here he is looking at me so expectantly.

I shrug. "I don't know. Last night was a mess, and I have to figure out what to do with Lily. Do you know where my phone is?"

"Yeah, here." He turns around, regrettably letting go of my arm, and takes my phone from the nightstand. Before he returns it to me, he says, "I turned it off last night when you were changing in the bathroom. It wouldn't stop ringing, but I didn't think it was the right time for you to have to deal with it, so I took the liberty."

"It was Lily?" I ask, my anxiety rising. I don't remember a single time when I turned off my phone. Shit, what if my dad tried to reach me because there was an emergency, or something happened to Lily.

"Yeah. But don't worry, I told Andrew to go get her before I came after you. She wasn't alone in case of an emergency," he tries to reason as if hearing my spiraling thoughts. I snatch my phone from his hand and turn it back on.

"She still could have needed me. You shouldn't have turned it off. You had no right," I rebuke. Then I focus on my screen when it lights up with about a million messages.

The first thing that catches my attention is the amount of missed calls I have from my best friend but also from Andrew and even some from Mattheo, though I guess he called me to ask where I vanished off to rather than because he knew what I saw. He wouldn't understand my reaction anyway.

Then there are all the texts from Lily, and finally, I see a missed call from my dad. That's what really scares me. I mean, something terrible must've happened if he called me at four a.m.

I clench my fingers around my phone to stop them from shaking but it's no use. I fail to enter my password two times before I manage to unlock my phone. Before I can call my dad back, a firm hand envelops my shaky one.

"The world won't fall apart if you're out of reach for a few hours. You deserve a break from time to time," Sebastian tries to reassure me. It does little to ease my rising panic, and when I speak next, I can hear the emotion in my voice.

"My world might. I have people depending on me, Seb. I can't just go off the grid. Now, please, let go of my hand. I have to call my dad back." As I speak, I'm preparing myself to get up to leave the room. This is none of Sebastian's business. I know he's only trying to be a good friend, but this isn't his burden to carry.

Of course, we don't see eye to eye on that, and he pulls me back onto the bed even as he releases my hand. "Stay. You don't have to do everything alone," he tells me, eliciting a heavy sadness within me. It's weird to hear someone say that. It feels like I'm being recognized only it doesn't feel good because it only confirms things are wrong.

I don't say a word as I sit up on the bed and call my father. I don't look at Sebastian as I count the unanswered rings. Two, three, four.

My palms start to sweat as I listen to the even sound over the phone. A million scenarios occupy my mind. None

197

of them are good. In fact, they're bad enough that the comforting hand Sebastian places on my knee doesn't help.

Finally, the ringing stops. "Aliena?" my dad's groggy voice asks, sounding confused. I could sob. Instead, I swallow thickly to make sure my next words are even.

"Yes, Dad. You called me?"

"I did? Oh, that must've happened by mistake. I'm sorry for that, honey. I hope I didn't give you a scare."

"You're sure?" I ask, slowly feeling my tense muscles release.

"Yes, everything's fine here," he assures me.

"Okay, good. I'm sorry I woke you, then. Go back to sleep, I'll see you tomorrow," I tell him.

"Until then, honey." The line disconnects and I sag against the headrest, closing my eyes and feeling like a thousand years of stress bleed out of me.

"He didn't mean to call me. Everything's fine," I say without looking at the man next to me.

He gives my knee a squeeze. "See, you got some rest and there was no catastrophe. Will you agree to sleep a few more hours now?" he asks.

I worry my lip between my teeth. "I don't know. I should still get back to Lily." Even as I say it, I don't make a move to open her messages. I don't want to deal with that right now.

Sebastian takes my phone from my hands again and puts it back on my nightstand, making the decision for me. Then, wordlessly, he tugs at my hands to pull me into a lying position. I'm in his arms the next second, my face buried in the crook of his neck while his even breathing brushes against the top of my head, making tingles rush down my spine.

After a few minutes of stroking my back gently, he asks, "Do you want me to read to you again?"

"No, this is fine. Thanks," I mumble against his skin, already feeling my mind drifting off. I just faintly notice his soft shudder in response to the brush of my lips against his skin.

———

The next day passes in a blur. I wake up again at nine a.m., and Sebastian isn't awake to stop me from sneaking away this time. I almost feel bad for just leaving but I have things to do before my shift starts, and I can't chance him talking me out of it again. Besides he deserves some more rest after I kept him up so late last night. I left him a note to express my gratitude and hopefully leave him in a good mood for the day, at least.

I get breakfast bagels at my favorite café and then head to Lily's place. Is she awake at this time the day after her party? No, she probably isn't. Do I care I'm waking her up? I can't say I do.

I ring her doorbell about fifty times and wait in the brutal late-December cold for several minutes until the door flies open and I come face to face with my best friend's disheveled boyfriend.

I smile at him. "Hey, there. Would you mind letting me in? I'm here to see my bestie," I chirp too cheerily. Andrew doesn't return my smile.

"Aly, it's really early. I'm sure Lily would be over the moon to know you came but she's still sleeping," he explains at the same time as a crash sounds from inside the apartment. He turns around to look for the source while I crane my neck to see inside in vain. The damn giant is blocking my view.

Lily curses inside and then appears next to her boyfriend the next moment, looking even worse than him. Her eyes are red and puffy as if she cried all night and there are dark circles under her eyes. Still, she smiles tiredly at me.

"I'm awake. Sorry. I'm up." Her eyes drop to the bag in my hands, and she beams a little more, despite her obvious nerves. "You brought me breakfast."

"Consider it your late birthday gift," I say. At the mention of her birthday and the memories of her party, an odd silence descends over us.

Finally, she clears her throat. "Right. Andrew, baby, why don't you go back to bed? Aly and I will be in the living room." Andrew nods, kisses the side of her head, then leaves with one unsure smile in my direction. I follow Lily into her living room and take a seat at her dining table, unloading the bagels.

Before I can even think to speak, Lily breaks the silence, her smile dropping and giving way to an anguished expression. "I am so sorry, Aly. Really. God, I don't know what I was thinking. I'm so sorry I exposed you to that. I can't imagine what you must've felt like.

"I tried coming after you after Sebastian left but Andrew found me first, and I didn't think you wanted to see me. I am so sorry. Are we okay?" she asks right as she starts to cry.

No matter how disappointed I might be in her, I have never been able to see my girl cry. That's why I quickly round the table and pull her into my arms, squeezing her to me.

"We're okay. Just never do anything like that again, okay?" My voice cracks but I press on with one steadying breath. "You have to promise, Lily. I know it's selfish but I can't lose another person to drugs. Not you."

She nods vigorously. "I won't. I promise. It was stupid, really." She hiccups and wraps her arms around my waist. "You looked so horrified," she adds.

"I was, Lily," that's all I say, refusing to lie. It's not my place to be angry at her for what she does to her body, but I won't give her an easy way out and lie about what the sight of her with those drugs did to me. That's not how our relationship works.

After staying a bit and talking until things felt normal between us, I left her apartment with less weight on my shoulders. I have just enough time to go home, take a shower, then go to work. There, my body easily follows my routine, and I do my chores and visit my patients on auto pilot.

Before I know it, it's lunchtime and I'm eating side-by-side with a few seniors, trying not to burst out laughing when old Mary Louise accuses poor Nelson of having stolen her peas even though I just watched her finish the last of them.

Yeah, I really love my job at times.

My good time is interrupted by a coworker, who tells me someone is asking for me at reception. A little reluctantly, I thank her and leave the table, telling Mary to take my peas as I go.

I'm not sure why I'm so surprised to see Sebastian once I reach the reception area, and I understand the way my heart starts doing somersaults even less. It's just Seb. My friend. Whom I'm attracted to, sure, and who held me all night but still. It's weird seeing him back here where it all started.

His gaze trails over me as I walk closer, perhaps looking for a sign of the pathetic girl I was last night. Not that he'll find her. After a great night's sleep, I've been able to reinforce my walls and pull myself together.

It does nothing to quench the flutter in my stomach when his eyes lock with mine, though.

"Hey, you. What are you doing here?" I ask, keeping my voice level to mask the effect he has on me.

"Lecturing you about sneaking out on me. That was rude," he pouts playfully.

I roll my eyes at him. "Oh, poor baby. I'm sure you never snuck out on a girl."

He says nothing to that, just grins and brushes me off. "That's not all. I thought we'd figure out the details of your move this morning but since you just left, here I am. I think it'd be best if I got some of your essentials before you get off work tonight so you can come straight home. Can you take a quick break so we can go over what you need me to pick up?" he asks, stunning me into silence for a good few beats.

I mean, really? He just barges in here, my move into his place all figured out while I wasn't even aware we were really doing it? I brushed his offer off as him wanting to comfort me last night but this? This is freaking me out.

Not to mention he plans on it being that soon. Jesus Christ, is he crazy?

I take a step back from him, laughing nervously. "Look, Sebastian, I really appreciate everything you did and said last night but you don't have to offer me a place to stay. I have it covered, really." Not strictly true, but I'm certainly not ready to move in with him.

Sebastian smiles patiently as if he knew how this conversation would go. "Listen, *friend*. I'm not doing this out of charity, and I'm not doing this to get into your pants. You'd obviously have your own room and between my classes and your job and visits to your parents' place, we'll barely see each other. Not to mention we hang out every other weekend as it is, so it really won't make much of a difference.

"I have the space and you could save a lot of money and spend it on more important things than rent. Am I wrong?" he challenges, and I stay quiet. No, I guess he's not wrong. Still, it seems impossible that I could move in with him, the guy who, until recently, acted like he couldn't stand me.

"That's what I thought. Now, I spoke to your landlord, and he said your next month's rent is due in a few weeks, but you can move out after a three-day notice and save those costs already." He pauses and sighs, studying me closely.

He takes a step closer and softens his voice impossibly more as he takes my hands into his. My brain short circuits when his thumb brushes over the back of my hand, my panic wavering for a second at the calming gesture. "Can you try not to freak out and listen to me, Aliena?" he asks, still caressing me. I look into his dark eyes, equal parts scared and amazed at how easily he makes me want to give in. I swallow and nod.

"Yes. It's just…damn, you have it all figured out, don't you? I won't ask how you contacted my landlord. I don't care. Still, I don't think I can save next month's rent. There's no way I can be out of the apartment in three days."

"Why not? I can call a moving company. It's not like you live in a castle. It shouldn't take too long to move everything. Besides, you said it yourself, tomorrow is your day off so you can pack everything up then, no?"

Right on time, a headache starts pulsing in my temples, pushing against the false sense of security his touch has lured me into. I've never been a fan of hasty plans.

"I told my parents I'd visit tomorrow, and I don't know when I'll be home. Besides, I don't have the money for a moving company that will work so quickly on such short notice right now."

"What about the money you could save on the rent?" he asks.

My cheeks burn with shame, but I try to hide my embarrassment as I respond, "I don't have it yet. I wanted to ask for a waiver," I explain, mortified when Sebastian's surprise becomes apparent. I pull my hands from his grasp and avert my eyes.

Finally, he pulls himself together. "All right. I'll pay for the movers, and you'll pay me back when you have the money, okay?" he proposes even though I'm already shaking my head.

"I don't want your money. If I wanted money, I might as well have told Lily about what's going on. Look, Seb, thank you, really, but I can't accept your help on this. I'm sorry I dumped all my drama on you yesterday, but it would be best if you just forgot all about it," I tell him, pulling away even though it's the last thing I want to do. The last thing I should do.

I don't know what I'm doing. I need his help. Desperately. By the rate I'm going at, the only question left is whether I'll have a burnout or be kicked out of my home first. I've just never been good at accepting help.

"Aliena, you're a few days away from asking for a rent waiver. You'll go into debt if you don't change something soon. Accept my help. Besides, I'm not giving you my money, I'm lending it to you until you're in a more stable spot. There's no harm. Can you come to terms with that?" he asks.

Slowly, very slowly, I feel myself cave. This talk alone just reminded me of how tiring my current situation really is, and he's right, maybe there is no harm in letting him help. I can make it up to him somehow else, I'm sure.

"Yeah. I guess we have a deal," I concede.

He smiles. "Great, I'll make the calls then. Do you want to give me your keys? I could start packing up your dishes or something since I have nothing better to do. It's no big deal," he assures me hastily when he sees me open my mouth to protest.

I snap it shut, choosing to trust him on this. We're on a time crunch and I don't see myself being able to pack up my entire apartment in a few days by myself. Reluctantly, I nod and hand him my keys.

"Thanks, Seb. Really."

Chapter 21

Sebastian

"Sebastian?" Aliena calls out when she enters her home hours after my arrival.

"In the kitchen," I reply loudly, turning away from the carton box I'd been filling with her belongings to see her step around the counter. I fight to keep an easy smile on my face even though the sight of her is a punch to my chest.

She's standing at the entry of the kitchen, her golden hair up in a messy bun, that has more hair falling out of it than in it, her clothes wrinkled and disheveled after a long shift, but that's not what calls to my worry. No, it's the sight of her posture, her shoulders hunched as if the weight of the world was resting on them, that makes me want to frown.

A part of me had hoped last night was the product of alcohol-induced sensitivity and maybe, Aliena isn't constantly feeling so overwhelmed. Seeing her now, I'm not convinced. In the very least, I hope that even though she's struggling financially and worried about her parents, things will look up since she won't have to pay rent anymore. It's the only thing in my control at the moment.

I get to my feet and don't think about it before pulling her into a hug. My instincts are driving me, screaming at me to make her feel better. My arm slides around her back to pull her as close as possible and my other hand comes up to the back of her head to cradle her. Her soft sigh brushes against my chest as her arms close around my back, her body melting into me. It does something strange to my chest, something foreign and unsettling, but it's not enough to overshadow my need to shield her. I lean down and rest my chin on her head, so close that I catch a whiff of her flowery shampoo. *It's intoxicating.* I suppress the sudden urge to bury my nose in her hair until she's all my senses can focus on and scold myself for losing my mind. What the hell was that thought?

I've noted the way she melts into my touch and soaks up every embrace she gets. It's clear physical touch is one of her love languages. That's why I'm hugging her, I tell myself... *And because you found yourself thinking back to how nice it felt to have her in your arms last night several times today, and you've been longing to get another taste,* a treacherous voice in the back of my head adds.

Yeah, this girl I agreed to be friends with, which I'm very attracted to and know feels the same way, is messing with my head. That's why I hold her for a second longer than I should. Reluctantly, I pull away until we're an arm's length apart. I keep my hands on her thin arms, another reminder of the weight she's lost, and meet her tired eyes.

"I moved everything from the cupboards into boxes already. I only have the cutlery left and then the kitchen is done. Do you want to start on the other rooms or would you rather just get your essentials and let me take you home?" I ask. Funnily enough, I don't even have to think twice about calling my place her home. I like the ring of it. It just rolls off my tongue.

207

I'd never tell anyone this but sometimes living alone in that huge apartment is lonely. That's why I started throwing the parties. To bring some life to the huge space that felt more like a showcase then a home. It was a makeshift solution to a bigger problem, but now when I think of sharing the space with Aly, it doesn't feel so lonely anymore.

Oblivious to my selfish thoughts, Aly glances around the rest of her apartment with tired eyes. "I should start with the other rooms. It's probably best if I just stay here tonight so I can pack things up until I pass out and then keep going tomorrow before I go to my parents' place. You should go home, though. You've done more than enough."

Like that would do. I don't like the thought of leaving her alone like this. Not now when I know about everything and she's only just letting me in enough to see how exhausted she is. "I'll stay too, if you let me. I don't mind helping some more," I insist quickly.

"I don't have a guest room," she argues.

"Luckily, I think we proved we can share a bed just fine last night, no?" Am I inviting myself to sleep in her bed with her? Yeah. I guess I'm that guy now.

Aliena doesn't protest any further. "Sure, suit yourself. When are the movers coming?"

"Whenever I tell them to."

That draws the first soft smile from her, the familiar spark entering her eyes as she rolls her eyes at me. "Privileged prick," she teases.

I shove her lightly. "Careful, this privileged prick knows where you keep your cutlery."

She arches an amused brow, clearly glad for the momentary distraction of our banter. "You're threatening me in my own home? Bold, little boy. Real bold," she says, trying to stare me down with a hand on her hips like a primary teacher or something. Never mind that she is way shorter than me, especially without her heels on.

I make a show out of looking down at myself, trying not to laugh out loud. "Little, huh? I don't think anyone has described me as such in a decade."

"Yeah, well, you're not that pleasant to talk to. I'm sure there are many things the people around you never dare to describe you as, no matter how true they are," she fires back without pause.

"Okay, rude. I am very pleasant." My classmates would disagree. In fact, her observation is very on point. I'm sure people have said or thought things about me they'd never dare to say to my face simply because I'm the dean's son. It's ridiculous considering my dad wouldn't care if anyone cussed me out. He'd probably like them more if they did. Invite them for dinner and create a club exclusively to rant about me and all my faults.

"Mhm, sure you are." She pats me on the arm and gives me those bright eyes of hers, her lips stretching into a small smirk. It's all sorts of distracting. She never lets me forget how gorgeous she is.

"Little troublemaker, I've had about enough of your big mouth," I chastise playfully.

Her eyes light with challenge. "That's something I haven't been told before. Usually, men can't get enough of it," she drawls, her double meaning clear and the implication sending a burst of heat to my stomach. I curse myself for not having thought my words through more carefully before speaking because now, my gaze flicks to those sinful lips and her innuendo has bad ideas coming to my mind. Even worse images.

I clear my throat. "There's a first for everything," I reply lightheartedly in an attempt to steer this conversation back into more innocent waters before we can slip into flirting.

Aliena goes along with a sigh. "I guess there is. Now, let's get back to work. This place might be small but I'm a hoarder."

———

Way past midnight, I've finally had enough of packing boxes. Here I thought I was in form, but no, boxing stuff up is what exhausted me. I head to Aliena's room where she's currently working her way through every nook and cranny.

She doesn't hear me approach and I take a second to watch her, unguarded as she is now, lingering in the doorway. She looks tired, her back hunched and her steps slow. Still, her heavily lidded eyes are determined. She's a fierce one, that's for sure. Too fierce for her own good.

I finally walk up to her and place a gentle hand on her shoulder to get her attention. She must not have heard my approach because her muscles tense under my touch for a beat, and I curse myself for sneaking up on her. It's not the first time I've noticed how jumpy she is, but her body loosens under my palm too fast for me to dwell on it as she turns to look at me.

"It's time for bed, sweetheart. Come on," I say softly, the term of endearment falling from my lips like it tends to do whenever she seems so small and tired. It's a weird urge to make things better, to take care of her so she never has to worry about a single thing again. It rears its head at the sight of her red-rimmed eyes and takes control of my tongue.

I'm already steering her over to the bed. She doesn't protest and practically collapses onto the mattress. I shimmy out of my jeans and take off my socks and shirt before asking her, "Where's your pajamas?" She's still wearing her work clothes.

She lazily points to the dresser, and I catch sight of a stack of neatly folded clothes on top of it. I get them for her, but she just blinks at them and doesn't move. "Thanks," she says, melting further into the mattress. She looks like she's seconds away from passing out.

I shake her softly and tug at her arm. "Come on, baby, you have to change. You'll be more comfortable."

She blinks up at me in the most adorable way. "Yeah. Totally," she agrees right before she shakes her head. "Don't want to move, though." Then, her eyes close again.

I sigh loud enough for her to react to it.

"Help me if it's so important to you," she mumbles. I blink at her.

"Help you change?"

"Yes." Then she opens her eyes. "Not if you're uncomfortable. I can easily sleep like this. I just can't move my arms anymore."

I nearly chuckle at that. Yeah, lifting all those boxes made even me feel a bit of a burn, and I doubt Aliena spends as much time as me working out her upper body.

"I don't mind. I'll just open your blouse, okay?" I warn so she won't flinch away from my touch again. I can still remember when she thought I'd hit her after I walked in on her and Mattheo, even if only for a moment. I don't ever want her to feel threatened by me again.

She nods, so I slowly bring my fingers to the delicate buttons, trying not to let my mind go anywhere that isn't platonic. It's no easy feat. Especially when I reach the middle of her shirt, which reveals her cleavage and navy-blue bra.

Once all the buttons are open, I help remove her arms from the sleeves, then say, "There, you have to help me a little with the shirt now, okay?" I slip her oversized sleeping shirt over her head and then help her raise her upper body enough for me to pull it down her back.

Hesitantly, I ask, "Do you want me to take off your bra?" It's no big deal, anyway. I'd just reach beneath her shirt and unclasp it, then help her arms out of the straps. I'd see nothing, and yet, my voice sounds nervous to my own ears.

Aliena rolls onto her back and says, "Yes, please." So I do. I platonically take a girl's bra off for the first time in my life. I don't let my fingers linger at the feel of her soft back, nor do I allow myself the contemplation of how such smooth skin might look spanned over her slender back.

"Thank you. The scrubs are just fine. Come here, now," she demands softly, patting the mattress next to her without ever opening her eyes.

With a chuckle, I untuck the blanket and cover her with it. Only then do I climb into bed with her, holding her like I did this morning. I'm oddly content now as the weird fuzzy feeling returns and settles deep inside my chest. I've never spent a night cuddling with a girl. Ever. I had no idea what I was missing out on.

———

The next night, I'm already asleep by the time Aliena comes home. My home. Or ours, maybe, now that most of her belongings are already here. I planned on staying up, I really did. I even left the door to my room open so I'd hear her when she returned from her parents' house, but after reading for over an hour, I must've finally lost the fight against sleep.

But now I'm waking up to the sound of soft footsteps. I rub my eyes and blink at the doorway where my new roomie is standing, looking hesitant. I sit up, growing worried something might be wrong when she doesn't speak. I texted her earlier asking how long until she came home, but she never answered. Maybe I should've called her, but I didn't want to interrupt anything.

"You're home. How was the visit? Is everything okay?" I ask, trying to stifle a yawn. Shit, I'm sleepy. I look over at my clock to see it's three a.m. Jesus, did she just come home now?

"Can I sleep here?" she asks rather than replying to my questions.

My heart grows a little heavier at how small her voice sounds and there are a million questions I'd like to ask. Instead, I simply say, "Of course, sweetheart. You can sleep here every night if that's what you want."

She nods absently and crawls under the sheets with me, instantly curling into a ball.

213

I don't move for a second, unsure as to whether she wants me to hold her or not. When, finally, she wordlessly reaches behind her and pulls my arm over her middle to clutch my hand close to her chest, I get the hint and snuggle up to her.

"Do you want me to read to you?" I ask softly. She shakes her head and takes a deep, uneven breath. When she releases it with a heavy sigh, it's like a world of tension bleeds out of her, and she melts against me.

I'm dying to know what happened. Dying to know if there is anything I can do for her, but this is not the time. Who knows, maybe just being here is enough for now.

———

Over the next few days, the two of us settle into an easy, comfortable routine. All her belongings have arrived, and Aliena unpacked most of the boxes in her room. Still, she sleeps in my bed every night, though we don't really talk about that. Sometimes, I read to her. Others, I just hold her. It seems like both are enough to help her sleep.

During the day, we barely see each other since we're both busy with our usual lives. Despite that, there hasn't been a second where I forgot she lived here too now. It's surreal, yeah, but she never lets me forget it, leaving me leftovers or little notes in the kitchen.

It's frightening how much I like it.

I've already established we could never be more than friends. I don't want a relationship, and I doubt I'd be good at one. I'm my father's son, after all, and I'm scared his indoctrination of how love makes you powerless has messed up a fundamental part of me. I can feel it every day, this need to control my surroundings. Whether that be the way my classmates see me by putting on an act or by never taking the passenger seat in a car.

I'm scared his words have gotten through to me even more than that. What if my need to control spreads to controlling my girl one day? Controlling a woman like my father controls my mother by dangling the threat of leaving her over her head every day, reminding her she's not special. That she's replaceable. What if I inherited his disloyal traits and end up putting the woman I'm supposed to protect down instead of lifting her up? I could take a chance, give into my attraction with abandon and one day wake up and realize I'm exactly like him.

It would break me, and I care about Aliena too much to put her in danger of that. I will protect her even if it is from myself. She doesn't need another person who can't get their act together in her life, so I will be her friend. I can do that.

Besides we don't have time for anything more complicated than this.

Aliena gets home late almost every night since she likes to visit her parents after work, and I get up early to go on a run and hit my gym before my classes start. Yeah, there's no way we would work, and yet sometimes, my treacherous mind plays out a scenario where maybe we're more.

A scenario where I can touch her in a non-platonic way. Where her body is molded to mine every night because we both want it, not because she needs it to sleep. Where maybe she trusts me enough to confide in me again and talk about how her situation is developing now that she's moved places or how her mother is doing.

215

But those thoughts are just slip-ups. Things are best this way.

Our friends don't know about our new living arrangement judging by their lack of interrogation. I guess Aliena still hasn't told Lily about her family problems and doesn't want to explain why she had to move at all. I'm used to not sharing anything too personal anyway, so it's no big deal to keep my mouth shut about my new roomie whenever I see my friends at school.

I'm just glad she seems to be doing slightly better, shooting me a few weak smiles or teasing me whenever our paths cross. It feels like spending time with the old Aliena. I won't do anything to jeopardize that progress by exposing her to our friends' curiosity.

"Seb? I'm home!"

Speak of the devil. I look at the time on my phone, surprised when I see it's just seven in the evening. I get up from the couch I was reading on and go to meet her near the entry, feeling my lips curl up in a smile.

"Hey, you're home early," I observe, leaning against my elevator as I watch her struggle out of her boots.

When she straightens up and takes off her jacket, she rubs her hands up and down her arms. "Yeah, no visiting my parents today. I need a break. I hope it's okay I'm back so soon?" The question surprises me.

"Yes, of course. You live here. You're free to be home whenever you want. Don't ever feel like you can't, okay?" I try to assure her, hating the idea she might've spent more time elsewhere because she thought she'd be a burden when she just wanted to come home and rest.

Searching my face closely, perhaps deciding if she believed me, she finally nods. "Yeah, sure. Thanks. Now, have you eaten already? I went grocery shopping, so I'll probably cook anyway, in case you want to join me," she offers.

Warm anticipation washes over me at the thought of eating dinner with her, but I eye the bags of groceries with a frown. "You didn't have to do that, Aly. Between the two of us, I'm the one with the more time on my hands. You can just make me a list of things you need, and I'll do the shopping. I've always done it myself." Not to mention she shouldn't spend her hard-earned money on my food when I have enough to cover it without feeling a dent.

But this time, she just brushes me off. "I already don't have to pay any rent. Let me at least do this so I don't feel like a stray you had to save from the streets," she argues.

Like I'd ever accept that sort of reasoning. "You're not a live-in maiden or cook, Aly. You live here, and it's not your job to get my groceries. I have the time and the money to spare, it's really no big deal. It just makes more sense if you don't have to worry about food on top of everything else."

Of course, like every other time I've tried to talk about her financial problems since the night she told me all about them, she gets defensive and dismisses me with a hard look. *Shit.* I should have known better than to go there.

"This is nonnegotiable, Sebastian. I want to contribute somehow. Now, can you help me get the other bags up, please? I left them downstairs since my hands were too frozen to hold onto the thin straps any longer."

Like a puppy beaten into obedience, too scared to upset her, I drop the subject and take the elevator downstairs in silence.

217

Chapter 22

Aliena

I'm drained and it's barely nine p.m. After I unloaded the groceries with Sebastian's help, I shooed him out of the kitchen and made dinner. We ate in comfortable silence and when we were done, I insisted he couldn't help me do the dishes. It was a quick chore, after all.

I went on and cleaned the kitchen, anything to stay busy since I don't know what else to do with myself anymore. When I tried to simply clean some other parts of the house, Sebastian stopped me, reasoning he had a very capable crew of cleaning ladies coming over once a week and I didn't have to do their job.

Now, we're locked in battle. He has my arms pinned at my sides with his hands around my wrists to keep me from moving away and cleaning another counter while I stare up at him with childish defiance. Whatever, I get cranky when I'm tired and it doesn't help I'm supposed to get my period in a few days. At least I have a day off tomorrow and the day after that.

It doesn't lift my mood enough to be compliant now, though.

"Aliena, stop fighting me on this. You're clearly tired. Why won't you just rest?" he asks, softening his voice so he sounds less demanding.

The answer would be I don't trust my mind not to go dark places when I give it the chance. Like, for example, how my mother is still not recovering. Instead, she's looking more and more like a ghost from my past.

On top of that, my dad's mood has been becoming darker by the day. I know he's mostly mad at himself because he thinks it's his fault our family is struggling once again and maybe a bit frustrated with my mother for being such a screwup.

Just yesterday, he snapped at me for dropping a fork when I did the dishes. His face got all red and a vein appeared at his temple. When he raised a hand to run it through his hair in agitation, I flinched away.

That sobered him up a bit and he apologized for losing his temper. Still, for a second, I was scared he might hit me again. I don't know what I'd do then. When I was younger, he never used much force on me so I'm sure I could take it. I'm just not sure if I want to.

Of course, I need to be understanding and help my parents as much as I can, but there are things I don't ever want to experience again. Too much already feels like old times. I want to feel like myself again.

Instead of saying any of that, since I know being a bitter pill all the time is how you bore friends into leaving, I just shrug. "I don't have anything better to do." I'm being stupidly defiant at this point. At least, it's good entertainment to get a rise out of Sebastian.

He scans my features thoughtfully. Finally, he smiles and lets go of my wrists to softly touch one of my shoulders instead. "I think you do. Or have you forgotten all about the unlimited access I granted you to a specific part of the house?"

At that, I perk up a little, and he chuckles.

"That's what I thought. Come on, I'll explain how everything works again," he proposes, already turning to walk up the stairs. I beam and follow him, feeling some of my energy returning at the prospect of some good old me-time. I can't believe I forgot about baths. Such a fool.

When I enter the master bathroom after the owner of the house, I halt in my tracks, gaping at all the new candles placed around the tub and the array of scented bath oils lining the wall.

"What is all this?" I ask, then turn to him. "You bought all that? Why? You had more than enough already," I protest, unsure what I'm feeling. I'm touched, yes, of course. Still, it feels wrong that he spent money on me. There was no need for any of this. The bathtub itself was enough, and he had scented oils he swore he wouldn't use on hand.

I was fine with the thought of using them. But this, this is excessive, the kind of ambience supposed to stay in fantasies and dreams.

Sebastian raises his hands in defense. "I didn't buy any of it. This was all my mom," he argues, making me frown in confusion.

"Your mom?" He told his mom I like baths? And she bought things for me?

"Oh right, I didn't tell you. She's a housekeeper and occasionally comes here with the other cleaning ladies. She saw someone had moved into my guest room, so I told her about you. I should have known she'd do something like this when I told her the oils she's been giving me for years are finally going to be used. Please, don't be upset with me. My mother surely got a lot of pleasure shopping for all that."

"I don't know what to say." His mother knows about me. His mother is his housekeeper? He told his mom, who'll be around the house unannounced from time to time and whom I might meet accidentally, about me.

She got me gifts.

"You have to give her my sincere thanks. Please. Oh god, and is there a way you could make her never buy anything for me again without offending her? I don't want to seem ungrateful, but I can't accept all this." Shit, why am I getting upset? The more I speak and think about this nice, thoughtful gesture, the more the lump in my throat grows.

Sebastian must notice it too, the attentive idiot. He takes my hands in his and lowers his voice to a softer, more intimate tone. "Aliena, there's nothing wrong with letting people that care about you spoil you from time to time," he tries to explain to me. Before I can protest his mother doesn't even know me, he goes on. "And no, there is absolutely no way my mother wouldn't take offense if I tried telling her anything of the sort."

I chuckle softly and nod, pulling myself together. "All right then. At least tell me when she's coming over next time so I can leave her some flowers."

"I'll let you know. Now, let's get your bath started," he proposes, only to hesitate for a beat. "You're sure you're okay, right? You'd talk to me otherwise. Or someone else. Whatever," he rambles, and I'm instantly mortified.

Great, now that I've nearly burst into tears because of a gift I deserve in no way, he's worried about me. I hate that. Making someone worry about me is easily the worst thing I can do to a person. It's such an unnecessary headache.

"I'm fine. Just tired. I get stupidly sensitive, and I don't know how to react to gifts. I was just surprised," I tell him. Eager to deflect, I add, "What about that bath now?"

———

After taking advantage of Sebastian's gigantic bathtub filled with soothing hot water and bubbles for over an hour, I dried myself with one of his fluffy towels and put on my pajamas. Then I climbed into bed with him, and he read to me until I fell asleep, stroking the back of my hand soothingly as I drifted off,

When I wake up, we're in the same position as always. My back is to his front, one of his arms is curled around my chest while the other is under his head. Only this time, my mind instantly focuses on something at my back. Something I'm no longer used to feeling so close to me.

Oh, god. Yeah, there's no mistaking the erection Sebastian is sporting. And it's placed perfectly against my ass, too. My sleepy mind doesn't have enough self-control to shut down the road my thoughts are now going down, and I nearly burst out laughing as I realize why Sebastian is as cocky as he is.

Yeah, I find that very funny. Until I become aware of the two fingers moving beneath my boob when my torso shakes softly with laughter. After that, I'm careful to stay very still.

Technically, I didn't mean to wake up so early. Judging by the grayish light streaming through one of the windows, it's way too early to start my day off.

I planned on sleeping in to an outrageous degree, maybe late afternoon if I could. I was fully intent on it...until now. Now, it feels impossible that I could fall back asleep with my awareness rising. The way my skin is tingling is both familiar and yet so much more intense than I remember.

Maybe it's because I know I can't act on it. That indulging in the way he's making me feel with this unconscious show of arousal is off limits. I've never been much of a rule breaker, but I hear it's a common inclination when it comes to sex.

And it's been quite a while since I've had that... Or maybe it's just that I'm feeling *Sebastian's* erection against me, something I've been fantasizing about more since I met him than I'd ever admit. Not just in the short time between meeting him in the nursing home and then at his party. No, he remained the lead in all my fantasies even when he acted like he couldn't stand me.

The tingle on my skin wanders lower, gathering between my legs as those unbidden fantasies rise to the forefront of my mind. He's so close and so warm and so *safe*. What would it feel like to have him cage me to the bed, shield me from the entire world while he made me forget everything so thoroughly I wouldn't even remember my own name? To have him sink into me and kiss me, to worship my body and own me entirely.

Shit, stop thinking crazy things like that. Abort. Abort before you get too attached to an ideal you can never have.

223

What do I do? Do I just wake him? It's not that I mind the position I'm in, and I'm not sure it would be fair to wake him now only because I'm up. But maybe it's wrong to enjoy this. Sebastian agreed to be my friend, after all. That's what we shook on. I have no permission to enjoy the way his erection makes my blood heat.

It's easy to forget how long it's been since I last had sex, and with sharing a bed with a very attractive man every night, tension sure has been building.

But Sebastian is just a friend. I can't let my mind go places.

Slowly, very slowly, I try to move my ass away from his front to put at least a little distance between us. Maybe then, I can go back to sleep and forget about this slip up.

When I move, his fingers brush against my boob again, and hell, if my body doesn't react ridiculously to that simple, accidental touch. It's always the same with Sebastian. My attraction to him intensifies with every touch we share, and the fact he told me nothing could ever happen between us only adds to my desperation.

His words return to me and in the clarity of the morning, they hit me a lot harder than they did at the party when he'd first said them.

Because one kiss wouldn't be enough. Nor would two, or ten, or fifty. Once I felt your kiss, I'd want to feel it all, Aliena.

You are so beautiful, it's hard to believe you're real at times.

Make that sound again and I'll fuck you up against the closest wall. Don't test me.

Don't pull away. I'm not ready for this to end. We said one kiss.

I feel myself getting turned on and grit my teeth, trying to carefully move my hips away again. This time, the arm around my chest tightens, damn near bringing Seb's hand close enough to cup my breast. It does nothing to stifle my uncalled-for lust. Sleepy me a few days before my period is a horny bitch.

I don't give up my task to put a little distance between the man behind me and myself, but when I finally create the smallest of gaps, he's quick to scoot back all the way against me with a sleepy rumble of protest.

Great, so much for not waking him. Although I'm not sure whether he's really conscious or if the reaction was mostly instinctual; the urge to stay in a comfortable position in his sleep.

When I move again, he really does wake up and speaks in that deep, husky voice of his. "What are you doing?" he grumbles into my hair, tightening his hold on me some more. I nearly make a sound of appreciation when his arm brushes against my stiffening nipples.

"Nothing, I'm just warm," I lie, resorting to just clenching my thighs to get at least a little relief. My neglected clit is pulsing weakly as she recognizes the feel of an excited man at my back. Unbelievable.

Sebastian hums and moves a little in preparation to go back to sleep. What he doesn't realize is I'm a burning, needy mess by now and his move basically pushed his dick right between my butt cheeks. It makes me want to wish it was somewhere else.

I cross my legs but the move isn't as subtle as I hoped. I feel Sebastian stiffen behind me as he notices what has me shifting around so restlessly.

225

For a second, he doesn't act at all. Then, he clears his throat and loosens his hold on me. He whispers a curse. "Shit, I'm so sorry. Didn't mean to make you uncomfortable." He tries to let go of me and maybe turn away, but I hold his hand in place before my mind can settle on a game plan, keeping him from getting away.

"Aliena?" he asks softly after a few beats of silence, still seeming hesitant to get closer. "I'll just take a quick cold shower and I'll be back. It's no big deal," he tries to reason.

"You didn't make me uncomfortable," I argue, my voice breathy and low. It feels forbidden to say. Absolutely reckless. Sebastian doesn't speak but I can feel some of the tension bleeding out of his body.

"No?" he finally asks. I shake my head and ever so slightly move back against him, not so accidentally rubbing my ass against his erection this time. He releases a low, anguished sound and his arm flexes around me.

"What are you doing, little troublemaker?" he asks into my ear. I shudder but don't reply. Memories are rushing back to me now, reminding of all the times the tension built between us only for him to shut me down. Then more recent images resurface of how Sebastian took care of me since we made peace. In all sorts of ways. I suddenly get the urge to return the favor.

I rub myself against him again, more conscious of the movement now, and more heat goes straight to my clit at the sound Sebastian makes. Yeah, I missed this.

He doesn't try to restrict my movements, similar to when we danced. Instead, he lets me work both of us up as his hand cups one of my breasts. That's what finally draws a soft moan from me and Sebastian curses, giving my nipple a soft pinch.

226

"I've been dreaming about that sound," he confesses breathlessly. The validation is all I need to finally untangle my body from his and push him onto his back. He blinks up at me as I kneel at his side, still looking slightly sleepy and hot as hell.

I move to kneel between his thighs, and he finally asks, "What are you doing?"

I grin. "I can think of a better way to take care of this than a cold shower," I tell him.

He closes his eyes briefly as if picturing it. "You don't have to do that," he assures me even though his want is clear. It still turns me on that he tries to assure me there is no pressure.

"I know," I confirm, placing my hands on his knees at my side and moving them up to fiddle with the end of his boxers. "I just really want to."

Chapter 23

Sebastian

I'm almost sure I shouldn't let this go on. I'm not sure why but there is that small, cautious voice in the back of my mind telling me to keep a clear head. That is enough to soothe my conscience and make me refrain from protesting. At least I know I'm not doing the right thing, right?

Besides, Aliena seems sure enough for both of us. With the way she is looking at me, her loose shirt rumpled while her face is beautifully flushed, I don't stand a chance resisting this. Not when she's finally touching me like I dreamed about for longer than I care to admit. Certainly not when her hand cups my stiff dick through my boxers, giving it a tentative squeeze.

Why did I ever think I could stay away from her? My good intentions seem incredibly frail in the face of her insistence.

"How many times have you come in this bed?" she asks me, smiling coyly as she strokes me.

"Too many since I met you," I confess. She's clearly satisfied with my answer. She likes knowing I haven't been with anyone because she's been messing with my head.

"How many times did someone else make you come in this room?" she goes on, despite knowing the answer.

"Not once," I confirm, secretly grateful for that decision when it visibly pleases her.

She smiles more and gives the waistband of my boxers a tug. I lift my hips wordlessly, letting her bare me completely. It's weird how after all the innocently intimate moments we shared, this is what makes me shy.

I'm used to being the one leading. Now, here is Aliena, kneeling between my thighs and shamelessly drinking in the sight of me in the broad daylight.

"Are you just going to look or are you going to touch me?" I tease her, trying to force my voice to be even. Truth is, my nerves are buzzing and anticipation is wrecking my brain. There's always been a strong sexual tension between me and this woman, even back when we were hardly friends. The wait made me impatient like a teenager about to have his first time. Christ, I need to get a grip on it.

"Oh, I have every intention of touching," Aliena drawls cockily, bringing her hands so close to my shaft I can almost feel the ghost of her touch there. This is a new side of her. A side my body reacts horribly excited to.

Finally, her soft, delicate hand wraps around the base of my dick and she gives me a long stroke, drawing a breathy version of her name from my lips before I can stop it. I don't even have it in me to be embarrassed about it. Not when the most beautiful blush creeps up her neck.

"I'll tell you what," she goes on, leaning forward to lick a trail down the curve of my neck before whispering against the wet skin. "I have every intention of tasting, too." Before I can turn my head to bring her lips to mine, to kiss her like I really want to, she's back to kneeling between my legs, grinning wickedly.

"No tasting for you. Just lean back and enjoy," she instructs, her hand's movement on my erection never faltering. Not trusting my voice, I don't protest and lean back as she told me to, never taking my eyes off her while all the ways I can return the favor are rushing through my mind.

I want to put her in the same position once she's done with me. Want to see her sweat and tremble beneath my hands, my tongue, and maybe even my dick. That last option isn't for today, though. No. There's too much I want to do to her first.

My train of thought is cut off when she leans down to press a kiss to my skin just below my belly button. Her warm lips linger, and when her eyes meet mine, I feel chills break out on my skin. I grab the bed sheets at my side.

She peppers my skin with kisses, following the trail of hair leading to my shaft. Finally, she grabs my erection in one hand and takes her eyes from mine as she takes the first few inches into her mouth. Her warm tongue glides against the vein on the underside of my dick and her shaky breath fans against my skin. Suddenly, I'm glad she isn't looking at me. Otherwise, she'd see the way I have to close my eyes and take a deep breath to restrain myself.

While I am more than eager to make this moment last forever, I'm also dying for her to move. To suck me down further and make me come. Heaven knows I need a release. I'm already aching for it, and we've barely started.

Finally, blissfully, Aliena brings those beautiful honey-colored eyes back to mine and stops the torture, pushing her face lower until her nose is brushing against my skin, and her throat constricts around me.

I grip the bedsheets more tightly, forcing my hands to stay where they are rather than let them guide Aliena's head. She knows what she's doing, clearly. If she wants to play with her prey first, I won't stop her. No matter how painful it is to be her prey. It's also the most exciting feeling I've experienced in years, if not ever.

I realize I've closed my eyes when the vibrations of her humming around my dick have my legs twitching in response. My eyes fly open, and when Aliena has what she wanted, meaning my eyes on her, she finally starts bobbing her head, using her tongue to accompany every stroke.

The rhythm is heavenly. The way her nails are digging into my flexed thighs as her tears drop onto my hot skin makes it even better. Soon enough, my blood is buzzing, and I'm high on the pleasure. My brain has completely shut off. All there is to focus on are the sensations.

I've never experienced anything similar. Not that I'm surprised. I knew Aliena was special from the day I met her. My body has never reacted this way to anyone before her.

As the pleasure builds at the base of my spine, I grip the sheets so tightly they finally can't take it anymore. They tear audibly, but if Aliena notices, she doesn't care. She keeps working me up, taking me all the way down her throat again and again. I curse.

"If you don't pull away in the next three seconds, I'll come down that pretty throat of yours," I warn her through gritted teeth. My hands are now clenched tightly at my sides, every muscle in my body stiff in anticipation of my release.

Aliena doesn't pull away and as promised, my orgasm washes over me while she's still sucking me down. My

231

eyes close, my back stiffens, and my hips buck. There's no stopping it.

When finally, the last of my tremors end and I melt back onto the bed, I take a second to collect myself. Shit, the amount of time I lasted is embarrassing. My only saving grace is Aliena knows of my long dry streak.

Besides, I'll have tons of opportunities to make up for it. That's for sure. Whatever my arguments were against taking my relationship with Aliena to a physical level have been eviscerated. Blown into tiny, incomprehensible pieces. There's no way I'll give this up now that I know how good she can make me feel.

Plus, now I have a challenge to complete. Make sure I can make her come even faster than she managed to do with me.

I open my eyes to see Aliena standing a few feet away, laughing silently at me. Damn, I didn't even realize she got off the bed. I'm sure this does wonders for her ego.

"You ripped the sheets," she observes helpfully, her shoulders shaking with her amusement. I sit up.

"Why, thanks, Sherlock. I hadn't noticed," I tease. "Now, get back here. We're not done. I promise the shredded sheets won't swallow you whole." I might, though I don't say that.

To my surprise, she shakes her head. "I wish I could but I'm desperate to take a shower. We need to start sleeping with the window open because it feels like a damn furnace is stuck to my back every night. I hate waking up sweaty."

"It's January. We'll get sick," I argue. I mean, come on, better to wake up a little sweaty than with a sore throat and a runny nose. The latter is often inconvenient for a much longer time. Or at least that's the case for me with my weak immune system.

"You better replace those sheets then. We need a proper blanket if we want to survive the dangerous subzero temperatures," she teases. Brat. Then she turns and heads to the bathroom.

"Care to invite me to join? Save hot water and all that," I say with the cheesiest wink I can muster.

Aliena bursts out laughing though she doesn't relent. "No, I think I'm good, thanks," she assures me sweetly, then disappears into my bathroom.

I startle a little at the sound of the key turning. She *locked* the door. As if she was scared I wouldn't take the hint. My gut twists a little. Does she still not trust me after everything? Does she really know me so little to think I'd invade her privacy when she said she doesn't want me there?

I brush those worries to the side, convinced I'm overthinking this. It's early in the morning and my heart is still racing from my orgasm. This day is already full of turns. So what if Aliena isn't in the mood to let me return the favor right now? That's completely fine. As long as she doesn't regret anything, I'm good.

When Aliena emerges from the bathroom forty minutes later, during which I read a bit to drown out my doubts, she looks fresh and happy.

I set my book down and give her my undivided attention. "So, do you have any plans for your day off?" I ask.

"Nope. I'm very open to suggestions, though. I hate being bored. What is your to-do list for the day?"

I could tell her what certainly wasn't on my to-do list; sitting in my bed so long after waking up. I should have started my day forty minutes ago, but I had to see Aliena again before leaving for my run. I was worried things might get weird if we didn't see each other for hours.

Maybe I just wanted to see her to be sure she was fine.

"Well, I should already be halfway through with my run by now so that's up next, I guess. I should work out after that since I've been slacking. Then comes lunch. I have two classes in the afternoon and then I'm free. If you're bored, you can run with me?" I propose unsurely. To be honest, I have no clue what her relationship with sports is.

When she groans, I have my answer. Not a fan, then. At least not of cardio. "There's no way I can possibly keep up with you, but if you're willing to run a few circles around me so I can tag along, I guess it's worth a try. The last time I was supposed to run from a stranger in the night, I cursed myself for not working out more."

The unwelcome reminder of the time I picked her up unconscious after she was robbed is like a bucket of ice over my good mood. "Good point. Do you have running shoes?" I ask, hiding my impacted attitude as well as possible.

She blows out a breath. "Yeah. In one of the boxes that remain untouched. I'll go look for them in my room," she says, already heading out.

"Good, and hurry!" I yell after her. So much for no longer slacking. I'm sure inviting her to join me on my run won't lead to a more efficient workout. Still, I've noticed how restless Aliena is, and if she wants a distraction, I'm happy to provide that.

Another twenty minutes later, my roommate and I are finally leaving my house. We barely talk. Me, because I'm anxious to finally get on with my routine, and Aliena for whatever reason. I'm glad for the silence this once. Not because I don't care about what she might have to say or be thinking but because I'm still busy sorting out my own thoughts.

No matter how hard I try not to, I'm stressed out about my father's possible reaction when he finds out I've been neglecting his carefully constructed workout plan. It's ridiculous, really. I'm a twenty-three-year-old man. I shouldn't care. Not about his disapproval or his opinions about my life. But it happened without my permission, and that should freak me out. Between helping Aly unpack when we were together and spending every evening I was home alone in my room so she'd find me when she returned, I slacked.

The thought of my father questioning the source of my sudden change in behavior makes my palms sweat because I know what he would say. I can hear his gruff voice in the back of my mind without having to talk to him. *"This is exactly what I was always talking about. Your savior complex always comes back to bite you in the ass. You're a slave to your soft heart. Entirely powerless."*

I try to push away all thoughts of my old man, but by banishing those worries, I make room for others to cloud my mind.

Should I address what happened this morning with Aliena? I mean, we shook on being friends. Those lines might've already been blurring with every night she spent in my bed, but this morning, something significant

235

happened. Something way out of those drawn lines. I'm confused about where that leaves us.

No matter how attracted I am to Aliena and how much I care about her, or perhaps because of it, I haven't changed my mind about entering a relationship. I haven't forgotten all the cons speaking against it.

Still, I get excited at the prospect of maybe repeating what happened this morning. The only problem is I don't know where my roommate stands on all this.

For now, I allow myself to focus on the burn of my muscles and the strain on my lungs as I try to motivate Aliena while running my route through the woods. It's a lot more fun than I thought, seeing her struggling to breathe when all she clearly wants to do is snap at me. My challenge for the duration of the run is to not let her catch her breath enough to give me hell for proposing she joined me.

"If you're down, you can always join me in the gym afterward," I tell her, half-joking because she certainly doesn't look in the mood for more exercise right now.

"I. Will. Murder. You," she gasps in between deep breaths. And to think I'm already slowing my tempo down enough to be running backward.

"Bap, bap, bap. Less talking, more breathing, sweetheart. We wouldn't want you to pass out, now, would we?" I reproach playfully. She glares at me but shuts her mouth, taking deep breaths through her nose.

———

"That was the worst idea I've had in my entire life," Aliena exclaims as the elevator doors shut behind us.

236

I walk inside to get two bottles of water, amused to find her slouching on the floor when I return from the kitchen. She's still catching her breath.

"You were right, you really do need to do more cardio," I tell her, handing her a bottle.

"If you think I'll ever run with you again, you're sorely mistaken," she declares instantly.

I just keep smiling. "All right. I'll always have my phone on, then. In case you need picking up in the middle of the night again."

She gasps. "You didn't just joke about that!"

"Oh, but I did. Too soon?" I ask.

She simply bursts out laughing and shakes her head. "Just right. I hate taboo topics. Coping with humor is my favorite deficit. There's nothing worse than being treated with kid gloves."

I'm tempted to ask if that applies to all topics, including her family because I'd rather have her jokingly tell me what's going on so I can read between the lines than not getting any information at all.

But one look at the sparkle in her eyes tells me I won't formulate the words. I don't want to do anything to jeopardize her rare good mood. She looks more like herself than she has in days, the skipped visit and bath last night combined with her day off today doing her wonders.

"All right, good. I'm going downstairs to the gym for a bit. You know where to find me, right?" I ask.

"Walk all the way back there, then take the stairs, right?" she recites before adding, "I can't believe there's a third floor to this monstrosity of an apartment."

237

Since I don't have a reply to that, I simply tell her, "Don't forget about the bathtub, yeah? If my mother comes around soon and finds none of her gifts used, she'll blame me. But eat a big breakfast first. All those glares you shot at me while trying to run burned more calories than you'd think."

———

After a few days, I become aware of a pattern. Considering I've been woken up the same way every morning since Aliena first made me come eight days ago, I'd say it's safe to say she's happy to touch me.

Since I haven't been allowed to return the favor so far and couldn't so much as steal a single kiss, I'll say she's not so interested in letting me touch her. Sure, she insists she got her period soon after that first morning, which I believe since she's been a lot grouchier recently. Grouchier and more affectionate at the same time. It's kind of cute, to be honest.

Every evening when she comes home, I ask her about her day. Her first reaction is to snap something rude at me, and I figured out quickly it's best to just let her be. On the nights she eats dinner with me rather than spending time with her parents, we eat in silence until she finally caves and apologizes.

She does the dishes, refusing to let me help as always, no matter how exhausted she clearly is. Then, something that surprised me the first time but quickly became something to look forward to, Aliena usually finds me on the couch and snuggles up to me.

So yeah, I get she's not in the mood to let me touch her while she's on her period, even though I assured her I couldn't care less about a bit of blood. Plus, she's busy with work and her parents again. And yet I can't shake the feeling those are excuses. At least partially. It's enough to drive me crazy with doubts.

I haven't forgotten how hard it was for her to accept my offer to move in. How she insisted it was too much and how she's been taking up all these chores around the house since. The cooking, doing the dishes, and the grocery shopping.

I know she still thinks it's not enough, no matter how much I try to convince her otherwise. Now, as much as I hate it, I wonder what her motives are for waking me up by kissing my neck, my chest, or, well, my more southern region. I don't doubt she's attracted to me. I've known differently from the day I met her. And yet, every time she denies me to touch her like I want or finally kiss those sinful lips again, I grow a little more worried. So much so that I've settled on the plan to talk to her tonight. I have to do it. Maybe then, I'll be able to focus on school again. Or, more importantly, stop messing up at practice.

Yesterday, I was distracted enough to hit my punching bag with my pinkie and my ring finger, like an idiot. The result was a whole lot of pain, some of which still lasts to this point. The only silver lining is I haven't heard from my dad in a while. My mom called me once, asking to see me on my upcoming birthday. Other than that, my parents have left me in peace.

The same doesn't apply for my friends, who've collectively been grilling me about why I haven't thrown a party in a while. After I ditched them on New Year's, they've been suspicious of me. I can't blame them. It's not my style to blow them off, but I knew Aliena wasn't in any condition to see everyone again so soon after Lily's party, so I stayed home with her.

Not that our friends know that. I told them I went to another club with some girl I supposedly met while Aliena came up with some different excuse. No one pushed her about it. Lily made sure of that, still feeling guilty about what happened at her party even after they made up.

Long story short, my friends know I'm keeping something from them. I doubt they'd ever guess what, though.

"Hey, I'm home," Aliena yells from upstairs, dragging me from my thoughts. My eyes flick to the clock on the wall, and I curse to myself, seeing how late it is. I'm still downstairs, working out. I should have finished up and showered by now so I'd be ready for dinner.

I grab my things and jog upstairs, greeting my roomie with my most dazzling smile. So much so she rolls her eyes.

"It's great to see you too, gorgeous," I tease as I head for the stairs leading to my room. "I'll just take a quick shower, try not to miss me too much," I add, jogging away before she can retort anything snappy.

As soon as I enter my room and turn on the shower, my mask of ease drops away and nerves bubble up within me. For the whole duration of my quick shower, I give myself a pep talk for the conversation ahead. When I step out, I'm still nervous and unsure.

How do I ask my friend and roommate if she's been sucking me off every morning because she feels obliged to repay me for letting her live here? This is bound to go wrong.

I don't bother drying my hair before I rush back down the stairs, beckoned by the heavenly smell of something that must be Italian. Honestly, I don't know where she learned to cook, but she needs to teach me one day.

"So, I'm back. Did you manage all right without me, or do you need a hug?" I taunt her, opening my arms welcomingly.

She throws me a withering glare. "I'm good, thanks."

Ignoring the sting of her rejection, I make sure not to let my disappointment show. Instead, I take advantage of her lack of attention to take her in. At first glance, she seems the same as always. A little grumpy and certainly tired.

She's gained back some of the weight she'd lost before she moved in with me, her body no longer looking at the verge of collapse. I've been obsessed with making sure she was eating enough, sometimes telling her I was full after eating half of my plate so she'd finish it, so that's good.

I notice her hand is shaking as she stirs the bubbling sauce in the pot. I frown and look back at the side of her face, seeing her pale, bloodless lips. It takes everything I have not to reach out and ask her what's wrong. Sadly, she hasn't eaten yet and I know better than to push her when she's hangry and on her period.

I opt to simply ask, "You came home late. Did you swing by at your parent's first?"

A tight-lipped nod is the only answer I get. I bite my tongue, desperate to ask more questions when I know I should just drop it. In the end, I sigh and leave her to set the table. We'll talk later. About more than just what I prepared myself for all day, it seems.

Chapter 24

Aliena

Sebastian is staring at me weirdly throughout dinner but says nothing. It's enough to set me on edge.

I know I've been acting like a bitch for the past few days, and as much as I'd like to blame it on my period, that's no excuse. Especially since I've been in uncharacteristically little pain. Usually, I get excruciating cramps, and my back aches badly enough I've called in sick at work because of it, unable to move. Not this month, though.

It's a good thing too. I don't think I could have handled that on top of everything else. Most of all today, when I visited my parents only to learn my mother was out and my dad was pissed. I just dropped off some groceries and cleaned a little, but the atmosphere was strained enough to drain whatever small bit of energy I had left after work. When I finally announced I had to leave, my father yelled at me, mad at me for not making dinner. Mad at my mom for being a screwup, and mad at the world because he's lost everything.

He didn't say all that, of course. I know him well enough that he didn't have to.

When I'm done cleaning the kitchen, I wordlessly get onto the couch next to Seb, taking my place under his welcoming arm and watching the show he put on tonight.

We sit in silence for a few minutes, both watching the screen before a squeeze on my shoulder has me turning my head to face him. Seb's eyes flick over my face, taking in what I know are signs of my exhaustion. I look like shit, no doubt, and his scrutiny makes me want to hide from him all the more.

"How was your day, sweetheart?" he finally asks, his voice unbearably soft.

I grit my teeth against my flood of emotions and look back at the screen. I really can't wait for my period to be over. I hate being so sensitive.

"Fine, yours?" I reply unconvincingly.

"Boring enough. It seems nothing is able to hold my attention when the alternative is thinking about you," he says, bumping his shoulder against me to make us sway. It's enough to drag a laugh out of me. God, he's an idiot.

I tell him just that.

"I'm serious. I couldn't stop thinking about you," he admits. I refuse to acknowledge what those words do to my heart. This isn't some love confession, not that I would want that, anyway. We've both made it clear where we stood. No, this is him trying to initiate something sexual, I'm not stupid.

"What did you think about?" I go along, innuendo thick in my voice. I mean, it's not far-fetched that he thought about me in connection to what I did just this morning. All these orgasms are bound to get to his head at some point. It's a good thing too. I might be tired, but I'd welcome this sort of distraction. Touching Sebastian is about the only time all the worries leave my mind, the sinful noises me makes when he praises me banishing all other thoughts.

Only when I turn my head, I don't see the expected smirk on his face. No, he looks thoughtful. Hesitant, even. My nerves come crashing back, and I pull out of his embrace.

Just when I think the worst would happen and he truly was about to confess his undying love for me, he says, "It's about what we did this morning. And all the other times."

So, my hunch is confirmed. Only he still doesn't look like the conversation is about to go where I thought it would.

"Okay…" I trail off, waiting for him to go on and bracing myself for the worst. God, is this where he tells me I should stop? That he doesn't want me to touch him like that anymore?

No doubt sensing my unease, he softens his voice even more as he asks, "Why do you do it, Aliena?"

What now? If his face wasn't so earnest, I would have laughed. As it is, it feels like my insecurities are tightening a noose around my neck, making it hard for me to answer as I try to think of why he's talking about this.

"Because I want to," I tell him unsurely, despite it being the truth. I've been wanting to touch Sebastian since the day I met him. Wanted to hear him moan my name and come because of me. Still, my voice is unable to convey my surety of that.

Sebastian doesn't look convinced but he nods to himself. I can tell he has more to say before he opens his mouth. "Why won't you let me touch you?" he asks slowly.

Oh, I guess he noticed that. I didn't think he'd pay so much attention. Truth be told, I'm scared to let him touch me. Not because I'm scared he'll hurt me. I know he would never do that. But I'm afraid of things changing. I'm afraid it'll be too good and I'll want more, again and again.

I've never done that. One-night stands, yes, easy. But I live with Sebastian. I can't sneak out on him before he wakes up. Worse, I wouldn't want to sneak out. Not when I sleep best in his arms. So yeah, my reply would be that I'm a coward. What I end up saying is the same shitty excuse I sprouted every other time.

"I'm on my period, Seb." My voice sounds more defensive than it should, which only makes me less credible. I know he notices too.

"So, what happens when that's over?" he asks, no anger or impatience in his voice. Just curiosity and maybe a little concern.

I don't say anything, averting my gaze when his big hand comes to settle on top of my own.

"I'm not trying to pressure you," he says.

"I know," I interrupt him quickly.

"If you never want me to touch or kiss you, I won't blame you for it. I'd just like to understand what we're doing." He pauses, sighing as his thumb caresses my cool skin. I don't dare raise my eyes to his. "I've just been wondering." He hesitates some more.

Finally, his free hand finds my chin, tilting it up, making me look at him. "You know you don't have to do anything for me, right? I appreciate the cooking and everything else you do, of course, but those aren't requirements for you to stay here. You don't owe me anything."

His words hit me in the chest like shards of broken glass, and I can't hide the puff of breath that swooshes out of me. His unspoken meaning is more than clear to me, no matter that he's too polite to spell it out for me. I've been acting like a live-in hooker. He thinks I've been doing those things to him as a way to make up for not paying rent. While I've been looking forward to waking up and being close to him again, knowing I'll get just as much pleasure from it as him, he's been worried I had some demeaning ulterior motive.

I swallow, feeling sick. It's not like he did anything wrong. I don't know why I'm even taking this so badly. I guess it's just harsh to have something you thought was good turned into something so ugly.

I keep my emotions off my face, determined not to make myself seem even more pathetic. If Sebastian truly thinks I'd go so far to feel like less of a burden, he doesn't know me how I thought he did. He doesn't have to deal with my sentimentalities.

I smile weakly, acting like I found this misunderstanding amusing. I take his hand atop mine with my free one, patting it twice before I push it off my other. "I know that, Seb. That's not why I've been sucking you off every morning. That has everything to do with wanting to feel you shudder and writhe beneath me. Nothing else," I tell him, ignoring his slight flinch at my vulgar words. Then, I get to my feet, no matter how that may betray my act. "I'm beat, so I'll just take a shower and go to bed."

Before I can walk away, his hand is on my wrist, holding me in place. He's frowning slightly. "I didn't mean to offend you or imply anything," he tries to assure me.

247

I gently free myself of his grip. "I know. I'm just really tired."

He doesn't look convinced. "Are you okay? Did something happen at your parents'? You seemed a little shaken when you returned."

"Same old," I reply honestly, knowing he doesn't know what that even means. We haven't talked about my parents since I spilled half my secrets after Lily's party.

Resigned, Seb concedes with a nod, "Right. I'll be up later."

———

By the time Sebastian's birthday rolls around, nothing has changed between us. I still wake him up with an orgasm whenever we have the time, but I still haven't let him touch me. I know he wants to. The desire to reach out, maybe flip us around and finally kiss me is written all over his face whenever our eyes meet. The only difference is my withering restraint. Whenever I'm cooking something and he steps up behind me, bracing his hands left and right of me as he leans over my shoulder to see what I'm preparing, I fight the urge to step back against him. To beg him to touch me too.

Even worse, so much worse, was the time I was completely drained after a full day at work and a long visit at my parents'. I came home that night, barely able to stay on my feet and Seb stepped up to me without hesitation, lifting me in his arms and carrying me upstairs. He prepared the tub for me, helped me strip with my consent, and took charge of getting me clean.

I will never forget how gentle his fingers were in my hair and on my skin as he leathered me up with soap. During all that, we didn't talk. I just closed my eyes and soaked it up, trusting him completely. He didn't so much as try to make it sexual, and I have no inhibition about him having seen me naked. That night, I fell asleep in his arms as usual.

It's bad enough that my reasons against it are being erased from my mind. There are times where I don't remember why I'm so stubborn at all. The only reason I haven't caved yet is because I know at some point, before my hormones took over, I had very valid arguments against letting him touch me like that.

Honestly though, this morning after Seb came down my throat, never taking his eyes from mine, he caressed my face tenderly, and I nearly jumped his bones right then. Instead, I dragged myself out of the house, saying I was going shopping. Which I am, though shopping seems less fitting than just longingly looking through the shop windows as I wander through the mall. No matter how tempting it is, I can't let myself enter a store. I barely have any money saved even without having to pay my own rent, and spending that on shopping would be idiotic. That remains my firm belief until I pass a lingerie store and spot a matching set of lace underwear in the most stunning dark green teal. My steps falter, and I allow myself to envision myself in it. Envision Sebastian's reaction to me wearing it.

He told me once that his favorite color was dark green because it reminded him of his runs in the forest. It doesn't take a genius to realize those runs are his safe haven, a time where he can let go and relax, even as he pushes himself to the limit. Seeing that matching set, I can't help but think it's a sign. I mean, really, how often do you stumble across that color in clothing items?

Before I can overthink it, I walk inside the store, pick my size, and try it on. It's love at first sight. I haven't felt like myself in a while, but here, standing in front of the mirror wearing perfectly-fitted lingerie, I recognize myself. The party girl that enjoyed the attention of strangers so much. Enjoyed the attention of anyone, really, as long as it was good-natured. I don't let myself dwell on it. Not when my heart is still racing excitedly. I buy the matching set and walk out of the store with new-found anticipation for this evening. Sebastian's not throwing a party. He said he doesn't like his birthday that much and it's a Tuesday, after all. He has school to attend the next morning. That means I have him to myself tonight. And yes, I shouldn't, but I know exactly what I signed up for when I bought that set.

So what if I give in and let him touch me? The tension between us has been building for long enough. More than that, I know he cares about me, and I'm not so scared he'll ditch me once he's had me anymore. I doubt things would be weird between us if we slept together. I don't think there's a reason to panic about the possible change.

We're both adults. It'll be fine. At least I know where we both stand. He told me he has no interest in something serious, so if I let us take the step, nothing will change. We'll remain friends with benefits.

I repeat that to myself all the way home, trying to quell my lingering worry.

When I get home, I'm relieved Sebastian isn't here yet. I put my new clothes into the washer and then take a shower, do my hair, and dress in my new, clean underwear, throwing on a tight dress over that.

I'm just finishing up my makeup when Sebastian comes into the bathroom. He startles when he sees me, and I meet his eyes in the mirror, smiling. "Hey. How was your day?" I ask, happy to be the one to ask it first this time.

He doesn't reply for a second, too busy running his eyes over me in the black dress to speak. I watch him in the mirror, shifting on my feet when I feel myself getting turned on under his heated gaze. Shit, he's on the other side of the room and my skin is burning up. If I didn't already plan on finally giving in tonight, I sure would considering it now.

"Sebastian," I prod slightly, unable to hide my satisfied smirk. His eyes snap to mine, letting me see his blatant approval before blinking it away.

"Sorry." He clears his throat. "Yeah, it was good. Though, the others gave me shit when I told them I was busy tonight."

I set down my mascara and turn to face him. "If you want to see them or ask them to tag along, that's fine. I totally understand." I hate to think I'm the reason he can't spend his birthday with his best friends. I know he's been seeing them a lot less than usual since I moved in, and while I feel guilty, I don't know what to do about it. I never asked him to stop throwing parties or inviting his friends over.

Sebastian smiles softly and steps closer, shaking his head. "We have a reservation for a table for two and I have no intention of changing that. I told you, I'm not a fan of my birthday. Besides, I'm throwing a party this Saturday, they can stop being up my ass then."

251

I chuckle at his assessment and nod my agreement. It's his day. If he wants to spend a quiet evening with me, that's more than fine.

"All right, then, I see you have a head start when it comes to getting ready. I have to take a shower, do you mind?" he asks.

I shake my head, smiling wider. "Please, go ahead. I do remember the offer of a show if I'm not mistaken," I tell him.

The second he realizes what I'm referring to and that I'm proposing to stay right here while he takes a shower, he blushes. "Right." He chuckles, getting over the shock. Then, I have the pleasure of watching him strip, revealing more and more of his golden skin peppered with ink and those carved muscles of his.

Yeah, that's a sight for sore eyes. I don't even try to conceal my ogling when he pulls down his boxers and discards them. Without looking at me, he walks to the shower and turns on the water, giving me a great view of his defined backside. I'm tempted to discard my plan for tonight and just join him right now. I just barely manage to restrain myself.

Sebastian groans and my eyes flick to his, realizing he's staring at me now as he steps under the steaming water. "Stop looking at me like that. Especially now when I know exactly what that look means," he tells me, seeming almost anguished.

I smile innocently. "How?"

"Like you damn well want me to get a boner without even touching me. Wicked troublemaker."

My eyes flick to the apex of his legs, and I nearly laugh when I spot his semi. It's good to know my attention has the same effect on him as his has on me.

"It's a shame we don't have time to take care of that now, I guess. Well, better hurry up or we'll be late for dinner," I tell him, my voice sickly sweet. He has the heart to laugh with me, shaking his head as he turns around to get clean.

Jarah Aurel

Chapter 25

Sebastian

Dinner at a restaurant with Aliena alone is surprisingly easy. I was worried it might feel forced and uncomfortable, coming across as a date when I invited her, but it's not. I should have known Aliena wouldn't mistake this for anything it's not.

As the waiter takes away our finished dishes, asking how we liked our appetizers, Aliena picks up her phone, smiling to herself at whatever she finds there. I try to quell my curiosity but the question as to who texted her is on the tip of my tongue, something close to jealousy turning my stomach. Forcing my gaze from her face, I thank the waiter and tell him the food was great. By the time I'm done saying as much, Aliena has put her phone down again.

"Sorry for that," she tells me, a soft smile still playing on her lips.

"Don't worry about it," I assure her right as my phone chimes in my pocket.

She smiles more widely and gives me a pointed look. "Check it. It's only fair," she insists and while I usually wouldn't, the way she's looking at me is enough to convince me otherwise. Her eyes hold something

254

mischievous. Like she's in on something funny but won't tell me.

I check my phone, cocking a brow at Aliena when I see the message I've received is from her. She sent me a picture.

Wordlessly, I click on it, nearly choking on thin air when it is done loading. Because there she is, the girl currently sitting opposite me, wearing nothing more than a matching lingerie set in my favorite color.

I swallow thickly, having trouble taking my eyes off the photo to look at Aliena. "What is this?" I ask hoarsely.

She shrugs elegantly, throwing me a feline smile. "Consider it your birthday present. Do you like it?" she asks.

My eyes flick back to the picture almost without my permission. I turn my phone off after a few long seconds, chuckling as I try to pull myself together. "Yeah. Fuck, Aliena, yes, I like it. I hate that you showed me this now, though, when we're still a course away from the privacy of our home."

"Two courses," she corrects me. "Don't forget about dessert."

"Oh, sweetheart, I just looked at my dessert. Don't worry, I won't forget," I tell her, satisfied when a blush creeps over her cheeks.

Thankfully, our main course arrives soon, granting me a distraction when all I can think about is how the colorful lace adorned her subtle curves. In the picture, she was sitting on the edge of a bed—my bed—and the thought that she was there wearing it there is enough to make the blood in my body rush south.

Every time I close my eyes, I see her thighs and the swing of her hips, her narrow waist, and, of course, that goddamned cleavage. Her face wasn't in the picture. Smart girl. Not that I'd ever entrust anyone with the sight of her like that. Hell no, that's all mine.

I've seen her in skimpy dresses at parties and I've seen her naked when she was too tired to take a bath by herself but that was different. I barely allowed myself to look at her, too caught up in my concern. This is the first time I've seen so much of her smooth skin in a sexual context.

"You all right there? You got so quiet," she asks halfway through the main course, still smiling. Yeah, she's really satisfied with the reaction I'm giving her.

"I'm brilliant. Just asking myself whether or not I'll get to unpack my present later…," I trail off, hoping damn well she tells me yes. Not that I'd be mad if she sticks to not letting me touch her, but god, I'd love to worship her body the way she deserves.

Aliena's blush is the only thing hinting at her lack of full control and confidence. "Mhm, that's generally how it works," she agrees, watching me closely.

I can't help the small, triumphant groan to slip from my lips. "You're a temptress," I announce, despaired at the thought of another course being in the way of me taking her home.

Aliena merely shrugs, looking very proud of herself. Swallowing the last bite of my meal, I decide the tables need to turn before I lose my mind, so I hook my feet around the legs of her chair and pull her more flushed against her edge of the table. She startles.

I lean forward over the table, lowering my voice as I brush a strand of golden hair behind her ear. She shivers,

256

her eyes fluttering, and I want to kiss her right there and then. That's not the plan, though, and part of me is still scared of her rejection.

Instead, I say, "How about this, sweetheart, I take you home right now, you let me have my dessert, then I'll make you whatever you want myself. Something sweet and sugary since you'll need your energy after that. Then, I show you what we've been missing out on all these weeks. On every counter and up against every wall you'll let me."

When I'm done, she just blinks at me and swallows, her eyes glazed as she thinks about the picture I just painted in her mind. Satisfied I regained some control, I lean back in my chair.

She finally shakes herself and nods. "Yeah. Yes, that sounds good," she confirms hoarsely.

I smile and wave the closest waiter over, asking for the check.

On the ride home, I ask her what she'll want for dessert later, remembering my promise despite my desperation to get home. The only thing keeping me sane enough to think about the possibly missing ingredients is the knowledge that it'll be a lot more annoying to get out of the house again *after* I've made Aliena come.

"Anything with chocolate," she answers quickly.

I nod, settling on a plan for what I'll make later and that I have all the ingredients in my pantry.

It's a good day to know my way around the oven, I'll say, since I have every intention of making good on my promise to fuck Aliena on every flat surface of the damn house. After months of not having touched a woman, I'm

257

eager to make up for lost time with her. God knows I have a lot of orgasms to catch her up on.

Like the gentleman I am, I open the door for Aliena and help her out of the car, only to sling my arms around her waist and lift her over my shoulder as soon as she's on her feet. She yelps, demanding I let her down, but I just laugh and shake my head.

On the elevator ride up, she doesn't stop slapping her hands against my back. Her protests only falter when we're in my apartment, nearing the stairs. Then, she holds on to me for dear life.

"Seb, please. You can't carry me up there. We're going to fall," she tries to reason.

I pat her thigh softly. "Come on, sweetheart, a little trust, please. You know I won't let anything happen to you," I say, taking the first few steps. I work out every day for a reason. Surprisingly enough, the girl over my shoulder doesn't protest anymore, going pliant in my arms.

Once I'm atop the stairs, I head straight for the last room down the hall, throwing Aliena on my bed as soon as I reach it. She bounces twice before getting up on her elbows to glare at me. I smile down at her, my heart racing a mile a second as I wonder what to do next.

I want to kiss her. Fuck, I've been wanting nothing more than to kiss her for a long while now. I just hope today is the day she actually lets me.

I climb over her, nearly groaning when she smiles and lets her knees fall apart to make space for me. My hips settle between her legs and my arms brace on either side of her head, one hand caressing her cheek.

With a voice so hoarse I barely recognize it, I ask, "Please, tell me I can kiss you."

She nods. "You said I was dessert. You can taste me wherever you want."

With an anguished groan, I smash my lips down on hers, the caress on her face becoming a possessive grip. The kiss isn't slow or gentle. No, it's a desperate press of lips, deepened by her when she arches her neck to come closer to me. I nip at her lips, letting my body melt further against hers, and she opens her mouth with a sigh. My tongue seeks entry immediately, greeted by her own as we settle on a fast pace.

God, the times I've imagined this. Imagined her beneath me, her soft body pinned to the mattress as I learn all the ways to touch and please her. My imagination had nothing on the real thing, though.

Aliena's hands unbutton my shirt, never once breaking the kiss, and I follow her lead, rolling up her dress. My fingers brush against the hot skin of her outer thighs, over the lace underwear I know to be green, and finally squeeze her waist. I let go of the black fabric to take in the feel of her, enjoying the way she shudders beneath my touch.

I take my hands off her long enough for her to rip off my shirt. Then, she lifts her upper body, a silent command for me to take off her dress. I do, and when she tries to pull me back down to connect our lips once more, I deny her and lean back, wanting to take her in.

And what a sight she is. Smooth, fair skin, interrupted only by the occasional beauty mark. Almost without my notice, my hands reach out to touch her again, to caress her tummy and feel the sway of her hips. At the gentle contact, something enters Aliena's eyes and she shivers.

Reaching out to grab my wrist before I can reach the waistband of her panties, she breathes out, "Seb." A command to do what, exactly, I'm not sure. All I know is my name on her lips is my new kryptonite. I'd do anything to make her keep saying it.

"Let me look at my present," I protest softly, leaning down to kiss her. "You're beautiful," I whisper against her lips. She shudders again.

I press another chaste kiss to her lips, pulling away a few inches before she can deepen it. Her gentle fingers find their way into my hair, and when she realizes what I'm doing, she goes along, meeting every short contact of my lips readily.

Once my heart rate has finally calmed enough, I take my lips from hers and kiss her cheek instead. Then, the edge of her jaw, the sweet spot below her ear, and her throat, loving the way her pulse flutters beneath my lips. I kiss my way over every inch of her skin, wanting to know it all. To taste it all. When I reach the edge of her bra, I look up to make sure she's still with me. What I didn't expect was the clear need in her eyes, silently urging me on. My resolve to take things slow dwindles, and I pull down the cups, bringing my lips to one of her stiff nipples while my hand plays with the other.

Aliena arches her back, her fingers tightening in my hair as she moans softly. That sound goes straight to my throbbing dick. I'm hyper aware of every reaction. I want to learn just what she likes.

I experimentally skim my teeth against her pebbled skin, and she sighs, squeezing my hair. With a parting kiss, I move on to her other breast, carefully daring to bite the swell of her breast. When that draws a startled sound of appreciation from Aly, I can't help but smile against her skin.

I move on, kissing the valley between her breasts and trailing a line down to her navel. Her breaths are wholly uneven now, something I take great pleasure in. After all the times she got to exert this power over me, I'm happy to have the roles reversed for once.

Reaching the edge of her panties, I take the fabric between my teeth, pulling it away before letting it snap back into place. I bring my hands to her thighs, moving her knees further apart on each side of my face. Already, the scent of her fills the room, and my mouth waters.

Unable to wait any longer, I press a close-mouthed kiss on the most drenched part of her underwear. Aliena gasps, trying to close her legs, but I hold them in place. When her hands leave my hair to grip my wrists, trying to pull them away, I reproach her playfully.

"Little troublemaker, this is my time to play. Now, can you behave, or do you need me to tie up those pretty hands of yours?"

She swallows, her fingers returning to the top of my head and when she caresses my scalp, I nearly melt.

"That's my good girl," I purr. Holding her gaze, I bring my lips back to her center, kissing her through the lace.

When I finally slip off her panties, my mouth wastes no time finding the apex of her legs. I lick her up and down once, parting her folds for me before finding her clit and sucking it into my mouth. Her back arches off the bed as I tear another one of those sinful sounds from her. I shift my hips, never taking my mouth off her as I try to readjust my throbbing erection in my pants. It's pressing painfully against my zipper, and I quickly find moving makes it worse, and stop, trying not to focus on my own pleasure as I feast on her.

She's addictive. I play with her clit, circling and flicking it until I can feel her pulsing beneath my tongue. Before she can come, I pull away and change tactics, unwilling to let this end so quickly. No, I intend to have a lot more fun with her first. My tongue runs through her weeping slit, nudging her entrance.

"Sebastian," Aliena whines as I tease her. I groan at the spark of pleasure hearing her say my name brings me. But, deciding I've been cruel enough denying her orgasm, I stop the teasing and start fucking her with my tongue instead. I do that until I feel she's on the verge of an orgasm again, only this time, I don't deny her the pleasure. Instead, I suck her through it, lapping up every last drop of her release as she spasms and jerks beneath me. Again, her thighs try to close around my head. Again, my fingers dig into her flesh to hold her still.

Without letting her come down, my mouth latches onto her clit again. She cries out, her body jerking at the stimulation on her sensitive bundle of nerves.

"Shh, relax, sweetheart," I whisper against her soaked skin, granting her a short break.

When her breathing is just even enough, and her hands start absently massaging my scalp, my tongue finds her clit again. I go slower this time, making sure her pleasure rises gradually. One hand releases her thigh as I bring two fingers to her entrance, wetting them before slowly pushing inside. A long, deep groan tears from Aliena as she arches her back, clenching around my fingers.

I keep circling her clit, locking eyes with her as my fingers rub against her G-spot. Her breaths start coming in shallow pants, her legs tense against the sides of my head, and her fingers tighten in my hair. This time, when she comes, I don't stop her from squeezing my head with her thighs. No, I keep up my steady assault as she writhes beneath me, coming for longer than before.

When she slumps against the mattress, breathing heavily, I finally raise my head and pull my fingers out of her. I take a second to look at her, face flushed, skin glistening with a sheen of sweat, and eyes closed. She looks perfectly sated.

With one more kiss, I wrap her up in my blanket and say, "Rest for a minute, I'll be right back with your dessert." The only reply I get is a soft hum.

Chapter 26

Aliena

I haven't moved a muscle in the time Sebastian was gone, only stirring when the smell of hot chocolate wafts over me. I open my eyes to see Sebastian walking toward me with a tray. I sit up on the bed, my mouth watering as I take in the small cake.

"One lava cake for the lady. I hope you like it," he says, seeming almost nervous as he settles down next to me and hands me the tray.

"None for you?" I ask, picking up the spoon on the tray.

"Oh, no, I just had dessert. Besides, I might've licked the bowls and spoons clean while the cake was in the oven," he admits, smiling sheepishly.

My eyes latch onto the tilt in his mouth and without thinking, I lean over to kiss him. He doesn't have time to kiss me back before I pull away, but I see a flicker of pleasant surprise on his face before I dig into my cake.

My eyes close as the flavor explodes on my taste buds. "That's fucking awesome," I tell him.

He chuckles. "Such a filthy mouth," he taunts.

I merely glare at him and keep eating. I don't even care that I'm fully naked beneath the sheets. I don't care I gave in and let him kiss me. Well, and a lot more than that. Hell, I'm not even panicking about what I know will happen once I'm done with this. As long as I don't dwell on the fact that I can't sneak out before morning, or that I have nowhere to go when this thing goes to hell, I'm fine.

"So, tell me what's next on your plan?" I prompt before my doubts can creep up on me in the silence.

Sebastian grins, kicking my heart rate up a notch. He muses, "Well, I was thinking once you're done, I'll put away the tray and lay you flat on your back." His fingers gently tug at the edge of the blanket covering me, drawing awareness to it.

"Then, I'll kiss you. We have a lot of that to do to make up for lost time." He arches a brow while I swallow another bite. "Let me think, what's next…" He trails off, humming as he pulls down the sheet to reveal more of my skin. It drops off my breasts, letting the cool air brush against my stiffening nipples.

I manage to swallow two more bites before I'm completely exposed and without the shield of the blanket to save me from his hungry stare. Slowly, teasingly, his fingers start caressing their way across my skin, making it hard for me to focus on finishing the last bit of the cake.

"There, there, sweetheart, finish up," he tells me, even as his fingers brush against the side of my boob.

I swallow another bite and clear my throat. "What comes next?" I ask.

"Mhm, let's see. I think I'll tease you with my fingers for a while, get you all nice and wet for me."

As he says it, I swallow the last bite of the cake with great difficulty. When he sees I'm done, he smiles, his eyes flashing.

"Drink a bit," he urges, nodding to the glass on the tray. I do so without arguing.

Satisfied, Seb reaches for the tray even as he says, "And then, my little troublemaker, I'm going to fuck you so hard you'll leave an imprint on my mattress."

Before I can utter a sound in response, his lips find mine, hungry and demanding. I meet him kiss for kiss, happy to open my mouth and let him deepen the encounter. My hands find his hair again, gripping the thick, dark strands as he lays me down as promised. And then, he's hovering above me again, his knees spreading mine apart to make space for him.

When he leans in, pressing his body to mine, I can feel how hard he is beneath his pants. As if he couldn't help himself and with none of the restraint he showed when he was eating me out, he grinds against me. We share a moan, and I arch my back, pushing my naked chest against his and marveling at the heat coming off him.

The hand cupping my face slowly lets go of my cheek and slides down my body until he's cupping my pussy. When he finds me already wet, he groans against my lips. "So responsive, sweetheart. Look how ready you are for me."

I pull his face back to mine without responding, grinding against his hand. He slips two fingers back inside me, massaging my inner walls and making sure I really am ready. I want to tell him to hurry, that I'm wet enough and aching to have him inside me, but he keeps up his slow coaxing of my pleasure.

266

It's only when I feel the familiar tingles spread from my womb to my toes that he pulls out of me, the bastard. I try to clench around his fingers to keep him there, to make him make me come since I'm *so* close but he merely chuckles.

"No, no, Aliena. The next time you come, it's around my cock," he says in that deep, husky voice of his.

I nod, reaching for his zipper to finally take him from the confines of his pants. My hand finds his erection, wrapping around the silky-smooth skin and pumping it once.

He searches my face, looking almost pained as he stops my hand on him. "With or without a condom?" he grits out, losing that grip on his self-control. We live together, so he knows I'm on the pill and we talked about both being clean.

Since I don't want him to move away from me now, I breathe out, "Without." I grind against his hand again, whispering, "Please," for good measure.

He curses, then kisses me with a new ferocity, and the next thing I know, his broad tip is placed at my entrance. Pulling away, Sebastian trembles all over as he says, "I'm not going to be gentle, baby. Not the first time." With that, he pushes into me with one deep, brutal thrust.

I grit my teeth and breathe through my nose as I try to make my body relax and accommodate the feeling of him inside of me. He's long, painfully so, with a girth that goes with it, and while I knew that already, it doesn't lessen the slight sting as he stretches me. I might be far from a virgin but it's been months since I've had sex.

Sebastian's lips hover over mine as he keeps himself still, seeming to hold his breath. After a second, my body finally relaxes, and his hand starts caressing my cheek.

267

"That's it, sweetheart. Relax for me," he mutters against my lips. Then, starting to move slightly, he adds, "Fuck, you're tight."

Despite his warning that he won't be gentle, his first few thrusts are slow, experimental. When I've finally relaxed fully and the sting of him turns into pleasure, he asks, "Okay now?"

I nod, keeping my eyes closed as I hold his hands where they are next to my face. He leans back, sitting on his heels as he grips my waist tightly, adjusting me, all without ever pulling out. When his hands move from my waist to my ass to hoist me up a few inches, his tip hitting the end of me, an embarrassingly guttural moan tears from me.

"Spread your feet apart," he instructs roughly. I do as he says, finally opening my eyes to see him looking down at where he's entering me. Following his gaze, my toes curl.

He squeezes my flesh, his pace picking up enough to make me scoot up on the bed. "Grip the headboard," he finally tells me. Once I do, the last of his restraint seems to bleed away, and he pounds into me as roughly as he promised.

I cling onto the headboard for dear life, my limbs shaking with the effort to stay in this position even as he does most of the work. It's worth the strain, though. The angle at which he's hitting me is heavenly.

"That's it, sweetheart. So fucking good," he moans. His praise worms its way through my body, warming my chest and adding to the pleasure gathering in my womb. My inner walls clench around him, eager to please, and when he groans, I nearly smile.

"Aliena, I won't last long if you keep doing that. It's been six months," he grits, his nails digging father into my skin. I like the sting of it, like that he's being rough on me, so I repeat my earlier motion and enjoy the way he grunts.

"You like that, don't you? You like making me lose it. You like it rough?" he asks and although his words are vulgar, they turn me on impossibly more. As if feeling it too, Sebastian treats me to an exceptionally hard thrust. I cry out softly, my toes curling as the pleasure within me reaches a high.

"Again. Please. I'm so close," I gasp, desperate for my release. My hands grapple with the sheets, twisting them in my fingers as my muscles strain. Sebastian seems only too happy to deliver, thrusting down into me again and again, his grip on my ass keeping me in place as he does, in fact, fuck me into the mattress.

I take in the vein pulsing on his neck, his strong, clenched jaw, and those dark, determined eyes. Our gaze locks as I feel myself tumbling over the edge, but as I reach my peak, I throw my head back and close my eyes firmly, unwilling to show myself too vulnerable.

Sebastian doesn't stop his ruthless thrusts, and he doesn't fall over the edge with me as expected. Instead, he pulls out of me when my body goes lax and the waves of my orgasm subside. Before I can wonder about it or feel bad, he effortlessly twists my body so I'm lying on my stomach. Then his hands are pulling up my ass, and his tip is back against my entrance. "I'm not done with you yet, sweetheart," he tells me, and I hear the strain in his voice. He curses under his breath. "I wish you could see yourself right now. So fucking beautiful with your back arched and your swollen pussy on display for me."

269

His body covers mine as he leans over me, kissing the curve of my neck. With one smooth thrust, he's back inside me, seated to the hilt. He sighs against my skin. "You feel like heaven. For fuck's sake, Aliena, why do you have to be so perfect? You make me want to come so badly, it hurts," he admits.

Every word nuzzles itself deeper into my chest, making me feel all warm and fuzzy. My sex clenches around him, the only reply I can manage.

Pulling back, he says, "One more, baby. Give me one more."

While my legs shake at the mere thought of another orgasm, I nod against the sheets. In this moment, with my body and control rendered over so entirely, I think I'd agree to anything he asked, and the thought doesn't scare me as much as it should.

He pulls out almost completely before slamming back in to the hilt. Again and again, he hits the end of me, making my fingers dig into the sheets desperately as I try to stay upright. The sounds leaving me are barely human, and I'm glad they're muffled by the mattress. Sebastian, at last, moans almost mindlessly, his praise for me the only interruptions.

When his hand curls around my hip and two of his fingers press against my sensitive clit, my body jerks, my muscles locking up as the pleasure that's been steadily building explodes through my body. I might've moaned his name, but I can't tell for sure. My mind is barely functioning as my skin sparks and the waves of my fourth orgasm tonight wreck me.

Behind me, I'm faintly aware Sebastian has stopped thrusting, holding himself deep inside of me and grinding his hips against mine as he comes. If his hands weren't holding me in place, I would collapse for sure.

When he is coming down from his climax, he pulls out of me, finally letting me do just that. With a sigh, I curl up in a ball, trying to gather my bearings and bring my mind back into my body from whatever cloud it's currently on.

Two gentle hands caress my skin, the gesture so tender I can hardly stand it. I know I should get up, if not to leave like my first instinct tells me to do, then to go to the toilet before I make a mess of things.

But when I try to get up, I wince and the hands on my shoulder gently ease me back down. "Tell me what you need," Sebastian asks, kissing my shoulder.

I sigh, soaking it up before I shake my head and get up again. "I need to go to the bathroom. I'm afraid you can't help me there," I tell him lightly. He just cocks an eyebrow at the challenge, and the next thing I know, I'm in his arms and he's carrying me to the adjoined room.

"Sure I can," he retorts as he walks. Meanwhile, my cheeks flush red when he sets me down right in front of the toilet. Again, I wince slightly at the discomfort he left between my legs, no matter that I like feeling sore. Sebastian, for his part, looks a little worried.

He cups my cheek, frowning. "I'm sorry if I hurt you," he says, but I'm already shaking my head, smiling softly.

"Don't be. I like it. Now, get out. I'll manage to get back to bed by myself," I tease, desperate to end this confusingly tender moment. I don't need him to take care of me, to look at me like he cares. Not right now, at least. It's too intimate and feels like a violation of the rules.

No, I need a second to push away my lingering panic of change or rejection and remind myself it's all right. That I don't have to walk away first because this is Sebastian, my *friend*, and he won't be weird about seeing me in the morning. Not when he's been doing that every day for a while now.

Chapter 27

Sebastian

For once, I wake up before Aliena. It's all the confirmation I need to know I must have really powered her out last night. Satisfaction curls in my stomach like a fuzzy animal as I hold her naked body against mine. She's soft and warm, absolutely heavenly.

Thoughts of last night flash through my mind, making enough blood rush to my semi to make me fully hard. God, I can almost still hear her moans and whimpers. Knowing I was the reason for them is enough to make me feel a foot taller.

I press a lingering kiss on her shoulder, reveling in the way she nuzzles closer even in sleep. If only her round ass didn't push up against my erection, making a new wave of need rush over me. I sigh and untangle myself from her before the temptation to wake her up with my dick in her tight heat becomes too great.

While we touched up on a few fantasies, we haven't cleared *that* particular idea, and I'd die before I fucked her without her consent.

Instead, I resort to something I know I'm allowed to do. I gently turn her on her back and peel the sheet from

273

her body like she's done to me in my sleep many times. I kiss my way down her breasts and her tummy so gently she doesn't stir and finally position myself between her legs. With my first kiss on her clit, she startles awake, and her wide eyes find mine.

"Morning, beautiful," I tell her, spreading her legs for me. With the granted access, I place a kiss on her entrance.

Aliena bites her lip. "Morning," she murmurs. Her chest is already rising and falling with heavy, uneven breaths and for a second, I'm too weak to deny my gaze to lock onto her moving breasts. Memories of how beautifully they filled my hand rush through my mind, and I reach up to cup them.

Aliena's eyes flutter shut, and she barely makes a sound as I slowly coax an orgasm out of her by teasing her clit and breasts. Once her body relaxes again, I come up to give her a deep kiss.

"Are you still sore?" I ask.

The corner of her sinful lips tips up, and she shakes her head, opening her legs for me and letting me bury myself inside of her.

This time, I'm not driven by the same desperation and pent-up need. No, this time, I take it slow, enjoying having Aliena beneath me as long as I can , so damn compliant for once.

I know without a shadow of a doubt that after this morning, our old routine will change.

——

By the time Thursday rolls around, I could blindly draw a map of Aliena's body and all the places she likes to be touched most. After round one on Wednesday morning, I went for my jog while Aliena got ready for work. Our evening looked the same as always but after dinner, while she was doing the dishes, I came up from behind her and started kissing her neck, something I'd been dreaming about for weeks. Every time we were in a similar situation, honestly. She seemed to like it too, tilting her head to grant me more access and leaning back into me.

Then, well, I did a little more than kiss her neck, and the dishes were forgotten. When we were done, I set her on the kitchen counter, finished doing the dishes, and put everything in place. My roommate seemed very happy with me once I was done and pulled me in for a kiss, opening her thighs to let me step in between. The woman's insatiable, and since I *did* promise to fuck her on every surface of our home, I was happy to discover it.

She slept in my arms as always, but when she turned that night to lay her head on my chest and sighed contently, I couldn't deny the dangerous adoration spreading through my mind and body like a wildfire.

It wasn't lust or attraction. It was something deeper and entirely foreign.

This morning, she woke up before me again and then treated me to her usual wake-up call. Although, before she could make me come, I pulled her up my body and let her ride me instead. With the way I know she can dance, it was no surprise she moved on top of me with an ease I'd never witnessed before.

Now, I'm at school, trying and failing to stop thinking about her.

"Dude, did you hear a word I just said?" a gruff voice breaks through the fog clouding my mind as someone shoves me.

My head whips up to glare at Andrew. "What?" I snap, a little harsher than intended.

"I told you to get up. Class is over," he points out, unbothered by my bad mood. I look around the room and realize most of my classmates have already filed out. Shit, I don't think I heard a single word the professors said today.

"What's up your ass? You've been weird all day. Did something happen on your birthday?" Mattheo chimes in, looking at me funnily.

"No, all good. I'm just tired," I deflect.

"Right. Tired. I don't even want to know what you were doing all night," Lily says, looking like she has a suspicion she's not happy about.

"You mean who. You don't want to know who he was doing all night to leave him this tired and agitated," Andrew provides helpfully, earning himself a punch from his girlfriend and me at the same time.

Mattheo, for once, resorts to merely glaring at me, clearly sharing Andrew's theory and not liking it. He still thinks there's something going on between Aly and me, and that I should be loyal to her.

He's right, of course, and I have been. Since I met her. He really has no reason to glare.

"It's whom, you idiot," Lily mutters under her breath, so quietly I feel like she's trying not to be a know it all, but she just can't help it. She changes the topic. "Anyway, let's talk about your party on Saturday. I checked with Aly, and she said she has Sunday off, so she'll be there."

I know that, of course. That's why I'm throwing the party on Saturday in the first place.

"Cool. Yeah, there's not much to talk about. It's the same as always," I tell them. When I see Lily's mouth open to argue, I cut her off. "It is, Lil. I don't celebrate my birthday, certainly not with a party. I mean it, don't try to bring gifts or something along the lines."

It's a tradition, of sorts, but not a very fun one. Like all things that have gone to hell in my life, my father was the cause of this certain rule. After what might have been my eighth or ninth birthday, the year where I wanted nothing more than a mountain bike so I could ride through the forest alongside Mattheo, I decided I'd been let down one too many times to keep getting my hopes up.

I'd been hinting at my wish for a long time, and my father indulged me. He confirmed I would have so much fun with Matteo on our new bikes, spun a whole tale until I truly believed my happiness *depended* on that stupid materialistic possession. He even paid someone to all but sculpt a mountain bike with wrapping paper so on the morning of my birthday I thought that's what I would get. But there was nothing under the wrapping paper, and when I turned my confused gaze to my father, he clicked his tongue and told me I better not start crying.

Honestly that might have been the only reason why one treacherous tear rolled down my cheek, just his words and the quick way he could snatch away my good mood. It was stupid and I only have myself to blame for the way he lashed out with harsh words as he always does when I show weakness.

"I just told you not to cry like a little girl. Are you so dimwitted you can't even follow a single simple

instruction? God, I've let you spend too much time with your weak hearted mother and your rotten grandmother. They've spoiled you senseless. It's time you realize life isn't sunshine and roses and if you want something you have to fight for it. Go to your room and don't you dare come down for dinner. I don't want to see you for the rest of the day."

He'd done similar things before, isolating or manipulating me, anything to make me feel humiliated or like a disappointment. Frankly, he'd managed to ruin every birthday I'd ever had as long as I celebrated them, so instead of allowing him the power to ruin a special day, I decided it should stop being one.

And my friends aren't my father, sure, but expectations only ever lead to a letdown, and I'm tired of giving that one particular day any more energy than it needs. I'm over it.

She pouts. "So, no cake?" she asks slowly.

I laugh and shake my head. "Sorry to disappoint, but no. There won't be cake."

Andrew throws his arm over his girlfriend's shoulder at the same time she turns around, mumbling something that sounds suspiciously close to, "Monster."

Still laughing, I follow my friends to our next class, glad that for even a second, they got my mind on something other than a certain honey-eyed woman.

I'm once again in bed with Aliena, only this time, before she can reach for my belt, I stop her gently. "Hang on. I had an idea I wanted to talk to you about," I tell her.

She pulls away so she can look at me without craning her neck. "Sounds saucy. Hit me," she demands, and I chuckle at the impatience thick in her voice.

To placate her, I offer her a short kiss, which she accepts happily. It's funny how she refused to let my lips so much as brush against hers for weeks and now she seems to enjoy few things more.

"Well, I have this box in my bedside drawer with some stuff in it," I admit, smiling sheepishly when Aliena's eyebrows rise. "It was a gift from the guys a few years ago, but I've never used it. Well, not the things in this particular box, but I have done things like that before. And I liked it, so I was wondering if maybe you were interested in trying something out." To my great despair, I can feel my cheeks burn up as I stumble over my words like a moron.

"What sort of things are we talking about?" Aliena asks carefully, reminding me just how badly I just was at explaining.

Instead of repeating the fiasco, I simply grab the box and set it on the bed, revealing the ties and ropes that lie on top. As I said, harmless stuff. Basically vanilla.

Of course, beneath those things are a few whips and crops of different sizes, but while I've spanked past partners with my hand or a belt, I've never tried using actual whips. I'd have to read up on it before ever using it on Aliena. The same goes for the other toys beneath.

Aliena takes a long second to look at what I revealed. Finally, she reaches for a red silk band that would be just perfect to bind her wrists.

She smiles shyly when she meets my eyes. "I've never really used accessories in bed, to be honest. Well, other

279

than my toys but only when I'm alone. I think I'd let you tie me up, though. If only to try," she explains.

My heart skips an excited beat. "Yeah? You're sure? I don't want you to feel any pressure to agree if you don't feel like it. I'm happy either way," I assure her.

"I know. I'm sure. I trust you. Besides, I have always been a little curious and since I like it when you pin my wrists, I'd say this is a safe bet."

At her admission, my heart doesn't skip a beat. It stumbles over itself and then misses two. She trusts me. I don't think three little words ever made me feel prouder.

"Okay, if you're sure. Now, let's backpedal to those toys you mentioned. Are they here?" I ask, watching her cheeks burn up crimson. There's my answer. "Tell me, have you used them since you moved in?"

Aliena shrugs nonchalantly but it doesn't contain the ease it usually does. I narrow my eyes, my amusement heightening. "Oh, you did. What about this room? Have you used them in this bed?" I go on. If she says yes, I might as well forget all about tying her up and take her right now. Some possessive part of me likes the thought that she pleasured herself in my room, on my bed when I wasn't here. Breathing in my scent on the sheets, remembering how I held her…

Sadly, Aliena shakes her head now. "Of course, not! This is your bed. No, I…they're in my room," she finally admits.

"First off, this is *our* room. You sleep here every night. Second, do you want me to use them? On you?" It would be a lie to say I didn't get excited at the prospect of it.

I can work her up to an orgasm perfectly fine without any assistance, but a toy can add some extra variety.

If anything, her blush deepens, and I don't understand why she's so shy all of a sudden. I always figured she'd be as loud and outspoken about all things concerning sex. She owns her body like she knows exactly what she wants, but maybe that was a misconception. I hate the thought of making her uncomfortable.

I reach for her hand and give it a squeeze. "Sweetheart, if I'm crossing a line, just let me know."

"No, you're not. It's just, I mean, you don't really need them, do you? It's not like you have trouble making me come," she mumbles. When she looks up and sees me smiling like a Cheshire cat, she glares at me. "Ugh, forget I said that. Your ego really doesn't need any brushing up to."

"Right, right. Already forgotten. Now, will you answer my question if I'm not making you uncomfortable?"

"Yes, Sebastian. I'd gladly let you use them," she drawls, shoving my shoulder. "Let's move over to my room. I don't want to move my things." I don't mention that it's not her room again. That the room we're currently in is *our* room and that's the end of it.

Getting off the bed, I reach out my hand to help her follow my lead. She accepts it and walks ahead down the hall. As I follow her, something else crosses my mind.

"Oh, I forgot to ask you something else. About Saturday when our friends come over, do you want to tell them? That you live here, I mean? I know that would come with a lot of explaining more private things for you but maybe it's time to stop lying to all of them."

I see her shoulders move with a sigh rather than hear it. "You're probably right, but I don't think I can do it. Those private things you mentioned are complicated as hell, and I honestly don't want to spend my evening explaining my family drama. For now, I'd rather keep those things to myself."

"And what if someone asks to give you a ride home? I doubt Mattheo will let you walk home alone again." I bite back a smile as I remember how I beat him up the last time. Sure, it wasn't my brightest hour as a friend but a vindictive part of me still takes great pleasure in it.

"Then I'll tell them I'm spending the night. I've always had a room, after all. It's not so unimaginable I'd take advantage of it."

Deciding this is her choice to make, I give in. "As you wish." And then I follow her into her room, perking up at the prospect of exchanging the daunting memories of banging on her door as she let my best friend fuck her with some good ones.

Chapter 28

Aliena

Sebastian is silent as I dig through my underwear drawer, reaching for the very back of it where I know my toys are hidden. Even with my back to him, my skin pricks with awareness of his gaze on me. I can't believe I really agreed to this. I don't know whether to be proud of myself for having let him in enough that I trust him with this or mortified.

When my fingers finally grasp onto the smooth surface of one of my toys, I let out a triumphant "aha" like an idiot. Slightly sheepish, I turn around with three different things in my hand. Three objects I never thought I'd show another living being, and yet a part of me is turned on by this perceived taboo.

I get on the bed next to him and lay them out. "You pick," I offer.

His answering smirk is wicked. "Do I have to?"

God, his unabashed flirting is turning me into a nervous, shy wreck. I'm so unused to these feelings, it's not even funny.

Usually, I'm the unflappable one. The flirt, the tease, the seductress, as Mattheo used to call me. I wear my confidence like a shield, using it to come across as though nothing could hurt me.

I don't have that safety net around Sebastian. Too much has happened between us, too many secrets revealed and walls lowered to put on an act around him. It gives him the kind of power over me no one else has ever had, and I don't possess the will to stop it.

Trying to cling to a semblance of normalcy, I act nonchalant as I shrug. "You can try your way through them and then decide which one you prefer, I guess." I keep my voice level even though the thought makes me nervous as much as it excites me.

"Oh, I have every intention of seeing which one you prefer in action, sweetheart." A soft shiver rushes down my spine at the promise. "Now, take your clothes off," he adds, his voice unnaturally deep and authoritative.

Of their own free will, my hands follow the order and I find myself topless in a few seconds. When I reach for the waistband of my pants, I'm a little more tentative.

I've never been particularly shy in the bedroom. Maybe this is just my being eager to please Sebastian. I feel like with him, it matters. Not that he would judge me more harshly than any one-night stand. I believe the contrary to be true for sure. I just never cared what any of them thought since I knew I'd never see them again.

I shrug out of my pants and underwear and then hesitate. Sebastian, probably seeing my nerves written all over me, reaches out and cups my face. He presses a tender kiss to my lips, and when he pulls away, he's smiling. It sends an uncomfortable pang right through my chest.

"Do you trust me, sweetheart?" he asks softly, and I know no matter my reply, he'd accept it.

I nod.

"Good. Lie on your back." His words are rough. Hot. I shiver and follow his command easily. Leaning close, he speaks against my skin as he adds, "Put your hands above your head so I can tie them."

He watches as I do and then carefully starts wrapping the silk around my wrists in a figure-eight, just tight enough to prohibit getting free on my own but not so tight to restrict the blood flow to my hands. He tugs gently on the silk and then looks at me, seeming satisfied.

"Is it comfortable?" he asks.

"It's perfect," I confirm, my voice shaky.

"If you change your mind at any given time, just tell me."

"Of course. Seb, you're not introducing me to god knows what. I can still move my arms when it comes down to it. Stop worrying," I tell him, no matter how cute his concern is. I can't deal with that sort of thing.

Nodding, his lips turn into a dazzling smile once again. "Okay, then. I'd say we start with the black one. It looks the most harmless," he announces, referring to my black, tear-shaped vibrator. Looking at me for approval, I merely nod.

He picks up my toy and turns it on, startling when it buzzes to live almost aggressively. I can't help it, I laugh at that. "There are different settings," I provide.

He beams at me. "How lovely. So much to try out." He quickly clicks through the settings before spreading my legs for him to kneel in between. A glance at my center is enough to tell him that although nothing has happened yet,

I am already glistening with my arousal. He swallows, his eyes growing dark with obvious lust.

"Be a good girl and don't move your hands, okay? Lest I have to get the rope from the other room and tie your wrists to the bedpost." Not trusting my voice to be even anymore, I nod. He's killing me here, letting me wait naked, tied up, and spread before him but not touching me. His words are the only caress I get, and every time he speaks in that deep, husky voice, it feels as if his lips are attached to my throbbing clit.

Finally, the rumbling of the vibrator breaks the silence in the room. Sebastian brings the pointy tip to the side of my right breast, watching me carefully as he draws a tight circle around my nipple. He repeats the motion on the other breast, never quite touching my nipple, and that alone has me whining for him to get on with this. When the silky tip finally does brush over my pebbled skin, my back arches off the bed and my legs try to close on instinct. Of course, Sebastian sitting in between them stops me from getting that sort of relief, and I am left to lie there, writhing uselessly as he plays with my sensitive flesh.

By the time he moves on, trailing the toy down my stomach and heading where I really want him, I'm dripping onto the bed beneath me. He widens his kneeling stance, forcing my legs apart too, and then moves the tip of the toy down the outside of my pussy. Left and right, he repeats that slowly without ever touching my clit or entrance.

"Sebastian, please. Enough teasing," I eventually beg. At the sight of his satisfied expression, I don't even have it in me to feel embarrassed.

"But of course, my sweetheart." He brings the vibrator to my center, wetting it with my arousal before moving it up to circle my clit. At the first contact with my swollen bundle of nerves, my body jerks violently. Sebastian's unoccupied hand finds my stomach, pressing me down to keep me in place.

"Mhm, maybe this is the wrong setting," he finally muses, clicking the button to change it. The vibrations turn faster, almost so much so that the buzzing is numbing. "No, this one won't do," Sebastian quickly realizes, pressing the button again.

This setting is inconsistent, going from soft to hard vibrations every few seconds. Sebastian clearly likes it. "Now, this looks like something suitable for edging," he guesses right.

And so he does, repeatedly driving me to the edge with tight circles until my body is buzzing and I'm not even sure what a full-blown orgasm feels like anymore. Hell, I'm so sensitive that every time the vibrator presses directly onto my clit, I damn near thrash on the bed.

"Seb, please, it's too much," I finally whimper, slumping against the mattress when the buzzing turns off.

Sebastian comes down to kiss me. "I love the way you beg," he whispers against my lips. Then, pulling back, he adds, "Let's grant your clit a short break and move on to this. Tell me, does this vibrate too?" he asks, motioning to the long, curved, slender vibrator.

I nod, and despite my hypersensitivity, my anticipation grows.

"Good to know. First though, drink this. Can't have you dehydrated after losing so many fluids," he teases, making me blush embarrassedly.

Between how he has me sweating and my pussy weeping, I guess he's right, but it's still a reality I've *never*

287

talked about with a sexual partner. I mean, just the word *fluids* sounds taboo.

Maybe that's the downside of never having a steady partner. I am not used to having any sort of trust and casual comfort toward my hookups. Hence, the communication aspect of the entire ordeal is entirely new to me.

Sebastian, oblivious to my wandering thoughts, nudges a cool glass of water against my lips. I oblige, despite my discomfort at needing his help for such a mundane task. It's not like my own hands are of any use right now.

Once he deems me hydrated enough, he sets the glass back on the nightstand and picks up the second vibrator. This time, the foreplay doesn't last as long. No, he wets the toy by running it along my slit a few times before slowly starting to work it inside me, all without turning it on. When he meets an initial resistance, he pulls the toy out and circles my entrance again. Then, he slowly pushes it further inside of me, making me gasp and arch off the bed. Shit, that's really freaking cold.

"You okay?" he asks, running a soothing hand down my thigh.

I nod. "Just cold."

"Oh, it'll warm up in no time, I'm sure. I remember how hot your perfect pussy is," he insists, starting to move it in and out of me. It's shorter than his dick by far and has a smaller girth. Still, the curve of it repeatedly hits all the right spots inside me, and I quickly feel tingles return.

When Sebastian turns on the vibrations, I finally cry out. Within seconds, I'm on the verge of an orgasm, and realizing that, Sebastian quickly turns the toy off again.

"Well, shit, sweetheart, I think you just revealed your favorite. Or did all my edging before make you get there so fast?" he tsks.

I don't answer, can't answer. I'm too frustrated. I want to come so badly, it's almost painful. So, I do the only thing I can do, I desperately clench around the toy inside of me, making myself moan.

Sebastian tuts playfully. "There, there, don't go all solo on me. I decide when you come tonight."

"Please," I whine.

"Soon, baby. We have one more toy to try out. One I am very eager to try out," he muses, looking where I know my wand lies.

Slowly, he pulls the second toy out of me, leaving me empty and aching but before I can be too sad about it, a dull buzzing noise bounces off the walls and my eyes snatch onto the wand he's now holding. "I've seen this a lot," he confesses, smiling wickedly.

And so he brings my last toy, already turned on, to my wet entrance like he's done with those before. Once it's wet and glistening, he turns it on and brings it to my throbbing clit.

Again, my legs try to close without success and so they shake around Sebastian's body. My hands ball into fists with the effort to keep them above my head, my nails digging into my skin deliciously.

Feeling my pleasure build in my womb, immobile as I am, spreading tingles all the way to my toes, I moan, "Seb." Whether it's meant to tell him not to stop or to warn him of how close I am, I don't know. All I know is that the next thing I know, my back is arching off the bed, my muscles tense, and my toes curl as I come hard. Sebastian keeps the wand in place, riding me through the waves of pleasure until I'm slumping on the bed, my legs shaking and my hips writhing to get away from the stimulation.

The toy finally shuts off and I groan, unwilling to open my eyes again. I'm beat. I hope the next thing on Sebastian's plan is to give me a break because I need a second to regenerate.

I feel the bed dip under his disappearing weight and open my eyes to see him gather my toys. Then, he moves my arms so my tied hands are in front of me and covers me with a blanket, kissing my cheek. "I'll clean these up and be right back to take care of you, okay, sweetheart?"

Tired but happily sated, I nod, glad for a second to just lie here. Then, without another word or kiss, Sebastian rushes out of the room to go to the nearest bathroom, I assume.

I rest my eyes for a bit, listening to the water run nearby. It's only then I realize that I could use a bathroom break too, so I hope Sebastian will be back soon.

When his steps finally come closer, I'm so relieved I could cry. I really need to use the bathroom and the sound of continuously running water isn't helping. If my guess is correct, I'd say he's filling the tub for me. For all my discomfort with intimacy, I find myself smiling at the thought. He'd said he would take care of me. Just this once, I guess I'll let him.

But when he steps into my room, I instantly know something is wrong and my smile drops. I try to straighten and sit up, bracing myself for whatever he's about to say only to find myself incapable since my hands are still tied up.

The knot in my stomach tightens as I watch him pace the room, searching the ground for something. Finally, he finds his shirt on the floor next to the bed and hurriedly puts it on.

I swallow around the rejection clogging my throat, forcing myself to ask, "Seb? What's wrong?"

As if he'd forgotten I was there at all, his eyes snap to mine, and he winces at the sight. That alone is like a bucket of ice dumped over my head. I mean, really? He winces at the sight of me?

"I'm sorry. I'm really sorry, Aliena, but I have to go," he rambles barely able to meet my eyes. It's a good thing too because mine are currently blurring up and I can't seem to stop it.

"What?" is all I ask, a broken whisper that makes him grimace again. Still, he won't look at me, already inching toward the door.

"I know this isn't what I promised but my mom just texted me. It's an emergency. She needs me, I'm really sorry. I'll make it up to you, I promise. Your bath should be done soon and I'll try to be back before long," he mumbles weakly, meeting my eyes just fleetingly, and I realize he's really leaving. Right now. While my hands are still tied up.

The lump in my throat is painful but I force myself to swallow around it and say, "Wait, Seb," trying to get him to look back and realize I need his help to free my hands. Only he is no longer standing in the doorway, and wherever he is, my voice isn't loud enough to reach him.

So, I just lie there for the minute it takes him to leave and get to the elevator below. As soon as I hear the ding announcing his departure, the first sob wrenches itself from my throat, unreasonable betrayal settling deep in my chest and chasing away all the warmth he placed there before.

He just left. After promising he'd take care of me. He left first. That realization hits me like a ton of bricks. As does the rejection that follows closely. This is what I've always been scared of, why I have all those rules about leaving first set in place. So I don't feel like an unwanted ragdoll, tossed to the side and done with.

I try to tell myself not to take this so personally. His mother is family, and if she needs him, she's his first priority, rightly so. After all, he's not my boyfriend. Cuddling after sex is boyfriend stuff. Our mistake was disregarding those lines by sleeping together every night.

But I'm still tied up and incapable of getting out on my own. I can feel myself panicking at my utter helplessness as I try to tug my wrists apart. They don't budge, the silk not giving me an inch to possibly slip out. My next breath stalls in my throat. *I can't get out of this.*

The sense of dread washes over me and I can sense the color draining from my face. It makes me feel powerless and weak. Incapable.

It reminds me too much of my incapability of changing my shitty situation growing up. Too much of my mother and the times my father would take his anger out on me. *Always out of control. Always helpless.*

A familiar weight settles on my chest, heavy and suffocating. I scream through the tears, trying and failing to rip my hands from my restraints. I can't believe this is happening. Can't believe I'm having a panic attack, tied up, naked, and alone.

Chapter 29

Sebastian

"It's happening again" that's all I can think about as I race toward my parents' estate. For god's sake, thirty minutes. That's how long it took for me to see my mother's message. I was so wrapped up in Aliena that, of course, I didn't check my phone. Still, I can't help but blame myself.

My mother needed me thirty minutes ago and I was too busy to notice.

"It's happening again" I know what she means, of course. My piece of shit father is out, cheating while my mother is crying about him.

Growing up, my mother often tried to hide that part of her marriage from me, but every once in a while, when she was unable to stifle her sobs, I'd find her, head in her hands and curled up against a wall, nearly hysterical.

She's scared he'll leave her. That one of these times, his affair will turn into her divorce and his new marriage like it did with her, and she's so scared to lose him, despite the fact that he's a jerk.

I don't get it, I never have. Why would she fight for him when the way he treats her barely meets the bare

293

minimum, and yet I could never ignore her when she felt bad about it either.

When I reach my parents' place, I jump out of my car and get into the house, my worry spurring me on. I can't believe this is where I am now. Not when I had so much planned for Aliena. I feel like a piece of shit just thinking about her and that sad look on her face when I told her I had to leave.

I told her I would take care of her and then I flaked. I know it's unacceptable. Especially after I asked her to trust me. The only thing soothing my guilt just slightly is knowing I already prepared her a bath before I left, at least. It's not how I wanted things to go but she can soak a while and maybe, if my mother's not feeling too bad, I'll be back at my apartment before she knows it.

But something hits me at that moment and my steps falter, dread washing over me like a bucket of ice. I come to a halt in the middle of the stairs leading to the first floor, slowly shaking my head to myself as I realize Aliena can't take a bath. Not really. Not with her hands still bound.

Oh, god. A wave of nausea hits me, my mistake dawning on me. I can't believe it slipped my mind to untie her. *Did I really forget?* Maybe I didn't? I can't remember if I went through the motions in my hurry or not.

The possibility that I did sits entirely wrong with me. Fuck. I reach for my phone with shaky fingers, intent on calling her when a pained sob hits my ear. My head snaps up, looking in the direction of my mom's room and then back at my phone. I'm conflicted only for a second before my mother sobs again, sounding as if she is choking on something. I pocket my phone again and rush up the rest of the stairs to reach my mom.

I find her curled up in the far corner of her room, her sweat-slicked, dark hair sticking to her face as she cries desperately. Cursing to myself, I crouch down in front of her, reaching out to pull her into my arms as my heart breaks. I hate seeing her like this. Hate to think she's been like this for over half an hour already.

"Shh, Mama. I'm here. You're not alone. It's okay," I murmur against the top of her head, squeezing her tightly in an attempt to hold her together so she can stop falling apart. It doesn't seem to matter how old I get, whenever this happens I feel like a little boy all over again, following the sound of his mother's sobs just to find her in a position that made him scared she was dying. Barely breathing through her sobs and entirely unresponsive.

"Please, calm down. You need to breathe," I urge when I realize just how choppy her breaths are. I pull away enough to wipe her hair from her wet face, cupping her cheeks to get her to look at me. Only to have her looking right through me as she trembles and sobs.

My brows crease with worry. She's having a panic attack, and I don't know what to do. I've never seen her like this. I've never let it come to this before.

"Mama, listen to me. Just listen to my voice. You need to breathe, okay? Do it with me. Come on," I beg her, trying to do what I did to help Aliena that time she had a panic attack.

Slowly, painfully slowly and after a lot of desperate convincing, my mom finally catches on to what I'm saying and slows her breathing in time with mine.

"Hijo," she finally sobs, recognizing me at last. She throws her arms around my neck. "I'm sorry. I'm sorry I had to text you. That you had to come here. I should be able

295

to handle this alone," she speaks choppily, each broken word tearing deeper into my chest.

"No, Mama, don't say that. Don't apologize. You did nothing wrong." It's not her fault I left Aliena the way I did. She couldn't have known I was with someone. That's all on me. I'm still glad she texted me, though, as messed up as it may be. I hate to think what might've happened if I hadn't come to help.

As she keeps crying in my arms, my hate for my father festers. He knows what he's doing to her, and I'm sure he gets off on it, this power play of his. After the first time I saw her like this, she made me promise not to tell him anything, but stupid as I was, eager to help my mom and unaware of the true nature of their relationship, I went to my dad and told him she was upset that night. I had still been under the impression that despite all his faults, he was a hard worker and that's why he was working late. I didn't know it was only an excuse to fuck other women. That day when I told him I'd found his hysterical wife on the cold bathroom floor while he was off cheating, his eyes lit up. *Happy* she was so hooked on him, so scared of losing him she couldn't even breathe. He knew then he had absolute control over her, and it was my fault for confirming it.

I want to tell her to stop wasting her tears on such a screwup, that he's not worth all her love and pain, and that she should get a divorce and move on. Knowing it would only upset her further, I don't say any of that. Instead, I eventually move us to the bed where she cries herself to sleep, still clinging to me. As she quiets and drifts off, my mind goes back to the girl I left at home.

Did she manage to get out of her binds by now? I really hope so. I don't care if she cut the silk up into a million pieces, I just hope that she's fine.

I want to call her, but I couldn't do that without waking my mom, and now she's finally resting, I can't risk it. I want to text her but don't, out of fear it would be considered a cowardly move. After all, what I did isn't something I can apologize for over text.

In the end, I convince myself she's fine and asleep by now. Surely angry as hell at me but I can deal with that. So, pushing the memory of her hurt face far, far away, I let myself doze off uncomfortably next to my mama's bed, her frail hands still gripping mine too firmly to leave.

Chapter 30

Aliena

I didn't get a wink of sleep all night, which only made me despise myself more. I can lie to myself all I want, but I know that as I tossed and turned, the thing missing to make me fall asleep was the comforting warmth and weight of Sebastian at my back.

Which means I've grown dependent on someone.

I finally accept defeat and drag myself out of bed shortly before dawn, deciding if I have to look like shit and feel like the dead at work all day, I might as well evade a confrontation with Sebastian first. No need for him to know how much last night wrecked me.

His departure was followed by one of the worst panic attacks I've had in years, during which I freaked out enough to get out of my restraints, at least. Not without chafing the skin around my wrists raw, though. No, the angry red marks still adorning them are proof of that.

I'm still not sure how I managed to get out. All I know is I felt like a caged animal and eventually started acting like one, biting and tearing at the restraints like something rabid.

I'm glad Sebastian didn't return last night to witness it. The humiliation of the whole situation, the panic attack, and the fact I almost wet myself, would have been too horrifying to bear.

I'm dragging my feet at work, barely managing to reply to the simplest questions of my patients. On my lunch break, I have nothing better to do than just pass out for a minute. I take my phone out of my pocket only for a second to set an alarm, ignoring Sebastian's texts and missed calls like I've been doing all day. I don't care if he wants to see me or talk. I'm afraid if he confronted me now, I'd be an open book and just spill all my secrets and feelings without any thought or restraint. If that happened, I'd have to change my name and leave the country, and I really don't have the money for that.

All too soon, my alarm goes off, ripping me from the brief, sweet relief of unconsciousness. As I get up and go back to work, I quickly realize sleeping only made me more exhausted, and by the time my shift is over, I'm barely seeing straight. I just have enough active brain cells to text my dad that I won't make it to their place tonight. I'm not a glutton for punishment and no amount of responsibility could get me to make *that* detour right now.

I take an excruciatingly long bus ride home, the only thing keeping me going is the prospect of making it to my bed.

My hope that I'll make it to my room without meeting Sebastian is crushed as soon as the elevator doors open to reveal him pacing the living room. He stops in his tracks when I step inside the living room, a whole lot of different emotions I don't care to analyze crossing his face.

Finally, he smiles at me and steps closer. "You're home," he says in a way of greeting, reaching out to hold both my arms as he studies me. I don't even have it in me to fight his scrutiny, and realizing that, he frowns. "Tough day at work?" he asks softly.

I brace my hands on his chest and push him away to get past. "Yeah. I'm exhausted. I think I'll just sleep now," I slur, nearly toppling over as the living room tilts on its axis. Damn, I'm dizzy.

Suddenly, the hands are back on my shoulders, turning me around to face Sebastian once more. "Sweetheart, you're looking a little pale there. Are you sure you're all right?" he pushes, and I hate the way my chest reacts to his term of endearment or his concern. I *don't need* him to take care of me.

"Yeah, fine. I just forgot to eat today. I'll do that after I've slept," I say, trying to walk away once more.

"Wait, as in, you haven't eaten at all today? Come on, sit down. I'll get you something," he insists, trying to steer me toward the dining table.

Fighting his strong grip is not what I want to spend my empty strength reserve on but following him is out of the question. In a last ditch effort, I use my words to tell him to let me go, my voice surprisingly sharper than I thought possible when I snap at him.

"I said I'm fine. Let go of me. I just want to sleep."

That, at least, finally gets his attention. Still frowning and with a crease marring the skin between his brows, he nods. "Okay. Sure. Let me help you get upstairs, then," he says, his voice still so horribly soft. This time, I don't protest as he steers me to the stairs and steadies me on the way up. I don't have a death wish, and I doubt I could make it to the second floor by myself in one piece.

When Sebastian tries to drag me down the hall and past my room, I stop him again. "I think I'll stay in my room

300

tonight," I tell him, even as a part of me screams at the prospect of not having him to cuddle up to again. Not when I feel this bad. But I'd hate myself in the morning if I caved now. I need to prove to myself that I don't need Sebastian. I'll get by just fine without him.

Looking up at his face, my stomach twists at the thought that I'm the one who put that sad look there. "Aly," he starts softly, and I know that's his way of trying to introduce a talk I know we'll have to have eventually.

Eventually isn't now. Not when I can barely keep myself upright. I shake my head. "Not now, Seb. I'm too tired. Just know that I'm not mad at you for leaving when someone you care about needed you."

"Then why won't you come to our room?" he asks.

Yeah, Aly, why? Because I'm a damned coward, that's why.

"I really need sleep tonight. No distractions," I tell him instead, feeling just a bit of petty satisfaction when I see my words hitting their mark as Sebastian winces just slightly.

"You think I can't keep my hands to myself when I know you're feeling bad?" he asks, clearly hurt by my lack of faith.

I don't tell him that I don't think that. A tired shrug is my only reply.

He presses his mouth in a thin line, nodding curtly before steering me back to my room. I manage to take the last few steps to the bed by myself, collapsing onto the soft mattress without another thought of the man that led me here. Only when he pushes me further into the middle of the bed and tucks me in do I open my eyes.

301

"I'm really sorry for last night, Aly. As horrible as it is, I forgot about the ties when I read my mom's text. I never would have left you like that on purpose," he says softly, stroking the back of my hand with his thumb.

"It's fine," I mumble when it really isn't. It's not my problem now, though. I just close my eyes.

Distantly, I feel his thumb come closer to my chafed wrist. He pulls the sleeve of my sweatshirt back just enough to reveal the irritated skin, no doubt, and his answering gasp is enough to make me pull back my arm to get it out of his view. Then, I blissfully let exhaustion drag me under.

———

When I come home from my morning shift the next day, Seb is preparing the apartment for the party tonight. I see the bar is already restocked, the couch is gone, and other valuables are currently being stowed away by the host.

"Hey," I greet him, my voice sounding a lot more like my own than it did yesterday. It's a good thing too. I hate how pathetic I was. "Is there anything I can help you with?" I offer.

He looks up, wiping the back of his hand over his sweat-slicked forehead, and gives me a dazzling smile. "Hi there. No, that's okay. I'm fine here, almost done." He observes me for a beat. "You look better today."

My cheeks heat involuntarily. I cringe at the vivid reminder that he remembers last night probably better than I do, tired as I was. The only good thing is I was able to sleep despite being alone. That does wonders to soothe my lingering fear of co-dependence.

"Right, if you're sure. I'll get ready for tonight, then." It's the first party I'll attend since Lily's catastrophic birthday but despite my nerves, I'm looking forward to it. Not only am I eager to dance again, but I can't wait to get ready. There's little I enjoy as much as dressing up and looking great. Or at least that's how I know I used to feel.

I'm trying to gaslight myself to get that version of myself back because these days I barely feel the ghost of her. She had her life together, and I'm a hot mess of unresolved feelings and reoccurring issues.

Since it's still hours until the party starts, I head straight for the last door down the hall. I might've been avoiding Sebastian since the night he ditched me but that doesn't mean I can't enjoy his dreamy bathtub.

As the water runs, I take a quick shower to wash the grime of the day off me. I was too tired to take one yesterday and was in a hurry this morning, so I feel dirty, and I'd rather not stain the bath with that.

Ten minutes later, I'm soaking in the warm water, absently playing with the bubbles as I try to think of what to wear tonight. I'm considering a midnight blue mini dress with an open back and slits from the bottom up to my waist on both sides when the door opens.

"Oh, sorry, I didn't know you were in here. I'll wait until you're done," Sebastian bursts out, turning around as if he's never seen me naked. Something about that gesture sits very wrong with me.

Sure I was the one to distance myself from him last night, but I'd hate to think he no longer wants me. Maybe that's why I chuckle coolly, telling him to turn around.

"No need to feign modesty now," I tease.

He smiles a little, doesn't tease me back, though. Instead, he asks, "How are your wrists?"

"Fine. A bit sensitive in the warm water but it's okay."

Looking almost uncomfortable, he asks, "I know it doesn't change anything now, but I truly am sorry. Can we please talk about it?"

"I already told you yesterday, there's not much to talk about. I believe it slipped your mind and you didn't mean to leave me like that. As I said, I'm happy you helped your mom when she needed you. I would have done the same thing."

"I think your exact words were, that someone I care about needed me. You know I care about you too, right? And I hate to think I left you when you needed me."

The knot in my stomach tightens, my defenses rising. "Don't worry about me. I managed just fine," I lie.

He gives me a pointed look, seeing right through me like he always does. "The bruises on your wrists say something different."

My stomach hollows out, and my default defense mechanism is to resort to anger. I straighten up, steeling my voice as I demand, "Why are you pushing this? What's done is done. Nothing we say can do anything about it now, so it doesn't matter."

"It matters to me. I messed up, but I can't make it up to you if you give me the cold shoulder instead of communicating. Why is it so difficult for you to just talk to me?"

"What do you want me to talk to you about? Do you want to hear that yes, I needed you too, that night, if only for ten more seconds? That I broke down as soon as you

304

left and spiraled until I had a fucking panic attack since you left me tied up like a sacrificial animal? Does it help you to know that?" I snap, my hands balled tightly beneath the water and my chest heaving with deep breaths that do little to calm my frenzy.

Instead of yelling back at me like I thought and maybe secretly hoped, Sebastian frowns and takes a step closer. I can already tell he's about to apologize again, his emotions are written all over his face. "I know you're sorry. I'm not mad, Seb. That night just made me realize a few things."

He stops in his tracks. "What things?" he asks cautiously.

"I think I should stay in my room from now on," I say first.

"I thought you had trouble falling asleep?" he interrupts me.

"I slept just fine yesterday." Whether that was just an exception because I was dead on my feet or not has yet to be determined, but I don't mention it.

"You could've slept anywhere yesterday," he protests.

"Either way, I can't stay dependent on you forever. Especially not when it comes to something as vital as sleep. I'm a big girl. I can stay in my own bed."

His frown deepens. "So where does that leave us?"

"Nothing has to change. We're still friends, and I'm not opposed to the whole physical thing we've got going on. The only difference is I'll go to my room once we're done," I say, trying to soften my tone when a shadow of hurt crosses his eyes. I'm the first one who gets how rejection can sting, and I don't mean to hurt him after everything he's done for me.

Slowly, he asks, "And what if I don't want that?"

"Don't want what?"

What if he doesn't want me anymore? Is that what he's about to tell me? The tables turn and already the rejection churns in my gut. I grit my teeth, steeling myself against the full force of it.

"I've learned I'm quite fond of having someone to hold at night. What if I don't want to give that up and act like a simple one-night stand?" he challenges.

Despite the fuzzy feeling that replaces the fear of rejection inside of me, I force myself to say a string of words that leave a bitter aftertaste in my mouth. Interesting how he's opposed to being a one-night stand but doesn't want to be something serious either. "Then I guess you better start looking for a new person to do that with."

His eyes narrow. "No."

"No?" I repeat, dumbfounded. What does he mean, no?

"No. You said nothing changes, so we're still exclusive. I told you a long time ago that I don't share and that goes both ways. Besides, you know I want no one else."

I sigh, equal parts content to let the soothing words wash over me and panicked. "You can't say stuff like that. That's boyfriend talk," I protest.

Seb shuts his mouth firmly, looking like he agrees with me and doesn't like it one bit.

He huffs. "Fine. We're just *friends* who mess around, but I'm serious about the no-sharing part. Another guy touches you and I break his hand." With that, he turns around and flees the bathroom, leaving me alone to stew on my conflicted feelings.

Chapter 31

Sebastian

"There you are, birthday boy. I know you said no presents, but it's not wrapped so it doesn't count," Lily says, hugging me tightly before shoving a box into my hands. A look confirms it's from my favorite bakery.

Despite hating presents, with the exception of the one Aliena gave me, my chest warms at the sight. The bakery is across town, so I rarely go, but my mom used to take me there a lot as a child, knowing the owner and all that, so it holds some sentimental value.

I lean down to kiss Lily's cheek before she saunters deeper into the private room to greet her best friend.

"Damn, babe, you look fantastic," I hear her tell Aly, who's waiting on the couch. I don't have to turn around to know she's right. The memory of her coming down the steps to meet me in the living room before the party started is burned onto the back of my eyelids.

I thought green was my favorite color but after seeing her in that midnight blue, I might have a change of heart. The dress, while beautiful, is risky as hell. The slits on the outside of her thighs up to her waist make me wonder

307

where the hell her panties are, and her low back lets me know with certainty she's not wearing a bra.

To say I got hard just thinking about it would be the unfortunate truth. She drives me crazy. Even more so because my attraction to her is now clouded with a mess of conflicting feelings.

Despite her brushing me off whenever I tried to mention it, I feel like absolute shit for having let her down after she let me tie her up. She might say she doesn't care, but it's clear I broke something vital between us in the way she's been distant.

I miss her. I miss waking up with her in my arms and most of all, I miss seeing the shimmer of trust in her stunning eyes when she looks at me.

With her breaking the news that she no longer wants to sleep in our room anymore before I could say everything I needed on my mess-up, it slipped my mind. Now, things are still strained and unspoken words hang in the air between us. I don't know how to fix it.

Even less so because as much as I try to understand it's my fault we're in such a strained place, I'm still fed up with her for what she said. She refuses to communicate, insists we're all good but still creates new rules neither of us wants. No more sleeping in our bed? Her insistence of calling me a friend. It helps neither one of us.

"What's got you scowling like that, Willy?" Andrew teases, clasping my shoulder in a way of greeting. From behind us, I hear Aly ask about my nickname.

"Willy? What's that all about?"

"That, dear Aly, is Sebastian's favorite nickname of all time," my best friend provides.

"Oh? How come I've never heard it?" she asks, intrigued.

"Sebastian hates it. His middle name is William, you see, which is also his father's name. Andrew likes to tease him with it," Mattheo explains, walking past me with a pat on my shoulder before leaning down to kiss Aliena's cheek. "Hey, *amo*. Long time no see," he adds, a sultry note to his voice that wasn't there a second ago. I grit my teeth against my growing irritation and look away before anyone can notice it, getting myself a drink.

When I come back, my friends are all happily conversing. For once, at least, I see Aliena and Mattheo aren't touching.

By the end of the hour, the private room has filled with a few selected outsiders. One of them is the red-haired girl Mattheo chewed my ear off about at school one day, Miriam or something. Once she arrived, I felt the tension ease out of my body. It's clear he's head over heels for her. He hasn't taken his gaze off her since she settled on the couch between him and Aliena. Or his hands, for that matter.

Aliena is mostly catching up with Lily and I'm glad to see they seem fine again, no strain in their talk.

At one point, my best friend grows sick of me and gets to his feet, reaching out to take Lily's hand. "You guys, it's been a pleasure, but I feel like dancing with my girl for a bit. See you later," Andrew announces, already dragging a giggling Lily behind him.

Right on cue, Mattheo shoots his date a questioning glance and the pair get to their feet too. "Well, I think we'll join them downstairs," Mattheo says, looking at Aliena sheepishly.

309

Realizing he probably feels weird or guilty for ditching his old dance partner, Aly smiles comfortingly. "Have fun," she assures him. Seeming relieved, Mattheo leaves with his new girl, leaving my roommate and me alone with a few near-strangers.

"So," she starts awkwardly. "I'm guessing you don't care to dance?"

"You're guessing correctly. All our friends are downstairs, and I don't feel like making up lies for their million questions when they eventually see us," I confirm more harshly than intended.

Because that is exactly what I'd have to do since Aly doesn't want them to know what's been going on.

It occurs to me I should pick my words with more care, but it seems our earlier talk is bothering me more than I thought. Suddenly alone with her now, my frustration and the sting of her rejection make me sound angrier than I am. All I really want is for things to just be easy between us, but I don't have a single clue where I'd have to start to get there.

She huffs and gets to her feet, clearly fed up with my tone. "Right. Have fun sulking up here, then." She tries to head to the door but as she passes me, I reach out to gently grab her wrist.

"Where are you going?" I ask, trying and failing to soften my voice so she knows I'm not trying to be a jerk.

"To dance." Her eyes narrow on me, the defiance I thought we'd gotten past rising in those honey-colored eyes. "I'm not going to stop doing what I love just because you refuse to do it with me."

"Mattheo is dancing with Miriam," I try to reason with her, my words rough as a thread of panic worms through my veins. Dammit, we talked about exclusivity just this afternoon.

"Then I'll just have to find someone else to dance with," she retorts, the challenge thick in her words. All my thoughts of keeping the peace go flying out the nearest window as my blood pressure rises. *I'm losing her.*

"I told you what happens when you let another guy touch you, Aly. I wasn't kidding," I say like a controlling, violent bastard I never thought I'd be. *Just like your father. The first hint of trouble and you're turning into the man you despise.* My heart pinches painfully in my chest, blood rushing in my ears.

I always thought my need to be respectful with women at all times was ingrained into my very last cell, so why am I losing my temper now when I want to make things *better.*

Just the other day, after I'd left Aly to help my mom, I thought I had confirmation I wasn't like my dad. He got off on seeing my mother crushed over him, but when I saw Aliena clearly upset after my screw up, I felt nothing but shame and the strong urge to make it better. To make her feel better.

It was like a puzzle clicking into place, taking the weight of the world off my shoulders for the first time since I realized I wanted this girl to be more than just my friend. I thought she felt the same way, and I wanted to talk to her about it after I had made-up for leaving her the way I did, but then she had to go and talk about me finding someone else because she no longer wanted me. Speaking of rotten luck. And now instead of keeping my cool, I can feel myself going off the deep end.

It's like I'm a bystander, watching myself from outside of my body. I know what I *should* do, and yet I lack the control to make myself comply.

"Then grow some balls and join me," Aliena fires back, her words more cutting than I've ever heard her.

For a second, I gape at her. *Stay calm. Fix this.* But a much louder voice in my head bursts at the seams with indignation. Where the hell is this coming from? It's like she has to prove a point again, same as when she refused to sleep in my bed anymore.

"You're the one that doesn't want to tell our friends where you live!" I remind her, hissing under my breath so the rest of the room doesn't hear.

"Yes, I know. But you not dancing with me has nothing to do with that. That's all you and your stupid fear of damaging your image. I thought we were done with this after we shook on being friends. I guess what you meant was that we'd be friends in private. What a shame it would be if the great Sebastian, grinch of Hartford U, was seen dancing and having fun with the same girl twice in a row," she spits.

I lose my temper entirely, my grip slipping. "Oh, you're talking about stupid fears now? Never mind your fear of being dependent on anyone but yourself is full-on self-destructive," I snap right back.

Something flashes in her eyes, but she just huffs and crosses her arms. "You know what, I don't feel like arguing with you right now. I'm going dancing." This time when she turns, I don't stop her, glaring at her back until she slams the door shut behind her. If anyone in the room wasn't staring at me before, they sure are now.

Fantastic.

———

I brood in the room for about twenty minutes before I can no longer stand it. My mental clarity is still lacking and maybe it would be best to wait until I'm feeling more rational, but I can't sit still anymore. Not while some bastard might actually have his hands on my girl. Because whether she wants to accept it or not, that's what she is.

Not even sure what my intentions or next steps should be, I walk down the hall and gaze upon the dance floor. My eyes look for a certain golden-haired woman of their own accord. Quicker than should be possible, I find her swaying figure. My rage dims, my thoughts come to a stop, and my breath catches. I almost forgot how mesmerizing she is when she dances.

So much has happened since I last saw her like this.

The short moment of admiration is interrupted when she turns to look over her shoulder, her features lighting up with a megawatt smile as she faces the guy behind her. The guy, who I now realize has his hands all over her as she pushes her body up against his.

The kindle of good feelings snuffs out in my chest.

I can't believe this. Of course, I can understand she went dancing without me, but is it so hard to just do it by herself for once? To be surrounded by strangers and not dry hump one of them?

I grip the railing with both hands, my knuckles turning white as I try to think of what to do. I want to stop them, but the reminder that Mattheo and Andrew are downstairs makes me falter. Aly might have forgotten all about her wish to keep us private, but I haven't.

Besides, Aliena said she wanted space and if I went down right now to dance with her, I know the night would end with her in my bed. And I'm not sure I'd be willing to let her leave it again to sleep down the hall like a meaningless one-night stand.

Finally, I see Aliena's movements falter as she leans in to whisper something to the guy behind her. She starts walking away in the direction of the bathrooms and for a second, I think she invited him to join her somewhere more private. Luckily, he stays where he is, turns in his place, and carries on dancing. I lose a sigh of relief, no matter that I'm still fuming, and follow Aliena down the stairs and into the nearly deserted hallway.

I wait there like a creep for a few minutes until she finally reappears, stopping in her tracks as she sees me.

"What are you doing here?" she demands, her mood clearly souring.

"I saw you with that guy, Aliena."

"So? I told you I was going to have to find someone to dance with since the stick up your ass doesn't allow you to entertain me."

Entertain her? God, she's making it sound like I'm her personal clown. Like my reservations about dancing don't count at all. "And I told you not to let anyone touch you," I say through gritted teeth.

She huffs. "You're the one that told me that we are nothing serious and never will be!" she snaps. "Guess what, maybe I don't want to be your toy forever, Seb. You can't demand the privilege of my fidelity without the commitment."

314

"My toy? Seriously? When have I treated you with anything other than respect?" I demand, only to keep talking before she can reply. "I warned you before we started this that once I had you, I didn't want to see you with anyone else, and still you climbed into my bed every fucking night! Some things might have changed since then, but that hasn't and it won't. I told you as much just today," I yell, my blood heating. After everything, I can't believe this is what we're arguing about.

She never gave me the impression she wanted to be in a relationship with me. Quite frankly, with the way she's keeping everything about our situation a secret, I was closer to believing she was ashamed of me rather than that she wants me like I want her.

I wanted to talk to her about what we could be, but she shot me down like every other time I've tried to talk about something real, and right now, I'm entirely too angry to question her revelation.

"Is what I give you really not enough? Is it that hard for you to be happy without constant access to any random dick?" I snap instead.

"Oh, my god! You're acting like I slept with him! We were just dancing!" she protests, her hands flying wide and her face turning red.

"Just dancing! Your ass was all over his dick, Aliena! Trust me, he had a lot more in mind than just dancing." My voice lowers dangerously and while a reasonable voice in the back of my head is trying to tell me to shut up now, I can't keep my next words from slipping past my reckless lips.

"I'll tell you something, if you pull the same shit you did with Mattheo again, I won't just sit by idly and feel bad

315

about it. If you go and fuck another guy, I'm done. And you better believe I won't go back to being celibate out of respect for you." The words taste like ash on my tongue, but I don't try to take them back. Maybe I am exactly like my father, always defaulting to being a jerk. Maybe this is how he started out as well. My stomach churns.

For a fraction of a second, she looks taken aback at my promise. Then, she steels her expression, squares her shoulders, and pushes past me without another word. A second later, I move too, heading back up the stairs to my room since I'm officially done with this party.

Despite knowing better, my treacherous eyes search the crowd one last time once I reach the second floor. When I see just who Aliena picked to dance with now, my anger doubles. Great, not only is she dry-humping another stranger, but she had to pick the biggest jerk in my school to do it with.

Whatever, he's a slime bag. They deserve each other.

———

It takes fifteen pages to calm me down. Sure, I barely soak up any of the words and it took me way too long to read them, but once I reach the end of the chapter, I'm no longer angry.

Truth be told, I just feel bad about how things went down between Aliena and me, and all I want to do is find her and talk it out so we can be on good terms again. It seems we have a lot to discuss, considering all the things she said about not wanting to be my toy but needing actual commitment.

I should be over the moon. I care about Aliena a lot, more than what's usual for a friend, and I do think of her as mine. Still, the downsides and risks haven't changed. I've never had a girlfriend and today's fight reinforced my worries that I'll be as shitty as my father. But maybe if I apologize first, if I admit I was a jerk it means I'm different. That I inherited some of my mother's goodness because I know my father sure never apologized for any off the damage he's done.

And we're both so busy and with everything going on with her family, I can't imagine we'd have time to date and whatever else you do in a relationship.

Thinking about it is just giving me a headache. It's time I talked to Aliena about all this, to hear where she stands so we can figure it out together. Maybe she has answers to some of the questions I don't. The only thing I know for sure is that I don't want to lose her.

I set my book down carefully on my bedside table and with a centering breath, I remind myself to stay calm no matter what happens. *I am not my father.* I want to talk to Aliena like an adult rather than snap at her when things aren't going my way. It's the only way we can possibly resolve things.

I return to the top of the stairs, searching the crowd for my roommate with my heart beating in my throat. The dance floor isn't as packed as earlier, the students either catching their breaths on the chairs lining the wall and bar or gone by now. Still, I can't seem to find the one person I'm looking for.

Deciding she probably retired to her own room, I head there next, only to find the door locked when I quietly try to open it. I tell my racing heart to calm down as the déjà

317

vu hits me, reminding myself she's probably asleep and didn't want any partygoers to stumble inside.

I'm ready to leave when a muffled sound reaches my ear through the wood. I freeze on the spot, my heart dropping to my stomach as I wait for confirmation. And then it comes, another silent moan I recognize as Aliena's.

My spine straightens, my hands balling to fists as acceptance mingles with rage and resolution. Fine, she really took someone into her room with her? I warned her what would happen if she did that. Forget about considering a relationship with her. I was stupid for ever thinking it could work.

Chapter 32

Aliena

My blood still boiling from my argument with Seb, I don't waste time getting back to the dance floor and grabbing the first dude I see. He's tall, looking slightly cocky but attractive enough. Most importantly, he seems happy to dance with me.

So, I do, losing myself to the pounding music, moving along and nearly forgetting all about the guy behind me. That is until he restricts my hips' movement, pulling my ass against his front and grinding into me. My stomach lurches, and I jerk at the sudden ballsiness of this stranger.

I quickly scramble out of his hold before he can even think of repeating the motion, refraining from snapping at him by sheer will. Honestly, what is wrong with certain people? There's a difference between dancing provocatively and straight-up dry-humping someone. What this guy just tried is a big no-no.

I shoot a tense smile over my shoulder and excuse myself, ready to forget about that little incident and the queasiness lingering in my gut. *Wrong hands,* is all I can think. I debate straying to the other side of the dance floor, far away from this jerk, but quickly realize that's not what I desire. Not really.

There's no better buzzkill than having someone cross a line, and call me sensitive, but that's what this guy just did. I can feel proof of it in the itchy feeling in my bones and the growing guilt as my mind drifts to Sebastian.

I can excuse dancing with others since he's the one so set on not committing to me. I meant what I said about the two-way street between fidelity and commitment, and if he's set to never lock in with me, why should I wait around? But just because I'm fed up with Sebastian and our situation doesn't mean I want another man's hands on me. Not like that. Not only is it vulgar and rude, but the only man I want getting that close to me is still the host of the party.

I swallow the lump in my throat and decide it's time to retire for tonight. At least from the party. Maybe I'll stray by Seb's room and check if he's still up. I doubt I could sleep now anyway, not without apologizing for tonight.

I said some things I shouldn't have, and I hate parting on bad terms, even if it's just for the night.

By the time I reach the top of the stairs, I'm sure I'm doing the right thing by talking to Sebastian. The added bonus of knowing I'm being the bigger person doesn't hurt either.

I'm just passing my room when I become aware of a shadow next to mine. My head flies up, turning to look over my shoulder just in time to see the guy I danced with before reaching out for me, a smile playing on his lips. My heart starts thudding painfully.

I open my mouth to yell at him, maybe scream, but his hand covers my mouth roughly as his other comes around my arm, grasping me tightly and yanking me against his chest. I yelp into his palm, shoving against his chest with my free hand.

He merely smiles, sneering, "Hey, beautiful. Missed you too. Such a tease, making me hard and then coming up here so we can be in private." He starts shoving me toward my room, ignoring that I am shaking my head frantically.

He pushes me the final step inside, following closely behind before he turns to lock the door. When his eyes meet mine again, he looks like a predator, and an unpleasant shiver runs down my spine.

"Get out of my room!" I demand, glad when my voice doesn't betray any fear.

"I will, don't worry. Once you finished what you started," he taunts, leering at me.

"You're sick. I don't want you here, get out and look for someone willing!" I snap, crossing my arms to shield myself.

"No. I don't think I will. Not when you're right here, so easy and ready for the taking." His eyes trail over my skimpy dress and for the first time I can remember, the warning about not dressing provocatively rings true.

I can already hear the accusations. *She wasn't wearing underwear. She was asking for it.* A cold shiver rushes down my spine, tears springing to my eyes. I danced with him, now he's in my room with no one around to hear my protests over the blearing music. He'll do whatever he wants to me, and no one will believe I didn't want it.

My panic rises as he strides toward me now, pressing me up against the wall and shoving his lips against mine as I try to scream. His tongue brushes against the roof of my mouth and I gag and whine, biting down hard just as he retreats. I barely manage to do any damage, and I curse myself for my slow reaction. His tongue is gone, all that is left is the repulsive taste of his last drink.

When his rough hands find the bare skin of my hips, trying to slip beneath the fabric of my dress through the slits, my instincts take over and I lash out, shoving him away with enough force to make him stumble. I don't hesitate as I rush past him, trying to get to the locked door and cursing my damn heels for slowing me down. Just a step away from freedom, a hand wraps around my ponytail and yanks me back. I go down hard, the stark change of direction making me fly back. I cry out, my scalp burning and my tailbone screaming as I land on my ass. Tears blur my vision, but I can still make out the figure of the guy standing before me, palming the bulge in his pants now. Like this is turning him on. Like seeing me on the floor before him, crying in fear, is making him hard. I gag again, nausea rushing through my body as I realize just what kind of sick man followed me to my room.

He never misunderstood my intentions when I walked away. He didn't think for a second I was inviting him upstairs to let him touch me more. He *knows* I don't want this.

When he gets on his hunches to come closer, I kick my legs out to bury my pointy heels into his thighs. I'll be damned if I let him touch me again. Despite my racing heart and frantic mind, I refuse to go down without a fight.

"Get out!" I repeat as he falls back, clutching his thigh.

"Bitch," he spits as he gets back to his feet. At the sheer rage in his eyes, I grow warier, fear gripping me by the throat. Strength-wise, I don't stand a chance.

But an angel must be by my side because he takes a step away from me. "Fuck it. You're not worth the trouble," he concludes, turning and getting out of my room without another look my way.

I slump on the floor, the gravity of what could have just happened hitting me. My heart is still racing, the tears still streaming down my face, and the aches he dealt me registering fully.

I know I'm a hair's breadth away from falling apart. Looking around my dark, empty room, I know this is the last place I want to do so. Again. So, I force myself to get to my feet, repeating that I just have to walk a few steps to reach Seb's room.

No matter how angry he is right now, I know he'll make it better. He'll make me feel better.

I wobble down the hall, trying to keep my tears in check in case I meet any of my friends. Luckily, I reach the last room without meeting anyone and with great relief, I open the door. I don't even bother to knock. I can't muster up the strength.

But I should have because I'm not prepared for what I find inside. The world comes to a halt entirely when I try to take in the scene. Because there he is, the person I trust most, despite everything that's happened, holding my gaze while he takes a deep drag from something that certainly isn't a cigarette.

A small, broken sob escapes me. Still, Sebastian's expression doesn't change, his face remaining cold.

He's just standing there, not appearing the least bit chastised at being caught doing drugs when he knows what this means to me. He knows what he's doing with this. I just don't understand why. Our argument wasn't so bad he should want to trigger me like this.

Where did he even get the drugs on such short notice?
What even is he smoking right now?

If small mercies exist, it's weed, but my nose is already stuffy from crying, and I can't tell if it's something stronger like crack.

Oh god, what am I even thinking about right now. What is happening? I shouldn't have to worry about what drugs another person I care about is poisoning themselves with. I take a shaky step back, my head spinning and my legs weak. He sees it all happen but doesn't react. Just keeps smoking. At the sight of his indifference, the shards of my heart only crumble further, disintegrating into nothing.

Before another sob can force its way past my lips, I hurl the only words I can think of at him. "What the fuck is that?" I demand, wrapping my shaking arms around myself to hide just how much I'm trembling. My body doesn't feel like mine.

If Sebastian notices, he doesn't care. He neither acts nor speaks, simply watching me fall apart with his nose turned up. As if I were overstepping and overreacting and he can't believe I think I'm in any position to make demands. As if I were dirty.

I feel dirty right now.

"In our room?" I go on, feeling sicker than I ever have. The fact he is taking drugs is bad enough in itself, but that he had to do it here? Knowing there was a good chance I'd find out. He did that intentionally to hurt me. He wanted me to find him like this and break me.

"It's my room," he retorts coolly. "Don't get things twisted just because I fucked you here a bunch of times." I recoil at his crude, cruel words, but he goes on, sounding less like the man that held me every night, allowing me to sleep, with every hateful syllable he throws my way. "Don't look at me like that. If you can fuck the biggest scumbag in my school, I think I'm allowed to take the edge off with a bit of weed. I had half a mind to find a beautiful woman to spend the night with since I sure as hell won't let you taint my fresh sheets after you let him touch you, but I figured this would do."

Fuck someone from his school? What is he talking about? He can't mean the guy I danced with tonight. He couldn't possibly know what he tried to do to me in my room just now. If he did, he wouldn't be acting like this. He wouldn't be calling me dirty and tainted. He wouldn't act like it was my fault.

But look at what you're wearing. And you danced with him. I shudder as my fears become truth before my eyes.

Shaking my head, I grasp my stomach tightly, feeling it turn. "I didn't. I didn't fuck anyone," I whisper, more to myself than anyone else. I can't get my voice any louder. Can't see anything anymore through the tears, and I can't breathe. A sour taste burns the back of my tongue. The nausea I've been fighting all along finally wins, and I feel my last meal rising in my throat.

I stumble to the bathroom, locking it desperately when I hear Sebastian's steps behind me. I just barely manage to make it to the toilet before my stomach rolls and expels its contents. I heave again and again until my throat is sore and there's nothing left inside of me to throw up. Then, I flush the toilet and slump against the nearest wall, willing my lungs to work and take in the air I so desperately need.

Distantly, I can hear Sebastian scream my name through the door as he bangs his fists against the wood, demanding to be let inside. I don't move. I can't move, I realize. I can't fucking breathe.

I panic, despite knowing that will only make things worse. I have no choice. I've lost all sense of control over my body as I curl up, gasping for shallow breaths.

The image of that stranger forcing me up against the wall, his nasty tongue down my throat while Sebastian was here getting high is wrecking my mind. I don't understand. Can't comprehend why he would do this. Why anyone would do this.

"Aliena!" Sebastian calls again, and I can hear the urgency in his voice.

Suddenly, I wish I hadn't locked the door. As my lungs burn and chest caves, I wish I weren't alone. I don't want to be alone anymore.

I think I'm dying. That's what is happening here, I can feel it. After everything I've been through, this is what kills me. This night. All because my lungs won't obey and do their job. I sob, pressing my forehead against the cold tiles of the bathroom floor. I don't want it to end this way. Not when that stranger was the last person who touched me. Not when the last thing I heard was hateful words.

I start dragging myself across the floor blindly, only stopping when I reach the corner of the shower. I turn on the water, not bothering to get out of the way of the ice-cold spray as it hits me first, or the too-hot water that comes next. I just stay there, letting the water wash away the stranger's touch and my falling tears.

326

To think that all I came to this room for was a hug from Sebastian and some reassuring words. I thought his arms around me could make things better, that he would tell me it wasn't my fault and tell me things would be all right, but look where it got me. I never should have started relying on anyone other than me.

Chapter 33

Sebastian

I startle awake the next morning to the sound of the door I was sleeping up against being unlocked. I jump to my feet as it slowly opens, taking the first deep breath since last night upon seeing Aliena. Her face is splotchy, her eyes puffy, and her hair still damp and clinging to her face, but she's unharmed.

For a moment there, last night, when I heard her pained, desperate sobs through the door, I was worried she'd do something stupid. Worried she would hurt herself. I've never felt such terror.

Unable to stop myself, I close the short distance between us and cup her cheeks, frantically searching her face as I say, "You're okay."

Aliena shakes her head, her throat bobbing as she swallows and takes a step back. I notice she's still shaking, still so horribly pale under the fluorescent lights, and the relief vanishes from my chest.

I stumble over my words. "Last night. I am so sorry. You knew I'd lose my shit if you fucked someone else again, but I didn't think this would happen. I just couldn't take it, knowing you were with him, and I dug out my old stash to take off the edge. I didn't know you'd come back so soon. I am so sorry, Aliena. No matter how angry I was, I never wanted you to feel the way you did last night," I tell her, desperately grasping for the right thing to say but failing greatly.

There is no right thing to say. Not after the way I wrecked her.

Last night, smoking the weed seemed like the smallest of evils. At first, I wanted to make good on my promise and find another girl to fuck just to give her a taste of her own medicine, but I couldn't go through with it.

I went downstairs and found a beautiful, willing woman, but the second she touched my arm, my every cell recoiled. I couldn't do it, and I hated it because it sure seemed easy for Aliena to let someone else touch her. I was spiraling when I remembered the old stash of weed in my sock drawer, so I dug it out.

I knew it would hurt Aliena more than anything else ever could, but I didn't think she'd come back to our room. Least of all so soon. I just hoped it would help my mind settle down for the night, enough to get at least a few hours of sleep before I'd have to face reality in the morning.

Aliena stares at me for a second, then clears her throat and says, "I didn't sleep with him."

My reeling mind comes to a halt. "What?" I ask, conflicted as I weigh my trust for her and what I know I heard and saw last night.

"I didn't sleep with him," she repeats, her voice a little steadier. "We danced but he got too handsy, so I left. I wanted to come here, to talk to you and apologize, but he snuck up on me without me realizing until it was too late. He ambushed me and dragged me into my room." She chokes on her words. "He tried…he wanted to take off my

329

clothes and touch me, but I didn't let him. I fought him off until he decided I wasn't worth it and left. I didn't want him to touch me. That *wasn't* my fault," she protests, holding her head high even as fresh tears stream down her face.

I can't comprehend what she's saying. My blood is rushing in my ears as I try to process her words. All I hear is *"I didn't want him to touch me."* Again and again, her shaky words play in my mind until my stomach is in knots and my own eyes sting.

"No," I finally whisper. That's all. One useless word of denial. "That's not true," I mutter softly.

As betrayal fills Aliena's eyes and she looks at me with her mouth agape, I quickly realize just how wrong those words came out.

Shaking my head, I try to salvage the situation. "I'm sorry. I didn't mean it like that, Aly. I believe you. I am sorry. I didn't know. I swear. I just heard you inside and I read the signs all wrong." My mouth clamps shut, horror cooling my blood as I realize I was *there*. I was there, right outside her door while someone assaulted her.

What I interpreted as a moan may as well have been a sound of struggle, but it never occurred to me something like that was happening. In my house, at that.

"You heard?" Aliena whispers slowly, taking another slow step away. It's a punch to my gut.

"I came looking for you. I wanted to talk, too, but I couldn't find you, and when I tried your door, I found it locked, then I heard you inside. I thought it was a moan. I swear to god, I thought it was a moan. I would have never left if I'd known what was going on." My words are desperate as I realize I'm losing her.

I fucked up so badly last night, I can't even grasp the depth of it. Not only did I not help her but I made it all worse by triggering her worst memories and taking drugs in this room. Our room, as Aliena finally called it. And then I went ahead and said all those things when she was already falling apart.

I might be sick.

Aliena's choked sob cuts through the silence. My eyes meet hers, desperately pleading, and I step forward. "Please, just let me hold you. Just for a second," I beg, needing to do something other than watching her cry. It's what I should have done last night.

Aliena shakes her head but doesn't move away when I reach for her hand. Instead of pushing her when she said no, I try to let my eyes convey everything I'm thinking as I open my arms for her. To my great surprise, she steps into them and wraps her own around my waist.

I hold her close, one hand on the back of her head and the other around her back as I kiss the top of her head. I stay like that for a few long seconds, with my lips on her hair as I breathe her in. She starts shaking again, her tears soaking through my shirt, and with every stifled sob and sniffle, I can feel the knife in my gut twisting.

"Did he hurt you?" I whisper slowly, hating the thought of it.

"Not more than I did him," she replies weakly, and despite the gravity of the situation, I'm proud of her for fighting. I hope he regrets having followed her, which I still don't know how he managed since there are guys at the bottom of the stairs to make sure no one who's not on the list makes it up. He sure as hell wasn't on the list.

Well, if he doesn't regret it now, he will once I'm done with him. If I kicked in my best friend's knee for not making sure Aliena got home safely, I'll do a hell of a lot worse to that disgusting piece of shit that tried to *rape* her.

"I think I'll move in with my parents," Aliena says, finally breaking the long silence, startling me.

I pull away enough to look at her face. "You don't have to do that," I insist, knowing it's the last thing she wants. Still, understanding she needs some space from me, I add, "I'll go. My mom will be happy to have me around. I'll stay away until you're ready to talk. You have my word."

No matter that being away from her and leaving her alone is the last thing I want. Especially when I know how bad she's currently feeling. Her sobs last night are still engraved in my mind, and I doubt I'll ever not be able to hear them.

"I can't let you do that. This is your home," she protests.

I won't back down, though. Not on this. "It's yours too. Tell me what I can do to convince you to stay. I won't let you go to your parents'. Not after everything you've told me."

Sighing heavily, she shrugs. "We can both stay. Just, please, get rid of the drugs. I can't live in another house filled with drugs." She pulls further away. "And we should try to stay out of each other's way. I don't want to see you right now."

Ignoring the way hearing those words hurt, I swallow any further protests and nod, stepping away. "Of course. I won't bother you. Just know I'm here if you need anything, okay?"

———

For six days, I barely see Aliena at all. It's weird how unaware I was of how much she infiltrated nearly every part of my daily routine until she was gone.

I no longer greet her as soon as she steps out of the elevator in the evening, waiting in my room or the gym instead, although I always keep my door open to make sure I know she made it home safely.

I no longer tell her about my day as she prepares dinner, hell, we don't share meals at all. I let her have the kitchen after she comes home from work, let her eat, and then follow suit once I know she's in her room. Still, she always leaves me a plate of whatever she prepared. It only makes not sharing the meals with her more painful.

I don't deserve her kindness and her leftovers. She shouldn't waste a single thought on me, not a second of energy, but I can't tell her that without going back on my promise to give her space. Instead, I silently appreciate every bite of her cooking, unsure of what else I could do.

The few times I've seen her in passing made my worry grow. She looks tired. Not as much as she did after I spent the night at my mom's place, but there are dark circles beneath her eyes and every smile she throws me is halfhearted at best.

I'm sure I don't look much better. She's not the only one that's been losing sleep. My mind is constantly reeling, trying to come up with ways to make things up to her, to make everything better but coming up empty. With every sleepless night, my worry that what I did is entirely unforgiveable grows.

But I try, nonetheless. I try everything I can think of to redeem myself because I can't just do nothing and lose Aliena for good.

On the Monday after my party, the first thing I did upon arriving at school was track down the bastard that hurt her. Brad, or Brandon, or something. I don't even care. All I know is that I dragged him into the alley between two of the school's buildings, waited for the first period to start, and did a hell of a lot more than break his hand like I promised Aliena.

I beat him into a bloody pulp. Not enough to be life-threatening. I had enough of a mind to refrain from that. Still, I made sure he learned his lesson.

Tonight, the night of that sixth day, my mind is once again too restless to let me sleep. I toss and turn for three hours, getting more and more pissed with every minute I get closer to hearing my alarm in the morning. I hate being up all night when I have school early.

Finally, I go downstairs and make myself some warm milk, chugging it once it's ready. Hell, if that doesn't work, nothing will. Well, something might. The comfort of another body curled up against mine. Aliena's body, to be exact. And only hers.

Since that is out of question, for the time being, I guess I'll just have to hope the milk helps. If it doesn't, I'll call in sick tomorrow. What's the worst that can happen? A call from the headmaster? Sure, I haven't talked to my dad in a while.

With that bitter thought, I reach the top of the stairs. I make sure to tread silently from there on, unwilling to wake Aliena as I pass her room. As I sneak by, a sound from the other side of the wooden door makes me pause though.

Maybe my imagination is playing tricks on me, but I could have sworn I just heard her groan. Or moan.

Remembering how easily I dismissed a similar noise the last time, I hesitate, pressing my ear to the door. Indeed, a few seconds later, I hear it again. Definitely not a moan, I realize. No, it sounds more like a pained whine. A sniffle follows closely. It sounds like she's crying, and I don't know what the hell to do. I want to go in, ask her if there's something I can do to comfort her, but I'm not sure if I should now. Sneaking into her room in the middle of the night isn't exactly the definition of giving her space.

In the end, I know I won't be able to ignore what I heard and just keep walking. I gently knock on the door.

There's no reply, so I repeat the notion. "Aliena?" I whisper against the wood like an idiot. The other side of the door has gone really quiet but that doesn't stop me from gently easing the barrier open to peek inside.

There she is, curled up in a ball in the middle of her bed, on top of her blanket and with her back to me. "Aly? Are you awake?" I ask as softly as I can in case she is, in fact, asleep.

Her reply comes in the form of a sniffle that goes straight through my chest. I close the distance between me and the bed but hesitate again instead of getting on.

"Sweetheart, I'm sorry to barge in here. I just wanted to make sure you're okay."

"I'm fine," she grunts breathlessly. It's anything but convincing.

I know I should leave, boundaries and all. It's just that my feet seem unwilling to move from this very spot unless it is to get closer to her.

"Doesn't really sound that way. Is there something I can do?" I ask gingerly. Slowly, it dawns on me what date it is, and I quickly do the math. Unless I'm way off, my guess is that Aly's on her period and while she didn't seem to be in much pain the last time around, I won't be bold enough to assume that's always the same.

"Go," she groans, not once moving. Sighing, I accept that I can't force her to let me help.

"I'm leaving my door open. Call out if you need anything, I'll hear you," I promise before stepping back into the hall and closing her door.

Instead of going to my own room, I head back downstairs to gather a few things. Once I have everything I might need, I return to the second floor. When I linger in front of Aly's room for just a second, I'm surprised to hear her call out my name. I'm back at the side of her bed in a second.

"I could hear you out there. What do you want?" she asks, sniffling after every word.

Suddenly feeling stupid and way more vulnerable than I'd like, I say, "I found a heating pad in case you'd like it." I fumble with my words. "And chocolate," I add quietly, feeling dumb. God, they don't prepare you for this at school. I feel like a nervous wreck. "And pain meds," I finally say. Those were the first things that came to my mind when I thought of what might help against the pain. Well, not the chocolate. That might just be a cliché, but I thought it wouldn't hurt.

With another sniffle, Aliena turns around, wincing as she curls up anew, this time facing me. I hate to see her small, puffy eyes and that stricken expression on her beautiful face. I wish I could hug her.

"Hey there," I say softly.

"Hi." There's a beat of silence. "That's very nice of you. That you brought me all that, I mean. You can just leave it here and go back to bed. I'm sorry if I woke you," she says softly.

"I was already up, don't worry. Is there anything else I can get you?"

"That's okay. Just, please take the pills away," she whispers hoarsely.

"Are you sure?" I thought those might be the most necessary.

"I don't like to take medicine. We never had it in the house growing up and the habit just stuck." She shrugs tiredly, and I curse myself for not having thought about that. It's not far-fetched that she's opposed to taking pills after seeing what drugs did to her mom. Not that it's the same, but I get where she's coming from.

"Of course," I agree, picking them up again. Then, before I can stop myself, I reach out to quickly caress her cheek, desperate to provide just a little comfort, at least. Her answering sigh makes my heart flutter, but I don't push it, pulling away and heading for the door.

"Goodnight, sweetheart," I tell her.

"Goodnight, Seb. You can close your door now."

Chapter 34

Aliena

The next week passes in a blur of work, visits to my parents' place, and coming home to small surprises from Seb. Ever since he helped me the night of my cramps, he's been making small gestures all the while still giving me space.

At times, he leaves little notes somewhere in the house he knows I'll stumble upon them. Yesterday, he printed a QR code and stuck it to my bathroom mirror. When I scanned it, a video of a cat falling into a toilet popped up, startling a laugh out of me. It was the first time I've laughed since his party.

So yeah, while I'm still sticking to my choice to stay away from him, I can feel my resolve crumble just slightly. I *miss* him like his absence is a physical wound. I don't want to keep fighting.

On my next day off, I wake up to the sound of my phone chiming. I check it groggily, blinking for a few beats as I try to read what the message says. When I've read it three times and the words still say the same thing, I sit up in my bed, squealing like an idiot.

He got me a ticket to another art exhibition. Persuasive idiot. He's making it hard for me to stay mad at him when he's so apparently trying to cheer me up.

But the reminder he got high in his room while I was being assaulted, all because he was so eager to think I would actually sleep with another man, on top of the things he said... Yes, reminding myself of those things does wonders for my grudge-holding and it dims my elation about the present. He wants to make it up to me. I know that's what he's trying with the thoughtful notes and now this, and while my heart is screaming at me to give in, my self-preservation hits me with a firm no. He burned my trust to shreds that night, and I don't want to put myself in a position where he can do it again.

That doesn't mean I'll refuse the ticket he got me.

———

I'm floating on cloud nine by the time I reach my parents' place that evening. I was at the exhibition for hours, staring at the art and thinking about Sebastian and what to do about him.

When the daylight streaming through the curved windows turned to a golden evening glow, I took the bus here, as much as I didn't feel like putting a dampener on my mood. It's been days since I've visited and checked in, after all.

I get in using my key and head for the living room, where I find my dad lounging on the couch.

"Hey, Dad. Is Mom home?" I ask, giving him a brief kiss on the cheek, trying not to notice how rough he looks.

He hasn't shaved in days and from the smell of it, he hasn't showered recently either. He looks despaired and drained.

"They took her," he mutters.

My thoughts come to a halt, and I whirl on my heels, gaping at him as my heart skips a beat. "Took her? What do you mean? Who took Mom, Dad?" I ask urgently. Hell, if she ran into trouble with a dealer, I don't know what I'll do. And why is my dad just sitting there?

"The people from that fancy rehab center. Took her two days ago."

Fancy rehab center? My relief doesn't outweigh my confusion. "What? How? Why haven't you told me?" My mind is reeling. Did Mom finally agree to get help? And how are we going to pay for that?

"I thought you knew. Your friend came here to explain everything to me and tell me she'll be in good hands," he mutters listlessly.

My stomach is in knots. "What friend, Dad? Lily?" *How did she find out?*

"No. No. It was a man. Tall, dark hair, nice clothes. Name starts with S. Or T, or something like that."

Realization dawns on me and I don't know whether to whoop with relief that my mother is getting help or scream in frustration at Sebastian's meddling. Sure, he means well, but I've looked into rehab centers. They're outrageously expensive. I've just recently been able to pay him back for the moving company. Now, I'm in his debt again. Not to mention the rent he's sparing me.

Sighing, I nod. "Okay, that's good, Dad. I'll just prepare dinner, yeah? Then we can celebrate."

"Celebrate that I'm alone? They took my wife," he murmurs as I get started in the kitchen. My heart breaks a little at his defeated tone. I wish he'd stop blaming himself for Mom's addiction. There was nothing either one of us could have done to prevent it.

"She needs help, Dad. She needs help so she can come back as the woman she was. She'll get better there. They can help her more than we can."

He takes several minutes to reply and when he does, it feels like he didn't hear a word I said. "I lost my wife," he repeats, his voice trailing off.

"You'll get her back. I'm sure we can visit her in the meantime. And, who knows, maybe now you can focus on finding a job," I try to sound cheery. When he doesn't reply again, I frown and start plating the food.

We eat in unnerving silence, and I'm glad when he swallows the last bite so I can do the dishes. Somewhere along the way, it feels like I haven't just lost my mother but my father too. He looks like a shell of himself, with no smiles, and no nicknames. Just emptiness and occasional anger. As I clean the dishes, I get lost in my thoughts again.

"You still believe I can get a job?" my dad asks from behind me, startling me into dropping a plate. Sweet heaven, I didn't hear him sneak up on me.

Taking a shaky breath, I try to assure him, "Yes, Dad. Of course, you can." Despite my best efforts, my voice comes out shaky. When has his presence become so unnerving?

He stares off into the distance as I pick up the shards of the broken plate. "I lost my job, I lost my wife, and I'm losing my daughter too," he recites brokenly.

341

I halt in my tracks. "What?" I ask, chuckling as a chill rushes down my spine. "What do you mean, you're losing me? I'm right here."

"You think I don't see how you keep eyeing the door. You don't want to be here any more than she did." His voice starts trembling with underlying anger, and I take a step back from him, hating that I'm scared. He hasn't hurt me in years. There's no reason for my heart to speed up.

"You want to leave. Everyone wants to leave! It doesn't matter how hard I try, does it? I will never be enough for either of you." He shakes his head to himself and steps closer, his hands grasping my arms. "So go, then!" He shakes me, making my breath stall in my throat as I stare into his wild eyes. He looks beside himself. Deranged.

I open my mouth to say something placating but before a sound can leave my lips, a loud slap rings through the house and a coppery taste explodes in my mouth. My teeth snap shut, my whole body going still and numb as shock washes over me.

He slapped me. My dad just slapped me.

I watch in silence as his eyes widen, the same horrible realization dawning on him. His hands start to tremble on my arms, his head shakes from left to right in denial.

His throat bobs. "I'm so sorry," he whispers hoarsely, all his anger bleeding out of him. His eyes turn pleading as his first tear drops. I don't move. Don't try to tell him it's okay when it's not.

"I am so sorry." Then he starts sobbing, wrenching me into his arms as he repeats how much he regrets laying a hand on me. After years of not doing it, I guess he just experienced a relapse of his own.

And I'm entirely back to being the girl I was growing up, trying to look after my addict of a mother and my abusive father. I hold him as he falls apart, my love and hate for him mingling until I can't even tell them apart.

Eventually, I move us upstairs into his room and hold his hand until he falls asleep. When I finally drag myself out of that house of memories and nightmares, I know I've missed my last bus home by a lot. I also know I can't stay in my childhood home for another second, so I do the only thing I can. I call Sebastian.

"Aly?" Sebastian asks when he picks up after the first ring. I guess he was already awake then, good. "Everything all right? Do you need me to pick you up from somewhere?"

My bruised heart sighs happily, soaking up his caring words. His willingness to get out of the comfort of his apartment so late at night just to help me. "That would be great. How did you know?" I ask.

"You haven't come home. I was worried about you."

"Oh," is all I can think to say to that. *He was worried. He cares.* I think it's nice to know that after missing the same reminders from my own parents, but I can't feel it right now. I can't feel much of anything other than this oppressive exhaustion.

"Yeah. So, where are you? Are you okay?" From the urgency in his tone, I can tell he's dying to get an answer to the latter question. Since he wouldn't like the true answer to that, I lie.

"Yes, my dad just held me up and I missed the last bus. I'm sorry for calling so late."

343

"It's no big deal. I was up anyway. I'm leaving right now."

"Thanks. I'll see you soon." And so I wait on my front porch, alone with my thoughts and freezing like a beaten dog.

When Seb's car pulls up, I quickly jump into the passenger seat, barely looking at him to say hello before I turn my face away. I checked my reflection in my phone earlier to see my split lip and a purple bruise already forming around it. If I can get home before Sebastian sees it, he'll never know.

The longer we just stay still in my driveway, the more my hope I'll get away with it dwindles. Finally, gentle fingers cup my chin and turn my face, confirming my plan has already failed.

Sebastian's worried eyes flick between my eyes, then drop back to my lip. He grits his teeth, though his touch on me is achingly gentle. "What happened?" he asks, trying his best to hide his anger.

"I slipped," I try half-heartedly, not meeting his eyes again.

"Aliena, don't lie to me. Or I'll have to go in there and find the answer myself," Sebastian threatens, his voice brimming with danger. I don't flinch at his gruff tone. There's not a nerve in my body that's on alert. Not with him. I know he'd never hurt me.

"My dad lost it a little. It's not so bad, though. It was just a little slap. Please, don't make a big deal out of this. I just want to go home," I plead with him, too tired for a charade.

344

After a silent second, something changes in his eyes. Like he's realizing something... Frowning, he mutters, "Nothing new," under his breath.

"What?" I ask, and his eyes snap back to focus.

"Nothing new. That's what you said when you called me from the telephone booth. You told me your attacker punched you, but that it was nothing new," he explains, his voice getting clearer with every word, and I can see him piece the whole story together.

I curse myself for slipping. Now and back in November. Especially when Sebastian's eyes meet mine, a deadly inferno of rage hidden in his. He lets go of my chin as if it'd burned him.

"He hits you?" he bursts incredulously. I have to suppress a flinch, not because I'm scared but because the words hurt to hear. *My father hurt me.*

"No. Not anymore. Not in many years, Sebastian. Today was an accident," I try to reason with him, the denial useless in the face of his palpable outrage.

"How do you accidentally hit your daughter?" he demands, nearly screaming now. "And what do you mean, not in many years?"

Sensing this isn't the time for games or lies, I say, "When my mother succumbed to addiction the first time around, my dad was under a lot of pressure, working and raising me. Sometimes, just when I'd mess up something or upset Mom, he'd lash out. But it was never bad, and he didn't mean any harm."

Sebastian bites his tongue, blows out a breath, and rubs his hands down his face. I can tell he wants to keep screaming. Hell, he probably wants to go inside my house and yell at my dad. I won't let him, though. That sort of stress is the last thing my father needs.

Finally, Sebastian sighs and slumps in his seat. His hands drop from his face to cup my cheeks with utmost care. "I wish you'd told me earlier. I don't care if you say today was a slip-up. I'd have accompanied you on your visits if I knew he was dangerous," he tells me.

"He's not dangerous," I protest. "He's just under a lot of pressure."

Sebastian's brows dip slightly as he shakes his head. "Don't make excuses for him, sweetheart. He doesn't deserve it." He sighs, studying me for a long moment.

I'm glad when the pity finally bleeds from his gaze, his expression changing as he searches my face. "Thank you for telling me," he finally says.

"It's not exactly a pretty bedtime story," I mumble, unsure why he'd be happy about me being a Debbie downer.

"I don't care. I'm happy about every piece you reveal about yourself. I want to know you, Aly. The good and the bad, and most of all the hidden pieces you keep so close to your chest. I want you to trust me enough to confide in me."

"You do know me," I tell him hoarsely. He probably knows me better than anyone at the moment.

Nodding slightly, he brings my hands to his lips and kisses my knuckles. Then, he says, "Let's go home."

So we do. Sebastian doesn't push me to talk more about tonight, and I appreciate it, using the silence to figure out my feelings.

"Can I stay with you tonight?" I ask warily when we arrive home. I didn't settle on many clear thoughts in the short ride home, but I do know for sure that I'm craving comfort. I've been craving it ever since I stopped sleeping with Sebastian, but tonight, I don't want to miss it. I lack the strength to deny myself.

Sebastian, though clearly surprised, quickly agrees, "Yes, of course."

I get ready as quickly as I can, washing my face and inspecting my bruise before meeting him in his bedroom. For one awkward moment, I hesitate in the doorway. Then, he saves the day with his most charming smile as he pats the mattress next to him.

"I promise I won't bite," he teases, and the sentence hovers between us like the ghost of old times.

"Not unless I ask," I add, finally getting closer.

To my surprise, he shakes his head. "No, sweetheart. Not tonight. As of tomorrow, when you're well rested and have a clear head, I'll do whatever you ask." He winks before reaching for my hand and dragging me down onto the bed. Within seconds, he manages to clumsily settle me next to him.

He holds my gaze as he slowly reaches out to brush his thumb over my bruised lip, a crease marring his forehead.

"It barely hurts anymore," I assure him.

"I hate that this happened. I hate that I wasn't there," he curses softly.

"You're the first person I called. Just focus on that. I know we have a lot to talk about, but for now, forget about this. Just hold me and go to sleep," I tell him, already turning around so we can settle in our old position.

Sebastian follows suit, his body curving against my back and melting against me with a sigh. "I missed you so fucking much," he confesses against my shoulder.

"Such a filthy mouth," I tease, ever my first instinct to deflect when things become too intimate. But I remind myself that's not what I want to do with Sebastian. Not anymore. With my heart in my throat, I concede, "I missed you too."

Chapter 35

Sebastian

Waking up with Aliena in my arms is like coming home after a long day. Like taking the first deep breath in months. I soak it up, breathing her in to reassure myself she's really here.

The days without her were hell. I was constantly thinking about her, equal parts worry and longing making my chest heavy. There wasn't a second when I wasn't thinking about her, and it was only my promise to her that kept me from getting too close against her wishes.

I take advantage of being the first one awake, watching her until she stirs, her change in breathing telling me she's awake. Still, she doesn't speak and doesn't try to change our position. For a few long minutes, we rest together as we wake up.

It's only when the tease in my bed starts shifting around, backing up with her ass until it's pressed tightly against my front. Weeks of waking up just like this, her teasing me until I was up and ready to fuck her taught me where this is going. I reluctantly pull away, much to my body's regret.

Grabbing her wrists, I pin them above her head so she's lying on her back before moving so I straddle her hips. "What are you doing, little troublemaker?" I wonder.

Her satisfied hum pierces the air. "I love it when you call me that," she replies, still looking at me suggestively through her lashes.

"Oh now, don't look at me like that, sweetheart. We need to talk first," I insist. She groans, making me smile a little.

"Okay, Grandpa. God, responsible people are the worst."

This time it's me that groans. "Please, don't call me that," I whine.

"What, you don't like it?" she teases innocently. "I think it's sexy, don't you, Grandpa?" she goes on, shaking with laughter when I fake gag.

"You make me want to get off you and move to the other side of the room," I ensure her.

"And yet you stay, pinning me down and all."

"Can I trust you to keep your hands to yourself if I let go?" I challenge.

"I don't know. Try it and find out," she fires back.

"Aliena," I chastise.

"Sebastian," she echoes, drawing out my name exasperatedly. "Yes, I can keep my hands to myself. You're not that irresistible."

I let go of her in time to place a hand over my heart. "You wound me!"

"Your ego can take the hit, I'm sure. Now, will you get off me to talk or would you rather keep me pinned so I can't walk away?"

"Why would you walk away?" I ask, hoping damn well that she's not planning on it.

She shrugs. "Judging how our last arguments went down, I'd say the chances are high one of us will storm off or flee at one point or another."

I don't indulge in teasing her about that. Not when I can still remember her rushing away from me and locking herself in the bathroom so vividly.

I slowly get off her. "There won't be any fleeing today," I assure her. That's a vicious cycle better broken sooner rather than later.

She straightens up, leaning against the head of the bed and watching me expectantly.

"I don't know where to start," I tell her honestly.

"Just don't apologize again. I know you're sorry. I knew that when you apologized, I knew it when you took care of me despite my asking for space, and I knew it every time you made a sweet gesture in the time since."

"Don't forget about the ticket to the exhibition," I cut in, grinning. I've got a lot of faults, but I do know my girl. She shoves my shoulder.

"That counts as a sweet gesture. Anyway, I'm no longer mad at you. Sure, you knew what you were doing when you took drugs in here and it hurt a lot, but the rest was said and done in the heat of the moment. I know you didn't mean it. Besides, it's not like I didn't do anything to provoke your anger. That's why I wanted to come talk to you at the party."

"I said such stupid things," I start, protesting against her letting me off the hook, and nearly flinching as I recall what words left my mouth that night.

Aliena stops me before I can go further down that road, though. "I know you didn't mean it," she repeats slowly. "Stop beating yourself up about it. People make mistakes. We both did."

I nod reluctantly, reaching out to take her hand. The urge to hold her is always right there. "Where does that leave us?" I ask.

"I don't know. Last I checked, you don't want a relationship, right? That didn't change?" she asks, and I swear she almost looks hopeful as she searches my features for any indication of my reply.

Swallowing around the nervous lump in my throat, I say, "I think it did, sweetheart. I think my view on all that has been changing for a while. From the moment you started sleeping in my bed, I suppose.

"We could have had this talk a lot sooner if you'd given me any indication you wanted something more from me. To me, you seemed even more hesitant to let things become serious than me, and I get it. With everything happening with your parents, I came to the conclusion that it wasn't the right time to demand anything from you that might take energy." Even more hesitantly, I add. "And I was a coward, hesitant to change the status quo, so scared of being like my dad despite how much I care about you."

My words linger for a second before Aly replies. "I was scared. Am scared. I've never had a relationship. You know all about my fear of leaning on someone, never mind that I crossed that bridge a long time ago when it comes to you, and it seems there's no turning back, no matter how hard I try. I'm starting to think the risk might be worth it if we give this a fair shot."

A slow, wide smile spreads over my face. I can feel it. "Yeah? You'd agree to being my girlfriend?"

She rolls her eyes, even as a smile of her own takes over her features. "Yes, Sebastian, I would gladly be your girlfriend."

———

To say the looks on our friends' faces are hilarious when Aliena and I walk into the private room hand in hand the following weekend would be an understatement. Lily gapes, instantly asking, "When did this happen and why the hell did I not know?"

Andrew is a little more subtle, his gaze jumping between Aly and me before he blows out a breath and takes a long sip of his drink.

Mattheo simply smirks, the bastard. "Look who finally came around. I must say, I was almost losing hope in you, Seb. After you ruined my knee, I was sure you'd man up and set to winning her over, but you persisted in being a little bitch. Now, here we are, months later."

Aliena stumbles a step, her head whipping around to look at me. "Pardon me, you did *what* to his knee?"

"Oh, oops, you never mentioned that?" Mattheo drawls, feigning innocence. Dumbass doesn't realize he's making his knee look horribly kickable again. "You remember how I couldn't dance with you on your birthday, *amo*? Yeah, you have that one to thank."

Before she can snap at me, I say, "He was the reason you got hurt. He should have made sure you got home safely that night." That, at least, placates her a little. She smiles and shrugs.

"We are all just accepting that? I thought you guys couldn't stand each other!" Lily protests.

"Your head is always in the clouds, my love. You're the only one who thought that," Andrew tells her. She glares at him before bringing her attention back to the girl holding my hand.

"You've been holding out on me! I always give you the dirty details about my love life. You two have been screwing around behind my back and I don't know a thing about it?"

Aliena laughs while Andrew has the courtesy to blush at the revelation that his sex life isn't as private as he might've hoped.

Before anyone can change the subject, Andrew seems to realize something that makes him jerk in his seat. "Whoa, you want to know how Sebastian is in bed?" His gaze swivels to Aliena. "No." Is all he tells her. I refrain from telling him she doesn't listen to orders. He'll realize that she does whatever she wants eventually.

"I'm still curious as to how it happened, though. And how you hid it from us," Lily persists, ignoring Andrew skillfully. I can't believe he didn't know women talked. Poor man.

"Well, circumstances kind of had me move in with him and one thing led to another," Aliena provides with a shrug.

"You live here?" her best friend exclaims. Now, even the guys look surprised.

"Since last December," Aliena admits, looking a little sheepish now as her friend's face turns red.

Lily takes a deep breath, and with a forced calmness, she says, "You and I will have a sleepover soon. At my place, apparently. Then, I will make you talk, you hear me?"

The whole crew laughs and as we settle into the couches, and the conversation eventually moves on from Aliena's and my new relationship status.

When eventually, the others start heading downstairs to dance, I notice Aliena eyeing me.

"Yes, sweetheart?" I ask, arching a brow.

"Well, aren't you going to ask me to dance?" she retorts with that attitude I love so much.

I bow my head in apology and get to my feet, holding out a hand to her. "Would you do me the honor and dance with me, milady?" I tease.

She swats at my hand, smiling cheekily. "You're an idiot," she declares, walking past me.

For a second, I just stand there and enjoy the view. *That's my woman.* I feel both unbelievably lucky and undeserving.

She finally looks at me over her shoulder and says, "Well, don't let me wait now."

My feet follow her obediently. "Sorry, sweetheart, just wanted to take in the sight," I say, moving her along with a hand on the small of her back.

"Oh, yeah? And, was everything to your liking?"

"Hell yes. My girlfriend looks devastating tonight," I whisper in her ear.

———

"I'm nervous," Aliena repeats for the hundredth time since I told her my mom was about to turn up at the apartment with the rest of the cleaning crew and demands to finally meet the girl that stole her boy's heart. Her words, not mine.

I've been managing to hold her off for a few days since telling her I had a girlfriend. Now, her patience seems to have run out.

"She'll love you, don't worry," I reassure her.

Right on cue, the elevator dings and opens to reveal a crew of ladies, all shorter than five foot five. I greet them with a smile as always, but they don't stop by to chat, merely sending curious glances toward the girl clinging onto my arm before they rush off to the second floor.

My mother is the last in line, her face lighting up as she spies us ready to welcome her. "My boy, hello," she exclaims, pulling me into a bone-crushing hug. She's seriously strong for such a small woman. Then, letting go, she moves on to study Aliena.

With my girlfriend's face in her hands, she gushes over how pretty she is in that thick Spanish accent of hers. Aliena, for her part, holds dutifully still, even as a vicious blush takes over her face.

I finally take pity on her and interrupt, "Mom, enough. You are embarrassing her."

Noticing I'm right, she lets go of my girl's face and resorts to hugging her. "Sorry, darling. I'm just very excited. Sebastian has never introduced me to a girl before, and I've been dying to meet you for half a year now."

Aly's brows shoot up and she turns to looks at me. I brush her off. She doesn't need to know I told my mom about her after our first meeting.

After a few minutes of chatting, my mom excuses herself to go help the others clean, but not before inviting us for dinner at my parents' place tomorrow night.

As soon as she's out of earshot, Aliena slumps against my side. "Oh god. I've never experienced anything more stressful. Do you think I made a good impression?" She groans before I can answer. "I was too quiet, wasn't I?"

Chuckling, I squash her against my chest and press a kiss to her forehead. Who would have thought I'd ever see Aliena Hart this shy?

Aliena

Dinner is tense. Sebastian's father, William Henderson, is as much of an asshole as expected and while I can brush off his demeaning comments quite easily, Sebastian's tight grip on my hand beneath the table tells me he isn't faring as well.

I feel bad for him. He warned me this would happen and apologized in advance. When I asked him why he agreed to come if he hates his dad so much, he simply said it would make his mother happy. My heart melted a little at that.

So that's what brings us here, into this beautiful mansion, sitting at this majestic mahogany dinner table, eating the delicious food Sofia, Seb's mom, prepared.

"So, Aliena, are you a student at my university?" William asks me, that deep, stoic voice disrupting the tense silence. Sofia looks nervously between her husband and me.

I smile sweetly as I tell him, "No, sadly not." Then, I keep eating, smiling sincerely when Sebastian squeezes my hand.

"Oh? May I ask where you study, then?" the old man at the head of the table goes on.

"I'm afraid the answer to that is nowhere. I chose to work rather than going to university." Never mind it wasn't much of a choice, in my case, but he doesn't need to know that. He's the kind of vulture that would jump at the notice of my dire financial situation.

He looks greatly displeased at that, and while his wife reaches for his hand, pleading with him with her eyes, and Sebastian glares, I keep my smile in place, completely unbothered by his rudeness.

So what if he doesn't approve of me or my life choices? I've never cared much for the opinion of little men who haven't known a single day of hard labor, and I don't plan on starting now. William is exactly the kind of privileged man that had one person or another cater to his every wish his entire life. I'd bet on it.

The two of us are locked in a staring contest, which I'm only willing to lose to look at Sofia when she speaks.

"I didn't study either," she throws in, smiling nervously at me. I smile back.

When her husband mutters a not-so-subtle, "Yeah, and look where that got you," my mask slips.

With a short apologetic look at Sebastian, I allow myself to lose it. Forget playing his game of forced niceties and backhanded comments. Where I come from, yelling is a much more popular way to express one's opinion.

"You never tire of hearing your own voice, do you? God, you make it so obvious no one has ever told you to *shut up*. The fact you were born with a golden spoon up your ass doesn't make you any better than your wife or me."

My outburst seems to snuff out the air in the room, but I'm not done. "You forgot to ask me where I work," I remind him sweetly. "It's a nursing home called Bloomfield Living Care. Does that ring a bell? It's a great place with lovely residents.

"You might know one. Her name was Rosie, and I got to take care of her for over a year before she passed. But you wouldn't know that. No, you never bothered to visit her, no matter how often she asked about you." My throat tightens at the mention of my old friend, but I buzz on.

"Don't worry, she didn't die knowing what an unlikeable, ungrateful disappointment her son turned out to be since I brought her flowers every month, pretending they were from you. Yeah, you're welcome." I take a deep breath, nodding to Sebastian before getting to my feet.

I turn to Sofia, who's gaping at me. "Sofia, thank you so much for the invitation. The food was fantastic. The company too, for the most part, but I think all in all, this was a successful dinner. I hope to see you around the house soon." Letting my smile drop, I turn back to William, nodding. "It's been a pleasure, old man. I can only hope you take what I told you to heart and stop being such an overgrown bully to the people you're supposed to care about. It's pathetic."

With that, I turn on my heels, trusting Sebastian is right behind me as I exit the mansion. Outside, I let out a startled laugh, feeling the adrenaline cursing through me. Holy shit, I can't believe I said all that.

I've never been a wallflower, sure, but talking like that to the father of my boyfriend? I can only hope Seb isn't too mad at me.

Speaking of the devil, two strong arms come around me from behind and a face nuzzles into my shoulder. "I don't deserve you," he mumbles against my skin. I turn in his arms, still feeling triumphant as I kiss his soft, inviting lips.

"Maybe, yeah. But at least now I know firsthand where you got some of your most questionable traits from." I peck his lips again, taking a deep breath as I cup his cheek, so I have his full attention. I remember the pain in his voice when he admitted to fearing he was like his dad. After meeting the man now, it's unfathomable to me that Sebastian would ever think they were similar. "You're not your dad, though. You're kind, and caring, and observant, and you've been taking such good care of me, Sebastian. It's a good thing too because if you ever tried undermining me like that, in front of others no less, I wouldn't stick around long enough for you to regret it."

He chuckles, tightening his hold on me. The gesture lets me know just how much my words mean to him. Even though his next words are teasing. I can feel the tension bleeding from his body. "Trust me, I know that. I wouldn't dare test you like that. Especially not after the show you just put on. I don't think my dad will ever recover, and Sweetheart, I've never been more attracted to you."

"Really? Me yelling at your dad turns you on but when I call you grandpa, it turns you off faster than a cold shower?" I tease.

He kisses me deeply, rather than replying. Then, resting his forehead against mine, he swallows thickly, as if bracing himself for something. "Aly?"

"Yes?" I reply, my voice lowering to match his as I keep my eyes shut.

"I love you," he whispers hoarsely. I smile against his lips, pecking them. He doesn't return the kiss. "This is the part where you say it back, sweetheart," he tells me playfully.

I huff and shove him away. "You're such an idiot. I was just about to do that, but you know how I feel about getting told what to do."

"Yes, I know, I know. You only like it in the bedroom," he announces loudly. I gasp, looking over my shoulder to make sure neither of his parents is there to hear.

"Shut up before I refuse to let anything happen in the bedroom until you forget what my preferences were in the first place," I threaten him playfully.

He raises his hands in surrender. "Okay, okay. I'm sorry." I'm granted another kiss. "Oh, by the way, that's another one of my firsts you snatched since you like them so much. You're the only girl I've ever loved."

My heart flutters happily. I hum against his lips. "I love that," I tell him. Then, lowering my voice, I add, "And I love you."

And since he's so great at ruining sincere moments, Sebastian pulls away, and whoops. That's right, he whoops and hugs me around the waist before lifting me so I'm slung over his shoulder. Then he skips to his car, no consideration for my newly filled stomach.

"You're an idiot," I declare, even as I cling to him.

"An idiot you love," he adds, whooping again.

Epilogue

Sebastian

6 months later

"Are you sure you want to do this, sweetheart?" I ask, unable to quench the worry that's been buzzing in my chest ever since Aliena came to me with her idea.

She huffs, her exasperation with me showing not for the first time in the last thirty minutes. "I am sure, Sebastian. Now, will you please finish tying me up? I'm getting cold because in case you haven't noticed, I'm naked here." Her fingers wriggle in her restraints, and I know if her hands weren't already tied, she'd motion toward her body spread out on our bed, not a stitch of clothing on her.

Letting my eyes trail over the sight is nearly enough to shut my mind off and let my instincts take over. My instincts which are very insistently screaming at me to get her nice and wet so I can sink back into her perfect pussy.

But this is about so much more than just sex, so I keep my wits about myself.

This is her way of showing me that she trusts me and my chance to heal the damage I did the first time around. My chance to prove she can count on me once and for all.

363

My chance to show her how good bondage can be so we might share that common ground in the bedroom. We have a *lot* of fun together as it is, but maybe if I do this right, we'll have even more things to try out in the future.

But I recognize this is a delicate matter because, as much as it pains me to admit, I caused Aliena some trauma with the way I left her tied up. The more I get to know her and everything about her past, the more that's becoming clear.

It's bad enough that I still sometimes dream about her chafed wrists, the red marks something I never want to see on her precious skin again. So, despite her insistence that she's all in, I want to be cautious. It's possible she's completely fine with being tied up one second but gets triggered somehow the next.

It's why I made sure she saw it when I left my phone downstairs after her proposal. Similarly to how I told her she was allowed to turn off her phone, I decided mine and all the possible distractions it could bring need to stay away this time when we do this.

Silently, obediently, I bind her hands to the headboard of our bed. Once I'm done, I tug on the silk. "Is this okay?"

She moves her arms a little, then repositions her hands so her fingers are wrapped around the bars for stability. She meets my inquisitory gaze with hooded eyes, her lips tilting up. "Feels like I can hold on perfectly when you finally fuck me like this."

I bite my tongue to keep it from saying something unhinged in return.

I haven't even decided on what I should do with her now I have her wrists tied up. Do I edge her like I did the last time? Or something tamer, like some good old head to ease her back into this scene?

"What do you want me to do, sweetheart?" I decide to ask. She'll know what she's in the mood for most, after all.

Her smile turns wicked as she gazes up at me. "Do I have to choose? It's unfair to ask that of me when you eat me out with the dedication of a starving man, you touch me as if I were a holy artifact, and you fuck me like you love me," she muses, feigning a pout.

Her words spear me through the chest, filling me up with warmth. I lean down to kiss her, suddenly needy to feel just any part of her. "I do love you, sweetheart. And you're worth more to me than any object could ever be, holy or otherwise." I brush my nose against hers and then lean back on my heels, admiring her once more.

"It would be a new experience to fuck you without having you claw at my back. Although I do relish in carrying your marks..." I trail off, mulling my choice over.

When her eyes light up like a Christmas tree, my determination grows. She doesn't want to choose? Very fine by me. This is all about her, after all.

My hands encircle her ankles wordlessly, and I revel in her sharp intake of breath. I spread her legs, slowly so she has time to feel my gaze on every inch of her. It doesn't matter how many hours I spend looking at her, the sight will always be addictive.

And it seems no matter how many hours I spend looking at her, *she* always gets turned on by it.

"Seb," she breathes out when her legs are as wide as they can comfortably go, her pussy bared to me where I'm sitting between her legs.

365

My voice is rough when I reply, "Can you manage to keep your legs like this, or do you want me to tie them to the bed posts as well?"

"Do it. I can never stay still when you touch me." Damn right she can't. I take more ties from the box only to hesitate a second. "Are you still cold?" I ask. I don't want to hurry while I make sure the knots are comfortable, and I can't have her freezing in the meantime.

"I'm burning, actually. Just keep talking to me and I'll be perfect," she assures. I grin to myself and start wrapping her calve up in a net of knots.

I keep her entertained, telling her all the things I plan on doing to her while I tie her legs in place, casually slipping in the question whether she's okay and comfortable when I have an opening. Glad when she confirms.

The sight of her once I'm done, so thoroughly at my mercy and trusting me to make her feel good, is enough to wreck my body with tremors.

"There we go, baby. Now, I can finally take care of your needy little pussy. I can see her weeping for me, already dripping onto our sheets when I haven't even touched you. My poor thing," I taunt, leaning over to kiss her.

She arches her neck to meet my lips halfway, clearly as eager as me to start this. My hands move over her body, touching every inch I can reach with the kind of reverence I've only ever dedicated to her. I spend extra time on the parts I know make her the weakest. Her sensitive breasts, a little squeeze around her throat, a firm grip on the meat on her hips.

By the time my right hand makes it to the apex of her thighs, she's barely kissing me back, damn near panting against my lips. I don't mind it, happy to put all my focus on the task of touching her.

I push two fingers inside her without any warning, meeting no resistance with how wet she is. Aliena's back arches off the bed when I curl them against her G-spot, and my next kiss lands on her jaw. I trail down her body until my face meets my fingers on her pussy, my lips closing around her swollen clit. I keep my eyes on her as I eat her out with exactly the kind of determination she deserves, savoring every lick and nibble at least as much as she does. She's got the most addictive taste no matter where I kiss her. I can never get enough of it.

My fingers stay buried deep inside of her tight heat while my mouth works on her clit until she comes apart underneath me, writhing against her confines. My attention sharpens on her every reaction, her every move, right down to the way she breathes. I don't stop eating her out as long as her orgasm is still rushing through her, not even when my worries arise again about her crashing because I ruined bondage for her the last time.

But she doesn't. She merely slumps against the mattress after a few more seconds, her breaths deep and her features relaxed.

I move up her body to get a closer look, dropping an occasional kiss in passing because it's like her very skin calls out to me with its siren song. By the time my lips meet hers, the hunger has returned to her gaze, her blissed out state only lasting a second. Insatiable as she is. She wasn't lying about wanting everything tonight.

I place a thick pillow underneath her hips, preparing to hit her at a better angle as I check in one more time. "You're doing so amazing, sweetheart. You can't imagine how stunning you are, tied up and flushed from your orgasm." I press another kiss to her lips. "Do you want me to fuck you now? Or should I make it a three-course meal? You know I'm perfectly happy with either." I pull back just enough to see her smile.

"Fuck me, Sebastian. I want you to wreck me, shatter me to pieces, then put me back together. I know you'll take care of me."

Her reassurance settles some deep-rooted anxiety I wasn't aware was there, proving she knows me better than I do myself. My heart pounds almost painfully, as if unable to handle the love and adoration constantly growing when it comes to Aliena.

"Always, baby. I'll be so good to you," I promise as I bring my dick to her entrance. The first touch of my sensitive tip against her soaked folds nearly undoes me, but I bite back my groan and kiss her instead.

My teeth dig into her lips with every inch I slide into her, further and further until I'm bottomed out. She sighs against me, trying to clench her legs in vain.

I move deep and hard, eventually sitting up on my heels to deliver her exactly the kind of rough fucking she asked for. My hands grip her hips, short nails digging into her smooth skin while her pussy sucks me so deep I'm already losing my mind.

The longer I fuck her, the more she tries to squirm. Her legs have just enough room for her to brace her feet against the mattress, but she can't move them otherwise, and her arms are entirely immobile. Still, her muscles flex, telling me if she wasn't tied up, her hands would be all over me right now. Scratching at my hands and arms, anything she could reach in this position.

I grip her more tightly, keeping her in place as my pace turns unforgiving. Her moans pitch higher the way they always do when she's walking the tightrope between pain and pleasure, my length hitting the back of her. Incomprehensible gibberish falls from her swollen lips.

"I know, baby. I got you. You can let go," I tell her, one hand moving to rub her clit in tight circles. She cries out, her back arching and her body tensing as she comes around me.

I grit my teeth, willing to hold on for a few more thrusts to drag out her orgasm. When her spasms come to an end, I allow myself to follow her over the edge, her name on my lips and my hips flush with hers. I brace my arms on either side of her face and just barely keep myself from crushing her as I catch my breath. My lips are on her cheek, lazily kissing her so she doesn't forget I'm right here. That I'm with her and I'll take care of her the second I can feel my legs again.

She nuzzles against the faint touch, giving me the reassurance I need as I bridge over the few seconds.

"That was amazing, sweetheart. You're so perfect. How are you feeling?" I ask, finally setting out to gently untie her.

She barely moves, keeping her eyes closed and her lips lightly pressed into a content smile. Her reply is barely more than a little mewl, but I take it as her way of saying she's fine.

Once the silk is a bundle on my bedside table, I help her move her arms down and place them at her sides. She doesn't wince, doesn't show any sign of discomfort. I

369

release a small puff of air. When I move to do the same for her legs, I make sure some part of me is always touching her. I don't want her to be afraid that I'm gone for a single second.

It's when she's completely free and I look at her face that I realize she's fallen asleep. My chest grows fuzzy and warm. She wasn't tense or afraid I'd let her down again. She really does trust me, even in her most vulnerable state.

I cradle her to my chest for a second, kissing the side of her face. She stirs and makes a sound of approval as her hands come around my waist to hug me back.

"Sorry to wake you, baby, but it's time for your aftercare." I scoop her up and get to my feet, ignoring her protests that she's too heavy for me. *As if.*

I carry her to the bathroom and set her down on the toilet. She doesn't screech in outrage the way she did the first time I ever carried her to the bathroom. She simply takes a seat as her cheeks stain pink.

"I'll just get everything ready real quick," I tell her as I start the water for her bath. Then, to give her some privacy and because I want the bed to be clean and ready for her once she's done with her bath, I go back into our room and strip the bed of the sticky bedding.

I replace it with a clean set and return to the bathroom as Aly flushes the toilet. I'm at her side in a second, offering a glass of fresh water as I brush a strand of her golden hair from her face.

"Thank you," she says, accepting the drink. She lets me wash and fuss over her without protest, soaking in the bath filled with new scented oils and bubbles until the water grows cool.

I help her out, wrapping her up in a fluffy towel before I quickly dry myself. She almost sways on her feet, so drowsy and relaxed. It really is time for bed now.

We get back to our bedroom, where I lay her down in the middle of the bed before joining her and dragging the blanket up to our chins. Aliena's quick to curl up against me, one hand on my chest where she caresses me gently with two fingers.

She glances up through drooping eyelids, but her words are clear when she says, "You can let go of what happened that night now, okay? It can't hold you back and drag you down anymore."

I startle a little, not having expected her to say something so serious, especially concerning me, when she's on the verge of falling asleep, but I still soak the words up.

"Okay, baby," I agree, kissing her forehead. It's her final undoing, making her melt against me. The next second, her breathing evens out against my chest and she's fast asleep in my arms.

Acknowledgements

Dear reader, I hope you enjoyed this short story covering Aliena and Sebastian's relationship. For updates on the upcoming interlinked books about Andrew and Lily, and Mattheo and Miriam, follow my Instagram; @Jarah_Aurel

It's where I keep my readers up to date on all things concerning my novels and their progress, as well as exclusive extra content like bonus scenes and character aesthetics.

Thanks for reading until the end. As always, I wish you a lovely day<3

Made in United States
Orlando, FL
06 July 2025

62682472R00213